MORE PRAISE FOR
THE TESTING

VOYA Top Shelf for Middle School Readers 2013 list

USA Today, Top Ten Summer Reads

★ "The rising tension, skillfully executed scenarios, and rich characterizations all contribute to an exciting story bound to capture readers' imaginations. . . . Charbonneau works action, romance, intrigue, and a plausible dystopian premise into a near-flawless narrative." —*Publishers Weekly*, starred review

"*The Testing* is a page-turner! Charbonneau has written a novel with that excellent combination of strong romantic heart and gripping plot that's sure to fully engage dystopian fans." —Emmy Laybourne, author of *Monument 14*

"A surefire favorite for dystopian fans, *The Testing* crackles with suspense, passion, and betrayal set against a scarred and brutal world." —Sophie Littlefield, author of *Unforsaken* and *Hanging by a Thread*

"Charbonneau jumps into the packed dystopia field with a mashup of Veronica Roth's *Divergent* (2011) and Suzanne Collins' Hunger Games trilogy, but she successfully makes her story her own." —*Kirkus Reviews*

"Charbonneau is a fantastic story teller and this book is a tribute to that background. The intrigue in *The Testing* passes evaluation of what a good dystopian novel should represent." —*VOYA*, 4Q 5P M J S

"The plot twists are well integrated and will keep readers on edge awaiting the next volume." —*Horn Book*

"The influence of *The Hunger Games* is obvious, and *The Testing* will satisfy readers who want similar dystopian adventures." —*School Library Journal*

THE TESTING

BY JOELLE CHARBONNEAU

Houghton Mifflin Harcourt
Boston New York

www.hmhco.com

The text of this book is set in Adobe Garamond.

The Library of Congress has cataloged the hardcover edition as follows:
Charbonneau, Joelle.
The Testing / by Joelle Charbonneau.
p. cm.
Summary: Sixteen-year-old Malencia (Cia) Vale is chosen to participate in The Testing to attend the University; however, Cia is fearful when she figures out her friends who do not pass The Testing are disappearing.
[1. Examinations—Fiction. 2. Missing persons—Fiction. 3. Graduation (School)—Fiction. 4. Schools—Fiction. 5. Colleges and universities—Fiction.] I. Title.
PZ7.C37354Te 2013
[Fic]—dc23
2012018090

ISBN: 978-0-547-95910-8 hardcover
ISBN: 978-0-544-33623-0 paperback

Manufactured in the United States of America
DOC 10
4500661835

For Stacia Decker, for so many reasons.

CHAPTER 1

GRADUATION DAY.

I can hardly stand still as my mother straightens my celebratory red tunic and tucks a strand of light brown hair behind my ear. Finally she turns me and I look in the reflector on our living area wall. Red. I'm wearing red. No more pink. I am an adult. Seeing evidence of that tickles my stomach.

"Are you ready, Cia?" my mother asks. She too is wearing red, although her dress is made of a gossamer fabric that drapes to the floor in soft swirls. Next to her, my sleeveless dress and leather boots look childish, but that's okay. I have time to grow into my adult status. I'm young for it at sixteen. The youngest by far in my class.

I take one last look in the reflector and hope that today is not the end of my education, but I have no control over that. Only a dream that my name will be called for The Testing. Swallowing hard, I nod. "Let's go."

Graduation is held in the colony square among the stalls

filled with baked goods and fresh milk because the school isn't large enough to hold all the people who will attend. The entire colony attends graduation, which only makes sense since everyone in the colony is related to at least one of the students crossing over to adulthood or celebrating their promotion to the next grade. This year is the largest graduating class the Five Lakes Colony has had. Eight boys, six girls. A clear sign the colony is thriving.

My father and four brothers, all dressed in ceremonial adult purple, are waiting for us outside our dwelling. My oldest brother, Zeen, shoots me a smile and ruffles my hair. "Are you ready to be done with school and get out into the real world with the rest of us slobs?"

My mother frowns.

I laugh.

Zeen and my other brothers are definitely not slobs. In fact, girls practically throw themselves at them. But while my brothers aren't immune to flirting, none of them seems interested in settling down. They're more interested in creating the next hybrid tomato plant than starting a family. Zeen most of all. He's tall, blond, and smart. Very, very smart. And yet he never got chosen for The Testing. The thought takes away the shine from the day. Perhaps that's the first rule I will learn as an adult—that you can't always get what you want. Zeen must have wanted to continue on to the University—to follow in Dad's footsteps. He must know what I'm feeling. For a moment, I wish I could talk to him. Ask him how he got through the disappointment that most likely is awaiting me. Our colony will be lucky to have one student chosen for The Testing—if any at all. It has been ten years since the last student from Five Lakes was chosen. I'm good at school, but there are those who are better. Much better. What chance do I have?

With a forced smile, I say, "You bet. I can't stay in school if I plan on running the colony by the time all of you are married."

Hart and Win blush. They are two years older than me and the idea of marriage and dating makes them run for cover. The two of them are happy working side by side in the nursery, growing the flowers and trees Dad has created to withstand the corrupted earth at the outskirts of the colony.

"No one will be doing much of anything if we don't get moving." Mother's voice is sharp as she heads off down the path. My brothers and father quickly follow. Zeen's and Hamin's lack of marriage prospects is a sore spot for our mother.

Because of Dad's job, our house is farther from the center of the colony than most. My brothers and father have made the ground around our small house bloom green with plants and trees, but a hundred feet past our front door the earth is cracked and brittle. Though some grass and a few scraggly trees do grow. Dad tells me the earth to our west is far worse, which is why our leaders decided to place the Five Lakes Colony here.

Usually, I ride my bicycle to town. A couple of citizens own cars, but fuel and solar cells big enough to run them are too precious for everyday use. Today, I trail behind my family as we walk the almost five miles to the colony's community square.

Square is really the wrong word, but we use it anyway. It's shaped more like a turtle with an oval center and some appendages to the sides. There is a beautiful fountain in the middle that sprays clear, sparkling water into the air. The fountain is a luxury since clean water is not always easy to come by. But we are allowed the waste and the beauty in order to honor the man who discovered how to remove the contamination from the lakes and ponds after Stage Seven. What is left of the oceans is harder to clean.

The ground becomes greener and birds sing the closer we get to the center of the colony. Mom doesn't talk much on the way. Zeen teases her that she doesn't want me to grow up, but I don't think that's the case.

Or maybe it is.

Mom and I get along fine, but the past couple of years she has seemed distant. Less willing to help me with my homework. More interested in getting the boys married and talking about where I will apprentice when I finish school. Any discussion of me being selected for The Testing is not welcome. So, I talk to her less and less and to my father more and more. He doesn't change the subject when I speak about going further in my education, although he doesn't actively encourage me. He doesn't want to see me disappointed, I guess.

The sun is hot and sweat drips down my back as we trek up the final hill. The sounds of music and laughter from just out of sight have me quickening my step. Just before we reach the top, Dad puts his arm around me and asks me to wait while the others go on ahead.

The excitement over the hill pulls at me, but I stay put and ask, "Is something wrong?" His eyes are filled with shadows even though his smile is bright.

"Nothing is wrong," he says. "I just wanted a moment with my little girl before things get too crazy. Everything changes the minute we go over that hill."

"I know."

"Are you nervous?"

"Kind of." Excitement, fear, and other emotions swirl inside me, making it hard to tell what I'm really feeling. "It's weird not knowing what I'm going to do when I get up tomorrow." Most of my classmates have made choices about their future. They know where they will apprentice or if they will move to another colony to find work. Some even know who they are going to marry. I know none of these things, although my father has made it clear I can work with him and my brothers if I choose. The option seems bleak at best since my thumb is anything but green. The last time I helped my father I almost destroyed the sunflower seedling he'd spent months creating. Mechanical things I fix. Plants I kill.

"You're going to get up and face whatever comes. I'll be proud of you no matter what today brings."

"Even if I don't get accepted for The Testing?"

"Especially if you don't get accepted for The Testing." He smiles and gently pokes me in the belly. When I was little, that never failed to send me into fits of laughter. Today it still makes me grin. It's nice to know some things never change, even though I doubt my father's teasing words.

Dad went to the University. That's where he learned to genetically alter plants and trees to survive in the blighted soil. He doesn't talk about it much, or the colony he grew up in, probably because he doesn't want us to feel pressured by his success. But I do.

"You think I won't get accepted."

My father frowns. "I think you're smarter than you give yourself credit for. You never know who the search committee might pick or why. Five of us from my grade were selected and tested. The other four always did better in class, but I was the only one who made it to the University. The Testing isn't always fair, and it isn't always right."

"But you're not sorry you went. Look at the amazing things you do every day because of it." The trees next to us are filled with blooms promising apples in the months to come. Bushes of wild blackberries grow next to daisies and other flowers I never learned the names of but know Dad was a part of creating. When I was small, these things didn't exist. At least not the healthy versions dotting the hills today. Even now I can remember the empty ache of going to bed hungry. Food had been scarce as Dad worked with farmers to make things grow. And they had. In Five Lakes Colony, we are careful not to waste, but hunger is no longer our primary concern. My father is the reason why.

"I can't be sorry about something I had no choice in." His eyes go far away as the birds chirp around us. Finally, he smiles, although his eyes never clear of whatever memories are capturing his attention. "Besides, I wouldn't have moved here and met your mother if I hadn't gone to the University. Then where would I be?"

"Probably living at home with your parents and making your mother worry that you'll never get serious about your future."

The clouds disappear from their depths and his eyes twinkle as he ruffles my hair. "Sounds like a fate worse than death." Which is what my mother makes it sound like every time she tells Zeen that life is passing him by. "Come on. Your mother is going to sound the alarm if we don't get moving. I just want you to remember one thing. I believe in you. No matter what."

Arm in arm we start up and over the hill to join the festivities. I smile, but deep in my heart I worry that Dad has always expected me to fall short of his achievements. That I will disappoint—no matter what.

Because the colony is spread out over many miles, this is the one guaranteed occasion every year when the entire population of Five Lakes gathers together. Once in a while we all congregate when there is a message from our country's leaders that needs to be delivered to everyone, but those occasions are rare. At just over nine hundred citizens, our colony is one of the smallest and farthest from Tosu City, where the United Commonwealth government is based. We don't rank much attention, which is fine by most of us. We do well on our own. Outsiders aren't shunned, but they aren't exactly embraced with open arms. They have to convince us they belong.

The square is quite large, but the space feels small with so many people dressed in their ceremonial finery. Shops for candles, baked goods, shoes, and all sorts of household items line the outside edge of the square. The shops will close when graduation begins, but now they are doing a brisk business as citizens who don't often get into town purchase or trade for necessary items. The United Commonwealth coin is rare in our colony, but the few people on the government payroll, like Dad, use it.

"Cia!" The waving hand catches my attention as my best friend Daileen comes barreling toward me. Her blond hair and pink dress flutter as she dodges groups of chatting citizens to reach me. She clutches a cone with rapidly melting pink ice cream in her hand. Squeezing me in a tight hug, she says, "Can you believe you're graduating? This is so exciting. They're even giving away free ice cream."

I hug her back, careful to avoid the melting cone. My mother will have a fit if I get a stain on my new dress before graduation begins. "Exciting and scary. Don't forget the scary part."

Daileen is the only one I've talked to about my fears of the future if I don't get chosen for The Testing. She looks around to make sure no one is listening and says, "My father heard there's a special guest who's supposed to speak today."

Graduation Day has a lot of speakers. Our teachers will speak, as will the magistrate and a number of other Five Lakes leaders. When the entire colony gets together there is never a lack of things to talk about. So the special guest doesn't sound all that special until Daileen adds, "My father says the guest is from Tosu City."

That gets my attention. "Someone from Tosu is here?" The last time an official from Tosu came to Five Lakes Colony was three years ago when our old magistrate died. Two men and a woman came to the colony to select the new colony leader. Mostly Tosu City communicates with us through proclamations or radio communications with our magistrate.

"That's what my father heard." Daileen licks the melted ice cream streaking the back of her hand. "Dad thinks he's here to escort a candidate for The Testing. That could be you." For a minute her smile falters. "I'll really miss you."

Daileen and I are only two weeks apart in age and have been best friends since the age of three. Her parents enrolled her in school at the mandatory age of six. My parents decided to send me at five, which is why we are not in the same class. She is the shyer, smarter, and gentler of the two of us. She is also the one less likely to make new friends unless someone else is there to get the conversation going. Without me pushing her to engage others in conversation during lunch and hang out after classes, she will probably eat alone and go home to an empty, sad house long before everyone else leaves the school grounds. Her mother died two years ago in an accident and her father, while nice, isn't home much, leaving Daileen alone to deal with the chores and the memories. I try to keep her in good spirits while we're at school, but some days the shadows overwhelm her. I worry one day those shadows will swallow her whole without someone to chase them away.

I give her another quick hug and say, "Every year there's a rumor about a Tosu official coming to graduation." Although a small part of me can't help yearning for this year's rumor to be true. To distract myself as much as Daileen, I add, "Now, I want to get some of that ice cream before it's gone. Okay?"

I enlist other friends, many of them going into their final year of school, in our search for strawberry ice cream, hoping that one of them will take Daileen under their wing when classes begin again in a few weeks. If not, I will find a way to make things easier for Daileen.

My mother waves at me and frowns, so I leave a smiling Daileen with the other students and cross the square to the fountain where she waits. Almost everyone I pass waves or says hello. Our family moves to new dwellings almost every year—to whatever section of the colony the magistrate thinks needs Dad's skill the most. All the moving makes it hard to feel attached to a home, but unlike most citizens, who know only their neighbors and former schoolmates, I know the majority of the people in our colony by sight.

Kids still too young for school, dressed in pale yellows and greens, dance around the twelve-foot-wide circular fountain, occasionally splashing each other with the water. But they avoid the area where my mother is seated. Her expression says that getting her wet will bring a scolding. Something I'm probably going to get no matter what.

My mother studies me. "Your hair is a mess. What have you been doing?"

My hair is always a mess between the curls and the frizz. I've suggested cutting it short, but my mother insists that long, cascading hair is a necessary asset for an unmarried young woman. If my hair came even close to cascading I might agree with her.

The sound of drums and trumpets compels my mother to stop her assault on my hair. My insides do a flip. Then another. It is time to take my place among the students. Graduation is about to begin.

My father and brothers appear out of the crowd and give me hugs before I head for the raised platform where my fellow graduates and I are expected to stand throughout the ceremony. It's often said that getting through eleven years of school is easier than standing through the two or more hours it takes to leave it. I am hoping whoever said that was just joking.

We line up as directed across the back of the stage. Boys in back. Girls in front. Which I am thankful for, because otherwise I wouldn't be able to see anything. My brothers inherited my mother's and father's height, whereas I am a throwback to another generation. At five feet, two inches, I am the shortest girl in my class.

Ms. Jorghen, our teacher, fusses with our positioning and reminds us at least a dozen times to smile, stand straight, and pay attention. This is her first Graduation Day in Five Lakes Colony so she is no doubt nervous. Once she is happy with our arrangement on the stage, she takes her place in the middle of the platform and the trumpets and drums sound again. Magistrate Owens appears in the doorway of her house—the only three-story structure on the square—and walks stiffly through the crowd. She is a robust, gray-haired woman with deep lines on her face. Her red dress is a darker color than most, more of a rust tone. The minute she reaches the podium at the front of the stage, she leans into the microphone that is set to amplify her voice across the square and announces, "Happy Graduation Day."

We all say the words back to her and several citizens applaud. Magistrate Owens waits for the square to grow quiet again before saying, "Graduation Day is an exciting time for us all, but especially for the students behind me. After today, they will become a very welcome addition to our colony's workforce. Twenty-five years ago, the United Commonwealth government decided to send 150 men, women, and children to this area. They created Five Lakes Colony in the hopes that our hard work could make the scarred earth that was once rich with farmland and forests thrive. The five lakes that we are named after were once called the Great Lakes. With the aid of our citizens, we are helping restore them to their original name.

We have needed every member of our community to make this happen. Graduation Day adds fourteen of you to our cause and for that we are fortunate. Each step we take forward creates the need for more hands to help cultivate progress. Trust me when I say we can never have enough hands. I know many of you have not yet decided what careers you will embark upon, but all of us are grateful for whatever work you will do here in the years to come."

The crowd applauds. My heart swoops with nerves and excitement as Magistrate Owens announces, "Let the Graduation Day parade begin."

I bite my lip to keep it from trembling as the trumpets and drums take up a marching melody. My eyes blur with unshed tears, blinding me for a moment to the entrance of my soon-to-be former schoolmates. Every year the students from the school parade into the square one class at a time to great applause. Each class makes a banner that two students carry at the front to announce what lessons were learned this year. After the ceremony, the banners will be displayed in the square and the favorite one will be voted on. There is often friendly betting among the adults as to which class will win. For the first time, I am not among those parading, and it hits me that I never will be again.

The youngest class leads the parade, followed by the next oldest and so on. They march around the fountain to the beat of the drums and over to an area left of the stage that is roped off for them. When all ten classes are standing near the stage, Magistrate Owens talks about the new train system that has been developed between Tosu City and ten of the other colonies and the plans to continue construction until all colonies are reachable by rail. From my place on the stage I can see the crowd's excitement at the news. When she is done relating news from the United Commonwealth, Magistrate Owens invites the citizens in charge of water, power, agriculture, and other revitalization projects to make announcements. These take more than an hour and range from reminders about proper water usage to requests for volunteers to help build dwellings for newly married couples. Even my father makes an announcement about a new, heartier breed of potato that his team developed.

I blink and try not to show my surprise. Not at the new potato. That I knew about. The old strain of potato had a half-inch hard skin that turned black when exposed to air. Something to do with whatever genetic enhancement Dad gave it to survive in the blighted soil in the first place. For the most part no one cared about the black skin. Once you cut away the outside, the potato was safe to eat. But Zeen decided to try his hand at a new version and succeeded brilliantly. So, no, it is not the potatoes that have caught me off-guard, but the words Dad uses to announce them. Last week he told us that Zeen was going to get full credit for the project.

But he doesn't. Zeen's name is never mentioned.

I crane my neck, trying to see Zeen in the crowd. Does he look disappointed? This was supposed to be a moment of triumph for him. Is he as confused as I am? I find him leaning against a tree in the middle of the applauding crowd. Several people are slapping him on the back because he is a member of Dad's team. But his smile doesn't fool me. The set of his jaw and the narrowing of his eyes tell me better than words that he has felt the slight.

Dad leaves the stage to more applause and our teacher takes

his place. My stomach clenches and my breathing quickens. This is it. I am about to graduate.

Ms. Jorghen smiles back at us. Then she says into the microphone, "I am very proud to read the roster of graduates who today pass from their studies into adulthood."

One by one she announces the names of our graduating class. One by one my classmates walk to the center of the stage, shake Magistrate Owens's hand, and then take their place back in line. The names are read in alphabetical order, so mine isn't called until the end.

"Malencia Vale."

My legs are unsteady from nerves and stiff from standing. I walk over to the podium and shake both Ms. Jorghen's and the magistrate's hands while the crowd applauds. Daileen's cheers can be heard above all others, and her smile makes me respond with one of my own. My heart soars. I'm officially an adult. I did it.

Still grinning, I return to my place with my class as Magistrate Owens takes the podium. The crowd goes silent. A ripple of anticipation makes my stomach churn. My hands clench and unclench in anticipation. If any students have been selected for The Testing, this is when it will be announced. I crane my neck, trying to spot an unknown face in the crowd—the rumored Tosu City official.

Only there is no Tosu City official. Magistrate Owens gives us all a big smile and says, "Congratulations to all of this year's students and especially to our graduates. I can't wait to see what your futures hold."

The crowd cheers again and my lips curl into an automatic

smile even as disappointment and tears lodge in my throat. I have been preparing for this day for years and now it is over. As are my dreams for the future. No matter how hard I worked, I wasn't good enough to be chosen for The Testing.

As I leave the stage and am given hugs of congratulations by my friends, I can only wonder, *What will I do now?*

CHAPTER 2

"HIDING?"

I startle at my brother's voice. Zeen's knowing smile makes the denial I was about to give die on my lips. Instead, I shrug. "Things have been kind of crazy today. I just needed a few minutes to catch my breath."

Guitars, drums, and several horns play music in front of the bakery while dozens of people dance and clap their hands to the beat. On the other side of the square, roasted meats continue to be sliced and carved. A combination of torchlight and electricity illuminates the rest of the square where people laugh, sing, and play games. But the light doesn't reach me in the shadows where I stand. For the past few hours, I've been dancing and singing because it is expected. To do anything less would be to show my disappointment, which would also reveal my arrogance in thinking I was smart enough to be chosen.

"Here." Zeen hands me a cup with an understanding nod. "You could use this."

The drink is sweet, but underneath there is the distinct flavor of something sharp and bitter. Alcohol. Since most fruits and grains that can be turned into alcohol are needed to feed Five Lakes Colony citizens, very little of the crop is turned into liquor. But a small amount is set aside every year for special occasions—like graduation night. Only adults are allowed to consume the special drinks, but my brothers have allowed me to sip from their cups in the past. The flavor isn't to my liking, so I only take a quick sip and pass the cup back to Zeen.

"Feel better, kiddo?"

I look down to avoid his eyes. "Not exactly."

"Yeah." He leans back against a large oak tree and drains the rest of the liquid from the cup. "Things don't always work out the way we hope. You just have to pick yourself up and find a new direction to go in."

The edge to his voice makes me ask, "Is that what you're going to do then?" In the past couple years Zeen had toyed with seeing what opportunities existed outside of Five Lakes. I would hate it if he did it now. Having him leave our colony would be sad. Knowing he'd be leaving mad would break my heart.

His hand tightens around the cup, but his words are mild when he answers, "I'm not sending an application to Tosu City, if that's what you mean. The magistrate asked Dad to change his announcement today, so he did. You know me. I'll be pissed for a few days and then I'll get over it." He shrugs, and his eyes shift to the party in the square. It's getting late. While some will dance and sing until morning, many are already starting to make the journey home. Graduation Day is coming to an end.

After several minutes, Zeen says, "You could do it, you know."

"Do what?"

"Talk to the magistrate. Send an application to Tosu City."

The thought is both terrifying and tempting. Any colonist interested in working in Tosu City or another colony can fill out an application and file it with the magistrate's office. The United Commonwealth government will then contact the applicant with an appropriate job assignment if one is available. In my sixteen years, I've known of only two applicants who were contacted and offered positions. After the disappointment of today, I'm not sure I'm ready to face another.

My uncertainty must show on my face, because Zeen throws an arm around my shoulders and gives me a quick hug. "Don't worry, kiddo. You have lots of time to figure out what you're going to do with the rest of your life."

Too bad Mom doesn't agree.

We all sleep late the next morning, but I've barely had a chance to get dressed before my mother says, "If you are determined not to work with your father, Kip Drysten has an opening on his team. You should talk to him before one of the other graduates takes the position."

Kip Drysten's team repairs farming equipment. While I like working with mechanical things, the idea of repairing broken-down tractors for the rest of my life is depressing. "I'll think about it," I say.

My mother's frown speaks volumes, which is why I find myself climbing on my bicycle and slowly riding toward town in search of Mr. Drysten.

The Drystens live in a small, pretty cottage on the other side of the colony. Knocking on the front door, I swallow hard. I can't help the swell of relief I feel when Mr. Drysten's wife tells me that Kip left early this morning for the Endress farm. He isn't expected back for several days. I've been granted a reprieve.

The day after graduation is a day of rest. Most businesses are closed. Families stay home to hold more private celebrations. My mother is planning a large meal later and even has invited a few of my friends over to share. I should probably go home and help with the preparations. Instead, I get off my bicycle when I reach the town square.

I lean my bicycle against a tree and sit next to the fountain. One or two citizens wave, but they are busy and don't stop to talk. Which I prefer. Resting my head on my hands, I watch the water gurgle in the fountain and try to ignore the hollowness that has taken root since yesterday's ceremony. I am an adult. Ever since I was little I watched my parents and the other adults and wished for the day I would be one of them — confident and strong. Never have I felt so unsure of myself.

The clock above the magistrate's house gongs. Three o'clock. Time to get home before my mother starts to worry. I'm over halfway there when I spot my brother Hart speeding down the dirt path toward me. Crap. If Mom sent him to find me, I'm really in trouble.

But it isn't my mother looking for me. "Magistrate Owens sent a pulse radio message to Dad just after you left the house. You're supposed to report to her house at four o'clock to talk about your future plans. When you didn't come home right away, Mom sent us all out to look for you." Hart gives me a wicked grin. "You'd better hurry if you're going to make it."

He's right. By the time I arrive back in the square, sweat is dripping down my face, my hair is a wreck, and my stomach is tied in knots. While my father and brothers have had occasion to be summoned to the magistrate's house to talk about their various projects, this is a first for me. My future plans? I can't help but wonder if this summons was prompted by my mother's concern. Did she contact Magistrate Owens and enlist her help or has my lack of career path been obvious to others? The idea that my disappointment has been noticed by those outside my family makes my stomach roil with shame.

Preparing for a lecture, I run my hands through my hair and straighten my white short-sleeved tunic and gray pants before knocking on the magistrate's front door.

"Good. You made it." Magistrate Owens gives me a smile that doesn't quite reach her eyes. "Please come in, Cia. Everyone else is already here."

Everyone else?

Magistrate Owens leads me into a large, carpeted sitting room and four faces turn to look at me. The three people who are seated are familiar. Gray-eyed, handsome Tomas Endress. Shy but sweet Malachi Rourke. Beautiful, artistic Zandri Hicks. They are fellow graduates. People I have known almost my entire life. The other is not.

Tomas motions for me to take a seat next to him and gives me a dimpled smile that makes it impossible not to smile in return. Magistrate Owens crosses the room, stands next to the stranger, and says, "Thank you all for coming on such short notice. I apologize for pulling you away from your family celebrations, but it was unavoidable." Her eyes sweep the room, looking at each one of us. "This is Tosu City official Michal Gallen. He intended on arriving yesterday for graduation, but was unavoidably delayed due to a mechanical problem."

Tosu City.

My heart tilts as Tosu City official Gallen takes a step forward and pulls a folded piece of paper from his pocket. He's older than us, but not by much. Around Zeen's age, with shaggy brown hair and a lanky awkwardness that belies the authority he must bring with him from Tosu.

His dark eyes are serious as he looks down at the paper and reads, "Every year the United Commonwealth reviews the achievements of the graduates in all eighteen colonies. The top students from that pool of graduates are brought to Tosu City for Testing to attend the University. Being chosen is an honor. The graduates of the University are our great hope—the ones we are all counting on to help regenerate the earth and improve our quality of life. They are the future scientists, doctors, teachers, and government officials." The paper lowers, and he gives us a smile. "You four have been selected to participate in The Testing."

A wave of excitement washes over me. I look around to see if I have heard correctly. Tomas's face is lit with a smile. He is the smartest in our class, so it is no wonder he has been chosen. According to this Tosu City official, I have too. Four of us have. This is real. I won't have to work with tractors. I have been chosen for The Testing. I did it.

"You will leave for The Testing tomorrow."

The glow of happiness fades as the reality of the Tosu City official's words slam into my chest. We leave tomorrow.

"Why tomorrow?" Magistrate Owens asks. "I remember there being more time in between selection and The Testing."

"Things have changed since your colony last had a Testing candidate," the Tosu City official answers. His voice is deep with a hint of impatience. "The candidates will begin the Testing process this week. I think you'll agree they stand a better chance of passing if they arrive on time."

"What if we don't want to go?"

We all turn to look at Zandri. Her face is almost the same crimson shade as her tunic. At first I think it is from embarrassment. Then she lifts her chin. By the way her blue eyes glitter, it is clear she is angry. The fact that four of us were chosen for The Testing is astonishing, but Zandri being one of the four is perhaps the bigger surprise. Not that Zandri isn't smart. She is, although many of us would think of her as an artist first and a scholar second. Zandri only excels at science when it helps her create new paints. And while she has never indicated a desire to continue her education, I am still surprised at her question. Who would turn down the honor of being chosen for The Testing?

The Tosu City official smiles, and I shiver. It is a smile devoid of warmth. "You don't have a choice. The law states that every United Commonwealth citizen chosen must present him or herself for The Testing by the appointed date or face punishment."

"What kind of punishment?" Zandri looks to Magistrate Owens, who glances at the Tosu City official.

The two lock eyes before Magistrate Owens says, "According to the law, not presenting oneself for The Testing is a form of treason."

And the most common punishment for treason is death.

Someone, perhaps Malachi, whispers a protest. My chest feels as though someone has wrapped his arms around me and squeezed tight. All my excitement about being chosen is gone—replaced with an icy fear. Only, there is no reason to fear. I want to be tested. Punishment will not be required for me.

Or for any of my fellow candidates. At the word *treason,* the fight goes out of Zandri.

Seeing our shock, Magistrate Owens explains that the law that governs the punishment for not accepting our place in The Testing goes back to the very early days of the United Commonwealth. There were lawless factions that wished to tear apart the new government and tried to convince Testing candidates to rebel. There is talk of the law being changed, but these things take time.

I feel a bit better knowing the law hasn't been invoked in decades, and the excitement that had been extinguished begins to resurface as the magistrate discusses the basics we will need to bring with us to Tosu City. Testing candidates are allowed to bring two changes of everyday clothing. Two sets of undergarments. One set of nightclothes. Two pairs of shoes. Two personal items. No books. No papers. Nothing that might give one candidate an advantage over another. Everything must fit in the bags we will be given when we leave the meeting. We are expected to be in the square tomorrow at first light, with our bags. Tosu City official Michal Gallen will be waiting to escort us to the Testing Center.

She then tells us how proud she is of our achievements and says she is certain we will all be successful in our Testing. But I know she's lying. My mother has the same forced, overly bright smile when she's upset. Magistrate Owens does not think we will all pass. Does she worry that our failure will reflect poorly on Five Lakes Colony?

I'm still wondering as we are escorted toward the front entrance.

Bright sunshine greets us as the door swings open. I am the last of the four to take a dark brown bag with the red and purple United Commonwealth logo on the front from Magistrate Owens. As I sling the thick strap over my shoulder, I realize the dinner party my mother has painstakingly planned will have to be cut short. Otherwise, I will not have enough time to pack and prepare for whatever tomorrow brings.

Zandri is already gone when I step outside, but Tomas and Malachi are waiting. For a moment the three of us stare at one another, uncertain what to say. I'm not surprised when Tomas is the first to find his voice. With one of his wide, heart-stopping smiles, he looks into my eyes and says, "I guess we should go home. Tomorrow's going to be a big day."

And I know he's right. It's time to go home and tell my family that tomorrow I will leave the house in the morning and I won't return.

CHAPTER 3

THE SOUND OF my family's laughter greets me as I open the front door. A congratulatory banner hangs on the far wall. The kitchen table is covered with plates stacked high with bread, meats, and sweets for my graduation celebration. Now it will also be a party of farewell.

"There she is," Zeen yells as he spots me in the doorway. "I told you she wouldn't be late for her own party. Not when cinnamon bread is involved."

My father turns with a smile. The minute he spots the bag hanging from my shoulder, the smile fades and recognition blooms in his eyes. "You've been chosen for The Testing."

The laughter disappears. Smiles falter as all eyes turn to me for confirmation. For all my happiness at being chosen, my throat tightens when I nod. University graduates go where United Commonwealth officials send them—where their skills are most needed. If I succeed in passing The Testing, the chances of my returning home are almost none.

The twins recover first. Before I know what hits me, the boys have me squeezed between them in one of their sandwich hugs, yelling congratulations. Hamin hugs me next. His excitement is less boisterous, but no less genuine. Then my mother is there. Her hands shake when she embraces me, but her smile is filled with pride as she asks what I'm allowed to bring and when I'm supposed to leave. I barely have time to answer or notice Zeen slipping out of the room before there is knocking at the door signaling the arrival of my friends.

I am so happy to see them, especially Daileen. So happy I get the chance to say goodbye in person. There are more shouts of happiness and far more tears as I explain about The Testing and the others who were selected. Daileen's happiness and sorrow are greatest of all. She tries to hide the sadness behind wide smiles, but as the party continues, I notice she slips more and more into the background, away from me, away from the others who she has always considered more my friends than hers. And I'm scared. While my family will feel the loss of my presence, they still have one another. Daileen will have no one.

Which is why, when my mother tells everyone the party has to end early, the first person I search out for farewell is Lyane Maddows. She isn't bouncing with excitement or yelling to get my attention. Instead, she stands quietly near the door, waiting for my brothers to escort her home. Lyane and I aren't the best of friends. We always say hello when we see each other, but rarely do we sit together at lunchtime or chat after school. But Lyane and I have a connection, which is why I invited her today. One I know she hasn't forgotten. I hope that memory means I can count on her help.

As the girls still squeal and chatter behind me, I wrap my arms around Lyane and give her a hug. Her shoulders tense with surprise, but she doesn't pull back. In her ear, I whisper, "Daileen needs a friend when I leave tomorrow. Will you watch out for her and keep her from being alone? Please."

Lyane's arms hug me tighter. I can almost feel her weighing my request. Her return whisper makes tears prick the back of my eyes from relief and gratitude. Daileen will not be alone.

Lyane walks out of the house without a backwards glance as I turn to say goodbye to the others. Daileen waits to be last. I can tell how hard she fights to hold back tears as she promises to see me next year in Tosu City. "I'm going to study harder than ever. They'll have no choice but to choose me."

It is only the sound of Lyane's voice from outside calling, "Daileen, will you walk next to me?" that keeps my heart from breaking as I watch Daileen slip out of view. Lyane knows what the darkness of too much solitude can do to a person. I helped pull her out of that black place four years before when I found her at the end of the colony limits, looking over the edge of the ravine, preparing to jump. Only, I wouldn't let her. Instead, I made her talk. About her father who was a government official in Tosu City and her mother who hated living in Five Lakes and took out her frustration and anger on her daughter. As far as I know, Lyane has never shown anyone else but me the scars she received at the hands of her mother. With my father's and the magistrate's help, Lyane's mother joined her husband in Tosu City while Lyane was taken in by another Five Lakes family and found reasons to smile. I trust Lyane to help Daileen find those reasons, too.

With my brothers acting as escorts for my friends, the house feels larger than usual as I help my parents clear dishes and tidy up the main room. Our current house is large by most standards. In addition to the central living space, we have two other rooms in the back of the house. The one on the right belongs to my parents. My brothers and I sleep in the one on the left, although Zeen and Hamin snore so loudly that I have taken to sleeping on a pile of blankets in front of the fireplace in the main room. I smile. Going to Tosu City for The Testing means I might sleep in a bed again.

While we work, Mom chatters about what I should take with me and how I should behave while in the city. More than once she stops what she is doing and tears up at the idea of me being the first of her children to leave home. My father says nothing during these moments, although I can tell he wants to.

When all the dishes have been washed and stored away, my father says, "Why don't we take a walk?" When my mother opens her mouth to protest, he says, "I know Cia needs to pack, but before the boys get back and things get crazy, I'd like to spend a bit of quiet time with my little girl."

My mom sniffles and my heart squeezes as I head into the darkening night with my father.

My father takes my hand, and together we stroll around the house to the back gardens. A hazy moon and stars are starting to shine above us. They say at one time the sky was clear and on a cloudless night the stars looked like diamonds. Perhaps that was true. It's hard to imagine.

Near the back of the house, Dad hits a switch. First there is a humming sound, then one by one lights flicker around the backyard, illuminating the beautiful daisies, roses, and vegetable plants behind our house. While the plants belong to Dad and my brothers, the lights belong to me. The colony has strict laws governing electricity usage. Production and storage of electricity in our area is limited. Most personal dwellings don't use electricity at all unless the citizens can create their own. Not many bother to try since candles and firelight work perfectly well. A few years ago, I decided to take up the challenge and talked Dad into letting me experiment with some leftover irrigation tubes, scrap copper plating, and wire. I conned Mom into giving me some glass jars, a little of our precious salt, and a bunch of other odds and ends, and got to work. The result is a network of fifteen lights all powered by the energy my solar panels harvest during the day. While I could create a much more sophisticated system now, Dad insists on using this one. This is the third backyard it has illuminated. For a moment, I wonder how long it will be before we have to move it again. Then I realize that I won't be here to help when the time comes.

Dad leads me over to the oak bench Hamin made Mom for her birthday and takes a seat. I sit next to him and wait for him to speak.

Crickets chirp. Wind rustles the tree branches above us. From somewhere deep in the lengthening shadows come the faint sounds of wolves and other animals prowling in the night.

After what seems like forever, Dad takes my hand and holds it tight. When he speaks, I have to lean close to hear him. "There are things I've never told you. I had hoped to never tell you. Even now I'm not certain I should."

I sit up straighter. "Is it about The Testing?"

Dad has never talked about his Testing or much about his days spent at the University no matter how many questions I've asked. For a moment I feel closer to him, knowing we'll share this experience. Then the moment is shattered.

"You should never have been chosen."

The words slap me across the face. I try to pull my hand free, but my father holds on tight. His eyes are staring into the darkness, but the expression on his face says he is not seeing anything. The glint of fear in his expression makes me forget my hurt. A knot of worry grows in my chest as my father's eyes meet mine.

"My parents and I dreamed of me being chosen for The Testing. Our family was barely surviving. Omaha Colony was one of the largest colonies in the Commonwealth. There were too many people. Not enough resources. There was never enough food for everyone. We all knew someone who had died from starvation. My parents believed I could help fix that. Restore balance to the earth. I wanted them to have the money the government gives Testing candidate families to compensate them for the loss of the student. And I admit that part of me believed my parents. I believed I could help. I wanted to try."

That the government compensates Testing candidate families is news to me. I want to ask if he and Mother will be compensated when I leave, but I withhold my question as Dad continues talking.

"There were only fourteen colonies then. Seventy-one of us assembled in the Testing Center. They tell me The Testing for my class took four weeks. I don't remember a single day.

Sixteen of us were chosen to move on. The head of the Testing committee said Testing memories are wiped clean after the process is complete to ensure confidentiality."

"So you can't tell me what the tests will be like?" Disappointment churns inside me. I had hoped my father's experience would help me prepare—give me an edge. No doubt this was exactly what the Commonwealth government was preventing by removing my father's memories.

"I remember arriving at the Testing Center. I remember being assigned a roommate, Geoff Billings. I remember us toasting our bright futures with full glasses of fresh milk and eating cake. There was lots of food and excitement. We could barely sleep that first night knowing our dreams could end the next day if we didn't perform well on the tests. The next thing I remember is sitting in a room filled with chairs being told The Testing was complete. I started attending University classes three weeks later. Geoff wasn't there. Neither were the two girls from my colony who traveled with me."

Somewhere in the night an owl screeches, but Dad doesn't seem to hear it. "The University was challenging. I enjoyed my classes. I liked knowing I was doing something important. My parents were able to send word that they were safe and well and proud. I was happy. I never gave a thought to Geoff or the other Testing candidates who didn't pass."

He closes his eyes and I sit beside him, wondering what it would feel like to lose the memories of my friends. To only remember the day I met Daileen. To not remember the giggles and the adventures we've had. The idea makes me want to cry, and I lace my fingers through my father's to make us both feel better.

"I went to Lenox Colony after I graduated. There was a botanist who was close to a breakthrough, and the Commonwealth thought my ideas might help. I worked there a year before I ran into a boy who reminded me of Geoff. That night I started having dreams. I'd wake up sweating, heart racing, not knowing why. Not a night would pass uninterrupted. My work began to suffer, and the government medics gave me pills to help with sleep. The pills didn't stop the dreams. They just made it harder for me to escape them. In the light of day I began to remember the dreams. Just flashes at first. Geoff giving me a thumbs-up from across a white room with black desks. A large red-numbered clock counting down the time as my fingers manipulated three blue wires. A girl screaming."

My father lets go of my hand and stands. I feel a flicker of fear as he runs a hand through his hair and then begins to pace.

"The flashes stopped. In their place was one recurring dream. Geoff, a girl named Mina, and me walking down a street lined with burned-out steel buildings. Broken glass covers the street. We're looking for water and a place to sleep for the night. The buildings are so badly damaged that we're nervous about using them for shelter, but we might have to because of the predators we've seen at night. Mina is limping. I spot a large branch and offer to make her a walking stick. While I'm working, Geoff scouts down the block. Mina tells him not to go too far. He promises he won't. A few minutes later he yells he's found something. Then the world explodes."

Dad goes still. My heart pounds loud in my chest. Dad's voice has gotten so quiet I have to lean forward to hear him say,

"I find Mina first—half buried under a slab of concrete, blood running down her face."

Dad swallows hard. His breathing is rough. His hands clench and unclench at his sides. I can tell he wants to stop talking. I want him to stop. This feels too real. I can see the blood. I can feel my father's fear.

"I find one of Geoff's boots ten feet away from Mina's body. It takes me a minute to realize his foot is still in the boot and I start to scream. That's where the dream ends."

For a moment the night goes silent. No more sound of owls. No bugs flutter. Just the image of a boy not much older than me in pieces on an abandoned street. A boy who went to be tested . . .

"It was just a dream." That's what Dad used to tell me when I had nightmares. I always believed it. I want to believe it now.

"Maybe." My father raises his eyes. The haunted despair in their depths makes me catch my breath. "For years I told myself it was just a dream. I consoled myself with the knowledge that I didn't have a single waking memory of a girl named Mina. We made breakthroughs in our experiments. New plants I helped create began to thrive. I never told a soul about the dreams. Then the Commonwealth assigned me to work in Five Lakes. God, I was angry. Being assigned to Five Lakes was like an insult. Only a handful of University graduates were stationed here. I didn't even have my own house when I first arrived. I had to sleep in Flint Carro's living room."

This part of the story is familiar. Normally, he tells it with a smile. Becoming friends with the colony's doctor. Being dragged into the tailor's shop by Flint. Seeing my mother sitting at a loom, weaving. Falling in love with her grace and kindness.

But that isn't the story this time. And my father isn't smiling.

"Flint's house is small. There was no hiding the nightmares. Flint waited a week before he asked about them. I tried to brush him off. That's when he told me about his own dreams. Not as scary. But disturbing. Faces of people he didn't remember. Waiting for friends to return from an exam, but they never come. Over the next year, Flint and I talked to the other University graduates. There were seven of us then. We had to be careful because every Commonwealth employee is in contact with the officials in Tosu City. We didn't want to jeopardize our jobs. I'm certain four of the others never lost a night's sleep, but one, the head of the school, had a haunted look that I understood. She denied she had nightmares, but she must have."

"You can't know that." I stand up and cross my arms over my chest, waiting for him to agree with me. I need him to agree.

His eyes meet mine. "No, but not a single student who graduated from Five Lakes was chosen for The Testing while she was in charge of the school. I don't believe it was a coincidence. Do you?"

A shiver snakes up my spine. I don't know what to believe. To believe my father's dreams are something more than dreams is unthinkable. Tomorrow I leave for Tosu City. At the end of the week I will begin my Testing. To refuse is treason and all that implies. I want to scream and shout, but all I can do is stand there and shiver.

My father puts his arm around me and leads me back to the bench. I lean my head on his shoulder like I used to do when I was small. For a moment, I feel safe, but it doesn't last.

"Flint says whatever process they used to wipe our memories could have caused the dreams. Our brains might be creating false memories to replace the ones that were taken."

"But you don't believe that."

He shakes his head. "I was grateful when your brothers graduated and no one from Tosu City came to take them to be tested. Yesterday, I upset your brother by not publicly giving him the credit due to him because the magistrate received word a Tosu official was on his way. I didn't want anyone questioning whether students should have been chosen before and whether past graduates should be reevaluated."

He pulls me tight against him and rests his chin on top of my head. A tear falls on my cheek, but it isn't mine. My father, who has always been so strong and smart and sure, is crying.

"So now what?" I squirm out of his arms and jump to my feet, angry. Angry that never once in all of our walks or conversations did he tell me these things. Never once when I was studying late into the night so I would do well on a test did he tell me what the consequences might be. "I leave in the morning. Why tell me this now? What good does it do?"

My father doesn't raise his voice to meet mine. "Maybe none. Maybe Flint is right and our dreams are just hallucinations. But if there's a chance they aren't, it is better you know. Better that you go to Tosu City prepared to question everything you see and everyone you meet. That might be the difference between success or failure." He crosses to me and puts his hands on my shoulders. I start to pull away, but then I notice the light reflecting off the tears pooling in his eyes. The fight goes out of me.

"Does Mom know?" I think she must, but at this point I'm not sure of anything.

"Your mother knows about the memory wipe and that I have nightmares, but not what they contain."

I roll the words over in my head, testing them for the truth. "So, is that why Mom didn't want me to be chosen?"

My father lays a hand on my face and rubs his thumb against my cheek. "Cia, I haven't seen my parents since the day I left to be tested. To have a child chosen is an honor, but it also means loss. Your mother didn't want to lose you."

I don't know how long we sit in silence. Long enough to hear my brothers' voices announcing their return and my mother's shouts chastising them for sneaking sweets. It all sounds so normal.

When my face is dry of tears, my father takes my hand and walks me back inside. We don't mention Dad's dreams or my new fears as Hamin teases the twins about my friends flirting with them. Mom puts out a platter of small cakes and sweetened mint tea as the boys pull out a deck of cards so we can all play one last game as a family. Even as I enjoy the laughter and warmth around the table, it feels incomplete without Zeen, who has yet to return. More than once I find myself watching the front door. I love all my brothers, but Zeen's the one I go to when I have a problem I need to talk about. Zeen is always patient and insightful. He asks questions, and without fail I feel better after any discussion. Tonight I have a problem, but Zeen isn't here.

When the game is over, my mother gently reminds me of the hour and of the task still in front of me. Excusing myself, I take the Commonwealth bag and slip into the bedroom I share with my brothers.

Knowing I may never see the room again makes me look at it with fresh eyes. A fire glows in the hearth nestled into the back wall. A square, worn brown rug sits in the middle of the room. Two sets of bunk beds are arranged on either side of the rug. Only mine, the bottom bed closest to the fireplace, has the sheets tucked in and the quilt smoothed. As soon as the boys graduated from school, Mom declared them old enough to tidy up their own beds. And they decided they were old enough not to care whether they slept in tightly tucked sheets.

We each have a wooden chest for our everyday clothes and shoes. The special clothes are hung in the large wooden armoire in the corner. Mother always talks about first impressions. I gnaw on my bottom lip and weigh the merits of all my clothes. Feeling confident is always easier when dressed in something special, but I hear my father's voice replay in my head. I imagine the abandoned city street he walked in his dream. The two dresses I own won't help me there. And even if the dreams aren't real, I know in my heart pretty clothes won't help once The Testing begins.

Ignoring the special attire, I walk to the wooden chest I've used since I was a little girl. I select two pairs of strong, comfortable pants and two sturdy shirts and my most comfortable boots. They are all hand-me-downs from my brothers. Knowing I have a piece of them coming with me helps ease the loneliness I already feel. I grab sleepwear and undergarments and carefully stow the selections in my bag. There is still plenty of room for the two personal items I am allowed to bring with me.

Sitting on the edge of my bed, I look around the room. Had my father not shared his dreams, I might have taken my flute or the silver necklace my mother gave me on my sixteenth birthday. Instead, I consider what might help me if The Testing is more than paper and pencil examinations.

After several minutes I slide off the bed and pull a small pocket hunting knife out of my chest. Each of my brothers has a similar knife—a gift from Dad. The knife also has a screwdriver and a few other gadgets attached. That's one. Now for number two. There is only one other thing I can think of that might help, but it doesn't belong to me. And Zeen isn't here to ask permission.

Last year, Dad began letting Zeen experiment at work with his own projects. Some of those projects take him outside the colony boundaries. The boundaries were designed not so much to keep people or animals out, but to remind Five Colony citizens that the land beyond is potentially unsafe. Poisonous plants and meat-seeking animals are only part of the danger. During the last three stages of war, violent earthquakes ripped the fabric of the land. A lone traveler who falls into one of the earthquake-made fissures can easily find death waiting at the bottom from a broken neck, exposure, or hunger. To prevent the latter two, Dad gave Zeen a small handheld device called a Transit Communicator sent to him by the Commonwealth government. The device has a compass, a calculator, and a communication system that allows Zeen to contact a matching device in Dad's office if ever there is a problem. I don't know how it works, but I'm betting if necessary I can figure it out.

When Zeen isn't working beyond the border, he keeps the device on a shelf next to his bed. Sure enough. My heart aches as my fingers close over the device. I wish Zeen were here to give me permission—to tell me he forgives me for being chosen when he was not. I want to tell Zeen that our father was trying to protect him when the announcement about the potato was made yesterday. That it wasn't motivated by ego, but by love.

I wrap the Transit Communicator in a pair of socks to keep it safe and slide it into my bag, hoping Zeen returns in time for me to tell him I've taken a piece of him with me to Tosu City. Even though I know he will not. Zeen is the smartest of my brothers, but he is also the most emotional. While Win, Hart, and Hamin are loving and kind, they possess a carefree attitude about life that frustrates our mother. Zeen, however, is fiercely passionate. His temper is quick to flare, but his love is all encompassing. Which makes the loss of one he loves almost unbearable. He barely spoke for a month when our grandfather died.

Sitting on Zeen's bed, I write a note that will serve as a request for his device and a reminder of my love. Not the farewell I hope for, but the only one I am certain I will have.

Now that my selections are made, panic sets in. Tomorrow I will be walking away from everything I know into something strange and potentially dangerous. What I want most in the world is to climb into bed and pull the covers over my head. Instead, I snap the bag shut, sling it onto my shoulder, and walk back out to my family, hoping to enjoy the last hours I have left with them.

CHAPTER 4

My brothers are still sleeping in their room when my father wakes me from a fitful sleep. I slip on a pair of tan leggings and a light blue cap-sleeve tunic, pull on my boots, and grab my bag. My mother holds a cup of milk for me to drink. Her eyes are red, but she isn't crying now. She tells me she's proud of me. I do my best not to cling to her as we hug goodbye. Suddenly, I am sorry for all the times I was angry at her for not encouraging my dreams of attending the University. Now I understand why she was scared for me to succeed. Now it is too late.

Fighting back tears, I drink my milk, take the apple Mom has waiting for me on the counter, and promise to write when I get to the city. My father waits at the door, and I give my mother one last hug before walking out into the moist morning air. The sky is still dark as we follow the same path we took yesterday. We walk about a mile before Dad breaks the silence.

"Did you get any sleep?"

"Some." Interspersed with anxious dreams.

"More than likely, Flint is right. The dreams are just dreams."

"I hope so."

"So do I." He laces his fingers through mine as we trek uphill. "You're smart. You're strong. I have every faith you'll pass whatever test they give you. Just don't let the other candidates psych you out. Some of the kids from my colony were vicious. They'd do anything to be number one."

"Like what?" Staying up all night to study was common in my class. I'd done it a few times myself.

"Poison was a favorite tactic of a couple of the girls in my class."

I stop walking. "Poison?"

"Not enough to kill. Just enough to make someone too sick to sit for a test. By my final year, I was careful to eat only what I brought with me to school."

"Were they punished?"

My father gives me a sad smile. "They were smart enough not to get caught. But even if they had been, I doubt they would have gotten more than a reprimand. It's hard to punish kids for trying to pull their family out of poverty."

We walk the next few miles without talking as I consider the implications of my father's words. I can tell myself there's no proof my father's dreams are real. But this . . . I can't think of a single student in the Five Lakes Colony school who would sabotage a fellow student in order to get a better grade. None of us are rich, but no one I know is starving, either. Not anymore. If a family is struggling in Five Lakes, the rest of the community pitches in to help. A world where you might poison the competition in order to feed your family is inconceivable to me.

Slashes of pink and purple light the sky as we approach the outskirts of town. Dad puts his arm around my shoulders and holds me close. "Make sure you eat right and get enough sleep. That's going to help you stay strong and think clearly."

I nod at the familiar words.

Just before we finish climbing the last hill he adds, "Be careful who you trust, Cia. You do that and everything will be okay."

Hand in hand, we walk into the square.

In front of the magistrate's house is an enormous black skimmer with the seal of the Commonwealth stamped on the side. Tomas, Malachi, and members of their families are standing near the back of it. Malachi is wearing his best clothes—stiffly pressed pants, polished black shoes, and a jacket over a collared shirt. The bright white of Malachi's shirt is in vivid contrast with his dark skin, and from the hunch of his shoulders I can tell he is fighting back tears. Tomas's clothing choice is more like mine. Faded gray pants and a white V-neck shirt make Tomas look like he is preparing to work on his father's farm instead of traveling to Tosu City. His handsome face is unreadable as his mother fusses over his unruly hair.

Magistrate Owens and the Tosu official are standing near the front of the skimmer and wave as Dad and I approach. Today, official Michal Gallen is wearing a fitted purple jumpsuit, also stamped with the Commonwealth logo. His shaggy hair is slicked back into a ponytail, giving the angles of his face more definition.

Magistrate Owens pulls my father to the side, leaving me

alone with official Gallen. He smiles at me, and I'm surprised to see warmth for the first time in his deep green eyes.

"Are you nervous about the trip, Malencia?"

For some reason I don't expect him to remember my name. That he does pleases me. "I'm more nervous that I'll disappoint the colony by not doing well on the tests, Mr. Gallen."

He laughs. "Call me Michal. And don't worry. That'll pass."

My nerves or caring about the colony? I don't get the chance to ask because he pushes off the vehicle and holds out his hand. "Can I stow your bag? You won't need it until we get to Tosu City." In his other hand is a transparent bag containing two thick silver bands—one larger than the other. "This is your identification bracelet. Each Testing candidate is assigned an identifying symbol that is engraved on the bracelet. You'll wear this one and the smaller band will wrap around the strap on your bag. That way no one can confuse their bag with yours."

He snaps the clasp of the identification band onto my left wrist and affixes the other to my bag. Once he disappears into the skimmer, I study the bracelet. It is about an inch wide and woven of thick metal segments. I know the bracelet has a clasp, but the fastening is impossible to distinguish. Turning my wrist, I study the large silver disk attached to the top of the bracelet. Etched in black on the disk is an eight-pointed star. In the center of the star is a stylized lightning bolt.

"The star represents your Testing group." I jump at Michal's voice. I hadn't realized he'd returned. "You'll find other kids with the same symbol on their bracelet, but yours will be the only one with a lightning bolt."

"Do the symbols mean something specific?" The words slip

past my lips before I can take them back. Maybe kids from other colonies who always have Testing candidates know what the symbols mean.

If he thinks the question is silly, Michal doesn't show it. "The eight-pointed star is the symbol for rejuvenation. The kids in that group show aptitude in a lot of different areas. It's a pretty good group to be in." His smile is warm and encouraging, and I find myself smiling back and wondering what group he was in.

A small beeping sound prompts Michal to look down at his watch. He looks around the square, and his smile fades. Zandri still isn't here, and I wonder if this is just her casual attention to time or if she has chosen to challenge the laws and refuse her place at The Testing. Does she believe laws so long untested will not be enforced?

Michal excuses himself and huddles with Magistrate Owens and my father. From the way Michal is pointing to his watch, he believes the time for Zandri to arrive has come and gone. My father and Magistrate Owens argue with Michal over giving Zandri more time. I turn away and hold my breath, knowing what the punishment might be. And I see her. I squint into the sunlight to be certain before yelling, "She's here."

"Thank God," I hear someone whisper.

The wind teases Zandri's gauzy multicolored skirt and peasant blouse as she strolls unhurried through the square. Her long blond hair glistens in the sunlight. A small smile tugs at her lips as she reaches us. She offers no apologies. And I know. She's planned this entrance. She's showing that while she can be required to perform, she cannot be controlled. While I admire her guts, the annoyed look in Michal's eyes makes me worry for her.

My father puts his arm around me as Michal gives Zandri her identification bracelets, and stows her bag in the skimmer. Gone is his warm manner as he instructs us all to get into the vehicle. It is time to go.

The swirl of emotions I've been holding at bay hits me full force as my father pulls me into a tight embrace. Tears threaten to choke me as I tell him I love him. I push aside the hurt that Zeen didn't say goodbye and ask my father to give Zeen my note and the entire family my love. My father tells me he loves me, too, and reminds me in one last whisper, "Cia, trust no one."

I am the last one to climb into the sleek skimmer. The door closes behind me. I hear the locks engage as the engine roars to life. My father puts his hand on the porthole glass, and I lift mine to mirror it. Our eyes meet for a moment, and one tear escapes my resolve as the skimmer begins to rise. Dad steps back from the skimmer, and a moment later we are moving forward—out of the square, toward Tosu City—away from anything familiar.

My heart races with excitement even as it is torn in two. I can see the same conflicting emotions on the faces of the other Five Lakes Testing candidates. Our graduation ceremony changed our status from adolescent to adult, but this journey makes it official. We are on our own.

I stare out the window until the last familiar sights fade into the horizon. I store up the memories of the fields and the hills for the days and maybe years to come. Then I turn and take in my new surroundings. My father and his staff have a couple of skimmers they use for work, so I've ridden in one before. But my father's vehicles are not as sophisticated or as fast as this. In fact, aside from the name and the fact that they hover several feet over the earth, the vehicles are nothing alike. Where the greenhouse skimmers are small and seat between one and four people, and only that if you squeeze, this one could seat twelve passengers in comfort. The couchlike seats that line the front of the passenger compartment are gray and soft. In the back of the vehicle is a small kitchen and a door that leads to another compartment. The roof of the skimmer is tall enough that I can walk around the cabin with room to spare.

I don't see our bags and consider asking Michal where he stowed them, but he is seated in a separate driver's compartment up front. From the set of his shoulders I'd say he's busy concentrating on driving. Which is good. While skimmers are designed to hover up to fifteen feet above the ground, the propulsion mechanism that makes the vehicle run requires there actually be ground somewhere underneath. If a skimmer travels over a large hole, it will stop gliding. Skimmers also have trouble over water, which is why someone adapted them to float if necessary.

"I've never ridden in anything like this before," Malachi says from across the cabin. His wide eyes are filled with anxiety. His father is an irrigation worker. His mother makes quilts. No, Malachi never would have had cause to ride on anything more sophisticated than a bicycle. Until now. I cock my head to the side to get a better view of the symbol on his bracelet. A triangle with an arrow in the middle. We are not in the same group.

"I think it's safe to say none of us have ridden in anything quite like this." Tomas gets up from his seat in the back and crosses over to sit next to Malachi. "At the rate we're going, we'll be in Tosu City before dark."

"You think so?" Some of the fear fades from Malachi's eyes. "Do you think they'll let us look around the city?"

"Probably not until after we're done with Testing. It sounds like they're going to have us on a pretty tight schedule." Tomas flashes a smile and claps Malachi on the back. "But once we're University students we'll have the run of the place and the girls. Right?"

Malachi smiles back. "Right."

"Some of us don't find University pedigrees attractive." Zandri tosses her blond mane and gives them both a look of disgust. Malachi shrinks back into the cushions. Tomas just laughs. After a bit of encouragement, he gets Malachi to talk about pictures they've seen of Tosu City, where some buildings are more than ten stories high. Eventually Zandri stops sulking and discusses the sculptures she's hoping to see.

I listen to the three of them chat, not surprised that it is Tomas who puts everyone at ease. As always, I'm very aware of being the youngest—and the least experienced. In class, I made sure to raise my hand only if I was certain of the answer so I would never look as though I didn't belong. Now, like in class, I hold back and listen. Tall, blond, and beautiful, Zandri exudes a prickly confidence, but her defensive posture softens when she talks art with Malachi. I'm surprised at the extent of his knowledge of artists long dead.

Now that Malachi and Zandri are filling the silence, Tomas sits back and only adds the occasional comment. He too is observing—weighing their laughter and their silences. Tomas notices me watching. Quickly, I look away as my cheeks burn. Not that Tomas isn't used to being looked at. Most girls in our class would spend the entire school day watching him instead of the blackboard. Since his assigned seat was directly behind mine, I never had the distraction. But I'd have to be blind not to notice the way laughter and the single dimple in his left cheek transform his angular face. More than once my fingers have itched to brush back the lock of hair that always falls across his forehead. Not that I'd ever have the courage to try. Which is okay. Boys and dating haven't been on my priority list. And they certainly can't be now.

The trio across the way laughs at something. Shrugging off feelings of being left out, I smile at the group and try to look interested in their chatter. After a while, Zandri and Malachi admit they didn't sleep well the night before. They stretch out on the cushioned benches in the front of the passenger compartment and are out almost immediately.

"Let's move to the back so we don't disturb them," Tomas whispers. My heart skips a little as I follow his lead. Tomas's first order of business is to explore the back of the cabin. I'm happy to open cabinet doors—which contain nuts, dried fruit, cheese, and crackers—and poke into the closet, which turns out to be a bathroom.

We grab a bag of dried fruit and some water and stretch out in the back. Tomas turns an apple chip over in his strong, calloused hands and says, "It's hard to believe they selected four of us this year."

I notice his bracelet design—an eight-pointed star with three wavy horizontal lines. My group. My surprise and worry must show because Tomas asks what's wrong. I explain about the identification symbols. Then, since Malachi and Zandri are both snoring, I decide to be completely honest. "You're going to blow everyone in our group away. Me included."

"Are you kidding?" Tomas's clear gray eyes sweep over my face. After a minute he laughs and shakes his head. "You really aren't joking."

"Everyone knows you were first in our class."

"Only because the teacher wasn't around last year. She doesn't know you built the wind and solar generators we use at school."

"My brothers helped." The achievement wasn't mine alone. I wouldn't have been able to do it without them. "My father says the irrigation system you designed is going to help revitalize areas outside our borders. That's huge."

He shrugs. "My father had been working on it for years. I just helped brainstorm a few ideas and set the thing up. I'm not saying I wasn't important, but I wasn't the genius Ms. Jorghen made me out to be. I got the impression she thought Five Lakes students were simple-minded. You know, since no one had been chosen for The Testing in years. My report on the new irrigation system during the first week of class made an impression."

Tomas is right about our teacher's preconceived ideas of Five Lakes Colony. For the first few days of the new school year every word she spoke was slow and deliberate. She sounded like she was talking to a group of four-year-olds. Then she gave us a "How I spent my break" assignment and everything changed. Ms. Jorghen's face never showed surprise, but the assignments got harder and she stopped talking in one-syllable words. Thinking about it now makes me wonder if my dad

the thought of my face being seen on some unknown television. We don't have much use for televisions in Five Lakes. The magistrate has one. So does my father's work and a few other select locations. Rarely are they used. Clearly they are not used so sparingly outside of my colony.

I move to the front of the cabin, feeling the camera following my every move. Does it also hear my words? If I had a chance to inspect the camera, I'd be able to tell. But I don't dare. I decide it's safer to assume it does and stare out the window in an effort to keep my discovery secret from whoever is watching.

The brown and cracked landscape we've been traveling over is transitioning to healthier, greener terrain. From several feet above, I can see the soil is also richer. Blacker. The signs of revitalization. The work of another colony. I move forward in the cabin to stand behind the driver's compartment. Sure enough. Far on the horizon are buildings. Some of them are tall. Much taller than those at home. I wonder what colony is ahead and realize I must have asked the question aloud when Michal answers, "That's Ames Colony. We'll stop at the outskirts and have lunch. The Testing committee arranged for it to be delivered to an outpost for us."

"We won't get to see the colony?"

He shoots me a smile. "You'll see it someday. Right now the Testing committee is keeping you contained so you aren't influenced by outside sources. Now you'd better sit down so you don't fall over when I stop this thing."

I return to the passenger cabin, take a seat, and relate Michal's words to the others—all while feeling eyes watching from somewhere behind a screen. The camera and the knowledge that my movements are being restricted makes my head throb and my shoulder muscles tense. The passing of scenery slows. After a few minutes the skimmer lowers and jolts to a stop, pitching Malachi to the floor.

"Sorry about that," Michal says, climbing from the driver's compartment. "I'm still getting the hang of landing this beast. They had to put new brakes on a couple of days ago, which makes it a little temperamental." He holds out a hand to help Malachi scramble to his feet. Then he hits a button and the skimmer door opens.

Warm air and the smell of fresh greenery beckon as Michal climbs out, followed by the rest of us. A small, squat log cabin sits about fifty feet in front of us. Surrounding the building are evergreen trees, hearty bushes, and lots of tall, flowering grasses. It's hard to believe dry, decayed earth is just over the horizon. Whoever cared for the land here did their job well.

We follow Michal down a concrete path to the wooden building. Inside is a small kitchen equipped with a table and five chairs. A small bathroom sits off the kitchen. The entire space is probably fourteen square feet and smells of roasting meat, garlic, and vegetables. There is also a large loaf of bread and a block of cheese sitting under a large glass dome on the counter. The air inside is chilly, and Michal warns us not to leave the windows or doors open or we'll upset the controlled temperature.

One by one we use the bathroom and wash our hands and faces. I opt to go last and wander around the room, pretending to admire the curtains at the windows. I spot the first camera in the light hanging over the large wooden table. The second is in the upper right corner of the kitchen. If there are more, I can't find them. Seeing the two is enough to take the pleasure from the meal. Still, knowing my every moment is most likely being judged, I eat the stew. I smile. I do my best to laugh. Out of the corner of my eye, I catch Michal watching me with an eyebrow raised. He glances up at the camera, then back at me, and smiles.

He knows that I know.

I shove a large piece of bread into my mouth so I have to chew instead of talk, which gives me time to think. Michal's smile was pleased. Proud. As though I had been given a difficult assignment and aced it.

He wants me to know.

I'm certain of it. That's why he told us about stopping for lunch when Tomas grabbed the crackers. Sure, it could be chalked up to a mistake. Michal is younger than any other Tosu officials I've seen. Still, he wouldn't have passed The Testing, graduated from the University, or been given this job if he made those kinds of careless errors. Is picking up on Michal's behavior and what it implies part of the test, or is Michal offering me an edge?

Michal opens a cabinet and returns with a heaping plate of cookies. They look like the cookies my mother made for my graduation celebration. Seeing the reminder of home tugs at my heart. The others grab for the unexpected treat. I push back my chair and ask if I can take a walk. "I promise I'll stay in sight. I just want to stretch my legs for a little while before getting back inside the skimmer."

"I don't see why not." He glances at his watch. "We have thirty minutes before we're scheduled to leave. Does anyone else want to go?"

When no one hops to their feet, I snag a cookie off the

table, head for the door, and step into the sunlight. The air is warm and wonderful. Better yet is the feeling of being free. No cameras. No judging. No worrying about saying or doing the wrong thing that might result in my failure. Knowing what I'm headed for, I vow to enjoy this one last moment of freedom. To store up the sweetness of it to keep me calm and steady through the weeks ahead.

I spot a grove of evergreen trees off to my right and head toward them. The tall grass brushes against my hips as I trek across the thriving ground. I enjoy the crumbly sweetness of the cookie as the trees grow closer.

"Cia, wait up."

Turning, I squint into the bright sunlight and hold my hand above my eyes. I'm surprised to see how far I've come in such a short time. The building that played host to lunch is at least one hundred yards away. Much closer is Tomas, who is moving fast through the tall grass. The idea of sharing my last few minutes of unobserved freedom makes me want to yell for him to turn back. And yet—these are his last uninhibited moments, too, even if he doesn't know it. I cannot bring myself to take them away.

I wait for him to reach me before turning to finish my trek.

"Where are we going?" His question is a bit breathless.

"Just to those trees." We walk the next few minutes in silence and have a seat on the shaded, cool ground. "You'd better be careful or Zandri is going to get jealous. She has her eye on you." I'm teasing, but there is truth behind my words. Every flip of her golden blond hair and bat of her eyelashes is designed to make Tomas notice her. So far, he doesn't appear to be cooperating. I'm not sure how I'll feel if he does.

"I'm not worried about her. I am worried about you." His hand brushes my arm, sending a shiver up my back.

"Why?"

"The set of your mouth, the worry in your eyes. I know your face, Cia. I can tell when something is wrong."

I shrug and try to deflect. "We just left our families and friends behind and might never see them again."

"I've seen you worry about your friends and family. I've seen you stress over getting an answer to a question just right. This is different." His hand settles over mine and gives it a gentle squeeze. "I know I wasn't your best friend back home, but you can trust me."

Can I?

My heart skips a beat and I look away from his intense gaze back at the skimmer—the cabin—where the cameras are waiting. I have known Tomas my entire life. We've worked on school projects together, played games, and even danced in each other's arms for one memorable hour at last year's graduation party. We haven't talked as much this year. My fault. More than once Tomas has asked me to take a walk or work with him on some assignment, but I've always found a reason to say no. My brothers' teasing after that party, the other girls' angry looks, my uncertainty over what those dances meant made me take a step back. Now I have to choose whether to step back again or take a chance and reach out to him. Technically Tomas is my competition, which should make me shut him out.

Soon the others will emerge from the building. Cameras will once again be watching and capturing our every move, possibly our every word. I know that here in the shade of the trees, where I am almost positive the cameras have not followed, is the last opportunity to share my concerns without being heard. My father said to trust no one. But looking back into Tomas's serious gray eyes, I decide to ignore that advice this one time. If it is a mistake, it is my mistake. The consequences will be mine to live with.

"There's a camera hidden in the skimmer. I spotted two more in the cabin."

"Are you sure?"

I nod.

A lock of hair falls over his forehead as he looks toward the skimmer. "I don't understand. Why would someone be watching us now?"

"Because," I say. "The Testing has already begun."

CHAPTER 5

Now that I've started, the words rush out of me. My father's missing memories. His fragmented nightmares. The belief that our former teacher shared the same nightmares and used her authority to prevent Five Lakes students from being selected for The Testing. I hold my breath and wait for Tomas to condemn my father's ideas. To tell me that we will be safe. This is only a test like all the others we've taken in our lives.

Instead, he says, "It's a good thing we're in the same group. We'll be able to look out for each other."

"You think my father's nightmares are real memories?"

"I think it's a good idea to be prepared for whatever might be coming. If they aren't real, then we won't be any worse off for keeping alert. If they are . . ." His fingers lace with mine, and we sit there as the unfinished words hang between us.

A whistle makes us jump. Michal is waving. He's ready to leave.

Tomas scrambles to his feet and helps me up. He doesn't let go of my hand as we trek back through the tall grass. Halfway to the skimmer, he stops and pulls something wrapped in a white cotton handkerchief out of his pocket. Cookies. He takes one and offers me the other. "Since we're partners."

The word makes me smile. Partners. As we have been so many times before. Every time we worked together, we scored the highest marks in the class. I find myself hoping this time will be the same.

"Well, partner," I say, taking the cookie, "make sure you turn down any cookies offered to you by our competition. Just in case."

As expected, Zandri looks annoyed when she sees Tomas and me climb into the skimmer together. While Tomas might not be concerned with Zandri, it is clear by the daggers she's shooting me that she doesn't feel the same. In fact, my partnership with Tomas might have just netted me a new adversary. Perhaps not as dangerous as those who would poison my food to get ahead, but still worrisome considering the length of her fingernails.

Tomas heads to the back of the skimmer to sit with the other two. A hand touches my arm as I start to join them. "Everything okay?"

Michal's eyes are filled with concern. I smile and am fully aware of the camera as I say, "Everything's great. It was nice to see the revitalization work up close. My father would be impressed."

He glances back toward the camera; then he returns my smile. The concern in his face is gone, replaced by pleasure.

Yes. For some reason, out of the four of us from Five Lakes Colony, Michal has decided to help me. And clearly he believes I have performed well.

Telling me to take a seat, Michal climbs into the driver's compartment. Zandri is busy talking to Tomas about some party they both attended a few weeks ago as I sink into one of the couches and feel the skimmer begin to move. She fingers her bracelet, a square with a stylized flower in the middle, as she leans forward drawing attention to the loose neckline of her blouse. I don't know if the people watching us are annoyed by Zandri's flirting, but I am. And worse, I'm certain her antics don't reflect well on her academic standing. Considering her reluctance to attend in the first place . . .

I wait for an opening and ask Zandri about the new windmill she had a hand in designing. While her primary passion is painting, Zandri has a wonderful eye for symmetry and balance that our town's architect has been happy to utilize. I'm betting her bracelet design has something to do with this skill.

Zandri gives me a curious glance, probably because I was also involved in the project, but doesn't dismiss the opportunity to talk about herself. Tomas asks her questions about the windmill and pulls Malachi into talking about the things he's been working on. For the next hour, Tomas and I trade off interviewing our fellow candidates, helping them look good in front of the invisible Testing committee. They are my competition, but because they are from home, I will do what I can to keep us all safe.

The conversation tapers off, and I find myself fighting to keep my eyes open after such a long day. "Why don't you get some sleep?" Tomas slides into the seat next to me and gives me a warm smile. "I'll wake you if anything exciting happens."

I follow his advice and stretch out on the cushions near the front of the cabin. I'm not sure how well I'll sleep knowing Tomas might see me drool, but I close my eyes and give it a try. The last thing I hear before the real world fades is Tomas telling Zandri and Malachi to speak softly.

My father talks to me in my dreams. The Dad I knew before I was selected. He patiently shows me how to splice flora genes. Holds my hands while I attempt to mimic his movements. Tells me the biggest failures typically come before the biggest breakthroughs. That no matter what, I should never get discouraged. Learn from my mistakes and all will be well.

"Cia. Wake up." My father's hands shake me. No. Not my father. Tomas. I am no longer home. Tomas smiles as I open my eyes. "Get up. Michal says you don't want to miss this."

Michal's right. Out the window I can see a shimmering, impossibly clear body of water. The dimming light cannot detract from its obvious purity. The five great lakes our colony is named after have been cleansed, but not like this. Not yet. The sight takes my breath away.

And then I see it. What the others are watching with shining eyes and open mouths. Up ahead—beyond the water. Silver buildings. Lights bright enough to be seen for miles and miles. These can only mean one thing—Tosu City. We're here.

In school we've been taught that ninety-nine years ago, Tosu City was created as the first tangible sign that we as a people had survived the Seven Stages of War—the Four Stages of destruction that humans wrought on one another and then the following Three Stages in which the earth fought back. This spot was chosen because its predecessor was deemed an unimportant military target by the wagers of war. While it could not escape the corruption of the earth or the earthquakes, tornadoes, and floods, much of the city still stood when the earth quieted, and those left alive began to rebuild.

As we move closer, the buildings seem to grow taller. How thrilling and scary it must be to view the world from the top. Some buildings aren't as tall, but the squat, perfectly cylindrical shapes constructed of steel and glass are no less impressive. Building after building after building. I cannot tell how many of them are new or which survived the wars. The buildings begin to blur together and everywhere there are people. Walking. Running. Laughing. Hurrying. Skimmers and bicycles crowd the streets. Old-fashioned cars and glide scooters. Most streets we pass look neat, clean, and new. Exactly what I expect from the city that serves as the center of our country's hope for the future. But as we travel, I catch a glimpse of other streets that are dirtier and in disrepair. The people walking to and from those areas look worn out and tired. Some appear hungry. Others look as though they haven't bathed in weeks, and I wonder why. From school I know the greatest concentration of our population is here—in this city. At least a hundred thousand people. Until this moment I never fully understood what that number meant. Now that I do, I am overwhelmed. I feel Tomas's hand slip into mine and hold on tight. His face is pale. His eyes are wide. I think I'm not alone in my feelings of insignificance and confusion.

Michal tells us we'll go immediately to the Testing facilities—no sightseeing will be allowed. But I notice he takes us past the towering capitol building and the cold, stone department of justice, both places Malachi expressed interest in seeing, before steering the skimmer through a large arching gate. A wrought-iron sign next to the arch reads THE UNIVERSITY OF THE UNITED COMMONWEALTH.

My heart skips. We are at the University. Here I can tell the buildings are old. Red brick. White trim. A clock tower. Some buildings made of glass. Others of stone. All speak of age and of wisdom. I see a large sculpture of two hands clasping each other—in prayer? In hope? Zandri might know, but I don't want to ask her. I just want to take it all in.

We pass a large stadium, and moments later the skimmer slows. It comes to a stop in front of a massive, sleek building made of black steel and black glass. The grounds around it are lush and green and filled with flowers, but they in no way soften the stark, imposing exterior. A small bronze sign in front of the entrance reads TESTING CENTER.

The skimmer door opens, and the four of us hop out. I look up at the tall structure and then at the heavy steel front door and my stomach clenches. I feel a large warm hand touch my shoulder. Tomas. Just knowing he is beside me helps keep the gnawing panic at bay.

"Here." Michal hands me the bag marked with my symbol. "Make sure you don't let it out of your sight." He says this in a low, quiet voice. His gaze locks with mine. There is no smile or amusement in his eyes. He is serious. I am to keep my few possessions with me no matter what.

Then the moment is gone. Michal turns back and his voice booms out, "Once we get inside, you'll be assigned your sleeping quarters and your roommates. Most of the other candidates are already here since their skimmers didn't have mechanical problems. The last few will arrive sometime tonight." He gives us a big smile and asks, "Are you ready to go inside?"

There is only one acceptable answer. "Yes." We all give it.

Michal nods and presses six buttons on a small keypad next to the door. There is the click. The door swings open, and we follow Michal inside. Tomas is the last to cross the threshold. The minute he does, the door swings shut behind him. The sound of locks being engaged accompanies our first glimpse of the Testing Center. Which, to be completely honest, is kind of a letdown. The lobby area is dimly lit—white walls with a scuffed, gray floor. Two gray, wooden chairs are arranged in a corner to suggest a conversational gathering place, but the chairs look as though they've never been used. We don't get to use them now because Michal is leading us down a long white and gray hallway to a bank of elevators. I've never been in one, but I've read about them, studied how they work.

The doors open the minute Michal presses a button, and we all step in. Whoosh. In a matter of seconds the numbers over the doors have gone from one to five. The elevator dings and the doors slide open to reveal a large, electrically lit lobby with shiny white tile floors. The side walls are painted blue, but the back wall is all glass, giving us a view of a large room beyond filled with tables, chairs, and people. People our age. My heart lurches. Dozens and dozens of other Testing candidates.

The sound of a throat clearing brings my attention to an overly large woman with long curly white hair and round, gold-rimmed glasses seated behind a large wooden desk. She gives us a smile and stands.

The woman begins to speak, and I relax. Her voice is warm and friendly as she welcomes us to Tosu City and congratulates us on being chosen for The Testing. "Most of the other candidates arrived yesterday or earlier today. Dinner is being served in the hall behind me. You can freshen up and leave your things in your rooms or you can just go straight in."

"I'd like to go straight in," I say. If I am shown to my room, I might never have the courage to come out. Zandri looks like she wants to fight about it, but Tomas agrees with me and that settles the issue. Michal gives me a subtle nod and leads us down the corridor, through a door, and into the large hall we saw through the glass. I don't think I'm imagining it when I hear the room go silent. All eyes dart to us. Take in our faces. Size us up as competition. Then the talking and eating resume.

On the left side of the hall is a buffet table piled with food. Three servers stand behind the table as though ready to explain the choices. Several types of bread. Apples, oranges, and grapes. A red stew made with lots of vegetables and beef. Carrots and tiny onions in a light sauce, and thick steaks of some kind of fish I've never seen before. Michal tells me the fish is called salmon. There is a separate table filled with cakes and other sweets.

"Grab a plate. Eat as much as you want." As if to demonstrate, he follows his own advice.

The four of us grab our own plates and make our selections. I take a roll filled with raisins and nuts, a small piece of salmon, an apple, and some of the carrots. Just what I can eat. But I can see other candidates do not follow that same rule. Many have more than one plate in front of them piled with food. Some are taking a taste of one thing then pushing it away in favor of something better. My father taught me to respect the food we grow and the neighbors we share our food sources with. The idea of blatantly wasting what has taken years to make, grow, and thrive makes me lose my appetite.

The tables closest to us are all filled with candidates. They eye us as we walk down the aisle to an empty table in the back. I put my plate down and turn in time to see a large, scruffy boy with mean eyes stick his leg out in front of Malachi. Malachi loses hold of his plate, which crashes to the ground. Were it not for Tomas's quick reflexes, Malachi would be face-first in stew.

Despite Malachi's dark skin, I can see embarrassment burning on his cheeks. He mumbles an apology and starts to clean up the mess, but Michal stops him. "This wasn't your fault." His eyes flick to the scruffy boy, who is busy shoving cake in his smirking mouth. "Why don't you take my plate while I find someone to clean this up?"

Malachi takes the plate and slides into a chair with his eyes cast down. His shame at causing an undignified scene is almost palpable, and I find my hands curling into fists. Rage, white and hot, burns in my blood. My family is close and encourages discussion to resolve differences. But I have four older brothers. When pushed, I know how to fight. I'm ready to do so now.

"Cia, your food is getting cold." Tomas's voice reaches me through the rage. The mild words hold a warning. We are being watched. Every move counts. Save my fight for later.

I feel my emotions deflate as I uncurl my hands, sit with my companions, and pick up my fork. Tomas nudges Malachi and whispers in his ear. Whatever he says knocks Malachi out of his stupor. He picks up his fork and starts shoveling in food. Michal returns with another plate and keeps a steady stream of conversation going while we eat. In the silences, I hear people from other tables talking about us. Wondering what colony we are. Someone speculates we are from Five Lakes, but that gets shot down with lots of laughter. Five Lakes Colony is a joke to them. The knot of worry in my stomach grows.

I finish everything but the apple. The salmon must have tasted good, but I wasn't paying attention to the flavors. Another group of six candidates arrives and takes a table in the back. They hurry to eat as the rest of our plates are cleared away by women in white jumpsuits. Then a voice begins to talk.

"Welcome to Tosu City and congratulations on being chosen for The Testing."

It takes me a minute to find who is speaking since the sound is being broadcast from speakers positioned in every corner of the room. Through the glass window I can see the woman who greeted us holding a microphone in her hand.

"One hundred and eight of you have assembled to be tested. At most, twenty will pass through to attend the University. I wish you all luck in being one of those who will pass."

Less than a one-in-five chance. Voices murmur around us. Some confident and cocky. Others surprised at the number, but trying hard not to sound worried.

The voice over the speaker continues, "Since everyone has arrived, tomorrow morning will mark the beginning of the Testing process. In ten minutes you will report to your designated sleeping quarters. If you haven't been assigned a room, please ask your travel escort, and he or she will get the assignment for you. I advise you to get as much rest as you can to help you in the days and weeks ahead. Good night and best of luck."

Michal presses a slip of paper with my room assignment into my hand and holds his there for several seconds longer than necessary. In his eyes, in the squeeze of his hands, I know he is wishing me luck. Then he is gone.

We head out of the dining hall and split up. Girls to the right. Boys to the left.

Zandri and I watch Malachi and Tomas disappear down the hall. Then together we look for our rooms. I'm in room 34. Zandri is in room 28. As she's about to go inside, I give her a hug. Who knows what tomorrow might hold. I want her to do well. Surprisingly, she tightens her arms around me, and we stand like that for a moment. Bonded by years of shared experiences and the fear of what is to come. When we step back from each other, she smiles. "Give 'em hell tomorrow. You hear?"

I nod. "You, too." She disappears into her room, and I go in search of number 34. I find it a few doors down. Someone is moving around inside. Taking a deep breath, I turn the handle on the heavy wooden door and push.

"Hi." The room is large, filled with two big beds, two desks, and some chairs. It takes me a minute to spot the source of the wispy voice. When I do, I'm surprised to see it belongs to a tall, beautiful girl with broad shoulders and long blond hair. She gives me a shy smile. "I'm Ryme from Dixon Colony. I guess we're rooming together."

I nod and take several steps into the room. The door clicks shut behind me. "I'm Cia from Five Lakes."

Her lips spread into a delighted smile. "That's amazing. Everyone at dinner was talking about Five Lakes and saying how no one from there has been tested in years. They thought it meant the colony died or failed or something."

"Five Lakes is still around. We're just small compared to other colonies."

"Dixon is small too." She sits on the bed against the far wall and curls her legs up under her. "We only have about fifteen thousand people. So it was really exciting when eight of us were chosen this year."

Her smile is warm, and I find myself smiling back. Taking a seat on the other bed, I say, "Fifteen thousand is big to me. Five Lakes is just under a thousand."

"How many of you are here?"

"Four. A quarter of our class."

She asks about Five Lakes. Where we are located. What kinds of foods we grow. What kinds of animals frequent the area. From what she says about her own colony, it sounds like Dixon is about three hundred miles southwest of Five Lakes. While her colony is larger, its resources aren't as developed. Maybe with so many people it's just harder to stretch the resources they have, or maybe it's because a large part of their adult population works on creating batteries and electrical supplies instead of developing the land. Since Ryme's family runs a farm they aren't hungry, but many in the nearby town are. Ryme says the compensation money her parents will receive is going to be used for more farming and food-storage equipment. Both will add to the food resources for her family and those around them.

Ryme sounds proud to have a hand in providing those things to her community. Even though I planned on keeping my distance from candidates from outside my colony, I find myself liking her.

We talk on and off for the next hour. Ryme shows me the design on her bracelet. A triangle with a decorative-looking A in the middle. Not my group. She offers to help me unpack, but I tell her I am keeping everything in my bag. Who knows when The Testing might come to an end for any of us? She smiles and agrees, although I can see two billowy dresses hanging in the closet in front of her bed. My mother would approve of the impression Ryme's clothes will make. We both use the small bathroom adjoining our sleeping quarters, change into our pajamas, and climb into our beds. Ryme asks if we can keep the lights on for a while. She is sitting cross-legged, flipping through a photo album she brought from home. The tears in her eyes tug at my heart, reminding me that I, too, left my family behind. That if this was any other night my mother would be sitting in front of the fire, asking about my day. My father would brainstorm ideas with my brothers while we played cards around the kitchen table. Swallowing down the wave of homesickness, I tell Ryme to leave the lights on as long as she wants before I curl up under the covers.

She thanks me. I'm about to close my eyes when she adds, "If you get hungry, I brought some corncakes from home. I made them myself. Help yourself."

I sleep with my bag tucked in beside me.

My dreams are troubled, although I can't remember them when I awake to a voice over a loudspeaker telling us that we have an hour to get dressed and eat before the first phase of Testing begins. I pull on a pair of dark brown pants, an off-white tunic, and my boots. Then I fold my nightclothes and the pants and top I wore yesterday and shove them in my bag. Ryme raises an eyebrow at my repacking, but doesn't say anything. She is wearing a flowing buttercup yellow dress and shiny white slippers. She's even added touches of lip stain and eye makeup.

Across the room, I can hear her stomach growling, but I notice she doesn't touch the corncakes. Maybe I'm paranoid, but I do a quick count. There are nine of them. If there are still nine after today, I'll know for certain not to trust Ryme with my possessions or my secrets.

I twist the bracelet around my wrist. Then check my bag one last time and hoist it over my shoulder. Ryme walks with me down to the dining hall, ignoring invitations from others to join them. I'm not sure why she wants to stick with me, but I'm guessing she's curious about the rest of the Five Lakes Colony candidates. From the way she was talking last night, it sounds like the other colonies have some communication with one another. Five Lakes is truly the unknown.

I fill a plate with strawberries, orange melon, a roll that smells spicy and sweet, and two strips of crisp bacon. Ryme kids me about nerves zapping my appetite while she piles a plate high with pancakes, waffles, eggs, sausage, and fried potatoes. We each grab a glass of milk, and I look around for my Five Lakes compatriots. They are at the same table we occupied yesterday, along with a few unfamiliar faces. I am not the only one who has picked up a passenger.

Malachi and Zandri introduce us to their roommates—Boyd and Nicolette. Both have dark hair, brown eyes, and tanned skin. I am not surprised to learn they are from the same colony to the east and south, Pine Bluff. Boyd is in Zandri's group. I can't see Nicolette's bracelet very well. Her dress has long, flimsy sleeves that keep fluttering over it. Something with a heart, I think. I slide in next to Tomas, who is the only other Five Lakes candidate with his bag in tow. Although I notice that at least a third of the candidates, including the two additions to our table, have theirs with them.

Letting the chatter swirl around me, I take small bites of the sweet fruit and try not to think about what is coming. If what I have learned thus far isn't enough, there is nothing I can do to change that. By the time I've finished my breakfast, I've learned that Nicolette and Boyd are cousins. Their two families operate a rice farm and have been struggling with their water management system. Rice is a crop I have never eaten and know next to nothing about. Tomas is unfamiliar with it as well, but hearing them talk about irrigation issues is enough to start a lively discussion. I even have a few ideas to add to the mix that Boyd thinks are of use.

We are having such an interesting conversation that I forget my anxiety until a voice announces, "Testing candidates, please report to the elevator banks, where officials will direct you to your first round of tests. Best of luck."

My heart swoops into my stomach, unsettling my breakfast. A hand takes mine and holds fast. I turn and look into Tomas's eyes. Is he nervous? I can't tell. But I am glad for the warmth and steadiness of his hand as I rise to my feet. Almost every girl is wearing her prettiest dress and her most polished and scuff-free shoes. I would feel out of place in my wardrobe if not for Tomas standing next to me. His black boots are worn. His cotton shirt and brown pants are faded. Regardless of what tests they throw at us, I can almost guarantee that Tomas and I will be the only comfortable ones taking them.

Testing officials in dark purple and deep red jumpsuits herd us into the two elevator cars and direct us to the third floor. Tomas tightens his grip on my hand as we stand in the back of the small silver room and descend two floors. Some of the other candidates give Tomas's and my joined hands a knowing look, and I start to pull away. But Tomas won't let me. I don't know why he has singled me out for his attention and support, but a small, terrified part of me is glad for it. Partners he called us. A word that doesn't begin to account for the bubbles of anxiety that have nothing to do with the tests and everything to do with the way my hand feels in his.

The elevator door opens, and we are greeted by more officials. It occurs to me that they are dressed in formal colors that announce their status. They are making it clear that they are adults. They are in charge.

We are directed into a large room filled with seats and a stage. The lights on the stage are bright, illuminating a gray-haired, bearded man wearing a purple jumpsuit. He holds a microphone in his hand and is clearly waiting for us all to be seated.

Hands linked, Tomas and I slide into seats in the back. We look for Zandri and Malachi, but don't see them. The last students sit. The Testing officials from the hallway come into the room and assume standing positions in the aisles. Finally, the man up front begins to speak.

"Welcome to Tosu City. My name is Dr. Jedidiah Barnes. I speak for myself and all of my colleagues when I say we are honored to have you here." His smile and voice are warm. "You are here because you are the best and the brightest. On your shoulders rest the hopes of everyone in the United Commonwealth. Here among you are the future leaders of our country. All leaders must be tested, which is the process that you will begin today."

People fidget in their seats. Nerves? Excitement? I admit I feel a combination of both.

The man smiles again. "The Testing process consists of four parts. Over the next two days, you will sit for the written exams. These will test your knowledge of history, science, mathematics, and reading as well as give us an idea of your logic and problem-solving skills. After these tests are evaluated, we will make our first cuts."

The tension in the room ratchets up a couple notches. I tighten my hold on Tomas's hand, which has to be uncomfortable for him, but he doesn't complain.

"Part two is a series of hands-on examinations that will allow you to demonstrate your ability to transfer intellectual knowledge into practical use. Those who pass will be asked to participate in part three—an examination that will test your ability to work in teams and assess your teammates' strengths and weaknesses. Finally, part four will test your decision-making and leadership abilities. Those who get high marks in all four sections of The Testing will then have a one-on-one evaluation with the selection committee. This final personality and psychological evaluation will help us determine who will move on to the University, where you will join with other outstanding minds to help restore the land and our country both to their former glory. This is a lofty goal, but from what I'm hearing about this class of candidates—especially those from colonies we haven't seen in years—I'm certain you can achieve it."

I see students in the rows in front of us looking around. For Malachi and Zandri. For me and Tomas. My roommate said everyone was interested in us because it was speculated that Five Lakes Colony was long dead. She would have mentioned if other colonies had been absent from The Testing. By singling us out, Dr. Barnes has most likely painted targets on our backs. Was it intentional? The polished quality of his speech tells me it was. Does he want to encourage the other students to trip us, or is he leveling the field so the others will not overlook us as teammates later?

Dr. Barnes hands the microphone off to a willowy woman whose red jumpsuit clashes with her bright orange hair. She introduces herself as Professor Verna Holt and says, "You will now be taken to your Testing rooms. All candidates have been assigned to groups based on your previous academic successes. The group you belong to is represented by the large symbol on your identification bracelet. When you see the symbol of your group on the screen behind me, please join the other members by the elevator banks. A Testing official will meet and escort you to your Testing room. I wish you the best of luck in your endeavors and look forward to working with you in the days and weeks ahead."

There is the hum of a motor and a large white screen unfurls above the stage. A black heart symbol flashes. You can hear people murmur as the symbol registers. Their time has come. I see Nicolette tromp up the aisle and disappear out the door with the twenty or so members of her group. Several minutes pass. A few people whisper. I hold my breath, waiting for the next group to be called.

A triangle. Malachi and Ryme.

I spot Malachi's small, slight body rise from a seat to our far left. His mouth is pursed in concentration or fear as he walks up the aisle. I give him a thumbs-up, but his eyes are plastered on the back of the girl in front of him and he doesn't notice.

There are fewer whispers. More fidgeting as we wait. My heart keeps pace with the seconds ticking by. The screen flickers. Another symbol.

Mine.

Tomas sucks in air, and I remember. Ours. Though I am certain he will outdistance all of us on the tests, I am so glad he is coming with me. He is a touchstone from home. I will do better knowing he is near.

We rise and join the others in our group. I can't help but notice that our group is much smaller than the others. Once we are in the hallway, I count. Ten. Half the size. Is this good or bad? The two Testing officials in their red and purple do not allow me the time to worry further. The blonde asks us to follow her. She heads down the hallway to the left and we follow. A dark-haired man brings up the rear.

The woman at the door instructs us to step inside and take a seat at one of the desks. The door is narrow. Tomas goes first.

I enter next. Two steps inside and I stop walking. My feet are planted to the floor as bile climbs up my throat.

I know this room.

White walls.

White floors.

Black desks.

This is the Testing room from my father's nightmares.

CHAPTER 6

I TAKE DEEP breaths. I force my legs to move. All the while I am wondering, *If this room from my father's subconscious is real, what else is? If my answers today don't make the grade . . .*

No. I yank my thoughts back to the here and now. Worrying about what comes next will not help me excel on this test. Breathing, focusing, relaxing—those are the things that allow my mind to work best. I start with the first. Deep and low. In and out. I finger the yellow pencil sitting on the desk and out of the corner of my eye see Tomas watching me with concern. Shaking my head, I smile to tell him not to worry. I'm fine. I will be fine.

While I wait for the test to begin, I take in the other members of my group. There is only one other girl in the room. She has long red hair and the fabric of her black dress is in perfect contrast with her pale skin. Her back is rigid, her eyes forward. The boys are no less focused. Two blonds. One redhead. Four with varying shades of brown. And Tomas. Several are of slight build, but the redhead in particular has muscles that speak of a life filled with activity. As I wonder briefly what colony he is from, a tall, bald man in purple walks into the room carrying a large stack of bound papers.

The tests.

Paper is precious in our community since so many trees were destroyed in the Seven Stages. All paper usage is carefully monitored in school. Once the paper has been used and is no longer needed, it is sent to Omaha Colony for recycling.

Silently, the Testing official circulates in the room, stopping at each desk, never once meeting any of the candidates' eyes. The large booklet lands on the shiny black surface in front of me. The cover reads *History.* In the right corner is the design from my bracelet—the eight-pointed star with a lightning bolt. My fingers itch to open the cover and see what lies beneath, but none of the other candidates opens theirs. Heart pounding, I wait.

The Testing official reaches the front of the room. He does not introduce himself but says, "Complete the pages in front of you to the best of your ability. If you need a drink of water, raise your hand and water will be brought to you. If you need to relieve yourself, raise your hand and an official will escort you to the facilities and back. You have four hours starting now."

He pushes a button on the front wall, which causes a small screen to descend from the ceiling. A timer. And the numbers are running backwards.

Our time has begun.

Fingers trembling, I open the booklet to the first page.

Question: Explain the First Stage of the War of the Nations.

Answer: The assassination of Prime Minister Chae, which fractured the Asian Alliance, sparked a power struggle among the other nations and a civil war. During the civil war, bombs were dropped on the Korean States, destroying most of the population and causing the meltdown of two nuclear reactors.

Question: Name the first two North American cities destroyed by the Mideastern Coalition.

Answer: Washington, D.C., and Boston.

Question: What group was the first to declare war on the North American Alliance?

Answer: The South American Coalition.

Question after question, I scribble answers. Hoping I'm correct. Hoping the details I provide are what the Testing committee is looking for. Questions about the bombs dropped, cities destroyed, people dead. More questions about the earthquakes, floods, windstorms filled with radioactive air. Events that cut the world's population to a fraction of what it was. It still amazes me that anyone survived the horrors I write about let alone had the strength and conviction to turn things around. I answer questions about the man from Five Lakes who created the process to purify the rivers. More about the woman who genetically crafted grass hardy enough to thrive in the earth. Questions about a people and a world struggling to find their way back from the brink of destruction.

I look up at the clock. Three hours have passed. I roll out my neck, trying to free the knots. Flexing my fingers that have been clutching the pencil so tight, I contemplate asking for a glass of water and decide against it. While water sounds good,

I don't want to risk losing precious minutes visiting the bathroom. Not while there are questions still to be answered.

Names. Dates. Foods created. Technology lost. Failures and deaths. All the happenings that contributed to me sitting in this chair. Taking this test. My eyes are tired and fuzzy, but I force myself to focus. To answer as many questions as possible. I flip to the last page when a loud buzzer sounds.

"Time is up. Please close your booklets and put down your pencils. The officials at the door will escort you upstairs to lunch."

My leg muscles are stiff. I stand and bend my knees a couple times before I brave moving toward the exit. By the time we get up to the dining hall, my muscles are feeling more limber, but the idea of sitting down again has zero appeal. Since I know I need fuel, I fill my plate with roast beef, fresh spring greens, and slices of grilled tomatoes, and take a seat at what I now think of as our table.

If I thought the tension was bad in the Testing room, I am in no way prepared for the level of anxiety that permeates lunch. All around is chatter about the questions, the answers. Did President Dalton order the first bomb dropped on London? Did the first Stage Five earthquake plunge the state of California under water or was it the second? Tears when a candidate realizes the answers she gave were incorrect. Elation over the smallest victory. I try to ignore the emotion swirling around the room and do my best to direct my table's conversation to something other than the questions we've been asked.

Zandri is delighted to change the subject. With little prompting she talks about our brief glimpse of Tosu City and the artwork it has inspired her to create. Soon everyone in the group is talking about the interesting things they've seen since being away from home. All but Tomas. He smiles and pretends to listen, but I can see by his eyes that his focus is elsewhere. Did he blank under pressure and fail the first test? I try to catch his attention to ask in silence what I cannot ask aloud, but his gaze is firmly fixed on the lemon cake in front of him.

We are all allowed to go back to our rooms to use the bathroom. I count the corncakes again. Still nine. Then it is time for the next written test. There are freshly sharpened pencils on all of the desks. The tests are passed out. This time the title of the booklet reads *Mathematics.* Word for word the Testing official gives us the pre-test speech about water, bathrooms, and the time we have to take the test. The clock once again descends, and everyone opens their booklet. The sounds of pencils scratching on paper and frantic erasing accompany my work.

If I finish a question too quickly, I check and recheck my work in case the question is not as simple as it seems. If a problem takes more time, I feel each second ticking by—stealing time from the other problems that are yet to come. I refuse to look around the room for fear someone is sitting quietly at his desk with his hands folded in front of him—done. I still have three pages to go when the buzzer sounds. My heart sinks in my chest. With so many questions left unanswered, I am certain I have failed.

The Testing official directs us to our escorts. I grab my bag and resist the urge to beg for more time. Ms. Jorghen at home probably would have given it. She loved when we showed dedication and determination. Here, they just want results.

We are allowed thirty minutes to freshen up in our assigned

quarters before we report for dinner. I'd rather crawl into bed and pull the covers over my head than have to eat and face the others. It's bad enough I have to confront Ryme, who's looking as fresh-faced as she did this morning. One glance in the reflector tells me what I already know. I am a wreck.

"How did it go?" Ryme asks with a sweet smile. "I thought the history section was a bit simplistic. Didn't you?"

I think of the final page sitting blank and shrug. "I think it covered the high points."

"And the math section was long, but really—if someone doesn't know differentiation, they shouldn't be here."

The calculus section was in the middle. At least she's talking about a section that I completed.

Ryme picks up the plate of corncakes and offers them to me. I just shake my head as she puts the plate back down and continues to chatter. "I would have thought the tests would have been more challenging. How else will they weed out the people who clearly don't belong here?"

The pitying smile she gives me makes my stomach roll. There is no question who she thinks should be the first to go.

I'm relieved when the announcement for dinner is made. I barely pay attention to what I'm putting on my plate before taking my seat next to Tomas. Our other colony-mates have yet to put in an appearance. Tomas gives me a half smile. He looks tired. The same tiredness I saw in the reflector a few minutes ago.

"How'd it go?" he asks.

Silverware clanks against china. People are laughing and talking louder and louder to be heard above the din. Everyone is either bragging about their intellectual prowess or steeped in misery. No one is listening to us. I decide to be honest. "I didn't answer all the questions. I ran out of time."

His smile grows wider as he runs a hand through his hair. "I thought I was the only one. I don't know how they expect anyone to answer that many questions in four hours. I thought my brain was going to melt out of my head by the end of the math test."

I laugh and feel some of the tension leach out of my body. If someone as smart as Tomas didn't complete the tests, I doubt many did. Tomas is that smart.

Malachi, Zandri, and their roommates arrive. Worry and fatigue color their eyes, and I wonder if they too left pages blank. I think of how relieved Tomas was to know someone else didn't finish the exams and weigh the reaction of those listening behind the cameras that no doubt are lurking nearby. After a moment, I come to a decision. "Well, I don't know about all of you, but I didn't finish either test."

They all look at me with wide eyes, forks halfway to their mouths. After several beats, Nicolette admits, "Neither did I."

"Me neither." This from Malachi. He looks at his roommate Boyd. "Did you?"

Boyd frowns at his mashed potatoes. "No. I left five pages of math unanswered."

"I still had five and a half." This from Zandri.

Two slender, fair-skinned male candidates sitting at the table behind Zandri turn to face us. Identical green eyes study our faces. Only their hair length distinguishes one from the other. One with long. The other with short. The one with hair pulled back at his nape asks, "Did you say you didn't finish the test?"

I see the others around the table stiffen, and I sigh. So much for thinking the noise covered our conversation. Lifting my chin, I answer, "There were just too many questions for me to finish them all. I got close on history, but I probably took too much time checking my work on math."

The green-eyed twins look at each other. Without a word they rise, gather their plates, and move to the empty seats at our table. The longhaired one says, "You have no idea how good it is to hear someone finally admit they didn't finish the damn tests." He sticks his hand out. "I'm Will. My brother Gill and I are from Madison Colony."

Madison. Only a few hours from Five Lakes. My father has traveled there a few times over the past two or three years. Something in the earth has been killing their crops. From the way the twins have piled their plates and the unhealthy cast to their skin, I'd guess there still isn't enough food to go around. I'm glad they have food now because I can't help but like them as they tease that they should have been allowed to take the tests together. They point out that everyone always says they share one brain. Gill excels in math and science. Will is strongest at history, English, and languages.

Once we are done comparing thoughts on today's tests, Will and Gill plow their way through three plates of food as they describe Madison Colony and their family. They live in the city the colony is named for. Their father works in the paper mill while their mother is employed at a dairy farm. Life is clearly difficult for some in Madison Colony, but the twins are optimistic and upbeat. They regale us with hilarious stories of their attempts to milk a cow and their own family's difficulty in telling the two of them apart until Gill took pity and cut his hair. The rest of us share our own stories from home, and I can see more than one envious face turned toward our table as we laugh. The laughter feels so good. It brightens our moods, eases the tension in our bodies, and replenishes our spirits. When dinner ends, most of the other candidates disappear into their assigned rooms, but we ask if we can remain in the dining hall for a while longer. None of us wants to leave the comfort of friends.

We sing favorite songs. Tomas and I perform a duet that we learned in school. The words speak of the hope of springtime and the world being born anew. Our two voices entwine and echo in the hall. The officials cleaning up after the meal stop and listen to us. When we go back to our rooms we all walk lighter. The lightness stays with me even as Ryme expresses relief that tomorrow's exam will send people packing. And when I sleep with my bag tucked tight to my chest I spend the night free of dreams.

We all gather again at breakfast looking rested but feeling tense. No amount of talk can take away the anxiety as we mentally prepare for our next test. *Science.*

Periodic tables. Balancing chemical formulas. Physics equations. Those questions are first and easy compared to the ones that ask for scientific explanations for the mutated insects and animals that now populate the world. But the section on genetically altered plants is easy considering my hands-on experience. While my thumbs aren't green, I understand the concepts behind creating hybrids and the factors that influence their success.

Too soon time is up. Two pages left unanswered. Lunchtime, then part four: *Reading and Language Skills.* My eyes are sore and my body numb with fatigue when I finish and realize the clock is still ticking. Ten minutes remain in the testing period.

Panic floods me. Did I answer the questions too fast? Did my hurrying cause me to give incorrect or incomplete answers? My fingers itch to open the cover so I can fix the mistakes I must have made. And yet, I hear my parents' voices inside my head. The advice they gave me when sitting beside me at the kitchen table, quizzing me for a test. Take my time. Never second-guess myself. Almost always my first instinct will be the correct one.

I put my pencil down. Fold my hands in front of me. Out of the corner of my eye, I see Tomas do the same. He's finished. Glancing over, he gives me one of his single-dimpled smiles.

Five minutes remain. Four. Three. Two. Pencils scribble. Eyes flick up at the clock and back to the paper in front of them, the candidates desperate to finish one last answer. The buzzer sounds. Round one of The Testing is complete.

We are escorted to the elevators. A few kids give one another high-fives and celebrate. I just feel tired and relieved. I did the best I could. Whatever happens now is out of my hands. Tomas gives my hand a quick squeeze as the elevator doors open. Then he disappears down the hall with the other guys. I head in the opposite direction and am disappointed to see Ryme has once again made it back to the room before me. She's seated at the desk, bent over a silver figurine she must have brought from home. There are still nine corncakes on the plate. Her smile is bright, if a little manic, when she sees me walk in.

"How did it go?"

I shrug my bag off my shoulder and decide to give an honest answer. "I didn't complete the science section."

Ryme's eyes narrow. She bites her bottom lip and studies me for several moments. I guess she's trying to determine whether I'm telling the truth. She'll probably decide I'm attempting to get inside her head since it's something she would do. Face it: anyone who brings a stack of corncakes with her and doesn't eat a single one isn't above screwing with someone's mind.

Finally she gives me a smug smile. "I guess Five Lakes Colony schools aren't as good as the ones in Dixon. Too bad. One of us won't be around much longer."

A flash of heat streaks through me. My nails bite into my palms as I fight for control of my anger. I can't help myself from saying, "Our teachers did well enough. Tomas and I finished the reading section with time to spare. Did you?" I can see by the surprise on Ryme's face that she didn't, and I flash a mean smile. "I guess you're right about one of us going home. Too bad. Don't forget to pack your corncakes when you leave." My tone is snotty—the kind I use when my brothers are ganging up on me and I decide to get in a low blow. A different heat fills me. Embarrassment. I wait for Ryme to take another verbal shot. I deserve it. But she doesn't. She just looks down at her hands.

"I'm sorry," I say.

Her eyes come back up to meet mine. Her lips spread in a wide smile. "Whatever for?" she asks sweetly. "You were just trying to make yourself feel better after admitting you didn't do well today. A lot of the inferior students at my school used to do the same thing, so I totally understand."

Ugh. The girl is asking to get slapped. To prevent myself from doing something else I'd just feel guilty about, I flop onto my bed, close my eyes, and keep my back to Ryme until dinner is announced. Before the announcement is complete, I am out the door.

Dinner is an exuberant affair. Everyone is tired, but the stress of performing under pressure is lifted for the evening. The food also contributes to the happy atmosphere. Pizza. Warm and gooey and better than anything I've tasted before. I eat six slices. Zandri gets the twins telling jokes, and we are all laughing as the loudspeaker hisses and crackles to life.

"Malencia Vale. Please report to the hallway. Thank you."

The dining hall goes silent. My heart slams in my chest. Have the Testing officials already decided I failed? Everyone at my table looks at me with questioning eyes. I must look freaked because Tomas takes my hand and says, "I bet they want to ask you to teach classes instead of taking them. Make sure they offer you a lot of money before saying yes."

Sure. I give him a weak smile and stand. All eyes are on me as I stiffly walk up the aisle, past all the other tables, and through the side door. Everyone in the hall is probably jockeying for position so they can get a good view through the glass wall. I clutch my bag and stand in the hallway, waiting for whatever comes next.

"Malencia Vale?"

I spin to my right at the sound of the familiar voice. The kindly gray-haired man from yesterday morning's assembly—Dr. Jedidiah Barnes. There are two officials behind him.

All are in their ceremonial purple. "Everyone calls me Cia," I say.

He smiles. "Both are lovely." I try to come up with a response, but fail. Thankfully, a response isn't required because he says, "Please forgive me for pulling you out of dinner, but Ryme Reynald's friends have expressed concern over her whereabouts. When was the last time you saw her?"

I blink. This is about Ryme. Not me. Not my Testing scores. Relief fills me. Confusion follows. "Ryme was sitting at her desk when I left for dinner."

"And she was well?"

Arrogant. Irritating. Irrationally confrontational. "I think she was stressed after finishing today's tests."

"Eight hours of tests for two days straight is enough to stress anyone out." Dr. Barnes's smile is apologetic. "We debate every year about spreading out the tests over the first week, but we feel it is best to get the first section of Testing over with quickly. Too much time to think about the tests also causes stress." He sighs. "Would you mind letting us take a look in your room? Ms. Reynald probably decided to skip dinner, but we would like to make sure."

"Sure." I mean, it isn't really my room. "Go ahead."

He smiles again. "You'll have to come with us. The law states that Testing officials are not allowed into any candidate's room unless the candidate is present or there is an obvious emergency."

I guess I'm glad they didn't test us on the United Commonwealth laws or I would have failed for sure. Irritated that Ryme has stirred up such drama and sucked me in for the ride, I head down the hall. Dr. Barnes's tread is soft, but the other two officials' boots clomp down the corridor. If Ryme is inside, she has certainly heard us coming.

Turning the knob, I push the door open and take a step inside. The smell, urine mixed with corncakes, hits me first. Then I see her. Dangling on a colorful rope. Hanging from the ceiling. Face red and blotchy. Eyes wide with horror. Neck gouged and bleeding where she fought from instinct or because she changed her mind.

I scream as the reality of what I see hits me. Hard.

Ryme is dead.

CHAPTER 7

HANDS HELP ME stand. Lead me into the hall. Someone asks me to wait and other people in jumpsuits come running from every direction. I clutch my bag to my chest like a security blanket as activity swirls around me. Ryme is cut down from the ceiling. A gurney appears. When she is whisked past me, I recognize the rope still around her neck: her dress, the one she looked so lovely in yesterday, tied to a bed sheet.

I can't help my stomach from emptying or the tears that flow hot and fast—for her, for me, for not seeing the desperation and depression under the arrogant façade. Did my taunting her with finishing the final written test push her over the edge? Could a kind word have saved her?

"Cia?"

I blink and realize Dr. Barnes is holding my shoulders. Looking into my eyes. I blink twice and swallow the bile building in the back of my throat. Mutely, I nod that I hear him.

"They are going to assign you a different room." He leans against the wall next to me. "Would you like to talk about it?"

No. But I will. I have to. Softly, I tell him about Ryme's arrogance and her taunts today. My reaction and the apology I eventually gave. Even the corncakes and what I suspected they might contain. He's a good listener. His deep brown eyes meet mine without censorship. His head nods, encouraging me to say more—never once letting his eyes travel to the officials walking in and out of the room, cleaning the floor next to me, talking in hushed tones about removing her belongings.

When I am done, I feel empty, which is better in a way than feeling smothered by guilt. Dr. Barnes assures me Ryme's death is not my fault. As we discussed earlier, stress is difficult. Some students handle stress better than others. Some can't eat. Some never sleep. Ryme took her own life. While this is a tragedy, it is better for the entire Commonwealth population to learn now that she is not capable of dealing with the kinds of pressure she would be forced to deal with in the future. This event is unfortunate, but The Testing served its purpose. He hopes Ryme's choice to end her candidacy will not impact the results of mine.

End her candidacy? Inside I am icy cold. An official in purple informs us my room is ready, and Dr. Barnes gives my shoulders a squeeze. I smile and tell him I'll be fine and that talking to him made me feel better. I hope he can't see the lie. Because while his tone was kind, I heard the indifference in his words. To him, this was just another test. One Ryme failed. If I am not careful, I will fail too.

I am shown my new room at the very end of the hall. The walls are painted yellow. They remind me of the dress Ryme was wearing when I first met her. The official asks me if I'm okay not having a roommate. If I don't want to be alone he is certain a female official would be happy to sleep in the spare bed.

No, I do not want to be alone. Awake, I am having trouble keeping Ryme's lifeless eyes out of my head. Asleep, I will be defenseless to stop her from haunting me. Knowing I will be alone through the ordeal makes me want to curl up in a ball.

But Dr. Barnes's words ring loud in my head. The Testing is about more than what happens in the classrooms. Asking for help through the night will be seen as a weakness. Leaders are not weak. The Testing is looking for leaders.

So I thank the official and tell him, "I'm fine being alone." He tells me to let the official at the desk know if I change my mind. They can even give me drugs if I need help sleeping. Then he shuts the door behind him.

I look around the room. Aside from the color it is an exact replica of the one I previously occupied. I hear muted voices and the sound of footsteps. Other candidates returning to their rooms from dinner. For a moment, I consider opening my door and going in search of my friends. A smile from Zandri, a hand squeeze from Tomas, or even one of Malachi's quiet looks would help ease the sadness. But I don't open the door because that, too, could be considered a weakness. Instead I shower, change into my nightclothes, wash the daytime ones, and hang them to dry.

Lying on the bed, I stare up at the ceiling, trying to conjure happy memories. Anything to ward off images of Ryme hanging from the light fixture. I can't help but wonder whether my father witnessed something similar. Whether his brain had made up an even worse memory of The Testing to compensate for the horrific one he used to have. At this very moment, I believe it is more than possible.

Everything is quiet. The others have taken to their beds and are sleeping in preparation for whatever is to come tomorrow. I am still awake. I keep the lights blazing bright and fight against the heaviness of my eyes. I am losing the battle when something catches my eye. A small circular glint in the ceiling. One that matches the one I saw in the skimmer.

A camera.

It is all I can do to keep the discovery off my face. I don't know why it should surprise me that there is a camera watching even when we are doing the most mundane chores like sleeping and getting dressed. But it does. Is this room alone being watched? Because I found Ryme? Immediately, I reject the idea. If they are watching one room, I am certain they are watching them all. The implication of that sucks the air out of my lungs. If there are cameras in every room, someone watched Ryme as she stripped her bed of the sheet. Tied it to her dress. Reasoned out the best place to affix it to the light fixture on the ceiling. They watched as she stepped off the chair. Saw her struggle against the rope, claw her throat in an attempt to free herself, and go limp as her body shut down.

They could have saved her. Instead, they let her die.

I force myself to appear calm as I walk over to the light

switch and cast the room into shadows. Whoever is watching, I don't want them to see the horror I feel. I bury my head under the covers and out of habit clutch my bag to my chest. I wonder if the people behind the screen are reliving Ryme's death while they sleep tonight. It is mean of me, but I hope they are because I am even before sleep pulls me under.

Ryme's blotchy red face and her glassy, blood-streaked eyes follow me into my dreams. Her voice taunts me with my inadequacies. She offers me corncakes and this time I take one and eat it. Each time I wake, I force myself to go still. Not to call out or thrash about. I keep my head under the covers just in case the camera can see more than I believe, and do my best to wipe my mind clean of the horrors before dropping into sleep again.

When the morning announcement comes, I am grateful to climb out from under the sheets. I go into the bathroom and study myself in the reflector. I look tired, but no more so than I did yesterday morning. Taking this as a good sign, I pull on my clothes and brush out my hair while scanning the bathroom for prying eyes. No cameras. At least none that I can see. The Testing officials must not be interested in our hygiene habits. I leave my hair loose around my shoulders, hoping it will pull focus from the fatigue in my eyes, grab my bag, and head down to breakfast.

Tomas and the twins are already seated when I arrive. Tomas's face is filled with relief and he wraps me in a tight hug before I have a chance to sit down. As I sit, Tomas gives my plate a long look. In my effort to appear normal, I have piled it with bacon, eggs, sliced potatoes, fruit, and sweet rolls. I immediately shove a piece of bacon into my mouth to discourage questions about yesterday. It works until Zandri, Malachi, and their roommates arrive. Once everyone is seated, Tomas asks, "Is everything okay? We kept waiting for you to come back last night."

They wait for me to reply. I replay Dr. Barnes's words in my head. Did he mean for me to keep silent? I don't think so, so I quietly say, "Ryme is dead. She killed herself last night."

The Five Lakes candidates show various degrees of surprise. The twins sigh and give each other knowing looks. After a moment, Will says, "We figured it might be something like that. Our teacher warned us about the pressure. He was a Testing official for a couple of years and said there were at least two or three suicides in every Testing class."

Ryme was one. I can't help wondering who might be next. Judging by their silence, I'm guessing my friends are doing the same.

We talk about it a bit then concentrate on eating. I give some of my extra food to Malachi, who has definitely added on pounds since coming here three days ago, and shove a sweet roll into my bag. I don't know if we are supposed to take food from the dining hall, but I figure if someone on the other side of the cameras objects, they'll stop me. No one does.

Another announcement is made. We tromp to the elevators and are whisked back to the lecture hall. Dr. Barnes is once again up front. He smiles at everyone as they take their seats and congratulates us on finishing the first phase of The Testing. "The tests are currently being evaluated by the Testing staff. Because we are aware of your unique skills, each group has its own set of requirements to achieve a passing score. After lunch we will meet with the Testing candidates and inform them whether they have been passed on or whether their Testing has come to an end. Until then, you will have time to spend as you like—either in your rooms, the dining hall, or the designated area outside."

Outside. The idea of fresh air lifts my spirits. Dr. Barnes tells us that all candidates going outdoors must stay within the fence surrounding the Testing Center. Breaking the rule is grounds for automatic dismissal from further Testing.

Candidates shift in their seats, getting ready to bolt for the door, when Dr. Barnes's expression changes. There is sadness. And though I am prepared for his words, my breath still catches and my eyes mist with tears. "I am sorry to announce that Testing candidate Ryme Reynald took her own life last night."

Some students gasp and cry out, but I notice more than one sly smile that says, *One down.* I try to remember the faces that go with those smiles just in case.

Dr. Barnes continues. "We know that this is a difficult process, but I hope that those of you who remain will talk to me or one of the other officials if the pressure becomes too much. We are here to help. Please enjoy your morning of relaxation. I wish you the best of luck this afternoon."

Based on where we want to spend our morning, candidates are directed into one of the two elevators. The left goes up to our rooms on the fifth floor. All of us from Five Lakes Colony head to the right.

The sun is shining, the grass is green and sweet, and a light breeze is blowing as we step outside. Two officials in purple are stationed at the front door, but otherwise we have the large fenced-in area surrounding the Testing Center to ourselves. We can see the University buildings shining in the sun—some only steps away from the fence. The buildings and the knowledge they hold remind me why I am here.

Only about three dozen candidates opted to make the trip outside. Since most are finding spots in the grass in front, the four of us from Five Lakes head around the building to the back. There, we find several tall flowering trees and three benches next to a small pond. The ripples of clean, clear water and the sun shining down have a rejuvenating effect on me. While the others sit on the benches, I take off my boots and socks, roll up my pants, and wade in. That's when I notice the metal piping in the middle of the water.

A fountain? I wade closer. Yes. I am certain of it. I wade around to the other side of the pond and find the power box nestled discreetly in a pile of rocks. The switch on the box says the fountain is on. So why isn't it working? Could this be another test?

I drop my bag onto the ground and pull out the small hunting knife I brought as one of my two personal items. Flipping out the screwdriver, I take the cover off the box and look inside. None of the wires or connections appears to be severed. There are no black marks indicating an overload or a burnout. The switch is connected properly. The trouble must be the pump.

Back at the center of the pond, I lean down and peer through the clear water at the pump. It's compact and looks undamaged. I consider removing it, but realize there is someone better equipped for the job. Someone who installed an entire irrigation system at his parents' farm.

Tomas is more than willing to leave his bench and take a look. Zandri and Malachi laugh at us as we poke around the pump, but after a while they fall into quiet conversation, leaving Tomas and me to our own devices.

Tomas thinks the problem might be the impeller. I guess the motor. We decide to remove the pump to find out who's right. Tomas uses my knife to unscrew the pump from its base, and we head to the shore. A few minutes later, we have the cover off and I give a shout of victory. The impeller is perfect. The motor has a loose connection. I tinker with it for a while and think I have the problem licked. Tomas puts the cover back on and installs the pump back in the pond. Minutes later, water shoots into the air, soaking us both.

Problem solved.

We lie on the grass, letting the sun dry our clothes, and I try to hang on to the happiness I feel whenever I make something work. I twist the bracelet on my wrist and use my fingernail to probe for the clasp as the four of us talk about our families and what might be happening in Five Lakes Colony right now. Zandri gets a faraway look in her eyes. She is missing home. I am too, and I can't help but wonder if all four of us will still be here to talk of home tomorrow.

I think I have found where my bracelet fastens when they call us to lunch. As I poke one of the metal segments with my knife, I hear a click that tells me I am right. I consider mentioning it to the others, but they have already started toward the building. Carefully, I refasten the bracelet as I walk to the other side of the pond and hit the switch. The fountain gurgles and stops. They might have power to spare here, though I can't help but heed the training I've had all my life. Waste is unnecessary. Tomas is waiting for me as I hurry to catch up. The warm approval in his eyes makes my heart skip several beats.

While the last two meals have been filled with chatter, the atmosphere at lunch is subdued. You can see the tension in everyone's eyes as they stare at the clock hanging on the wall behind the buffet. No one knows exactly when the results interviews will begin, but we know they will start soon. Everyone leaves food on their plates. I shove an apple into my bag as the twins try to keep the mood light by telling jokes. Everyone pretends to laugh.

The loudspeaker crackles. "Please return to your sleeping quarters. When your name is called, quickly exit your quarters with your belongings. An official will escort you to your designated results room. Best of luck."

Chairs scrape against the floor as candidates head for their rooms. Our table is the last to rise. I look from face to face. Tomas. Malachi. Zandri. Nicolette. Boyd. Will and Gill. The chances of us all making it to the next round are small. We say nothing. Wishing each other luck will not change the work we have already done—the results that have already been determined. So we squeeze hands and say we'll see each other later, knowing full well the words are a lie.

I wait in my quarters as names are announced over the loudspeaker, trying not to think about my father's words. I can't help but wonder why no one has ever mentioned what happens to past Testing candidates who didn't succeed. What became of them? What will become of us?

Unfamiliar names are called. But then I hear Malachi's name quickly followed by Tomas's. Time stands still although the clock says otherwise. Finally, my breath catches as my name is called. I enter the hallway. A woman in red silently escorts me down to the elevators. She pushes number two, and the doors close. When they open, a male Testing official nods and asks me to follow him down a long white hallway to a set of dark wood doors. He opens the door on the left and steps to the side. I enter the room alone.

The room is small with only a shiny black desk and two black chairs. The walls are white. The dark-haired woman behind the desk asks me to sit. I follow her command and wipe my sweaty palms on my pants. Her eyes meet mine, and for a moment she says nothing. My heart slams against my rib cage. I swallow hard and try not to fidget.

Finally, she smiles. "Congratulations. You have passed the first round of Testing."

Relief fills me. I let out a breath I didn't know I was holding in as she tells me I should get plenty of rest before the next round. An official walks me back to the elevators. The doors open on the third floor. I walk into the lecture hall and strong arms immediately swoop me close.

Tomas's voice whispers, "Congratulations, partner. I knew you could do it."

Then Malachi is giving me a shy hug. Of those at our dining hall table, the three of us are the first to arrive. Boyd arrives next, looking pleased. He high-fives Malachi, almost knocking him over. The room begins to fill up. Nicolette arrives, looking flushed with pride. We watch the door from our place in the back of the room, waiting for the next of our party. Will strolls in with a cocky smile. We wave to him. He breaks into a large grin and starts walking over. The grin fades as his eyes move from face to face. By the time he reaches us the smile is back, but I can tell something is wrong. I remember the way I could hear the names of candidates over the loudspeaker as they were called for their results before me. Will must have heard a name called. A name of someone not returning. Of our group only two have not returned. Dread coats my stomach.

Five minutes pass before the last two candidates arrive, followed by Dr. Barnes. One of them looks around the room, spots us, and breaks into a large smile. Zandri crosses to us and gives Malachi the first hug. Most of our group congratulates her, but I walk toward Will, who is still watching the door—waiting. Realizing his other half won't be returning.

Dr. Barnes asks us to take our seats and congratulates the Testing candidates who remain. I have to lead Will to a chair. Force him into the seat. Tomas and I sit on either side of Will as he begins to tremble. From their stories, I know Will and Gill have never been apart for more than a couple of hours. I've watched them complete each other's sentences. I wonder how one half will survive without the other.

Will holds my hand like a lifeline as we are told the second round of tests will begin tomorrow morning after breakfast—the first of a series of hands-on examinations that will allow us to demonstrate our intellect, unique skills, and problem-solving techniques. Dr. Barnes then warns, "If there is a part of the test you do not understand or do not know how to complete, please do not guess. Raise your hand and let the Testing official in your designated room know you cannot finish. Leaving a problem unsolved is better than giving an incorrect answer. Wrong answers will be penalized." He lets the words settle on us and dismisses us with one last round of congratulations.

Tomas helps me get Will up and moving. By the time we get to the dining hall, Will is telling us his brother probably failed on purpose so he could go home to his girlfriend. He tells more jokes at dinner. Every once in a while I see him glance to his left as though waiting for his brother to finish his thought before realizing he isn't there.

We go to our quarters early to get ready for whatever will come with the morning. I dream of Ryme with a makeshift noose tight around her neck, offering corncakes to Gill. She smiles at me as he takes one and falls to the floor dead.

In the morning I scrub with cold water to wash the grainy feel from my eyes and then head to breakfast. I'm the last of our table to arrive. Spirits are high. Especially Will's as he flirts mercilessly with Nicolette. Her cheeks and the tips of her ears are tinged with pink as she sips her glass of apple juice. Judging by the way she smiles back at him, I don't think his attention is unwelcome. I hope he isn't just using her as a way of coping with his brother's absence. Things are stressful enough.

The announcement is made and we all head to the elevators, back to the third-floor lecture hall. Dr. Barnes, with his smile bright against his graying beard, watches us as we take our seats. He tells us that there are eighty-seven of us left. He reminds us the second phase of Testing begins today and asks us all to remember that in this phase wrong answers are penalized.

We are called in groups of six. I am surprised when Malachi

and Will are called with me, and we trail down the hall after a testing official. The Testing room holds six waist-high worktables in two rows—three in front, three in back—each with a small stool seated directly behind it. On the left-hand corner of each station is a small sign depicting a candidate symbol. In the center of every table is a large wooden box.

A silver-haired female official asks us to find the table marked with our symbol. My workstation is the back center one. Malachi's is at the front to my right. Will is next to me on my left. He catches me looking at him and winks.

The official tells us to raise our hands when we complete the test in front of us. The box will be removed. When all candidates have finished the current box, a new test will be brought out. We are to complete as many tests as we can in the allotted time. This test will not break for lunch, she warns. Then she repeats Dr. Barnes's instructions about raising our hands if we don't know how to complete the test, stressing that we are not to guess at answers we are uncertain of. She tells us to solve the puzzle of opening the box and then follow the instructions for the test we find inside.

Seems easy, which is enough to make me nervous. The Testing is not designed to be easy. I study the box while out of the corner of my eye I can see several of my fellow candidates tapping and tugging at theirs. My mother has a puzzle box at home that her grandfather created for her. It requires the opener to slide pieces of the box to the side in a specific order—otherwise, the box will not open.

Slowly, I turn the box on the table so I can view every side. The wood is rich and smooth and has a swirling etched design that makes it quite beautiful. I'm sure Zandri would be able to identify the technique used to create the pattern, but I'm not interested in admiring it. I want to open the thing.

Ah. There in the bottom corner I see a small knot in the pattern. Nowhere else on the box is there that tiny circular shape. A button? I dig the tip of my index finger into the small spot and feel something give way. Sure enough—the side of the box is now able to slide up and off. I set that piece to the side and pull out the instruction sheet.

Test the plants inside the box for edibility. Separate those that are edible from those that are poisonous.

Again there is a warning: *If you do not know an answer, do not guess. Set the unknown plant to the side.*

I smile. This test was designed for me.

There are eight plants in the box. I recognize six immediately. The white flowers arranged in an umbrella-looking shape are water hemlock. My father says they were deadly even before the lakes were corrupted by biochemical warfare. The deep green leaf with the threads of red veins I believe is also poisonous. At least the rhubarb leaves that grow by us are not to be eaten. The branch of deep green oval leaves with brown nestlike shapes hanging from the branch has to be a beech nut. I'm also positive I recognize sassafras, wild onion, and nettle, which are often eaten by the bugs in our colony.

The last two species give me pause.

I sniff the first—a large, jaggedly shaped green leaf. There is a faint hint of a floral scent. I can see on the stem where a flower might have been connected recently. The leaf is soft and reminds me of a flower that my father pointed out to me a few years ago—not one he created, because it is poisonous and his work is to create things that will sustain life. Still, he thought the plant had value because of its fragrant beauty. Is this the same plant? If not, I believe it to be related. I put it in the poisonous pile and move on to the last—a dark hairy root with white flowerlike leaves attached to the top. I scrape away the outside of the root with my fingernail and sniff it. It smells sweet. Not like a beet or a carrot. Those are very different. But something about this seems familiar. I can hear Dad's voice as he talks about a variety of roots that have had luck growing in southern colonies. One called chicory that Zeen wanted a sample of to study in case it would help with the new version of potato. This is chicory or something near to it. I feel confident enough to place it in the edible pile and raise my hand.

The other candidates look at me as the official checks my work. She asks if I am confident in my answers. Wiping my palms on my pants, I look over the plants once more. Yes. I am as certain as I am going to get. She smiles and scribbles something in a notebook. Then she removes the nonedible plants and tells me to take a seat until the other candidates are finished.

Ten minutes later, everyone's work has been checked. The Testing official has removed the plants the candidates separated as not edible and has recorded those in her notebook. Back up front, she asks us one last time if we want to change our answers. She calls each of our names and waits for us to answer yes or no. None of us takes her up on her offer.

"Well, then," she says cheerfully, "you should have no

problem ingesting a sample of each plant you have deemed edible."

The room goes silent. Finally, I understand.

Yes—a wrong answer will be penalized. Dizziness. Vomiting. Hallucinations. Maybe even death.

I glance around at the tables in the room and see each Testing candidate has a different sampling of plants. There is no way to compare answers. Did I make a mistake? The boy in front of me seems confident he did not. He quickly samples each of his plants. Next to me, Will samples his four. I take a deep breath and eat the beech nut, a small piece of the sugary root I hope is chicory, and the other three plants. None of the plants I deemed poisonous would be fast-acting. We will have to wait to learn whether any of us has made a mistake.

There is no time to worry about whatever might be happening inside my body as Testing officials carry in the next box. This one has a complicated sliding pattern to remove the top and all four sides. Inside is a large pulse radio and a set of small hand tools. The instructions say to restore the pulse radio to working order.

We are told that before the Seven Stages of War, the world was able to communicate through devices that bounced signals to satellites in space. I don't know what happened to those satellites. Maybe they are still floating somewhere above us or maybe they have crashed into the earth without any of us knowing. And with the earthquakes that pulled apart the earth, all underground wires for communication were severed. After the war, scientists decided to use the much higher concentration of electromagnetic radiation to restore communication.

Pulse radios were born, although they can broadcast more than just voices. With the right receiver on the other side, pulse radios can broadcast images as well as sound. They record large chunks of communication and then create a pulselike signal that propels out to receivers. My father has a pulse radio to communicate with other colonies and Tosu City, so I have seen one before. My father even let me take a look inside it. Which means it is easy for me to find the wires that are mistakenly crossed, fix the solar-powered motor, and make a few tweaks to the transmitter. In between each adjustment, I pause and check my heart rate to determine whether the plants I consumed are making me sick. At any sign of illness, I plan on purging the other plants from my stomach. It won't impact the poison already in my bloodstream, but I have to try something.

While working, I notice a few wires that clearly don't belong in a pulse radio and some small metal hinged boxes that don't look familiar. If I were at home, I would poke around to see what they contained. But this isn't home. I will do only what I am certain of.

I screw the top back on the pulse radio and am about to raise my hand when I notice Malachi swaying on his feet. Fatigue or one of the plants he consumed? I think of the plants that I received and try to decide if one of them would cause this kind of reaction. Sweat pours down his face. His hands begin to shake as he starts work on an area of the radio that I ignored. One that contained an unfamiliar metal box. I know we are not supposed to help our fellow candidates, but Malachi's shoulders are twitching and I am worried the plants he ingested no longer allow him to think rationally. I open my mouth to call out—to tell him not to touch the metal box.

But he already has. A moment later a nail imbeds itself in Malachi's eye, and he drops to the floor like a stone.

CHAPTER 8

When I was a child, I once cut my finger to the bone. My mother tells me I didn't scream or cry out. I just froze as though staying still would stop the blood from flowing. The blood pooling on the white floor next to Malachi's head has the same effect. A scream builds inside me, fights to get past my clenched throat, but I make no sound. Someone else's shouts, maybe Will's, wake me from stillness, and I race from my station to where Malachi lies twitching on the floor. A pair of purple-clad arms grab me and pull me back. In my struggle to get free I barely hear the head Testing official talking to me. Asking me if I have completed my test. If not, I must return to my station. Otherwise, there is a risk I will receive assistance from observing another candidate's work.

I want to scream that the test doesn't matter. Not when life is draining drop by drop onto the tile floor. But I choke out a yes, and I am released. The Testing officials make no move toward Malachi as I take his hand and hold tight. From their posture I can tell they will offer no aid. This is the penalty for an incorrect answer. To them he has earned whatever comes next.

The twitching is getting worse. While Malachi's uninjured eye is open, I am uncertain if he can see or if the plant he ingested has caused some kind of coma as it wages war on his body. Still, I shift my position on the cold tile just in case. If he can see, he will recognize something of home. A girl who sang songs with him on the grass and asked him for help when she struggled with her homework. A girl who is his friend. Someone who can't imagine what will happen when he is gone.

Only, I no longer need to imagine. The twitching stops. His muscles go slack as his chest stops its rise and fall. Malachi is dead.

Do I cry? I must. Because when they tell me to go back to my station, I touch my face and find my cheeks are wet. How long they let me sit next to Malachi's unmoving body is uncertain to me. A while. Long enough for two of the other candidates to finish their tests—or perhaps, after what happened to Malachi, they chose to stop instead of taking their chances.

Giving Malachi's hand one last squeeze, I brush a lock of dark curly hair from his forehead and kiss his cheek. The room swoops and spins as I stand. After a moment, I am able to walk stiffly to my station. I balance on my stool and wait for the officials to move Malachi's body, but they don't. Not yet. Not until everyone has completed this phase of the test.

I wait for the other candidates to protest. To say this is wrong. But I know why they don't. It's the same reason I don't yell out. The reason is Malachi and his too-still body. We all want to live.

Several minutes later, Will raises his hand to indicate he has finished and then closes his eyes so he won't have to see the shell of a boy he shared meals with. The girl to my right finishes. The Testing official checks our work. When she is done, she signals the other officials to remove Malachi from the floor. My fellow candidates look at the tops of their desks or up at the ceiling. I don't. Malachi deserves someone who cares to bear witness. I force myself to watch every second—picking him up, carrying him by his arms and legs across the room, out the door. Away.

There is no time to grieve as the next boxes are brought in and placed on our tables. We are given permission to start.

My hands tremble as I smell the blood still staining the floor. I force myself to take deep breaths. Push myself to continue when I only want to run screaming from the room—leave the building—find my way back home. But I know that isn't possible so I rub my hands on my pants, swallow my tears, and examine the box. I need several tries to figure out how to open it. Inside are soil samples and several capped beakers of solutions. We are to identify any soil samples that contain radiation.

I use only the solutions I can identify by smell and color. Out of the ten soil samples, there are four I am certain contain radiation, three that do not, and three on which I will not risk wagering a guess. Had this been the first test, before the plants, before Malachi's twitching, bloody body, I might have been arrogant enough to feign confidence. No more. Malachi made a mistake, and he paid for it. The price he paid would be worthless if I didn't learn from his actions.

Four more test boxes appear in succession. There is a keypad to enter our answers to complex mathematical equations. I only answer half and am glad I didn't guess on the last when the boy in front of me starts to shake. Electrocution. The punishment isn't as severe as Malachi's, but the boy can barely balance on his stool to work on the next three boxes.

I identify about three-quarters of the slides they ask us to view under what I suspect is a rigged microscope. Thankfully, we never learn what the penalty for mistakes would be. There is a solar power converter that I easily build—though the girl next to me ends up losing the tip of her finger—and six samples of water that we must purify using the chemicals provided. The purification test takes two hours, and we are instructed to drink the ones we think have been done correctly. I drink two. The electrocuted boy and the girl next to me drink none.

With that, the second round of tests is over. We are free to leave the room.

Will can barely walk. From the stress, the water he drank, or one of the slower-acting plants he might have ingested? I don't know. But his legs tremble as he takes small, halting steps. I put my arm around his waist to lend my strength as we exit the Testing room. In the doorway, I stop walking and take one last look back at where Malachi fell—where his blood has dried on the floor. A tear falls. I say a whispered goodbye. Then, with a steadying breath, I lead Will away, wondering who else will be missing when we reach our table.

Boyd.

According to an ashen-faced Nicolette, he collapsed during the third exam and was taken for treatment. He never returned. They all look at me and Will, who is now seated but needs help staying upright. Tears prick the backs of my eyes and Tomas takes my hand and holds it. I am grateful to him for his support. For his survival. I share the story of our Testing room as quickly as possible, telling myself it is like pulling off a bandage. The quicker you pull, the less agonizing the pain. But I am wrong. Fast or slow, relating Malachi's death digs a knife deep into my heart. Watching Tomas's jaw clench and Zandri's eyes fill with tears twists the knife until I don't know if I can keep breathing.

The last of the Testing candidates straggle into the hall and an announcement is made. "All candidates who feel they are in need of medical attention, please report to the elevators."

At least one candidate at every table gets up and heads back into the hallway. Nicolette tells Will he should go. He starts to rise, but I push him back into his seat and tell him not to. I study his face. His pupils are dilated, but his breathing has become easier. While his skin is still clammy, color is returning to his face. My gut tells me whatever caused this reaction is leaving his system. Do I think the right medicine would help him get better faster? Of that I have no doubt. But I remember Dr. Barnes's words spoken in the hallway as Ryme was being cut down from the ceiling. About the Testing demonstrating the pressures a candidate can handle. About finding those who can deal with the pressures and still perform as leaders. I doubt those seeking medical attention will be deemed strong enough leaders to return.

Nicolette pleads with me, but I will not let Will go. I can't. Dinner is served. I tell Tomas to get Will food and something to drink. That will help. I hope I'm right.

Will does improve after drinking two glasses of juice and eating small bits of bread and fruit. Now that he can sit unassisted, I get food of my own—more than I can ever possibly eat despite the fact that I'm not hungry. I eat some vegetables. A few bites of chicken. Drink some juice. The two apples, the orange, the bags of raisins, and the rolls disappear into my bag one by one. I wait for my friends to finish eating and stow away anything they have left. Why? I'm not sure. At this point I'm not sure of anything. I just know that being prepared for whatever comes is better than not being prepared at all.

I notice most of the candidates stay in the dining hall until we are instructed to leave. The celebration of last night is a memory. Tonight we are just glad to be alive.

We return to our sleeping quarters. I sleep with the lights on, hoping Malachi and Boyd will not join Ryme and Gill in my dreams. But Malachi comes. They all come. Only this time the terror in their eyes is for me. They warn me to be careful. Ryme reminds me to trust no one while Malachi sings me a song from home.

The anxiety of the night mounts with the morning announcement. When it is time to report for breakfast, I tell myself I am as ready for the day and what it might bring as I will ever be.

Will gives me a smile as I reach our table. His eyes are sad, but no longer look sickly. Whatever strange plant he consumed has worked its way out of his system. He whispers a soft thank-you and says Tomas's roommate sought medical treatment. He has yet to return.

I force myself to eat, and this time I notice someone else slipping food into his bag. Tomas sees me watching and nods as the loudspeaker crackles to life.

"Congratulations, candidates, for reaching the team Testing phase. For this exam you will be placed in groups of five. Due to the number of candidates who remain, one group will comprise only four. When you hear your name called, please walk to the hallway to join your testing group. Best of luck to you all."

There are five of us at our table. I don't even have the chance to hope we will be called together when Tomas's name is announced along with those of four other candidates I don't recognize. Tomas touches my arm as he slings his bag over his shoulder and walks out. Several minutes pass before the next group is called. Both Will and Zandri promise to see us later and disappear out the door.

Nicolette and I stare at each other as group after group leaves the room. Finally, Nicolette's name is called along with four others. She and I will not be testing together. Dread churns my breakfast as I scan the room and see the scruffy boy who tripped Malachi on our first day still seated at a table. He, along with a tall, muscular blond boy and a red-haired girl I remember from my written exams, will be in my group for this test. The only group of four.

"Do we wait for our names to be called or save them the trouble?" This from the redhead.

I smile at her and stand. "If we haven't figured out our group by now, we probably don't belong here, right?"

The two boys stay seated, but the redhead rises. She joins me in the hall and holds out her hand. On her wrist I see a half circle surrounded by the eight-pointed star symbol we share. "Annalise Walker. Grand Forks Colony."

"Cia Vale. Five Lakes."

She gives me a wide grin. "I know. Five Lakes candidates

are all anyone from my colony has been interested in talking about."

I wince. "What have they been saying?"

"Most figure you're easy competition. They equate small colonies with simple-mindedness."

The self-satisfied smile on her face makes me ask, "And you?"

"One of the guys from my colony has the same eight-pointed star symbol. He's the only person who scored higher than me in class. I used to study for weeks in order to beat him, but I never could." She shrugs as though to show coming in second didn't bother her at all, but the glint in her eyes tells a different story. Smiling, she adds, "If two of you from Five Lakes made it into the same Testing group as the two of us, I'd say the rest of the candidates are pretty stupid to overlook you."

The loudspeaker announces, "Malencia Vale, Brick Barron, Roman Fry, and Annalise Walker—report to the hallway."

Brick. Roman. I try to decide which name belongs to which boy as they stride toward us. Before I can ask, a Testing official in red leads us into the elevator and pushes the button for the fourth floor.

We are led to a white room with a table surrounded by four chairs. On the far left side of the room is a large wooden door with a green light blinking above it. In the center of the table are four pencils and four booklets marked with our symbols. The knots of worry loosen as I see the paper. While I have no idea what the pages contain, I am certain of one thing—a written test contains no immediate threat. None of my friends will die from a test today.

Once we take our seats the Testing official explains, "Today's test will evaluate your ability to work as a team. On the table in front of you are booklets filled with five sample questions. Each sample problem requires specific skills to solve. As a group, you must decide which team member has the skills best suited to solve which sample problem or problems. Those same skills will be required to solve a corresponding problem in one of the five individual examination rooms. Once you have determined who the best person to solve each problem is, the person you have selected for the first problem will go through this door." She points to the door with the green light. "Once you have walked through this door, the light above it will turn red. Follow the hallway to the end. There you will find five doors marked with a number. The numbers correspond to the sample problems in your booklet. There is also a door marked EXIT for when you have completed your portion of the exam. Open the door marked with the number of the question your team selected you to answer. Inside, solve the problem as best you can. When you have completed your portion of the exam, indicate you are finished by going through the exit door. The light above this door will then turn green. This will signal it is time for the next candidate to begin. Everyone in the group will be given credit for all the correct solutions on the exam that are not only your own."

The idea of being scored based on someone else's work makes me uncomfortable, but Annalise's confident smile banishes some of the doubt.

The Testing official isn't done. "Because there are only four of you in the group, one candidate will be responsible for solving at least two of the problems. Once a problem has been answered, the door to that problem cannot be opened again. Any attempt to resolve an already completed problem will result in a penalty for the student making the second attempt to solve that problem. You have one hour to discuss your strategy." The official pushes a button and the green light is replaced by red. "Once the green light is turned on, you can begin the test. There is no time limit to the exam. Take as much time as you need to get to know one another's strengths and weaknesses. Good luck."

The sound of locks being engaged accompanies the Testing official's exit. The only way out of this room is through the Testing exam doors.

The four of us look at one another for a moment. I am the first to grab the booklet marked with my symbol. The tall, muscular blond boy grabs one with what I think is an anchor surrounded by a heart. The X surrounded by a circle belongs to the scruffy kid.

Something about this test makes me apprehensive. Maybe it is the simplicity of the instructions or the idea that someone else will get credit for my work and me for theirs. Whatever it is, my gut tells me there is more to this test than meets the eye.

I don't have to think about what that might be as Annalise takes charge. "How about we solve the sample problems one at a time? Once everyone is done with a problem we can compare notes. That should help us figure out who should do which problem. Right?"

Since none of us has a better idea, we take her suggestion and get to work. The first problem is mathematical—a one-dimensional heat equation to determine the flow of heat in a rod where everything but the ends are insulated. These are equations I have used often and make me smile as I get to work.

I'm surprised when the scruffy boy, whose name turns out to be Roman, finishes before me and has the same answer as mine. Annalise's answer also matches. Brick's does not.

One by one we work through the problems in the book. A history section that requires dates, names, and population sizes for the colonization of the United Commonwealth. A biology question that asks for the DNA mapping of a rock wolverine that resembles a wolf but is actually a mutated version of a Nebelung cat. While I'm answering the question about solar power, the red light turns green. Our Testing can begin at any time. Maybe the pressure of the light distracts me from fully concentrating on the last problem that details the principles of nuclear weaponry. I'm the last one in the group to complete the final question. Brick is first to finish. His answer agrees with the other two. My answer matches no one's.

Out of five questions, my answers match at least one of the others four times. Annalise also gets four matches. Brick matches answers on two. Roman's first answer is his only correct one.

"Guess that means I go first, right?" he says.

Of the members of the group, I am by far the youngest. At home my natural inclination would be to hear everyone else's opinions before offering mine, but something about his enthusiasm rubs me the wrong way. So instead of waiting, I say, "The Testing official didn't say the problems have to be completed in order. We just have to determine the order the members of our group go in to solve the problems."

Roman folds his arms across his chest and scowls. "That's not what I heard."

I look at Annalise. She chews her bottom lip and closes her eyes as though trying to recall the exact words. When her eyes open, they're filled with apology. "I think Roman could be right. We could try it another way, but if we do we could fail. That's a risk I'm not willing to take."

Roman smiles. Brick shrugs and nods. Three against one. Just like that the discussion is over.

Annalise leads the decision making. Roman will answer the first problem. She will answer the second and third. I will answer the fourth, Brick the fifth. I suggest that I might be better suited to the third question since my father's work has given me a strong understanding of genetics, but Roman and Annalise disagree. Brick refuses to give an opinion. Part of me wonders why as Roman gets up and says, "See you all after the test." He turns the handle on the green-lit door and walks out without a backwards glance.

The light turns red, and we wait.

At first, we try to chat. Annalise asks Brick about his home, and we learn he's from Roswell Colony. His parents are both University graduates. They work at a former military facility where together they develop weapons and security methods for colonies plagued by animal attacks. No wonder he excelled at the nuclear science question.

As the minutes tick by, though, our conversation becomes more stilted. There is more time in between questions. Shorter answers. Until we no longer talk. We just wait for the light to change.

There is no clock. No windows to measure the movement of the sun. No way to know if the time that passes is as long as it feels. My shoulder muscles tighten. I see Annalise roll out the tension in her neck. Brick is the only one who appears unfazed by the long wait.

He closes his eyes.

Annalise gnaws on her thumbnail.

I stretch my muscles.

Every minute feels like ten. Never do I lose sight of the light.

Finally, it changes. Annalise stands and smiles. "My turn. I bet I can do both my problems in less time than it took for Roman to do his."

"Don't rush," I warn, and I feel my face flush as I realize my words could imply criticism. "We're okay waiting," I say. "Take as long as you need."

Annalise's smile fades as her eyes meet mine. In their depths I see nerves and a touch of fear lurking behind the bravado that I have in this short time come to admire. Then the smile is back as she nods. "I promise to kick butt on questions two and three. The rest is up to the two of you."

The door closes. The red light returns. So does the silence.

Brick sits unmoving. His calm, silent demeanor has the opposite effect on me. I stand and pace the room as my stomach begins to growl. I am certain it is far past lunchtime. It is obvious that no meals will be provided until this test is complete. And maybe that's part of the test—to see if candidates will stay focused despite the desire for food.

My mother always insisted I eat everything on my plate on

mornings before important tests. She said the brain and body need fuel to operate at the highest level. I dig through my bag for my stash of food and find myself deciding between a roll filled with raisins and nuts, and an apple. Since the roll is easier to split with Brick, I start to pull it out when I realize they are two of the items I selected for dinner the first night of The Testing. I count back the days. Less than a week has passed, but everything has changed since that night when the four of us from Five Lakes arrived and took our table. Now Malachi is gone and I am working in a group with the boy who tripped him. Did Roman stick out his leg for spite? For fun? Did he think it would intimidate Malachi into doing less well on the exams, thereby giving Roman a better chance of passing? Maybe. Roman only got one answer correct today. How smart can he be? The work he did on the final problem was so illogical I found it hard to believe he had made it through the first two tests.

Wait.

I reach for the booklet marked with the X and the circle. Roman's handwriting is neater than I would have suspected based on his appearance. Hearing my mother's voice warn not to let appearances deceive me, I read through the pages of numbers and formulas for the first problem. The work impresses me. While I also got the correct answer, Roman was able to calculate several steps in his head, which is why he finished first. His work makes it clear why he was chosen for The Testing. He's smart. Very smart.

Which is why his answers to the other questions make no sense. Gibberish fills those pages. We had all been so concerned with who gave the correct answers to the problems we never bothered to check the pages that preceded the final solution.

Roman's scribbles made one thing obvious. He wasn't concerned with coming up with the right solutions. He was just wasting time. Why?

"Cia."

I jump as Brick's voice breaks the silence and follow his gaze to the light above the door. Green. If I were to make a guess, less than a half hour has passed since Annalise walked through the door. Could she have finished her problems in so little time? Hands shaking, I grab the booklet marked with the other eight-pointed star and start flipping the pages.

Yes. Her writing is clear. Concise. Confident. Her logic shows no flaws that I can see. If anyone could whiz through two tests in far less time than it took another candidate to do one, it would be Annalise. Still . . .

"Are you going to go in?" Brick asks.

"In a minute," I say. Going through the door is my only option. The only way to get past this test. It's what happens once I am through that door that is in doubt. I think back to the Testing official's instructions. Roman's insistence that he go first. One answer allowed per question. The scores to the answers provided count for all. Any attempt to resolve a question will be punished.

Annalise's testing booklet falls from my fingers and my legs go weak as the pieces click into place. Roman's lack of effort on the other problems. The length of time it took for the red light to turn green during his turn. Dr. Barnes told us the third test would evaluate our ability not only to work well with others, but to evaluate their strengths and weaknesses. If I am correct, Roman evaluated our group perfectly and has set the rest of us up to walk into a trap.

A trap Annalise must have already sprung.

I sit hard on the chair behind me and take deep breaths trying to stave off the panic. If I am right, I cannot attempt to answer the problem my team assigned me. If I am wrong, not answering the problem could result in my failure. I have to decide what I believe.

My heart pounds as I look at Brick. His calm demeanor and poor performance on the practice problems take on a sinister tone. Does he know about Roman's plan? Did they plot this together? Brick's practice book might present me with the answers, but the booklet is currently resting under his elbow on the table in front of him. To get the booklet, I have to explain my concerns. If he isn't involved in Roman's trap, Brick will learn about it from me and gain the opportunity to pass when he doesn't deserve to.

Shame. Hot. Deep. Oily, stomach-churning embarrassment fills me. My thoughts make me no better than the person I believe Roman to be. I will not stoop so low as to trick others in order to eliminate the competition. While I am horrified at the methods employed with The Testing, I seriously doubt the Testing officials who rate us at the end will approve of trickery either. What kind of leader would that type of person make?

Mimicking Brick's calm demeanor, I carefully explain what I believe Roman's plan is. What I think happened to Annalise. What could possibly happen to us if we attempt to solve the problems we have been assigned. Brick listens without interruption, and when I fall silent, considers me for a long time before saying, "We said we would answer the agreed-upon questions."

Does he not believe me? No. His expression is not one of disbelief, but of resignation. "Roman agreed to work as a team, but I don't think he is. If we answer an already answered question, we'll be penalized."

I can see the nail enter Malachi's eye. The blood. The trembling body crumpled on the floor. Knowing what could happen makes me want to shake Brick's stoic shoulders as his head moves side to side while once again saying he gave his word. His parents taught him to respect a promise. End of story.

Desperation claws at my heart even as I wonder if he's right. If I'm wrong. If Roman answered only his question. If not answering ours will be the biggest mistake we could make.

Hitching my bag onto my shoulder, I walk slowly across the room. I have done all I can to help Brick survive the day. If he doesn't . . .

"Please." Turning, I walk back to Brick and take his hand in mine. "You don't know me. There's no reason you should trust what I say. I can't tell you what to do. I can only ask that you look at Roman's booklet and think about who has the most to gain by betraying the others. If he solved all five problems, anyone who attempts to solve them again will be penalized. I don't know what the penalty is . . ." I see the nail enter Malachi's eye again and swallow the bile that rises in my throat. "But if I'm right, three of us could be eliminated from The Testing because we trusted our teammate."

For a moment the composed expression disappears, replaced by confusion. "I'm not from your colony. Why do you care what I do?"

"Because I don't want anyone else to die."

Brick looks over my shoulder at the door behind me. The green light telling me it is time for me to make my choice.

Letting go of his hand, I open the door, give one last look at my teammate, and walk through hoping I did enough to save Brick's life. Hoping I am confident enough in my own deductions to save my own.

The hallway is dimly lit. The shadows fill me with unease as I follow the corridor to the end. As promised, another hallway lined with six illuminated doors greets me. To my right is the door marked with the number four. The door I promised to walk through. To my left are doors one through three. I cross to door two—looking for signs of what? Blood? Hair? Something to prove my theory right. The silver doorknob gleams in the light. There are no smudges on it to bear witness that it had been handled. I check the other doorknobs. All perfectly polished.

I walk back to door number four and trace the black number on the snow-white door. Do I keep my word and turn the handle, or go with my gut and walk away?

How long do I stand in front of the door? I don't know. But when I finally make my choice my knees protest as I shift my weight. Touching the doorknob, I take a deep breath and step away from the door. Turn to the right. Walk two doors down to the one marked EXIT and turn the gleaming knob, hoping the choice I have made is not my last.

CHAPTER 9

A TESTING OFFICIAL is waiting inside a small room containing a dark wooden table, a chair, and a control panel of some kind. It's probably what makes the light we watched go from red to green. The official's expression is pleasant as she leads me through a back door, down well-lit hallways to the bank of elevators. The Testing official stays on the elevator as I exit onto the fifth floor wondering how and when I will learn my fate.

I hear the sounds of conversation from the dining hall and realize that I might not need to wait. The person with the answer to whether I made the correct choice is right through those doors. My heart leaps as I see Tomas, Will, and Zandri sitting at our table, but I do not join them. Not yet. Instead, I scan the room.

I spot Roman before he sees me. Laughing with friends. At a joke or at those of us who might have been eliminated because we believed him?

Tomas calls my name, but I don't move from my position in the doorway. The girl next to Roman jabs him with her elbow. His eyes turn and meet mine. And I know. The disbelief and anger in his eyes tell me I was right not to trust him. I just wish I had figured out the truth sooner. If I had, Annalise might be seated at one of these tables. There is no sign of her red hair and confident smile. A small part of me hopes she is relaxing in her room, though if she is, I am almost guaranteed a failing grade.

I feel Roman's eyes follow me as I grab a bag of crackers from the snacks on the table and walk across the room to sit with my friends. Tomas, Will, and Zandri tell me about the problems they solved. From the way they talk, I begin to understand that while we all had the same types of problems to complete, every group solved them in a different order. Tomas answered the third question for his team—the math question Roman was supposed to answer for ours. Zandri went first for her team and answered the history problem. Will went second and was assigned genetics. Everyone from Tomas's group has returned from the exam. Zandri and Will are still waiting for the rest of their teammates to arrive.

As I watch the door, they ask which question I was assigned. In a quiet voice I tell them about my belief in my teammate's betrayal. My decision not to open the door. To leave before answering my question. My friends stare at me. A knot forms in my chest. Will recovers first and says he's impressed I trusted my instincts. That he was glad he never had to make a choice about trusting his teammates since Zandri was the only one who went before him. And, of course, he trusted her. Tomas looks at Will for several long moments before saying he's proud that I alerted Brick to my suspicions. Will tells a joke to make me feel better, but I don't. Zandri's wide eyes and trembling lips and the way Tomas frowns when he doesn't think I'm looking remind me that the verdict to this test is still in doubt. There is still a chance that I made a mistake. That I failed. And when Brick appears in the doorway, I am certain I did. My heart drops. Brick had been adamant about following through with his promise. And when he passes my table without a glance, I'm positive he did exactly what he swore to do. Brick solved his question. He knows I was planning on not answering mine. Now I am forced to wonder—did I ruin the chance for all of us to pass this test and continue on?

Nicolette arrives full of stories about her teammates. Some were nice. One was pushy and arrogant. Her group made the arrogant boy go last—just in case he got any ideas about messing up the test for the others. I turn a cracker over in my hands and listen to everyone talk about the personalities of the candidates they were grouped with. Zandri shoots looks at the door as she watches for her other test teammates to arrive. I realize Tomas has fallen silent. He's watching our friends closely. Out of the corner of my eye I see him looking at me. Does he think I'm paranoid? Maybe I am.

Time passes slowly as more candidates arrive looking triumphant or tired. Sometimes both. Eventually, dinner is served. I force myself to eat. With every bite, I cast a look at Brick, willing him to make eye contact. To give me a sign of the choice he made.

As we finish with our meal, a voice over the loudspeaker says, "Phase three of Testing is now complete. Failing results will be delivered to candidates' rooms within the hour. For those who pass, I wish you a good night's sleep. Preparation for the final phase of Testing will begin tomorrow."

My friends rise and head for the exit. I pretend to adjust my bag's strap and remain seated until Brick walks past. He never looks in my direction.

For the next hour I watch the clock in my room as the minutes tick past. I hear the sound of someone crying. I flinch as footsteps come near, but no one knocks or opens my door. After the allotted time passes, the hallway grows silent. I know I have passed. I should feel joy, but as I climb into bed there is only numb fatigue and the hope that I am up to the challenge of whatever tomorrow will bring.

The morning announcement comes with the dawn. We are to bring all our belongings with us when we report for breakfast. I dress quickly and lace up my worn leather boots as a sense of dread grips my stomach. My friends are all at breakfast the next morning. We have made it to phase three, although Zandri's red-rimmed, tired eyes and withdrawn demeanor show that success has not come without a price. I look around the room and spot Brick sitting at the back table. This time his eyes make contact. For a moment we just stare at each other. When he nods, I recognize his gratitude.

An hour passes before the loudspeaker invites us downstairs. Around the room I see people suck in air. Some, like Zandri, let out low whimpers. Others, like Tomas, look concerned but resigned. Even the cockiest like Roman show signs of fear. Yes. The Testing has exacted a price from us all and that payment isn't over. There is still one test to go.

Dr. Barnes once again waits for us in the third-floor lecture hall. Today he is wearing a serious expression that makes everyone in the room fall silent.

"Congratulations to all of you for making it to the fourth round of Testing. There were one hundred and eight candidates in this year's Testing class. Fifty-nine of you remain. Tomorrow will begin the longest phase of our Testing—the practical examination. University students are the future leaders of the United Commonwealth. Because some of you in this room will soon be designated as among those leaders, we believe it is necessary for you to understand fully the challenges you will face. You will travel to a nonrevitalized part of the country and be placed in a designated starting location. When the test begins, you must then find your way from that location back to Tosu City. Those who return will be given a passing grade and will qualify for the final evaluation. That evaluation will determine the candidates who will attend the University."

Terror. That's the only word I can think of to describe what I feel. Alone in an unfamiliar part of the country. Or not alone. Not really. Animals. War-fallout mutations of animals that were once harmless but are no longer. And drifters—those who have chosen not to join the United Commonwealth. People who believed structured governments led to the Seven Stages of War and abandoned those who sought organization. Those people might be out there, too. And just me, by myself, to face them.

"Each candidate will begin the test independent of each other. That does not mean you have to remain alone. You may choose to team up with other candidates. You may also choose to impair the progress of your fellow candidates in order to ensure that you obtain a passing grade before them. What choices you make during the test will be considered in your final evaluations."

Tomas takes my hand and holds it tight. The pressure of his fingers and the implied support calm me enough to focus. If I am going to pass this test, I need to focus.

A screen descends behind Dr. Barnes. A map flickers on the screen. At the bottom left corner of the map is a silver star. Next to the star are the words *Tosu City.* On the top right is a large black star next to a blue body of water. The black star is labeled *Start.* Aside from the stars, the one body of water, and the name of Tosu City, the only detail provided on the map are two lines—one red and one blue. The red runs on a diagonal from just about the starting point to a few inches above the silver star. The blue line starts several inches below the starred location and runs to just south of Tosu City.

"All candidates will travel from your designated starting position through the area in between the blue and red boundaries to Tosu City. Both lines indicate fences that have been erected by Testing officials to help you understand and stay within the boundaries of the Testing area. Any candidate who leaves the Testing area at any time will be given a failing grade.

"Please do not make us enforce this rule."

Malachi's bloody face flashes in front of me. Ryme's bulging, bloodshot eyes. Annalise's now empty chair. Judging by Dr. Barnes's serious expression and the tone of his voice, there is no doubt what penalty a failing grade will bring.

"As soon as you are dismissed, each of you will meet with a Testing official who will give you further instructions." Dr.

Barnes sighs and slowly looks around the room, letting his gaze settle on each and every candidate. "Please be safe and smart. It is my dearest hope that each and every one of you returns to Tosu City." He straightens his shoulders and tells us to watch the screen behind him. When our symbol flashes on the screen, we are to stand and join our assigned Testing official in the hallway. He wishes us luck and then leaves the stage, walking down the aisle and out the door without a backwards glance.

The first symbol flashes on the screen and a boy down in front rises. Still holding my hand, Tomas leans over and whispers, "The starting point is Chicago."

I think back to the map that flashed on the screen, consider the water and the distance between it and Tosu City, and nod. I'd been too stunned to recognize it from the maps we'd studied in school. Even without any additional identifying landmarks, I'm certain Tomas is right and wonder how we can use that knowledge to our advantage.

Tomas is one step ahead of me. Talking quietly in my ear, he tells me to find the tallest building still standing. Go there. He'll meet me. If we don't find each other in the first twenty-four hours, I'm to travel due west until I reach the fencing that is the northern boundary of the test. We'll find each other there. Partners. We will do this together.

Two plans. Two hopes that I will not have to travel hundreds of miles on my own. I nod and squeeze his hand to show him that I agree, that I will do my best to find him, as a symbol of an eight-pointed star with a lightning bolt flashes on the screen. My mouth goes dry. I don't want to let go of Tomas's hand, but I convince each finger to uncurl. I move away from the strength Tomas's presence has lent me, and I stand. Hoisting my bag onto my shoulder, I touch each one of my friends—Tomas, Zandri, Will, Nicolette—on the cheek as I pass.

When I walk into the hallway, I can't help feeling a small burst of relief at the face waiting for me. Michal. His expression is stern, but I can see a spark of pride that I am still here. Or maybe I am just imagining that because, when he asks me to follow, his tone is formal. As though we have never met.

We take the elevator to the first floor and exit left down a long gray hallway. At the end of the hall, we stop in front of a large gray door. "This is the Testing storeroom," Michal says. "Each Testing candidate is allowed ten minutes inside this room. During that time you will select three additional items to help you successfully complete this test. I will log your choices as you make them. At this time, I am supposed to remind you to choose carefully. Your choices can mean the difference between success and failure. Of course, I doubt you would have made it this far if you hadn't already figured that out."

This time I am certain I don't imagine the glint of pride in his eyes. He tells me my ten minutes start when I open the door. I take a deep breath and turn the handle.

Outdoor clothing. Sensible shoes. Food. Compasses. First-aid bags. Travel gear. Fire-making kits. Fishing poles. Knives. Guns. And more. Everything you could need to stay alive. And I am allowed to take only three.

I feel Michal's presence behind me as I walk slowly past tables, racks, and shelves stacked with life-sustaining items. Once again, I am grateful for my broken-in boots. Most girls will need to exchange their fashionable footwear for something they can hike in. My thievery in the dining hall also has paid off. While a half dozen apples, rolls, and bags of dried fruit won't get me all the way to Tosu City, I know I have enough to get me by—for now. So I ignore those options and study the rest. All of it seems necessary. I feel the time I am allotted for my selection ticking away as I try to decide what I really, truly need.

Tucked in the corner is a deep green bag with a small stamp that reads *H_2O.* My hands pull the bag from the pile and investigate. Inside are two canteens filled with water and a small kit of the chemicals we used during the second test.

I think back to the map. The testing zone is large. I am certain the area must be filled with lakes, streams, and creeks, though they hadn't been marked on the map. Between conversations with my father and Dr. Barnes's words, I know most if not all of the designated Testing area has yet to be revitalized. That means the water within the boundaries is most likely contaminated in some way. Not all contaminations will kill, but many cause illness—especially in the tired and malnourished. I will risk both during this phase of The Testing. I will not risk dehydration as well.

One choice made.

Sliding the green bag onto my shoulder, I consider my other options. The tent with its rainproof fabric and insulated floor is oh so tempting. But just lifting the case makes the decision for me. While it doesn't feel heavy now, there are more than seven hundred miles to travel. After the first ten the tent will feel more burden than blessing. Comfort must take a back seat to survival.

I skip by the compass since I have one on the Transit Communicator I borrowed from Zeen. I also skip past the knives and the fire-starting kits. I have the pocketknife I brought from home. I will make do. As for fire, it will take me a while to build one without the assistance of matches or flint, but I can do it. It is one of the first skills they teach new students in Five Lakes Colony. For the fire kits to be included here among the survival gear, I have to wonder if our small size and remote location made this a lesson unique to us.

The stash of crossbows, guns, and explosives catches my attention. If an animal attacks, I do not want to be caught unprepared. I've never fired a crossbow and immediately scratch that off my list. The explosives are unfamiliar and scare the crap out of me. I have fired my father's shotgun, and Daileen's dad taught us to fire his pistol. Daileen is a much better shot, but I can hit the center of the target at least 75 percent of the time. I finger the shotgun, which I am more comfortable with, but it only comes with a box of ten shells. My fingers shift and close over a small black handgun that comes with two boxes of ammunition. Lightweight. Easy to carry. Enough bullets that I can take a few practice shots without worrying about running out.

Second choice complete.

The gun and the two boxes of ammunition disappear into my bag as Michal warns there are two minutes remaining. My heart skips as panic sets in. Two minutes and I have no idea what else to take. Signal flares to help Tomas find me? A sleeping bag? A raincoat? A manual on hot-wiring old-fashioned cars? Will there be cars? I don't think so — but how can I know?

Closing my eyes, I take two deep breaths and make a list of what I do have. Food. Water. Clothes. A knife and small tools. A Transit Communicator complete with compass. A gun for self-defense. But what if I get injured?

I open my eyes and head for the medical kits. Each one contains bandages, a needle and thread, and antibacterial ointments along with some radiation tablets, mild pain/fever medication, and other bottles I don't have time to examine now. I shove the medical kit into my bag and sling it onto my shoulder as Michal announces, "Time's up."

Turning my back on the supplies, I follow Michal out the door trying to ignore the nagging worry that I have made a mistake. But there is no going back. My three choices have been made. Whatever else I need I'll just have to find as I go.

Michal checks his watch and leads me down the hallway to a room marked with my symbol. He opens the door. Inside is a small sleeping chamber and an adjoining bathroom.

"You have an hour to repack your belongings or change clothes." He looks at me and smiles. He knows I won't be changing into anything, but his words and expression let me know this is a script he must follow. It also tells me something else—if Michal is being this careful, there are people listening to what is being said. "If you need anything during the hour, please let me know. I'll be right outside."

The door closes, and I sit on the small twin-sized bed. Everything in the room is decorated in shades of gray. Not exactly the most uplifting place I've ever been in, but it could be worse. In fact, I am certain it very soon will be.

I strip off my clothes, shower, and wash my hair. Once I'm

clean, I contemplate myself in the reflector before pulling my hair back at the nape of my neck and twisting it into a tight knot. I have no idea what I will be facing when the test begins, but I cannot afford to let my cascading hair get in the way. If during the test I have to cut it off, I will. Vanity has no place here.

Boots laced up, I empty my bag on the floor and repack. I remove one canteen of water to keep handy and store the rest of the kit on the bottom of the bag along with my clothes. The medical kit goes in next. Then the food I took from the dining hall gets wrapped in a towel from the bathroom (no one said we couldn't take them) and stowed. Last the final canteen, Zeen's Transit Communicator, and the gun. The knife I put in my pocket. I lift the bag. It isn't as light as it used to be, but I've distributed the weight well. I can run with it if I need to.

The end of my hour is signaled by a knock on the door. Michal is waiting. He takes in my hair, my unchanged clothes, the single bag hanging from my shoulder, and nods. "Follow me."

He leads me through a series of hallways until we come to an elevator. This time he pushes a button for a floor I've never seen before. UG. When the doors open it is very clear by the mildew scent what UG stands for: Underground. According to Michal, we will travel by an underground moving walkway system to the outskirts of the city. A skimmer will then transport us to my designated starting area.

The tension and worry I've been carrying diminish when I spot the underground walkway. It is a large conveyor belt that hums along the floor, and I can't help but ask Michal dozens of questions about how it works, how large the network is, and how it is powered. He smiles and tells me he'll answer what he can while we travel. I stumble as I step onto the belt, but Michal catches me before I end up on the ground.

The walkway ride lasts the better part of an hour, much of it traveling through dimly lit tunnels. Several times we have to step off one walkway and climb onto a new one. I'm grateful for Michal's presence as he continues a steady stream of conversation. Concentrating on his voice helps me ignore the anxiety blooming in my stomach.

We arrive at our destination and step off the walkway. An elevator zooms us to the surface, where Michal says our lunch awaits. The elevator lets us off into a large room bustling with Testing officials. One official in purple holding a clipboard spots us and hurries over. He makes note of my identification bracelet symbol, scribbles something on his board, and tells Michal to take me to number 14.

Number 14 turns out to be a well-lit but airless skimmer docking bay. In the corner is a small table holding a large picnic lunch. Michal will stay with me here in this room until I've gone through the next step of Testing preparation—whatever that might be. A tiny window next to the table looks out onto a green field of grass. Beyond the grass is sparkling water. After being inside for most of the last few days and not knowing whether I will ever see healthy land like this again, I ask Michal if we can eat lunch outside. He is about to say no, but I must look pretty desperate because he tells me to wait here while he asks one of the upper-level officials.

I take one look at Michal's face when he returns and give

a whoop of joy. Michal grabs the basket of food and tells me we have exactly one hour to spend outside. He presses a small button on the wall, and the docking bay door rises. A moment later we stroll into the fresh air.

Picking a spot near a large tree, I admit, "I'm surprised they let us come outside."

"As long as I'm with you and you aren't able to communicate with other Testing candidates, there's no reason to say no." He hands me an apple from the basket and smiles. "To tell you the truth, most Testing candidates are happy to follow instructions. The Testing committee is always interested to see which candidates show a bit more initiative."

Even now, before we are thrown into the wreckage of our country, we are being tested. It shouldn't surprise me. But it does. My eyes run up and down the length of the tree, looking for signs that our words are being recorded, that we are being watched.

Michal smiles. "Don't worry. Our conversation isn't being recorded out here. The Testing committee is too busy to monitor everything leading up to the fourth test. That's what I'm here for, and I don't plan on reporting this conversation. If you want to talk, this is as safe as it gets."

Do I want to talk? Yes. But do I trust Michal or is this just one more test to be graded? My father would instruct me not to trust him. As much as I want to be, I have proven over and over again since leaving home that I am not my father.

Michal hands me a sandwich from the basket and asks, "How are you holding up?"

My insides are churning, but I make myself take a bite

of the sandwich—beef, cheese, and a hearty wheat bread. It probably tastes wonderful. Swallowing, I say, "Malachi is dead. I watched him die."

"I heard." His eyes meet mine. "I'm sorry."

I believe he is. The sympathy I feel radiating off him makes me want to cry. "Why? Why is he dead?" A poisonous leaf. A nail to the eye. Those are the causes. But the reason . . .

Michal looks over his shoulder and then tells me to eat, to pretend to laugh and enjoy myself. Otherwise someone watching at a distance might wonder what we are saying. As I eat, he tells me that the Testing process was designed years ago by Dr. Barnes's father, who believed that the Seven Stages of War occurred because world leaders did not have the correct combination of intelligence, ability to perform under pressure, and strength of leadership to lead us out of confrontations. That the only way to ensure the United Commonwealth did not repeat past mistakes was to test the future leaders of our country and make sure they had the breadth of qualities that would not only help our country flourish but keep our people safe. Over the years, several Commonwealth officials have questioned the necessity of such strong penalties for failing The Testing. Some even say that the Testers rig the outcome of the tests so that those who are too smart, too strong, and too dedicated are weeded out. For those are the ones who feel not only compelled to rebuild the Commonwealth but also to question its laws and its choices. Anyone who voices negative opinions about The Testing either is relocated to an outpost or disappears.

Michal laughs as though he has said something funny. I laugh too, though nothing has ever seemed less amusing. What constitutes too smart and too strong? Does asking to go outside mark me a rebel? My head spins, but I continue to smile as though my life depends on it.

And it might.

I eat the entire sandwich, then another because it won't keep in my bag and I know I need to be well fueled when I start the next test. Michal leans back in the grass and watches. When the sandwiches are gone, Michal glances at his watch. Ten minutes of freedom remain.

"Are you scared?" he asks, handing me a bottle of water.

I take a sip and feel emotions crash against the carefree wall that I had erected. I nod. Yes, I am terrified. Trying not to lose my composure, I slide the uneaten apples, oranges, and rolls into my bag. My fingers tremble as I try to close the fasteners. Michal helps me and whispers, "Don't worry about being the first to arrive back. Every year candidates think the order you return in matters. It doesn't. Be smart. Be safe. Trust your friends from Five Lakes if you can, but no one else. Every year there are Testing candidates who think taking out their competition is the best way to ensure their entrance to the University. More often than not they are right. Don't let them be this time."

The bag closes. I sit down as the world around me starts to spin and then fades to black. The last thing I remember is feeling strong arms lifting me while a soft, warm voice says, "You're smart, Cia. You're strong. There are people like me on your side who know you can make it. Please, prove I'm right."

Then everything fades away.

The next thing I hear is water dripping. My eyes fly open. I am lying on a cot in what can only be described as a metal box. The whole thing is probably six feet by six feet. I try to squelch the panic I feel at being in such a small, confined space and take in the rest of my surroundings. There are electric lights illuminating the space. A small basket of food sits on the floor next to me. A toilet and tiny sink occupy the corner at the end of my bed. On the wall across from me is a countdown clock with a sign that reads: TESTING BEGINS IN THIRTY MINUTES. No. Strike that. Twenty-nine minutes.

I use the toilet. Flush the grogginess from my eyes and the metallic taste from my mouth that are clear signs I was drugged. I think back to the water Michal handed me and feel a stab of betrayal. Then it is gone as I remember the whispered words. The drugs were part of Testing protocol. His words and the care they contained were not. For whatever reason, Michal genuinely believes I will make it through this test. He even claims others I don't know are offering their support. I will not prove them wrong.

As the clock counts down, I strip the bed of its sheet and stuff it into the bottom of my bag. Who knows when I might need the warmth. I then check the food basket. More sandwiches. Dried fruit. A bottle of water. A small box of crackers and three perfectly ripe strawberries. I eat the sandwiches, sniff the water for traces of drugs, and then sip at it while storing the crackers and the dried fruit in my bulging bag. If nothing else, I'll have enough food to see me through a week. More if I'm careful. One by one I eat the juicy strawberries as I watch the clock tick down. When it reaches five minutes, I wash my hands, dig Zeen's Transit Communicator out of my bag, and turn on the compass. The compass swings wildly, searching for direction, and finds none. I can only guess the metal box is confusing the signal and hope the situation remedies itself when I am able to leave.

Two minutes left to go.

I take one last sip of water and store the bottle in my bag.

One minute.

I realize anything could be outside that door. After putting Zeen's Communicator in the side pocket of my bag, I reach into it one last time. When the clock hits zero, I stand with my bag on my shoulder and the small black gun in my hand.

The side of the metal box swings open as a recorded voice says, "The fourth round of Testing has now begun."

CHAPTER 10

THEY DIDN'T WISH us luck. Perhaps that is a strange thought to be having at this moment, but my mind can't seem to focus on anything else as I step from my tiny Testing candidate cell onto a patch of brown grass growing up through concrete. I can barely breathe as I look at the decaying devastation around me. Steel and rock. Glass and wood. Buildings broken and collapsed. Cars completely rusted and overturned. A layer of sooty grime covers it all. Here and there heartier plants are fighting to get beyond the rubble—yearning toward the sun. Vines cover the wreckage of broken cars and buildings. Trees that have been corrupted by the tainted earth but are determined to survive twist through the pieces of the broken city on their way to the sky. Not too far away from where my metal box sits is what looks like a collapsed brick arch that is partially covered by dark, prickly vines. In the rising sunlight, I think I can see words etched on the brick, and I cautiously take a few steps toward it.

I squint to make out the letters: CHICA O STOC EXCH E B

Even with one letter unreadable, I now know for certain where I am. Chicago. The third city destroyed during the Fourth Stage of War. The first two cities had some warning—announced evacuations. Hundreds of thousands of people died, but it could have been worse. Like it was here. Books tell us the attack was fast. Undetected until the first bombs had been dropped. Who the enemy was who breached the country's defenses and destroyed a city unprepared has never been confirmed, although the president and his advisers believed they knew. They struck back, and the world collapsed.

Wind whistles through the abandoned streets. But they aren't abandoned—not now. Fifty-eight other Testing candidates are here. Some are my friends, but according to Michal, others will happily cut me down with the weapons provided for our defense just to ensure their spot in the University class. How do I find one without risking running into the others? Or the weapons they might have selected? Being forced to use the gun in my bag?

Tomas said to meet him at the tallest building, but from my current vantage point, it is hard to tell what that might be. I walk back to my box and hoist myself up to the roof to get a better look. More broken concrete and twisted steel. Mountains of rubble that form the graves of the people who used to call this city home. The enormity of the destruction pulls at my heart, but I don't have time to grieve for the people who died here. I have to find Tomas.

As I prepare to climb down, I spot something that catches the light above the rest of the destruction. It doesn't look like a building, but it's the tallest thing I can see from my location. Distance is hard to judge, but I'm guessing it isn't too far away. I don't know if Tomas will head there, but I have to take a shot.

The Transit Communicator's compass is working now. So is the mapping tool that determines longitude and latitude. At least I know my coordinates. I can find my way back if I need to.

Jumping down, I set off with my compass directing me north to my destination. I scramble over piles of broken rock and avoid large gaping holes in the ground, stopping every few feet to listen. Do I hear other footsteps? Is anyone else nearby? All I hear is the wind rustling the dried, clawlike leaves on a nearby tree.

While my goal didn't appear to be all that far from my metal perch, the sun is much higher in the sky when I approach what I can now see is a grayish-looking spire shooting up from what used to be a building. How the spire survived destruction is a mystery. I wonder if Tomas can see it from his designated starting point.

I sit on a fallen piece of stone and take several sips from my water bottle. The sun is hot. Sweat is dripping down my back. I need to keep hydrated if I am going to survive this test. My stomach growls, and I break off a small piece of raisin bread while I try to decide how long to wait here for Tomas. He might not see the spire. He might have decided that the tall-building plan is a bust and is now trekking his way west to the fence line that was our second rendezvous point.

Checking the position of the sun, I decide it must be sometime after noon. Hours have passed since I first stepped onto the city streets. While I would like to wait as long as it takes to find Tomas, I also need to find shelter when night comes. The idea of sleeping out in the open with Testing candidates and whatever unknown dangers are lurking freaks me out. One hour. That's how long I decide I can give Tomas before I leave this spot. Then I will move on.

I finish my sparse lunch and decide to explore my surroundings a bit until it is time to leave. Hoisting the bag onto my shoulder, I scramble over debris. I almost trip on a tree root and end up directly on the other side of the spire, looking at a large metal box sitting on a broken street.

A Testing candidate box.

My heart picks up speed as I tread slowly toward the box, careful not to make any noise as I walk. It is too much to hope for that Tomas's box would be the first one I come across after leaving my own, or that he would still be in it hours after the test began. Still, I have to look.

The clock inside is no longer lit. The basket of food contains only a discarded apple core and the container the crackers came in. This is definitely not Tomas's box. He wouldn't have been reckless enough to eat food that could be stored for later. And he would have stripped the cot of its sheet like I did. I'm considering adding the sheet to my inventory when I hear a stone skitter over the ground.

Someone or something is outside.

I freeze and hold my breath, trying to decide my next move as I hear fragments of cement crunch under a shoe. Not an animal. Definitely a person. My heartbeats count off the seconds as I listen for sounds of advance or retreat. The minutes pass. I hear nothing. I tighten and retighten my grip on the gun in my right hand and count to one hundred. Still nothing.

Being trapped in this windowless box has me at a distinct disadvantage. Not only can I not see who is out there, but I have no method of escape if someone comes through the door. It is time to leave. Now.

I peer out of the entrance of the box. The opening faces an area that at one time must have housed a building but is now home to a few partially standing walls. A few of the walls are only three or four feet high, but one or two are taller than me. The tallest wall is probably fifty or sixty feet away. The walls could provide a place to hide from whoever is nearby. At least until I can determine whether the person means harm or not. The ground between the box and the wall is cracked but mostly flat. If someone is waiting for me outside the box, taking them by surprise is my best chance. I position my bag's strap over my head so it is more secure, shift the weight, take a deep breath, and run.

My boots pound against the hard stone ground. Somewhere, off to my right I think, I hear someone swear. My flight or my identity has taken them by surprise. If it is a friend, they would call out. When they don't, I run faster. I am about ten feet away from my destination when I hear a high-pitched, almost musical vibrating sound. Then a thunk. Embedded in the scraggly tree trunk to my left is a crossbow quarrel.

The vibrating whine sounds again. This time I flatten myself against the concrete. Seconds later a metal quarrel hits the wall five feet in front of me and clatters to the ground. More swearing. Definitely to my right. Whoever is shooting the quarrels either has amazing luck with the weapon or has had training with it in the past. I need to get to a safe place—fast. Scrambling to my feet, bag banging against my hip, I speed forward and duck behind the wall as another crossbow quarrel connects with stone.

There is no doubt: someone is trying to kill me.

Another Testing candidate? I have to believe so. A crossbow was one of the weapons in the selection room. And while I understand feeling scared and alone in this wasted city, I do not believe those are the feelings propelling this attack. Like Roman's sabotage of our group on the third exam, this attack is calculated. It is cold. It is an attempt to better the odds of making it to the University.

Anger and indignation cut through my fear. Whoever this person is, isn't relying on their own smarts to pass this test. Michal said that killing someone isn't against the rules, but in my mind it's a form of cheating. I'll be damned if I'm going to let a cheater win.

I remember the gun in my hand, get into a crouching position, and slowly move to the right, careful to keep behind the crumbling stone. When I reach the end of the wall, I calculate my best guess as to where the quarrels were shot from, peer around the wall, and fire.

The kick of the gun jolts my entire body as the sound tears through the silent city. Someone curses loudly—a male voice. I find it hard to believe my blind attack hit him. That wasn't my goal. I don't plan on surviving this test by killing the others. But that doesn't mean I'm going to go down without a fight. I shoot three more bullets out into the city and crouch behind the wall, listening for sounds of my attacker. The sound of feet connecting with rocks makes me hold my breath.

Rocks skittering across pavement.

The clang of something metal.

Silence.

Then the sound of heavy footsteps running. Not toward my position, but away. I am safe. For now.

My body shakes as anger seeps out, leaving behind hollow fear. I just shot a gun at someone. No, I wasn't trying to kill the shooter. But I could have. I could have killed someone. The fact that the person was trying to kill me can justify my behavior, but shame and horror still fill me.

I realize that I am huddled up against the wall, no longer listening to the sounds of the city, and tell myself to snap out of it. There will be time enough later to worry about what I have just learned about myself. First, I need to put distance between me and this place. The gunshots will have attracted attention from anyone in the vicinity. If there are other Testing candidates out there interested in taking out the competition, they might come looking for the source of the gunshots. I don't want to be here when they arrive.

Listening carefully for signs of life, I peer around the wall and scan the wreckage of the city. I see no one. Not near the candidate box. Not on the piles of broken buildings or hiding among the branches of diseased trees. As far as I can tell, at this very moment I am alone. While I would like nothing better than to have Tomas walking out of the city with me, I will have to make it out of here on my own.

Keeping low to the ground, I check my compass and slowly head west, careful to stop every ten or fifteen feet to scan the area around me. So far I see no one, but I know the crossbow shooter is out there somewhere. Climbing over rocks and pieces of steel makes travel slow. Eventually, I find a street that is mostly cleared of debris and pick up my pace.

The street leads to a wide river of dark, swirling water. There is no need for tests. This water is not drinkable. No amount of basic purification chemicals will make it so. The street I am following arches up and over the river. There are cracks and gaping holes in the bridge. Do I try to cross here or find another way to the other side?

I stow my gun in the side pocket on my bag and climb a tree on the riverbank for a better view. The river curves to the northeast. It's hard to see what lies in that direction. To the south there is another bridge, but it too appears to be in disrepair. And who knows how long it will take me to get there or what I will encounter when I do. Scrambling back down to the ground, I decide to try to cross here. I need to put as much distance as possible between me and any unfriendly candidates. If I start to cross and find the bridge is too unsafe, I will head south and try my luck there.

As I cross, I see evidence of a meager attempt to repair the bridge. Perhaps past Testing candidates placed the large planks of wood and slabs of rock over gaping holes when they, too, needed to cross to the other side. Pieces of rock crumble under my boots as I pick my way to the middle of the bridge. From this vantage point, I can tell the far side of the bridge is in even worse condition. Entire sections of asphalt are gone, leaving only small strips here and there that can be navigated. Whoever attempted to patch the bridge behind me must not have wanted to go back to land for materials to repair this side.

I contemplate my options: return back the way I came to try the south bridge or keep going and hope for the best. My current position on the bridge has me exposed. No doubt I am in view of any nearby candidate. If one has spotted me, going back will leave me open to attack. Either option holds risk.

Fear of the crossbow shooter keeps my feet moving forward. I shift the bag on my shoulder as the patch of pavement I walk narrows to a mere foot in width. The dark water rushes underneath me, waiting for one misplaced footstep to carry me away. I am twenty feet from safety when I hear the now familiar vibrating sound that signals danger. There is no choice but to run as what I can only guess is a quarrel whizzes past. There is a plunk in the water below as it is swallowed up by the current.

Five feet from safety the piece of road I have been traveling vanishes. The vibrating sound sings again. I don't have time to think as I leap up and over the gaping hole, hoping to make it to the other side. But only the top part of me makes it onto land. The rest of me dangles in the emptiness between the ledge and the river. Between the weight of my body and my bag, I feel myself sliding backwards. I claw at the concrete and dig my fingers into a fissure in the stone, bringing my backwards movement to a halt.

My arm muscles begin to tremble as I attempt to pull myself onto land. Only, after several tries, I have barely moved a fraction of an inch and my fingers are starting to lose their hold. There is nothing I can do to stop it. In a minute, I will be plunging downward toward the water. I'm bracing myself for the fall and hoping that the bank next to the river is scalable when something clamps onto my arm and pulls my fingers loose from their tenuous grip on safety. With all the dangers around me I know I should stay quiet, but I can't help it. I scream.

CHAPTER 11

"It's okay. Cia. It's okay."

It takes a minute for the voice to penetrate the fear. For the realization that I am being pulled up and not pushed away to bloom into understanding. I stop fighting and allow myself to be hoisted up—up—up to the safety of land.

My heart is pounding. I can hardly breathe, but I manage to croak out, "Thanks," as Tomas's face swims in front of me. His eyes are wary and filled with concern, but his tone is light when he says, "When we get back to Tosu City, we're going to have to work on your long jump."

It's a weak joke, but it makes me smile and helps me briefly forget where I am. Why I'm here. For a moment I am safe. Then the moment disappears. Scrambling to my feet, I peer back toward the bridge, looking for signs of the crossbow shooter. "We have to get out of here. There's someone with a crossbow looking to thin out the competition. He attacked me while I was looking for you. He must have followed me to the bridge."

Tomas's eyes narrow as he looks beyond me to the bridge. Is he looking for proof there was a shooter? Does he not trust my word? If not for my father's dreams, Roman's betrayal, and Michal's warning, I would not have believed another candidate would approach this test in such a way. Can I blame Tomas for doubting?

"Well, whoever it was must be trying to find a safer way across the river. It's amazing you made it at all. I almost lost it when I saw you jump." He shifts the bag on his shoulder and holds out his hand. I'm about to take it when I realize mine are bleeding. Tomas notices the cuts and says, "We'd better get those cleaned. The last thing you need is an infection. Come on. Let's get out of the sun and fix you up."

We travel west for over a mile before I'm willing to stop at a waist-high pile of broken metal and rocks. They will offer some concealment while I patch up my hands and get something to eat. Now that fear no longer gnaws at my stomach, I am starved.

Tomas sits next to me and says, "I can rip my sheet into bandages if you need me to."

"Not necessary." Although I'm glad to know I was right—Tomas did strip the sheet off his bed. "I have a medical kit in here."

Since I don't want to get blood all over everything in my bag, I ask Tomas to retrieve the kit and the half-full bottle of water. I wet a cotton bandage and dab at my wounds, grateful to learn that under the blood there are just a couple of scrapes. A smear of anti-infection ointment and a few bandages later, I am ready to eat. I stow the kit back in my bag, take out an apple, and offer one to Tomas. It's the least I can do after he saved my life.

He grins. "The medical kit was one of your three items, right?" When I nod, his smile grows wider. "I almost took one, but I figured you'd think of that. I didn't want to duplicate anything you had just in case we hooked up."

It was a risky choice. One that might not have paid off had we not found each other. But we did. Knowing he was thinking of us as a team while making his choices makes me inexplicably happy considering the circumstances.

As we eat our apples and the two cinnamon rolls Tomas pulls out of his bag, we compare equipment. I show him the water and purification chemicals, which he also figured I would take, but he did not guess my last choice. He'd been certain I would take a compass, since it was the one item almost every candidate would need on this journey. So his eyebrows rise in surprise as I pull the gun from the side pocket of my bag and admit that I already have had cause to use it.

"That was you?"

The shame I felt earlier at my actions resurfaces, and I drop my eyes so I don't see the censure that must be in Tomas's eyes. But he won't let me look away. Fingers lift my chin so I have to meet his gaze. In it I see understanding, caring, and pride.

"You did the right thing. It takes courage to defend yourself, and I'm glad you did. I can't imagine what I would do if something happened to you." He gives me a soft smile. Then he says, "Do you want to see my three items?"

A tool kit that Tomas was pleased to find also contains matches. A late-twenty-first-century map book of all fifty of the former United States containing detailed maps of the ground we will be treading. Last is a very large, very deadly-looking knife that Tomas slides out of a leather scabbard. I don't remember seeing that kind of knife, if you can call it that, among the weapons we were allowed to select, but it must have been there. Two hands can easily grasp the handle. The blade itself is at least two feet long. One edge is serrated on the bottom. The rest of it gleams with deadly sharpness.

"I thought it would be useful in case we need to cut our way through overgrown bushes." He slides the knife back in its scabbard and attaches it to something on his belt. As far as weapons go, it was a good choice even if it makes me cringe.

I store my belongings back in my bag and then show Tomas my brother's Transit Communicator and the pocket hunting knife I brought from home. Knowing we must be much better stocked for survival than most of the candidates makes me feel more confident as we set off through the wasted city to whatever lies to the west. Tomas thinks we should continue in this direction for a while before turning south, which surprises me.

"Aren't we traveling all the way to the fence?" I ask.

"Why?"

"To meet up with the others. You told Zandri and the others about meeting at the fence, right?"

Tomas stops walking. "You're the only one I told."

"But . . ." I'm about to ask why, but then I think about the crossbow shooter, Ryme's offer of corncakes, the way Malachi was tripped by Roman when we first walked into the dining hall. And Roman's trick. It comes down to trust. Tomas trusts me, and the kindness I have seen him demonstrate over and over again since we were children makes me certain I am correct in trusting him. Still, I cannot help but ask, "What happens if we run into Zandri or the others along the way?" Will we leave them to fend for themselves? Do we allow them to join us? Can we just walk away from people we call our friends?

I see Tomas wrestling with the question as we once again begin to travel west. After a long time, he speaks. "They say we're going to be evaluated on the choices we make. I guess that's going to have to be one of them."

We walk for several more miles, rarely talking as the landscape on the horizon becomes more barren. History says that town after town once fanned out from the outer reaches of the city. That hundreds of thousands of people lived and worked in close proximity to Chicago and thrived because of the city's heartbeat. There is little evidence of that now. Whoever destroyed the city also decimated the towns surrounding it. At least the ones we might be able to see from our location. All that is left are scraps of metal, broken walls, pieces of glass, and a lot of cracked, decayed earth—signs of the destruction man can cause against his fellow man.

The sun fades from the horizon and darkness begins to fall as we spot a small structure that stands amid a tall patch of weeds. A survivor of the war or something built after by one of those who escaped the destruction? Whatever the structure is, it appears to be intact. We look at each other and in that glance agree to head for the building. We could walk a little farther, but who knows if we will find another structure to camp in. The idea of staying outside, unprotected, with Testing candidates and animals prowling for victims is not appealing.

We are both hot and sweaty when we reach the building. The last vestiges of light are fading from the sky. The building is small and square—about eight feet by eight feet—with a hard concrete floor. All four walls still stand, but much of the roof is gone, leaving us with a view of the hazy sky. I'm glad there is no sign of rain. A charred area in the corner of the building suggests someone—probably a Testing candidate from a previous year—lit a fire there.

Tomas decides the walls provide enough cover if we would like to build a small fire. But while a fire would be comforting, neither of us wants to take the risk. In the blackness of night, any light will be seen for miles. We eat dried fruit and some bread for dinner. By the time we are finished with our meal, the light is completely gone, and though the moon is bright, I can see only the outline of the building's door. Nothing else. While I am used to the dark nights of Five Lakes Colony, this blackness feels different. Menacing. Filled with the monsters I used to think hid under my bed. And there are monsters out there. At least one Testing candidate is intent on killing. Tomas's hand finds mine in the dark, and I blink back tears of gratitude that I am not facing this blackness and fear alone.

"Why don't you go to sleep, Cia? I'll keep watch to make sure nothing happens."

I need to sleep. My body is trembling from exhaustion, but I know nightmares are waiting for me when I close my eyes so I opt for conversation instead. "How long do you think it will take to get back to Tosu City?" I used the Transit Communicator to track the coordinates of this shack. Compared them to the ones where my candidate Testing box was located. Walking all day, we had traveled just under eighteen miles. The enormity of the miles between us and our goal is overwhelming.

"Three or four weeks. The farther we get from the city the

easier travel will be. If we find some kind of transportation, it'll go even faster. Just remember one thing. Your dad made it back when he was tested, Cia. We will, too."

I use that thought to push worries about food and water and the actions of other candidates out of my head. With a picture of my father's smile in my mind and Tomas's fingers curled tight around mine, I slip into sleep.

I wake with a start and blink up at a sky tinged with a hazy purple and pink, uncertain where I am. Then I remember. Slowly, I glance to where Tomas lies next to me. His head is cushioned on his Testing bag. His breathing is slow and even. He must have fallen asleep before waking me for my watch. He did not hear whatever it was that woke me from my sleep.

The sound of a twig cracking makes my heart thunder. The wind? An animal or something more deadly? I squeeze Tomas's hand and put a finger over his lips as his eyes slowly open. His eyes widen as I point to the open door and mouth, "I heard something." Another snap, some leaves rustle, and my hand slides into the side pocket of my bag for my gun. Tomas reaches next to him for his knife. We wait in silence. If a Testing candidate is nearby, they will see the building. Will they feel compelled to look inside for anything that might be useful during the test? I would. My fingers tighten their grip on the gun as I wait for a face to appear.

None does.

Tomas and I sit and wait. The minutes pass, and I am reminded of yesterday when I was trapped in the candidate box with someone lurking outside. At least this time I am not alone.

How long do we wait? It feels like forever, although it is probably only fifteen minutes. We have heard no other sounds.

Tomas slowly gets to his feet and makes a motion to the door. He wants to take a look. I nod and quietly get to my feet. If someone is out there, they aren't expecting two of us.

Step by cautious step, Tomas crosses to the door. He adjusts his grip on his knife, takes a deep breath, and walks outside. I quickly follow behind him.

Nothing.

We circle the small building, looking for signs someone has been here, but find only our tracks and those made by small animals. Now that I am not terrified, I find myself smiling as I study the animal prints. Fox and maybe a rabbit. We are going to need a food source beyond the fruit and bread we have stored in our bags. I make a note to look for wires and other supplies to create traps and follow Tomas back inside the little building to gather our things. If we are going to make it to Tosu City, we need to get moving.

We eat cinnamon rolls with raisins for breakfast, and I open the first canteen of water for us to wash it down. With two of us drinking from my supply, the water will go fast. Especially in this heat. While yesterday I was concerned with putting distance between us and the wrecked city, today I am focused on finding the tools we need to survive the weeks to come. We need to find water that is uncontaminated enough for my purification chemicals to make drinkable, and we need to find it soon.

As we eat breakfast, we study the Illinois page of Tomas's map book. Though most of the cities, towns, and roads have been eaten away by war and time, we are hoping that at least a few of the lakes and rivers have remained constant. We decide to head toward a river that looks like the best option and punch the coordinates into the Transit Communicator. According to the device, the river is fifteen miles to the southwest. Bags on our shoulders, we start walking, using the compass as our guide.

All around us is flat, brittle land. A casualty of the biological weapons used on the city and the nearby towns. So different from the hilly part of the country I grew up in. As we walk, we take sips of water, trying to replace the liquid the sun is leaching out of us, and talk of unimportant things—our favorite childhood games, the songs our mothers sang us to sleep with, our favorite foods. Tomas is fond of honey-glazed carrots. I love fresh raspberries. We talk about celebrating our Testing success with both.

After several hours of walking, we find a grove of squat trees in which to rest. Just as Tomas dumps his bag, I give a shout of joy. Growing near the trunks of the trees are dozens of small white flowers with spiky petals reaching up to the sky. Clover. My father says it is one of the few plants that never had trouble growing no matter the condition of the soil. When I was little my mother often served clover salad when other foods were scarce. Funny how some things never change.

Tomas and I strip the ground bare of the small white plants, divide them into two piles, and sit in the shade, eating the fresh flowers and green stems with our bread and fruit. We leave the roots so the flowers will grow again—perhaps for the Testing candidates who come this way next year.

The afternoon sun is brutal as it bakes the ground beneath my feet. Sweat pours from our bodies. The dirt that swirls in the air adheres to our wet, sticky skin. Between us, we have emptied the first canteen and have opened the second. We need to find a water supply. The device in my hand tells me we still have two miles until we arrive at what we hope is a river.

It is late afternoon when we reach our destination. A dry riverbed. We check the map twice to make sure this is the right location. There is no doubt. An event, probably an earthquake, shifted the land and emptied the river between the time the map was created and now. And while it isn't surprising, I can't help the surge of disappointment that is rapidly followed by fear. I shove the fear aside and concentrate on solving the problem. Because isn't that what The Testing is about? Finding those who can solve the problem even when put under great stress? The Testing officials want candidates to succeed. There will be water somewhere. We just have to be smart enough and patient enough to find it.

I see a small hill to our southwest and say, "Well, the water from the river had to go somewhere. Why don't we see if we can spot it from up there?"

Tomas stows the map book into his bag and nods. "Sounds good to me."

The hill is farther and taller than it looks. The sun is starting to lose its luster when we reach the top. One look at the landscape below us makes me want to cry. More cracked grayish brown earth. More scraggly, diseased-looking trees with dry, parched leaves. More emptiness. Except off in the distance. I squint into the setting sun. Yes. There, far to our right, is a patch of green. Green that can only be created by thriving plants. And for plants to thrive they have to have water.

With a wide smile, Tomas takes my hand and we set off at a quick pace toward the greenery. It occurs to me as we walk that while our view from the top of the hill was helpful, it might have also put us in danger. Anyone in the vicinity looking our way will have seen us. I mention my worries to Tomas, but there isn't much we can do now. There is no place to take cover in this empty landscape. We have to keep moving forward and hope for the best.

The closer Tomas and I get to the greenery, the edgier I feel. The proximity of the hill to the greenery and the possible water source we spotted start to feel too much like coincidence. Because this part of the country has not been officially revitalized, there is the impression it's been left untouched by the United Commonwealth's government staff. But that isn't necessarily the case. Dr. Barnes and his Testing officials want to see how we think, how we identify and deal with problems. It only makes sense that they would set up smaller tests within the larger one, that they would not be willing to leave the obstacles we face up to chance.

As we approach the green patch, I begin to feel certain that this oasis is another kind of test. The perfect oval the grass grows in. The shimmer of a clear, clean, uncontaminated pond that rests in the center. Two trees filled with healthy leaves stand guard on either side. The entire area is only about twenty feet wide and half as long. There is no doubt. This small patch of paradise is man-made.

Tomas picks up his pace at the sight of the water, but stops when he notices I am no longer beside him. "What's wrong, Cia?"

I explain my suspicions, and his forehead wrinkles in thought. He looks at the pond with longing and says, "They know we need water. It only makes sense that they've added some water sources out here in order to keep us alive. Otherwise none of us would pass the damn test. Then where would they be?"

Tomas has a good point. But he wasn't the one who listened as Dr. Barnes rationalized Ryme's death. He didn't see Malachi die. If I hadn't, maybe I would believe this spot is a gift from the Testers. Instead, I see it as a trap.

"Let's walk around the grass line and take a look just to be sure."

Tomas wants to argue. I can see it in the set of his jaw. It's the same reaction he had in class when a fellow student or our teacher was wrong. Instead of arguing with him, I walk up to the vibrant green grass, careful not to disturb it with my foot. Flowers grow near the edge of the pond, filling the air with their sweet fragrance. The trees are tall and straight and provide shelter from the sunshine. It's a perfect spot to rest and be restored from travel. In this place where nothing is perfect, is it a wonder that I refuse to trust it?

"It looks okay to me," Tomas says from the other side of the oasis.

"Just a few more minutes. Please," I yell. I turn my back on him, hoping this will end the discussion. My gut tells me to get the hell away from this place, but I have to convince Tomas. He has always been so good, so kind to others—especially those who are sad or in distress. It is no wonder he expects the government that brought us here to be helpful, too. With this being the only water source we've seen since the contaminated river yesterday, I don't blame him for being tempted. If only there was another water source nearby. There's another hill not too far away. Maybe I will see something if I take a look . . .

"I'll be right back. Stay there," I say, and I set off for the hill.

My legs are tired, but I move fast. I'm at the top of the hill in less than five minutes and, though I am breathless, laugh when I see it. Not too far away—maybe another hundred yards or so—is a small river. The water doesn't gleam and the plant life surrounding it isn't lush, but I know by the path it sculpts through the ground that it is natural. Water. Contaminated? Probably, but I have my kit to deal with that. For the first time today, I feel a sense of relief.

Then the world explodes.

CHAPTER 12

Surprise and the force of the blast knock me off-balance. I hit the ground and roll, then scramble up to my feet, trying to understand what just happened. The ringing in my ears. The gaping hole where the oasis used to stand. Tomas nearby on the hard, cracked earth lying completely still.

Choking back a sob, I fly down the hill to where Tomas is sprawled on his back, eyes closed. I fear the worst. That once again I will hold the hand of someone from home as he slips from the world, leaving me behind. Then I see the steady rise and fall of his chest and sag with relief. He's alive. However the trap was sprung, Tomas was not in the middle of it when it happened. Otherwise he—like the trees, flowers, and water—would be gone. Just thinking of a world without his strong, steady presence is enough to bring me to my knees.

Still, he is not conscious, which isn't good. I sit on the ground next to him and gently check the back of his head for swelling that would indicate a concussion or something worse. I am relieved to find nothing. Then I notice the blood pooling on the ground next to his right hip and the inch-thick branch protruding from his body.

I stamp down my tears. Crying won't help Tomas, so I have to decide what will. Dr. Flint always says you aren't supposed to move someone with a head wound, but I don't have a choice. I have to stop the blood seeping into the cracked soil. Carefully, I shift Tomas onto his side. The jagged wood is buried deep in Tomas's backside. The explosion and the impact against the ground must have created enough force for the branch to impale him.

Taking a deep breath, I get a good grip on the tree branch and pull. The edges of the wood catch on Tomas's flesh. He starts to groan and wince as I work the wood back and forth in the wound to remove it. The flow of blood increases as the wood slides free from Tomas's body. I rip a strip of fabric off my cot sheet, press it against the wound, and hold it there with one hand while my other searches for the medical kit. The disinfecting ointment will come in handy. The needle and thread might, too, if I can get up the nerve to use them. I'm starting to roll Tomas onto his belly when he moans again.

His gray eyes blink open. "What happened?"

Hearing his voice, seeing him awake, makes me smile even as it unlocks a flood of tears. "The oasis blew up," I tell him, wiping tears with the back of my dirt-streaked hand. "You got impaled by a tree branch. I removed it, but the wound is bleeding pretty bad. Don't worry," I say, feigning more confidence than I feel. "I'll have you fixed in no time. Only . . ."

His eyes narrow. "Only what?"

I feel the blush heating my cheeks even before I say, "You're going to have to remove your pants for me to do it."

The grin he gives me is wicked and more than a little sexy, but quickly turns to a frown as he struggles to unfasten his pants and push them down. The wound is still bleeding, but not near as bad as it was. The puncture is over an inch in diameter and judging by the blood on the stick at least three inches deep. The area around the wound is a mangled mess of blood and tissue. An injury like this has to hurt like hell. And I have no idea how to fix it. Over the years, Dr. Flint closed several of my brothers' cuts, but those didn't look like this. Those had been tears in the flesh, which could only be brought together using a needle and thread. This is a gaping hole.

Still, I have to do something.

I dig several pain tablets out of the bag and prop Tomas up so he can swallow them. Then I clean the wound as best I can with water. Wiped free of blood and dirt, the injury looks even worse. I was right—there is no way I can sew this wound shut. Which leaves me with only one idea. Just thinking about it makes me want to scream, but I have no choice. Blood is still flowing from the gap in his flesh. If it doesn't stop soon, Tomas won't be able to travel. He won't finish the test and neither will I since I could never leave knowing he'd most likely die out here injured and alone.

Gathering bits of dried grass and pieces of wood into a pile, I light them with one of Tomas's matches. Once the fire is started, I pull the hunting knife out of my pocket. In addition to the knife and screwdriver, there is a nail file, a wood saw, a hook, and several other metal gadgets I've never found a use for. Until now.

I select the tool that is about an inch and a half long, less than a half inch wide, and flat on top. There is a hooked thing near the middle my father said he used as a child to open bottles, but we don't have those kinds of bottles in Five Lakes so I can only imagine how that works. It isn't the bottle opener I'm interested in, but the flat, unsharpened surface near the top. Now I just need to muster the courage to go through with my plan.

As the small fire crackles, I do something I've seen Dr. Flint do when the patient is conscious during a particularly unpleasant treatment. I hand Tomas his cot sheet to bite down on, then hold the bottle opener over the flames and wait for it to turn red. When it does, I ask Tomas to look away. Before I can lose my nerve, I pull the hot metal out of the flame and apply it to the wound.

Tomas screams into the sheet and bucks in pain. The sounds of his agony are muffled and my eyes fill with tears. But I have to keep working. I put the tool back into the flames with one hand while I wipe the blood from the wound and hold Tomas's legs down with the other. When the metal is once again hot, I place it against his flesh. A coppery, sulfurous odor makes me gag. The smell of burning skin.

Tears run down my face. My chest tightens so I can barely breathe. Tomas's muted screams rip through my heart as I heat the metal and apply it to the wound again and again. Until, finally, the burned tissue fuses together and the bleeding is stopped.

My hands shake as I use our precious water to dab clean the wound. Then I spread ointment on the area, bandage it, and help Tomas struggle into his pants. I fervently hope the bleeding is stopped for good because I don't think I can do that again.

Tomas's eyes are glazed and his forehead coated with sweat as he gives me a weak smile. "I barely felt a thing," he lies.

I go to place a kiss on his cheek, only he turns his head and the kiss lands on the corner of his mouth. Time stops as we stare at each other. Then, very slowly, Tomas leans forward and kisses me again. The kiss is light as a feather, but I feel it all the way down in my stomach. I've been kissed by boys before—I'm young for my class, but I'm not that young. None of those kisses made me feel the way this one does. Maybe because of the fear and adrenaline I've been operating under or because I don't understand why Tomas kissed me. Gratitude? Or something more? Something I have felt building since we danced last year and have been too scared to believe is real.

Confused by emotions I don't want to analyze, I turn away and start jamming supplies back in my bag. "It's going to get dark soon. When I was on top of the hill, I saw a stream. It's not too far away. Do you think you can walk or should we set up camp here? There's probably enough light for me to make it to the stream, fill up our canteens, and come back." I know I'm rambling, but can't seem to stop myself.

He shakes his head and slowly gets to his knees. "If your crossbow friend heard the explosion, he might come looking for us. We should put some distance between us and here before we lose light."

With everything else going on, I'd forgotten about the other

Testing candidates. The explosion will have drawn attention. If the crossbow shooter heard the explosion, he might assume whoever was caught in it is dead. Unless he heard Tomas's screams during my treatment. Either way, Tomas is right. We need to clear out.

I help Tomas to his feet and loop his arm around my shoulders so I can lend him support. He is almost a head taller than me, but we manage to make it work. It's slow going up the hill, though, and both of us are panting hard when we reach the top.

Finally the pain medication is starting to take hold and Tomas is able to walk a little faster as we go down the other side. In the graying light, I spot a clump of shoulder-high bushes thick with gray leaves and head toward them. The cluster of bushes is dense, but after breaking off a few lower branches I wriggle underneath the bush closest to the stream and find a small area that we can camp in. I ask Tomas for his scary-looking knife and use it to clear a bit more space for us. Then I spread Tomas's sheet on the ground and hold branches out of the way for him as he climbs inside. Tomas is asleep almost before I can tell him I'm going to get water. Which is going to be tricky since the sun is setting fast. I grab the three empty water containers and my bag of purification chemicals, and scoot through the underbrush to the stream.

Testing water for drinkability isn't difficult, but it does require time and light. With the last canteen of water almost at empty and the sun fading, I'm short on both. But I have to try. If Tomas develops an infection in the middle of the night, the last thing I want to be is short of water.

The tests for most contaminants are pretty basic. You fill a cup with water and then add drops of a variety of liquid chemicals that react to contamination. The small sample of water will turn either red, blue, yellow, or green to indicate a specific contaminant. Sometimes the color can be very faint. You have to be able to spot the subtle shifts in color in order to add the correct counteracting chemicals to make the water drinkable. The trick is to add only the chemicals necessary to counteract the contamination. If you add anything that doesn't belong, you could end up poisoning the water. It won't kill you, but it can make you really sick. Something I really would like to avoid.

After setting out my chemicals, I use one of the clear plastic water containers from our Testing box baskets and fill it with a half inch of water. I put a drop of the first chemical in and swirl the water around. If the water contains the bioengineered version of cyanide used in many of the Stage Four bombings, the liquid will turn red. After several minutes of swirling, I am certain the water is free of that contaminant and move on to the next. I make it through the first three tests without a color change. But the fourth, for a chemical cooked up by the Asian Alliance that causes the cardiovascular system to overload, turns the water a vibrant purple unmistakable even in the last vestiges of sunlight. I empty out the test bottle, refill the three containers, and then add the counteracting chemicals to them. It will take at least an hour for the chemicals to counteract the contamination. In the morning, I will retest a capful of the water to verify its purity before we drink. For now, I crawl back through the underbrush with my water containers, eat a few pieces of dried apple, and curl up next to Tomas on the sheet.

While I try hard to stay awake, I can't help the exhaustion of the day pulling me into sleep.

The sound of a bird singing greets me in the morning. For a moment, snuggled warm in the sheet, I think I am sleeping in front of the hearth at home after being chased from my room by my brothers' snoring. Then I realize that something behind me is moving and remember where I am. My eyes fly open to find Tomas's clear gray ones staring down at me.

"Good morning," he says with a soft smile. "I didn't mean to wake you."

"I wasn't supposed to fall asleep." And I'm annoyed with myself because I did. So much for keeping watch for the cross-bow shooter. If he had come across us in the night, we would both be dead. Stupid. Only luck kept us alive.

Tomas doesn't seem concerned, but he keeps his voice low as he says, "We're pretty well hidden here. I woke up a while ago and took a look around. If our fellow candidates have come by, I haven't seen any sign of them."

"Don't you think that's strange?" I ask. "That we haven't seen any of the other candidates?"

"I don't think so. The map they showed us at the Testing Center made it look like the fence lines around here were at least twenty miles apart. That means there's room for us all to spread out. At least at first." He reaches into his bag and pulls out his map book and flips to the page for Kansas. "If I remember correctly, the fence lines narrow near the end—around here." He points to a spot a fair distance from the city that was once called Wichita. "I'm guessing the Testing officials want to draw us together at that point—to see how we respond."

"Another test within a test. Like yesterday."

"Yeah, and look how well that turned out." Tomas's eyes flash with anger, an emotion I have never seen from him. He's normally so calm and logical. But his voice is loud and tight as he says, "I almost got us blown to pieces on that one because I couldn't believe you might be right. That the one hopeful thing we'd seen since starting this test was something designed to kill us. I kept telling myself you were wrong and I was right. I mean, why the hell would the Testing officials bring us all here just to kill us? It doesn't make any sense."

His fists are clenched, and I can see confusion and anger in his eyes as he demands an answer. Only I don't have one. Not really. So I take Tomas's dirt-streaked hand and hold it because I feel as lost as he does.

We sit hand in hand for several minutes before Tomas smiles at me, flashing the familiar dimple. "Well, you were wrong about one thing. I'm definitely not the smartest kid from our class, Cia. Although I guess I was pretty smart about teaming up with you. What other girl would have been willing to fix my ass after I got myself blown up?"

"Are you kidding?" I turn away and busy myself with pulling the sack of dried fruit out of my bag so he can't see the heat flooding my cheeks. "Almost every unmarried girl in Five Lakes Colony would have volunteered to patch you up. Especially if you thanked her with a kiss."

"Cia." I turn, and Tomas's eyes find mine. The humor in them is gone, leaving something more compelling in its place. "If another girl had helped me, I wouldn't have kissed her." The words hang between us. Deep inside I feel something shift and click into place. Then the humor is back as he says, "Come on. We should start walking. Tosu City is still a long ways off."

Before we leave, I test the water I treated yesterday, grateful to have something purposeful to do instead of obsessing about Tomas's words. Was he saying I was special to him or just flattering me? Considering all the girls back home who practically threw themselves in his path, I find it hard to believe he ever really thought of me in that way. And yet, I think back to that dance and to the moments last year when I caught him watching me across the classroom. Perhaps there has been something between us all along.

The water test comes back clean. Tomas and I take the opportunity to drink our fill and even wash the grime of travel from our hands and faces before refilling the containers from the stream and treating them. We eat a breakfast of crackers, apples, and some red clover we find growing next to our grove of bushes. Then, after I check Tomas's wound and apply more ointment to it, we set off to the southwest.

The day is cooler. I think storms might be on the way, but the lack of extreme heat makes travel easier. Our progress is marked not only by the change of our coordinates on the Transit Communicator, but also by the changing of the scenery. The flat, cracked earth with only small patches of plant life and angry-looking trees starts to give way to more hills, trees that are not quite healthy-looking but not as black and twisted, and far more plants. More than once I make Tomas stop as I spot wild carrots, hollyhock, and milkweed. We'll have to light a fire to boil the milkweed, which I'm not sure we'll have time for, but I gather it just in case. Our current food supply will last only another two or three days. We'll need all the food we can find.

We also begin to see more signs of birds, like the one that awakened me this morning with its singing, and other game. Tomas spots deer, fox, and rabbit tracks along with larger prints of animals we cannot put names to. We'll have to start hunting if we hope to stay strong enough to make it to the end of the test. But for now we walk. While the miles pass, we comment on the buildings we are now seeing. There aren't many, but a few here and there. Some with only partially standing walls. Others that look more intact. As night starts to descend, we decide to head toward a group of one-story structures that look like they might be in decent repair. Perhaps whoever once lived in these houses has left behind something we can use to travel faster. If not, we might find other things, like wire for animal traps, that will help us survive.

An animal family had taken up residence in the first house. There are tracks, claw marks, and droppings left behind that look fresh enough to make us rethink entering. The next house looks on the verge of collapse, but a small storage building behind it appears to be sound so we venture inside. The last streams of sunlight shine through a window long devoid of its glass, which helps us to see. The dust and moldy smell make me sneeze. There's a rotting bench on one side of the small, rectangular room. On the other side is what could have once been a tractor. The rust and the lack of wheels or a motor make it hard to tell for sure. I shift a large sheet of decaying wood that is propped against the back wall and smile. Behind the wood is an old wagonlike cart. The wooden cart itself is rotted and has a chunk of wood missing from one side, but there are two wheels at the bottom and both appear to be salvageable. Tomas gets out his tool kit and helps me detach the wheels. They are heavy, coated with a thick layer of cobwebs and grime, but they give me hope. If I can find more materials, I might be able to build something to help us travel faster.

Several more houses yield us a small pot, a skillet, and some nuts and bolts that were attached to some rotting cupboards. Not a lot, but more than we had when we started. We make camp for the night, eat two of our apples and the last of our bread, and fall asleep hopeful that we will find more treasures tomorrow.

The next day, a few miles away, we find a cluster of several dozen buildings—these made of mostly bricks and mortar—that have stood the test of time and weather. The way they are situated I can only guess they once formed the center of a town, much like Five Lakes' square. We search building by building. Bits of wire disappear into our bags. A wrench. Not much else.

We are about to enter the last building when Tomas points to the ground nearby. A partial boot print. My heart catches. Another Testing candidate? We have to assume so. My first instinct is to flee. To run as far and as fast as we can.

But Tomas wants to enter. "If there is another candidate nearby, it would be best to know who it is and what their intentions are. We don't want them catching us off-guard."

It's hard to deny Tomas's logic. The idea of an unknown person lurking nearby, waiting for us to let down our guard, gives me a chill. Swallowing hard, I slide the gun out of my bag and follow Tomas inside and into chaos. Several small, furry animals jump off a rickety table and go racing across the room toward a hole in the wall. With my nerves taut and fear pulsing through my veins, I don't think. I just react. *Bang. Bang. Bang.* Two of the white animals drop before the rest make it to safety.

Then I come to my senses and realize that if someone is nearby, I have just alerted them to our presence. I start to apologize, but Tomas just laughs. "Don't apologize. If someone is around, they're probably running as far as they can away from whoever has the gun. And if they knew you could shoot like that they would run even faster."

He tells me to guard the front door while he checks the rest of the building. After a few minutes, I hear him let out a loud shout. At first, I think he's encountered whoever made the footprint. But then I hear the happiness in his voice as he yells for me to join him. He's got a surprise.

And what a surprise. In what must have once been a vehicle storage unit are two bicycles. Tomas says he found them lying under a sheet of plastic in the back corner. The room is dark. One bicycle is missing the back tire. The other's chain and pedals have seen better days. Both have a fair amount of rust and dirt on them. But I can't help smiling from ear to ear. They might be old, damaged, and rickety, but these bikes are the most beautiful things I've ever seen.

Tomas and I carry the bikes back to the front of the building, and I laugh as I remember the animals I shot. Opossum. The fur is darker and rattier than on the ones we have around Five Lakes Colony, but the cone-shaped face, the rows of tiny sharp teeth, and the furless, scaly tail are unmistakable. And I know from experience, their flesh is edible. Between the bikes and the fresh meat, I am incredibly happy as we set up camp near a group of trees in the center of the buildings.

Tomas volunteers to take care of dinner and scout around for a water source while I assess the bicycles and their usability. Using a strip of cot sheet, I clean off the dirt, rust, and grease. One chain has a faulty link, but with a bit of tinkering, I'm able to remove the broken link and get the rest in working order. The three remaining tires of the bikes are deflated, but that's okay. I remove the rubber from the wheels of the first bike, and work for the next three hours to realign the gears, attach the chain, and get the brake unstuck. The seat cushion has been gnawed by mice or some other rodents, but after stuffing some of the holes with bits of dry grass and sewing a new cover made from the cot sheet, I deem it usable. By the time the sun is starting to descend on the horizon, I am coated with grease and dirt, but one bike is ridable. It might not last very long, but I'm pretty sure, even without the rubber tires, the wheels will cover a bunch of miles before giving out.

While I've been fixing the first bicycle, the problem of the second one and its lack of a hind wheel has been rolling in the back of my mind. There is no way two of us can ride on one bike like Daileen and I sometimes did at home. Not for the distance we need to travel. We need two. Which means I have to fix the second bike. I think I might have a solution when Tomas calls that dinner is ready. I do my best to wipe the grease from my hands before heading to Tomas and our campsite. When I get there, I'm in for another surprise. While I've been working on the bicycles, Tomas has also been busy. He's not only started a fire, but skinned and roasted both opossum, and boiled the greens and wild carrots with some pine bark. Perhaps the best surprise is the small, fresh, sweet strawberries he found growing wild near the side of one of the buildings. The warm, filling meal feeds the growing sense of hope I've been feeling all day.

During dinner, I tell Tomas about the bicycles and my idea to repair the second one using the two cart wheels we found yesterday. We talk about the best way to reconstruct the bicycle and decide to spend the next day here instead of traveling, which we hope will pay off in the end.

The next morning, we eat cold opossum and strawberries for breakfast and get to work restructuring the gear assembly on the second bicycle to accommodate the two medium-sized cart wheels I found. It takes most of the day and a lot of scavenging for parts in the town's buildings, but by the time the sun is low in the sky I am riding the second bicycle around the town square. We eat more strawberries and opossum, drink water Tomas found at a stream about a mile away, and attach scraps of metal behind the seats of our bicycles to create shelves for our bags to rest on while we pedal. When darkness falls, we settle onto the ground and watch the stars appear in the sky. With Tomas's arm around my shoulders, I can almost imagine we are sitting in the square back home, watching the heavens with our families somewhere nearby. I turn to say as much to Tomas when his lips find mine in a gentle kiss. My heartbeat quickens. I can't see his face in the darkness, but I know Tomas is giving me the chance to pull away. But I don't. I lean in and feel Tomas's mouth smile against mine before the kiss deepens.

I snake a hand around his neck and hold tight as a thrilling shiver travels through me. Despite our tenuous situation, nothing has ever felt this perfect.

A distant scream streaks through the night. A human female scream. The sound jolts us apart and into action. I hear Tomas slide his knife out of its leather scabbard as I find my gun. Side by side in the darkness we wait for the scream to come again.

It doesn't. Neither does sleep.

CHAPTER 13

At the first hint of light we are up, packing our bags, storing them on our new bicycles, and slowly riding off to the southwest. Arms wrapped tight around each other last night with our weapons a breath away, we whispered assurances that the screamer was far in the distance. That we were safe from whatever caused the outburst.

While Tomas's wound appears to be better, I can tell he is having a hard time finding a comfortable spot on his bicycle. Without the rubber tires to absorb some of the friction caused by riding over stones, twigs, and other debris, the ride is a bumpy one. There are also more trees, bushes, and intact houses the farther we get from Chicago. So we decide to head due south, where Tomas's map claims a large roadway used to exist. Even a road in disrepair will be easier to navigate than the terrain we're currently riding on. The other reason for our decision remains unspoken. Last night's scream seemed to come from this direction. We are looking for the girl whose scream kept us alert through the night. If she is injured, we have to help. I couldn't live with myself if we didn't at least try.

A flock of crows circling something from above makes my throat tighten. Without a word, we turn and pedal through the patchwork brown grass to whatever has attracted the birds. When we find it, there is no question about helping the screamer or what we would do if she asked to join our team. The body sprawled on the ground is past asking for anything. I think I remember the girl marching in front of Malachi and out the lecture hall door to take the first round of tests. Long white-blond hair that is currently matted with dirt and streaks of blood. Eyes that might have once been blue now bloody sockets as the birds feast. And there in her stomach, a sight that turns my nausea and pity to icy-cold fear.

A crossbow quarrel.

Her Testing bag is empty. Either she lost the contents, which I doubt, or the crossbow shooter took them after bringing down his prey. Which means he is out there somewhere, hunting.

"We should clear out of here." Tomas gives my hand a squeeze as I stare down at the girl. "The road can't be too far away now."

"You're right. We should go. The crossbow shooter might be nearby." And yet I do not move. I cannot leave this girl to be pecked away piece by piece. While she is beyond caring, I am not. She has family. Friends. People who love her somewhere—who think she is safely ensconced in Tosu City, showing off her skills in math and science. Those people might never know her fate, but their love for her and hers for them demand respect. This is what my mother and father taught me. It's the Five Lakes Colony way of life.

Tomas finds a crack in the earth large enough for this slight girl's body. Together, we chase away the carrion crows and carry her to what will be her final resting place. I fumble with her identification bracelet until I find the right place to press. The clasp opens and the bracelet with its symbol—a triangle with a small eight-spoked wheel—falls into my hand. We then set her body into the fissure. An hour of daylight is lost as we stack rocks over her to keep the birds and other scavengers from claiming the rest of her remains.

I mark the grave with a large reddish rock and wish I knew the girl's name so I could at least bid her a proper goodbye. Instead, I clutch her bracelet to my chest and offer my silent promise that no matter the pressures or fears that come, I will not put aside the beliefs I grew up with in order to pass. Nor will I forget this girl's fate.

Tomas's jaw clenches as he gives the grave a final look before we mount our bicycles. Silently, we travel through the rest of the day toward the road we hope to find somewhere over the horizon. We stop only to test and purify water, gather dandelions and wild carrots, and eat more of the opossum and our final apples. My legs are trembling with exhaustion, but the memory of the dead girl and her sightless eyes keeps me pushing the pedals over rocks and underbrush until darkness falls.

By late morning on the following day, we find the road. It's a wide paved path that travels far beyond what we can see, which should make me happy. Instead, the condition of the road fills me with dread. There are no holes. No breaks in the asphalt.

Other than recent patches here and there, I see no signs of disrepair. This time Tomas doesn't question me as I dismount my bicycle.

"Do you think this is another trap?" I ask.

"After the pond, anything's possible." He cocks his head to one side. "But I don't think so. Look down there."

I squint in the direction he's pointing toward and see it. Far in the distance is a line of bright blue cutting across the countryside. The southern Testing fence line. The one we are not supposed to cross beyond.

"I bet they fixed this road in order to install the fence." Tomas digs into his bag and pulls out his book. "According to the map, this road goes all the way to the southwestern side of the old state and connects with another road that leads right to Tosu City. The officials have to have an easy way of getting back and forth from Tosu City to the start of the test. I'm betting this is it."

The reasoning is sound. But it isn't Tomas's logic that sways me. It's the map itself, which tells me this road leads through several major cities on the way to Tosu City. My father's most vivid nightmare took place in a city where the buildings still stood. If the Testing officials are going to lay traps for us, those cities are the most logical places to set them.

"Let's throw a few rocks onto the road," I say. "If it doesn't explode, we should try it."

Tomas laughs and looks around for some ammunition. His arm is better than mine, but between the two of us we land about a dozen rocks onto the pavement without incident, and we decide to trust it. After riding over twigs, rocks, and tree roots, pedaling over the smooth surface is like heaven. After the horror of burying the unnamed girl, I am glad for the wind and sun on my face. The freedom of riding fast. No matter the daunting number of miles that we still have to cross, I am glad to be alive.

After the initial joy of riding on the pavement passes, I realize taking the road has not only improved our speed. It has also increased our visibility to whoever might be watching from the thickets of trees and abandoned buildings along the way. I hope the crossbow shooter and any others intent on removing the competition have not yet found speedy transportation.

We ride over a long bridge that spans a wide, opaque river, and I suggest we camp near the water for the night. It's earlier than we normally make camp, but I am dirty, my hair is matted with grime and sweat, and my legs are starting to cramp. The abundance of water means an opportunity to feel clean for the first time in days. It's also a good place to forage for food and maybe even trap game.

Tomas is more than willing to stop, especially when he checks Zeen's device and sees we've traveled just over forty-five miles in a single day. We are now a seventh of the way to Tosu City. While it's still far, the bicycles and the road we travel give us both a more optimistic view of this test.

The river—like all untreated water sources—is tainted. But one look into the swirling waters tells us that at least some species of fish have adapted to the contaminants. While the contaminants make it dangerous to eat the fish raw, a pan and a fire will make them more than edible. I roam the banks of the river, gathering plants for dinner, while Tomas attaches a hook from his tool kit to a braided strip of sheet. He goes fishing using the last bits of our opossum as bait. By the time I return with a pot filled with wild onions, pickerelweed, and cattail roots, Tomas has caught and cleaned three medium-sized fish—two catfish and one that looks similar to the wide-mouth bass we catch near home. We boil the cattail roots and pickerelweed, fry the wild onion and fish, and have a feast.

With the sun still an hour or two from setting, I decide to wash. Our tests have determined the water contaminant is mild and won't affect skin on contact so I strip down to my undergarments and wade into the cool water. The current is surprisingly strong. I don't venture far from the bank as I scrub the mud, dust, and sweat from my body and the clothes I've been wearing for the past few days. When I climb out, I give myself a few minutes to air-dry before pulling on my second set of clothing and hanging the wet ones over a branch to dry.

I'm about to call to Tomas that I'm finished with my bath when I see him still and quiet, positioned behind a clump of bushes on the hill that leads to the road. His muscles are taut. His hand clutches the hilt of his knife. He has spotted something.

Gripping my handgun, I am careful to step softly—avoiding the rocks and branches, keeping to the grassy patches that will deaden my tread. Tomas jumps as I touch his shoulder, but then he points far down the road in the direction we have already traveled.

People. Three of them. At this distance, it is hard to tell whether they are male or female. But their feet drag on the ground, telling us they are tired, hungry, and possibly dehydrated. Even with the slow pace the three will be here before the sun sets.

"Do you want to pack up and move farther away from the road or should we stay put and see if they notice us?" Tomas asks.

"What do you think?"

Tomas frowns. "They look pretty tired to me. If I didn't know about our crossbow friend, I'd say flag them down and see if we can help. They won't expect us to travel with them since they're on foot and we're on bicycles. Still . . ."

I can finish his thoughts. There are candidates out there willing to shoot. To kill. To get a passing grade on this test no matter the cost. But we are not like them. As if to prove it, I say, "Why don't you catch a few more fish in case they make it this far before nightfall. They're going to be hungry."

Tomas's eyes narrow as he studies the trio. After a moment, he agrees.

There are five fish roasting over coals when the three candidates step off the bridge onto our side of the river. All three look vaguely familiar. One gangly, freckled red-haired boy. Two girls. One is tall with olive skin and short dark hair. The other has long ash-blond hair and is several inches shorter. All three look as though they are ready to drop from exhaustion.

"Are you hungry?" I ask, stepping out from my hiding place.

Tomas is still behind the bushes with the knife poised in his hand. We agreed that the trio might be more inclined toward aggression if they saw both of us. I hope a single, smallish girl will inspire them to think before they react. The three don't look surprised at my appearance. I suppose the smell of food cooking alerted them to the presence of another human being. But their eyes gleam with terror as they notice the gun in my hand. I feel bad, but I don't lower it. I'm not that naïve. "You look like you're hungry and tired. I have fish cooking and some water down by the river if you'd like to make camp here tonight."

The tall redheaded boy speaks first. "Why would you want to help us?"

I give them the only answer I have. "It's what I was raised to do."

Whether they believe the honesty of my words or they are just so hungry they can't resist the smell of the cooking fish, the trio follows me off the road. I warn them I'm not traveling alone, and while the shorter of the girls looks terrified at the sight of Tomas and his knife, the others don't appear concerned. Especially not when they spot the food and water waiting for them. They keep their bags close at hand as they sit on the ground. The tall girl starts to cry when I say, "Help yourself to the food."

In between mouthfuls of fish, the tall girl tells us her name is Tracelyn. The other two are Stacia and Vic. All three are from Tulsa Colony. They were sitting together in the lecture hall when Dr. Barnes showed the map of the fourth test and, like us, they set up a meeting point. For them it was the fence line directly south of the starting location. It took them two days to find one another and they've been traveling near the road ever since, only leaving it to look for food and water. Food has been scarce, and they haven't wanted to venture far from the road to find more familiar plant life. The road has been their greatest source of safety since they can see people coming and hide if necessary.

"We were hiding in an abandoned building when you rode past," Vic admits, taking another helping of fish. "I thought you were miles and miles ahead, so it never occurred to me to look for bicycle tracks on the side of the road. I should have been more careful, but the smell of food distracted me. You guys seem to be playing things straight, but not everyone is."

"We know." Tomas meets Vic's eyes. The two seem to size each other up.

Vic looks at the knife in the scabbard on Tomas's belt, at the gun resting in my lap, and nods. "Someone took a couple potshots at me while I was getting out of the city," he says.

"With a gun or a crossbow?" I ask.

Tracelyn's eyes widen. "Someone's shooting at people with a crossbow? I just don't understand how anyone can do that kind of thing. I mean, the Testing committee said they're going to evaluate us on the choices we make. They can't possibly give someone a passing grade for shooting the competition. What kind of leader would that person be?"

"A strong one." This from Stacia, who until now has sat cross-legged on the ground, eyes firmly fixed on her food. "The Fourth Stage of War would never have happened if the president of the United States had attacked the Asian Alliance. Instead, he tried to broker a worldwide coalition even when his own advisers said it was useless. He was a pacifist when the country needed aggression."

Tomas shakes his head. "Striking first would have guaranteed a strike by the Asian Alliance. He knew the damage the first Three Stages of War had caused. He had to try and head off what he was certain would be the destruction of the world."

"Fat lot of good it did." Stacia laughs. "Isn't that the point the Testing committee was making when they dropped us in one of the destroyed cities? They're looking for candidates with a killer instinct."

"I don't believe that," I say. "My father passed The Testing, and he's a pacifist. He believes in creating, not destroying."

Stacia shrugs. "Well, maybe he lied in his evaluation and told the committee he took a few of the candidates out while making his way back to civilization. I mean, how are they going to know he lied? It's not like they can see what we're doing out here."

Or can they? I remember the camera in the skimmer. The ones in the log cabin we lunched in. The cameras in our sleeping quarters back at the Testing Center. The most direct route to Tosu City from Chicago stretches seven hundred miles. Tomas figures there is a twenty- or thirty-mile stretch of land in between the fence lines. There is no way the Testers have planted enough cameras in the landscape to cover every inch of ground. But what if they don't need to? What if there is another way to keep track of our actions?

The conversation shifts from The Testing to talk of home. Tomas, Vic, and Tracelyn share information about our two colonies. Tulsa Colony has more than seventy thousand people living in the southern half of what used to be Tulsa, Oklahoma, and the countryside that stretches beyond the city limits. There is an oil refinery still active in Tulsa that Vic's father works at. Tracelyn's parents both work at the power plant—the largest operational plant in any of the colonies. Stacia doesn't seem interested in sharing information about her family. She just lies back on the ground and stares at the sky as the stars begin to shine through the haze. I wonder what she is thinking as the boys compare weapons. Both girls have knives. Vic has a handgun like mine. I'm glad they've been honest about their protection, but I have to wonder if I will sleep knowing candidates I don't fully trust are armed.

We leave the fire burning as we assign pairs to keep watch as the others sleep—Vic and Tomas, me and Tracelyn. Stacia doesn't even question not being assigned watch duty as she curls up in a ball and falls asleep. I give my gun to Tomas, since he has first watch, and close my eyes while wondering if these people are worthy of the little trust we have given them. If not, I doubt I will live to see the morning.

But I do.

Tracelyn and I are awakened after several blissful hours of sleep and together watch the sun rise on a new day. In the peacefulness, I learn that if she makes it to the University, Tracelyn wants to be a teacher. She is also in love with a boy back home and was planning on marrying him. He wasn't chosen for The Testing, which means they will most likely never see each other again.

"You're lucky both you and your boyfriend were chosen," she says with quiet sincerity.

"Tomas isn't my boyfriend." I feel the blush on my cheeks.

"You could have fooled me." She gives me a wide smile. "I think he's in love with you."

"He's just watching out for me. You know, since we're from the same colony," I say, but I can't help the thrill I feel at her words. Deep down I hope she's right, because with every day that passes I am more certain that I am falling in love with him.

She changes the subject and we talk about our families, the tests we've taken thus far, and the distance we still have to travel in order to pass this test. She seems so genuinely sweet and a touch too trusting, which coming from me is saying something. I share our experience with the clean pond of water and the perfectly green glade of grass that ultimately exploded. Whether or not she believes me, I know I've tried to help make her aware of the dangers out here.

As the sun rises, so do our companions. Stacia sits far away from us as we eat breakfast. Tomas and I barely rate a glance as we say goodbye and head out before the others can follow. We find the thicket where we hid our bikes, carry them to the road, and begin to pedal. As the miles pass, I cannot help but think of the candidates we left behind and wonder if they will cross the finish line. There is a quiet determination about Stacia that makes me think she'll make it, but something about her fierce smile and the logic she ascribes to the Testing committee gives me concern for her companions.

As our bicycles eat up the miles, I think again about how the Testing committee will evaluate us when we arrive back in Tosu City. From everything I have seen thus far, I cannot believe Dr. Barnes and the other officials would be content with candidate reports on what occurred during the test. Which means somehow we are being monitored. If not all the time, then off and on. Enough for them to make their decisions.

By the time we pull off the road and find an abandoned farm to make camp at, I am certain I know how the Testers are keeping track of us. But I'll have to wait to check my theory until we have settled in for the night. If I'm right, the Testers will know if I deviate from the routine Tomas and I have set since starting our journey.

There are clouds gathering to the west that indicate a storm is coming, and neither Tomas nor I have any interest in sleeping in a downpour. A faded, gray wooden barn that tilts to the left catches our eye. Despite the leaning walls, the structure appears to be sound.

We step into the barn and startle a group of wild chickens. Four gunshots later we have three of them ready to be plucked and roasted. Their nests yield four light brown eggs, which we save for breakfast tomorrow. I try hard to act normal as we make and eat dinner, although Tomas shoots me more than one questioning look as we work. Finally, dinner is over. As I store leftovers in my bag, I use the opportunity to dig for something else. The minute my fingers close over it, my heart skips in anticipation and I pull it out into the light.

The identification bracelet I took from the girl we buried.

Every Testing candidate has one—two, actually, since a smaller band with our symbol is attached to our bags. We've all been instructed to wear them at all times. Since the clasps are hard to detect, I am certain most Testing candidates have heeded this rule. The bracelets are our identification. Could they also be an invisible leash designed to tell the Testers where we are and what we are doing?

The bracelet is a quarter of an inch thick and made of a silver metal. The disk affixed to the top contains an etching of the Testing candidate's design and the back . . .

There. In the middle of the area directly behind the etched Testing symbol are three small holes. Pinpricks, really. So small, I would never have noticed them if I hadn't been looking for something specific. But they tell me what I need to know.

Someone is listening.

CHAPTER 14

A SURGE OF satisfaction streaks through me, the kind I always feel when I ace a test. This time the pleasure is gone as quickly as it came, replaced by the slick, acrid taste of dread.

Have the Testers been recording every word we have spoken? Did they listen in on my conversations before I reached Tosu City or would they have not thought to bother since almost every move I made was recorded by their tiny cameras? I cannot help but pray for the latter to be true. Otherwise, they know. They know about my father. His nightmares. The warnings he gave me. He told me to trust no one, but I didn't listen. I decided I knew best. I trusted Tomas. I told him everything, and in doing so, I might have jeopardized my father's life. Because any government that is willing to stand by and watch as candidates commit suicide or ingest poisonous plants because they gave a wrong answer won't shrink from eliminating a man they might see as a threat. And Magistrate Owens. Dr. Flint. Our old teacher. Everyone who worked hard to keep Five Lakes

Colony graduates safe from The Testing is at risk. Because of me.

"Cia, are you okay?"

I whip around and see Tomas staring at me. I must look pretty awful to warrant the concern in his eyes. Forcing a wide smile, I say, "Yeah, I'm just worried about Tracelyn and the others. I hope they find shelter tonight. It looks like a big storm is coming." Then I put my finger to my lips, point to the bracelet in my hand, and show him the almost imperceptible holes on the inside. With unsteady fingers, I probe for the clasp on my bracelet, work the fastening free, and set it on top of my bag. I then take Tomas's hand and remove his before heading out the door into the swirling wind.

"They've been spying on us," Tomas says. "I guess it shouldn't come as a surprise after the exploding pond. Listening to private conversations is minor compared to that."

"But how long do you think they've been listening? Just this test or since the beginning?"

I watch him consider the question and see the moment he remembers our conversation under the tree—away from the cameras. "Maybe they weren't listening then. I mean, at that point, there were one hundred and eight of us. Most likely they were just using the cameras so they could observe us all at once. Listening to over a hundred different microphones would take a lot of time and people."

I can only hope he is right. I don't know if I can live with the alternative.

"Cia, I know this is hard, but you can't worry about what might be happening to everyone back home." His hand brushes over my cheek. I catch it and hold it like a lifeline. "The only way for us to help anyone at home is to survive this test."

My throat tightens as desperation takes hold. "If we pass, they'll remove all our Testing memories. We won't remember there's anything we need to help with."

"Not if we figure out how they do it." He gives my hand a squeeze and brushes the stray tears that have slipped down my cheek. "I've been thinking about it, and I have a few ideas. Now that we know about the bugs, we can make sure they won't always know what we're planning. You've given us an advantage. We just have to be smart enough to use it."

The doubts I have threaten to consume me. Are we smart enough? Can we out-think a system that has been in place for decades? That has controlled the lives of hundreds of the brightest minds since the world began to rebuild? That is currently controlling us?

Straightening my shoulders, I say, "Well, then we'll just have to be smart enough. Right?"

"Right." Tomas smiles. "With the two of us working together, how can we go wrong? And you know what? I'm glad you figured out someone was listening in for another reason."

"Why's that?"

"Because the first time I tell you that I'm in love with you, I'd rather not share the moment with Dr. Barnes and his friends."

The words and the way his lips touch mine make my heart shimmer. I know this is the wrong time to be thinking about love. The stress of the test—knowing our lives are in danger—means I can't trust my emotions. But the warmth in my veins and the strength I feel just being near Tomas are real. So when his lips leave mine, I'm able to say, "I think I love you, too."

"You think?" He laughs and hugs me tight against his chest. "Well, I guess it's good I have a couple hundred miles of road left to convince you." He drops a kiss on the top of my head and sighs. "We should probably go back and entertain our listening audience before they start wondering if we've passed out from eating too much chicken." He takes my hand, and we start back toward the barn. "You do realize I'm going to have to declare my love again for our audience. Otherwise, they might start wondering why I'm telling you how beautiful you are."

I can't help smiling as we walk back into the building and snap the bracelets back onto our wrists. But now that I know people are listening, I can't seem to come up with anything to say. Thankfully, Tomas doesn't have the same problem. "I thought I heard a noise outside, but I guess I was wrong. No one was there. Guess with the storm coming, the wind kicked up some debris."

For a second, I'm confused. Then I realize he's explaining the silence to whoever was listening. "Good," I say. "We could both use the rest after last night. I'm not sorry we invited the others to camp with us, but it was hard to sleep with them there."

"I know." Tomas lowers himself to the ground and pats the spot next to him, which I take. "I didn't get much sleep either."

"Then how do you explain your snoring?" I tease even though Tomas doesn't snore. Our audience will no doubt find it amusing. We talk about the other three candidates for a while, and then speculate on how our friends might be doing—whether they've teamed up with others or are traveling alone. The wind howls in earnest and raindrops begin to pound against the roof.

Once the barn is completely draped in shadows, we get ready for sleep. Settling into the back-corner spot we thought was best protected from the weather, we listen as rain pours from the sky. Water drips from holes in the roof, but the area we have chosen stays blissfully dry.

Tomas puts his arm around me and says, "You know, I really did lie awake for most of last night. I don't know if this is the right time to say this, but Tracelyn is right. I am in love with you."

Hearing it for the second time, even if he's saying it for Dr. Barnes, still makes my breath catch. Like last time, Tomas kisses me, but this kiss is longer, deeper, and stirs my blood. When he pulls away, it takes me longer to recover. Smiling in the dark, I snuggle up against him and whisper, "I think I love you, too."

His answering chuckle chases me into sleep.

Something's wrong.

Tomas's arm is still wrapped around me. His breathing is even and steady. A pale gray light streams through the barn. The rain has stopped.

I put my head back down and close my eyes, trying to catch a few more minutes of sleep. And that's when I hear it.

Panting. Something is here.

My eyes fly open, and I raise my head and look around the dim interior of the barn. Nothing. At least, not that I can see. The panting sound is nearby. I close my eyes to pinpoint the sound. It's coming from behind me.

Heart pounding, I slide out from under Tomas's arm, slowly sit up, and turn my head to look at the wall behind us. There's nothing there. But I can still hear the rapid inhale and exhale of air. There's a long crack in the corner of the wall where sunlight is streaming in. Being careful not to disturb Tomas, I quietly get to my feet, peer through it, and bite back a scream.

The animal is massive. Standing on its haunches it is as tall as I am, with black and gray fur covering most of its body. In places here and there, leathery pink skin peeks through. What captures my attention most, though, are the hooked claws and the teeth. Several rows of them. Yellow and sharp in a wide, protruding mouth.

Is it a kind of bear or a wolf? If it's either, this version is unlike any of the species I've ever seen. My father has shown me pictures that he took on the outskirts of one of the colonies he worked in. Pictures of animals twisted by the same chemicals and radiation that laid waste to the earth. Some of the animals developed extra limbs or lost their tails. Others lost their fur or gained skin almost impenetrable to weapons. Regardless of the change, every mutated animal became vicious. The smallest rodents with their hairless bodies and oversized ears would attack a human no matter their size. This animal—whatever it might be—outside the barn isn't small. It's huge. If it attacks, we will be in serious trouble.

And it is not alone. The large black head swings to the right, and I can see another grayer but equally scary animal standing behind it. It sniffs the air. Has it caught our scent? I think so. Which means we need to get out of here now.

I'm grateful we kept our things packed because we have to move fast. Kneeling, careful not to make a sound, I gently shake Tomas awake. His gray eyes open. His mouth smiles as he sees me, but the warmth and happiness leave his face as he notices the fear on mine. His eyes narrow as I lean close to his ear and whisper, "There are mutated animals outside. We have to get moving."

He nods and is on his feet, bag in hand, in seconds. Together we cross to the other side of the barn. Every scuff of our shoes or rustle of dry grass under our feet makes my heart jump. Once we are at the door, Tomas whispers, "We'll run with our bicycles until we get to the road. Then we'll ride. Okay?"

The barn is about 150 yards from the road. There are rocks, trees, and underbrush between us and the pavement. Not to mention the way back to the road slants uphill. I have no idea how the hook-clawed wolves move or how fast they can run. Perhaps they won't notice us. Or even if they do, maybe we will be far enough away for them not to give chase. If they do . . . well, I hope they lumber like bears. That might give us a chance. If they are swifter . . .

I clutch my gun, take a deep breath, and say, "Okay. Let's do it."

My feet pound the hard-packed earth, my hands hold tight to the handlebars as I keep my eyes focused on the road. The bicycle wheels bang and jump as they roll over the harsh terrain, but I don't look back to see if we have been noticed. That will only slow me down. If the animals and their vicious-looking teeth are in pursuit, I cannot afford the delay.

But Tomas does look back. I can tell by the way he sucks in air. The way he wills himself to go even faster as he yells, "Run, Cia. Run."

I do. I run as fast as I am able. My calf and thigh muscles burn as I propel myself and the bicycle up the hill that leads to the road. To our hope for escape that lies at least another fifty yards in the distance.

With his longer legs and superior strength, Tomas pulls ahead of me. He yells for me to keep running, and I am, but I can only go so fast. And then I hear it. Panting. Branches cracking. Yips and whines. They're close. Too close. And getting closer.

Fear, swift and fierce, helps move my legs faster. I climb the incline. Twice I almost lose hold on my bicycle as my feet catch in the underbrush, but I manage to keep climbing. Somewhere behind me the yips become growls. The sounds are closer. They are catching up, and I still have at least ten yards until I reach the road. A bicycle pedal catches on a bush, and I tumble to the ground. I look up and see Tomas at the top of the hill. He's already seated on his bicycle, poised to take flight.

"Come on, Cia. Hurry."

He doesn't say it, but I know the animals are moments behind me. There is nothing he can do to help me unless I make it to the top. So I scramble to my feet, pick the bicycle off the ground to keep it from catching on branches and grass, and force myself up the last incline. My feet hit smooth pavement and I want to cry with relief, but I can't. Out of the corner of my eye, I see them. A pack of them. Six or more. They are fast. Large, bulky shapes of gray and black matted fur. Ten or fifteen feet behind me. Jaws open. Ready to attack.

One leaps out in front of the others. Its wide, yellow eyes are focused on me as it closes the gap between us. I aim and fire. The thing growls in anger as the bullet hits it square in the chest. But it doesn't stop. The bullet doesn't even slow it down.

"We can't take them out. Get on! We gotta go."

Tomas's voice snaps me into action. I throw my leg over the bicycle frame. My feet hit the pedals and push. The sound of claws on pavement and the snarls of our pursuers get my legs pumping faster. The rickety metal beneath me protests as it picks up speed. I pray my handiwork won't give out on me now. Tomas is right. These creatures, whatever they are, are too strong for us to kill with a handgun or a knife. If we cannot outrace them . . .

Tomas yells encouragement back to me as the road slants downward. My wheels pick up speed. There are howls behind me, but they sound like they are dropping back. I keep pedaling. Willing the animals to give up the chase. To find a different, less speedy prey for their morning meal.

And they do.

The yips and growls grow fainter. When I no longer hear the sounds of the animals in pursuit, I brave a look behind and see in the distance that the pack is leaving the road. Heading north. Away from us.

Still we keep riding in case the creatures think to circle around and come at us from the other side. That kind of thinking takes higher reasoning and calculated determination. More than most animals are capable of, but there are stories told around campfires to scare children. Stories as well about humans who survived the radiation and the chemicals but were horribly changed. Never did I believe those stories were true, but I would never have believed the United Commonwealth capable of killing Testing candidates to aid in their selection process. So while the animals we are escaping showed no signs of human characteristics, we ride another fifteen miles before we stop and catch our breath.

I lay my bicycle on the ground and walk into Tomas's waiting arms. Pressing my head against his chest, I hear his heart hammering hard and know mine is pounding equally fast. We are alive. Since being shot at hours after the test began, I have been focused on the dangers my competition might bring or the ones the Testing officials have put in place. I had almost forgotten to worry about the animals roaming the damaged plains. Although, now that I think about it, I have to wonder if they are out here by accident or design. The Testers erected fences. If they are high enough to keep us in, wouldn't it stand to reason they would keep animals not welcomed by the Testers out?

Pulling away from the comfort of Tomas's arms, I dig out a water bottle and swallow the bitter taste of fear and fatigue. I hand Tomas the bottle and unwrap the food we intended to prepare for our morning's breakfast. Miraculously, the eggs, wrapped carefully in my clothing, have survived unbroken. Tomas suggests we make a fire and cook them since we need to rest for a while anyway. Our race to safety has left us both exhausted.

At least, that's what I think when we first gather twigs and sticks for the fire. As Tomas kneels down to light a match, I notice the blood seeping through the back of his pants. The sight stops me cold, and I realize how bloodless his face has gotten now that the color of exertion has disappeared. The match trembles in his hand as he lights the twigs and coaxes them into a crackling fire.

I pull my medical kit out and order Tomas to lie on the ground.

He flashes me a pained grin. "Tell a girl you love her and she automatically gets bossy. Well, I guess I can't complain since you're asking me to take off my pants."

I laugh, but a tear in the cauterized wound puts an end to my amusement. And once I wash away the blood, I can see a slight redness that speaks of infection. The infection isn't bad—yet. But it could be if we aren't careful. Seeing the possible contagion makes me decide to change treatment options. Not that this one will be any easier.

I make Tomas take several pain tablets and drink a lot of water before I sterilize a needle, thread it, and begin work. Tomas flinches as the needle slides into his flesh. Or maybe it was me who flinched. My heart thuds, my stomach clenches, and I grit my teeth as I push the needle back through tissue, pull the thread taut, and do it again. The tear is less than a half inch long, but each stitch is so small that it takes a dozen of them to complete the job. Tomas doesn't make a sound, but every wince on his face makes my heart ache. Dr. Flint told me once that it's hard for doctors to work on people they love, and that he hoped he'd never have to perform surgery on Dad or any of us kids for fear that love would get in the way of his training. Working the needle in and out of Tomas's flesh, I understand Dr. Flint's words. My fingers are slick with red when I make the last stitch and tie and cut the knot.

I am shaking and queasy as I slather the anti-infection ointment on the wound and place another bandage over it. Tomas is in worse shape. Traveling now isn't an option. I wash the blood from my hands and tell Tomas to sleep while I get food ready. His eyes are closed before I can dig out the pan.

I decide to postpone cooking for a while. After all that blood, the idea of handling or eating food doesn't appeal. Gun in hand, I do a search of the area for something to cook with the eggs and score some wild onion. I also find a patch of ripe wild raspberries.

I let Tomas sleep for more than two hours—as long as I dare. When his eyes open, I'm thrilled to see they are bright and clear and filled with annoyance at being left to sleep the day away. Although, when we finish eating, it's obvious that no matter how much he might want to travel, riding isn't a good idea. Tomas is weakened from the blood loss, and the injury is too tender. So we walk, wheeling our bicycles beside us for hours and taking short breaks for Tomas to rest. We find a river, but the water is poisonous and cannot be purified. At least, not with the chemicals in my bag. Our progress isn't fast, but it is constant. And by the end of the day, we can see buildings in the distance.

An abandoned city. And the road we are traveling runs right through it.

CHAPTER 15

THE SIGHT OF the buildings makes me shiver. The streets in between the buildings could house anything—wild animals, other candidates, or worse. From here the city looks to go on for miles. Even without the threat of danger lurking around every corner, I do not relish entering its depths. Tomas and I have been foraging for plants and treating water from the ponds and brooks we have encountered along the way. I doubt we will be able to do the same in a world comprising decaying stone and steel.

With the threat of the city looming in the distance, I set out dinner and say, "The city would be the perfect location for the officials to add some additional tests. Most candidates will probably pass through the city instead of going around because it looks like the faster route." I think of my father and his nightmare. Whatever happened to his friends took place in a city like the one sprawled out before us.

Tomas meets my eyes and nods. He understands what I

am thinking and what I am careful not to say with the Testers listening in. "Or they could place traps on the roads leading around the city to make sure candidates have to travel through it. They're going to want to see how we react when we come across other people. Look." He points to the south, and I squint into the setting sun. "The southern fence line bumps right up against the city. I can't see the northern boundary, but I'm betting it's closer than we think."

Weapons tight in our hands, we let sleep claim us and are up and ready to travel with the dawn. A survey of our supplies has us looking for water as the city looms closer. We find a small, murky pond coated with a black oily substance about a hundred yards from the road. Three of the purification chemicals are needed to treat the water, and even still I am concerned about its safety. Storing the water, I hope we find another source before we are forced to drink it. If not—well, we'll have to take our chances. While I don't relish being poisoned, I like the idea of dehydration even less.

Tomas insists he is okay to ride and grits his teeth as he takes his seat. His obvious pain makes me reevaluate my plan to go around the city. If Tomas's injury does not improve, we will need a better mode of transportation. A city with all of its abandoned stores and buildings could be the best place to find a vehicle.

The road we are traveling forks. The section that swings to the right and travels on the outskirts of the city is in serious disrepair. I doubt our bicycles would last more than a few minutes navigating the broken pavement. The fork that leads into the center of the city is perfectly smooth. The obvious sign of direction from our Testers makes my muscles clench. But there really isn't much of a choice. We will follow the road and get to the other side as fast as we can.

The road narrows, and we begin to pass the occasional building. Most of them are only two or three stories tall. None are in good repair. In fact, considering the number of holes in the roofs and walls, I'm amazed the structures are standing at all. We make a point to stay in the middle of the road in case the Testers have rigged the dilapidated buildings to collapse as we pass.

As the buildings grow taller and are spaced closer together, we see ones that have collapsed. In each instance, the building wreckage blocks a road leading off from the one on which we're traveling. At first I think I am imagining it, but when we pass the fifth different building collapsed over a fork in the road, I know I'm right. The Testing officials are herding us in a straight line. Toward whatever they have planned.

I yell to Tomas and stop in the middle of the road. He puts his feet down and turns to me. "What's wrong?"

I explain about the collapsed buildings and my worry about what might lie ahead.

"Do you want to go back and travel around the city?"

By his annoyed expression, I know Tomas does not. And to be honest, I'm not sure if I do. Going around might be equally dangerous. And we've already spent the morning coming this far. If we go back to where we started, we'll have wasted the entire day.

"No. Not really. I just want us to be careful."

He gives me a quick kiss and grins. "I promise not to throw rocks at any ponds unless I clear it with you. Okay?"

His smile makes my heart turn over, and despite my lingering worries, I find myself smiling back. "I'm going to hold you to that."

We set off at a slower pace, watching the buildings and pavement in front of us for signs of danger. Anything could be hidden ten or twelve stories up—cameras, traps. Anything. After pedaling almost four more miles we come to an intersection of roads. This time there are no piles of stone and metal to block our way. Instead, there are three unblocked paths. One that stretches in front of us and two that jut off to either side.

"What do you think?" Tomas places his feet on the pavement.

"I think now is a good time to start chucking rocks."

Tomas laughs but then climbs off his bicycle, grabs a large rock, and lobs it down the center path. It hits the ground and skips another ten feet across the pavement. He does the same for the other two. The rocks hit the ground and skid to a halt without incident.

"Now what?"

I don't know. We look down each path, trying to envision what it might hold. The path ahead and the one to the left are surrounded by buildings all similar in structure to the ones we've passed on our way to this point. Far to our right is a building that catches our attention. The gray structure is long. The center of the building stands several stories taller than the rest and is capped by a large dome. If for no better reason than we are curious to get a better look, we set off to the right.

And come to a dead end.

The domed building that once must have been magnificent is now crumbling. It and two collapsed buildings on either side block our way. Is part of the test figuring out how to get beyond these barriers or something else? While I consider the implications, Tomas picks up a rock and lobs it onto a set of broken stairs.

Nothing happens.

The two of us smile at each other, but before Tomas starts forward I say, "Try another rock. Just to be sure."

Tomas picks up another rock and hurls it toward the rubble to our left. For a moment there is silence before a faint ticking sound fills the air. A moment later the patch of ground where the rock landed explodes. There is no going around or over. Leaving the road is the wrong answer. A decision that will be punished.

Wordlessly, we follow the road back to the fork and choose the path that leads straight ahead. Another dead end. We don't bother to test this one for traps. We know they are there.

The left path takes us past several buildings that once might have been shops. A faded but partially legible sign boasts hardware. Part of me itches to stop and explore whatever inventory might still be usable, but I do not. The road that once terrified me is now a source of safety. The road zigzags around the crumbling gray buildings and eventually comes to another fork. Once again we have three choices. We take the middle one, pass more decaying structures, and come to a dead end that shows signs of a recent explosion. We turn around. And I realize what this reminds me of.

A maze. We are in a maze.

When I was growing up, my father used to draw me and my brothers complicated mazes and then ask us to solve them. Kind of like a race. All of us would be given the same maze and Dad would wait until we were all ready before telling us to start. Once we touched the tip of our pencil to the paper, we were not allowed to pick it back up. If we ran into a dead end, we were out of the race. Dad was teaching us to think and plan ahead. Not to rush into any decision too quickly without considering what the outcome would be.

Perhaps somewhere in his fragmented memory, he remembered this part of the test. Or maybe he was just giving us a game to pass the cold, snowy nights. Whatever the reason, I need to use the lesson it taught and think ahead. Already it is late in the day. If we aren't careful, we could be trapped in this maze longer than our supply of food and water will hold out.

I tell Tomas we should break for an early dinner. He's frustrated and hot enough to agree, so we sit down in the middle of the road and pull out the chicken since it will be the first to spoil in this heat. While we eat, I ask to see Tomas's book of maps. Together we pore over the pages. According to the book, the road we want to take out of the city is on the southwest side. That means we should choose paths in directions that should ultimately lead us to that road. The more straight- and south-traveling paths we can take the better.

Well, it isn't much information, but it is more than we had when we sat down. We hop back on our bicycles and start pedaling. Another fork. We take the left road. More undistinguishable buildings. A dead end. Back to the fork and straight ahead. Our shirts are soaked with sweat as we continue to search for the right roads. Even with the compass as a guide, the twists and turns are confusing my sense of direction. At nightfall, we have no choice but to make camp. Without light, we risk stepping off the road and tripping a trap. We opt to camp in the center of the road near a dead end. The three booby-trapped sides will at least limit the direction from which new dangers can arrive.

We eat the remainder of the chicken and save the greens and the last bag of dried fruit for morning. We will have to think our way out of this maze before hunger takes hold. In the heat of the day, we tried to ration our water intake but now our lips are cracking from a combination of heat and dehydration. We have no choice but to open the bottles that might contain contaminants. The taste is a little off, but neither Tomas nor I detect the metallic or bitter flavors that mean certain death. The one bright spot is that Tomas's wound seems better as I change the bandage and apply more ointment.

"That's because I'm being treated by the best," he says, and gives me a kiss. The hope of the healing wound and the warmth of his lips help me fall into a fast sleep.

Frustration returns with the light. Often we think we are on the right path only to find several turns later that we have to backtrack. More worrisome are the voices we begin to hear somewhere in the distance. Some voices sound as though they are just on the other side of a barrier or building. It is impossible to tell. But one thing is certain. We are not alone in this maze. There are other rats scampering after the seemingly illusive exit.

An explosion rattles the buildings next to us. A scream scrapes the air. Then another. Then silence. We pedal faster. Away from the explosion. Down one road. Dead end. Backtrack. Choose another path.

We try to make jokes when we come to the inevitable barriers that make us turn back. But hour after hour of searching and the jokes come less easily. Our laughter is more forced.

Until there is nothing left to laugh at. My scalp itches from the dirt and sweat. My body aches from the constant exertion that seems to be getting us nowhere. We eat the last of the dried fruit. Tomas finds a stale roll in his bag, and we split it to curb the hunger gnawing inside us. The only good news is that we are not yet feeling the effects of the marginally tainted water. And even that news feels grim when we realize that the water will not hold out for much longer. Not a single cloud dots the sky to offer the hope of rain.

My tired leg muscles protest when we choose a path that slants uphill. I force my feet to move the pedals. The higher up the incline we go, the better our view of the city. We aren't that high, but here and there, where buildings have collapsed from age, we can see beyond our patch of road. And when I squint into the distance, I think I can see the long, domed building that we encountered when we first entered the maze. It is far, far away.

I point it out to Tomas, who gives me the first genuine smile of the day. "Well, the end can't be that far away, right? Let's go find it."

The lure of freedom rejuvenates us. When we hit the next dead end, Tomas says, "Well, that's one less dead end until we find the exit." And we backtrack again.

And then we hear it. The sound of boots pounding on pavement. Someone is running close by. We move faster. Turn. Pedal.

Dead end.

The running feet are coming nearer. I look to Tomas. Fear and determination are bright in his eyes as he nods. We both step off our bicycles, lay them down on the ground, and draw our weapons. The pounding of leather on stone is more distinctive. Right around the bend. I raise my gun, hold my breath, and force my hand to steady.

I see the shadow first: the outline of a person. The outline of the gun in the person's hand. My arm muscles are taut. My finger poised over the trigger as the shadow comes closer. I know my weapon has the farthest reach. The runner could fire the minute he sees us, which means I will have to shoot first. Without knowing the person's intentions. Without knowing whether he or she means us any harm.

I will my finger to press the trigger as the shadow looms larger and a figure bursts around the corner. And I fail. I can't take a life. I barely register that the person is male. All I know is that if Tomas and I die, it is my fault.

Only, instead of a gunshot, I hear, "Cia! Tomas? Is it really you?" Before I can understand that we aren't going to die, I am swept up by a dirty pair of arms into Will's laughing embrace. His laughter is contagious, and I cling to him. My nose wrinkles at the scent of him—dirt and body odor combined with blood and whatever else he's run into since this test began. But I don't care. Face it: I'm not smelling like a rose these days, and holding him gives me hope that Zandri and Nicolette might also be alive.

"It's great that you and Tomas managed to hook up with each other out here. I never thought I'd find either of you."

His raised eyebrow asks to hear the story of how Tomas and I came to find each other. So I step back and say, "I had some trouble getting out of the drop-off city. Tomas arrived in time to rescue me from a swim in that river or worse." There's no point in telling Will that Tomas and I conspired to meet. It would only highlight the fact that we didn't include our other friends in the plan. Trust is hard enough in this environment. Now that my shock has worn off, I notice a bandage on Will's shoulder caked with dried blood. "What happened to you? Are you okay?" I ask.

Will flashes me a roguish smile. "I'm fine. Just a misunderstanding with a tree branch. No big deal."

"Infection can be a big deal," I say, reaching into my bag. "Why don't you let me take a look?"

Will shakes his head. "It's fine. Honest. Our time would be better spent getting out of this stupid maze. We have to be getting close to the end of this thing. I don't know about you, but I'm starting to run low on food and water."

I'm about to insist on stopping everything to treat Will's shoulder, but Tomas speaks. "Will's right. We need to get out of here. We can deal with the rest once we find the exit. Let's hit the road."

Tomas and I pick up our bicycles off the ground. We wheel them along as we walk next to Will, who is curious how we came by them. Tomas seems content to let me do the talking, so I give Will a rundown on finding the wheels and the bicycles and how we repaired them. It turns out Will found a nonmotorized scooter in a garage. One of the wheels wouldn't turn, but he managed to loosen it up and rode it on the same road we traveled into this maze.

"I kept hitting dead ends, and I was so frustrated that I forgot to be careful. I was going down a slope a little too fast, lost control, and fell off the scooter. The next thing I knew, the scooter hit the barrier at the end of the road and blew sky high. Guess I'll have to look for another set of wheels once we're out of this place. Especially if I plan on keeping up with the two of you."

As we search for the exit route, Will tells us about his travels, which sound uneventful compared to ours. The water he drank from the first source made him a little queasy, but thus far he's been able to find supplies and food along the way. When he shows me a spool of wire he found, I'm ready to kiss him. It's thin and flexible and perfect for setting snares. If we ever get out of here, we might have an easier time catching food. I'm so delighted with the wire that he gives it to me to carry in my bag.

As much as I want it, I shake my head. "You found the wire. You should have control of it."

"Think of it as a thank-you gift. If you hadn't stopped me from going for medical attention after the second round of tests, I wouldn't even be here. None of the candidates who went came back." Then Will leans down and whispers, "Besides, I don't know if we'll be traveling together after we get out of this city. Tomas looks pretty intent on keeping you to himself."

I start to deny it, but Tomas has not had much to add to the conversation since Will arrived. And when he does, there is a wary quality to his tone that makes me wonder what he is thinking. At the moment, Tomas is walking in front of us. Close enough to hear the conversation, but far enough away to avoid participating. I have to wonder if Will isn't correct. Not about keeping me to himself. Tomas knows this isn't the time or place for romantic drama. Survival—passing this test—has to take precedence. But maybe the fact that Will doesn't have a method of travel other than his own feet is making Tomas wary. Teaming up with Will means a much slower pace of travel than what we have set thus far. Although I don't know how well Tomas can ride with his injury. He has been limping more and more as the day goes on. If we get out of this maze, I'm hoping we can find a cool stream for him to soak in to help reduce the swelling.

There's no point in worrying about Will and Tomas now. Not with another dead end looming. We backtrack, take another path. At the next fork there are only two options. Left or right. The compass says the road leading out of the city is somewhere to our right. We head in that direction.

We follow the compass's direction and keep walking. It is Tomas who points out the size of the buildings that we pass. They are becoming smaller, similar to the ones we rode by when entering the city. The end of this maze must be near. I desperately want to jump on my bicycle and race down the road to see if he's right. Instead, we walk. A mile passes without a fork, without a choice to make. Two miles. Our smiles become more confident. There are fewer and fewer buildings. Finally, there is just hard, caked earth, the plants that have been able to survive in this landscape, and the road looming long in front of us.

When the city is several miles behind us, Will asks, "Do you mind if I camp with you guys tonight? I don't want to slow you down tomorrow, but it would be nice to have company for a little while longer."

"Of course you can camp with us tonight." Tomas beats me to agreement. But I notice he is careful to promise only to stay with Will for the night.

While I know it might annoy Tomas, I add, "Our food stores are low. We're going to need to search for food and water tomorrow on foot. Maybe we'll find some wheels along the way. Then we can travel together to the end."

"Sounds good to me." Will smiles. "But if we don't find wheels tomorrow, I don't want you and Tomas hanging back on my account. The quicker you get to the end the better. You know?"

Tomas seems to relax after that. We walk until the sun is low on the horizon. The southernmost fence line that marks the boundary of the Testing area is visible from the road. Beyond it I can see the glistening of water, clean and bright. I can't help but wonder if the sight of water is another test designed by the officials to see if we remember and follow instructions to not leave the designated Testing area.

We pick a spot behind a pile of large rocks to make camp. While Tomas and Will start a fire, I head off to look for food. The ground here is harder and more water-starved than on the other side of the city. But near the fence line there are signs of healthy plant life. On the other side of the fence I can see a lake. No doubt the reason for the health of the plants at my feet. Despite my frustration at being unable to reach the water, I'm happy to come away with several handfuls of dandelion greens, some wild onion, and a pot filled with white clover. I also put Will's wire to good use. Two hundred yards from our camp I set several snares, trying to remember everything my brothers taught me about trapping animals. If I'm lucky, a wayward animal or two will cross my snares. I can only hope because my stomach is already hollow with hunger.

Will's water bottle is empty. Tomas and I share our water with him during the meal. When night falls there are just a few swallows at the bottom of one of the canteens. Finding a water source will have to be our first order of business tomorrow. Otherwise we won't need to discuss who will travel with us.

Tomas insists on setting up a watch rotation for the night. "With three of us, we can each get a decent night's sleep and still have someone standing guard. Cia and I had a close call with some wild animals recently. I'd rather not repeat that experience if we don't have to."

We leave the fire burning and Tomas gives me a long kiss before climbing on top of the rocks to watch over us while we sleep. I'll take last watch.

In almost no time at all, Will shakes me awake and quickly sinks into sleep as I take my place on the rocks. The fire has burned down low, but it still casts enough light on my friends that I can see Tomas's shoulder muscles relax as Will begins to snore. Did Tomas stay awake during Will's watch? He must have. I am torn between frustration at Tomas's lack of trust and guilt that I trust so easily. Seeing Tomas's uneasiness, I am forced to reconsider my plans to have Will travel with us.

Birds singing signal the arrival of dawn. I promised Tomas to wake them at first light, but I decide to forage for breakfast in order to give Tomas a few more precious minutes of sleep. The sight of a skinny but very edible rabbit caught in one of my snares makes me grin.

I walk along the fence line on my way back to camp, on the lookout for other food. A handful of clover and a few wild carrots end up in my bag. I would like it to be more, but these will have to do. I turn my back on the fence and start to hike back to Tomas and Will when I hear a twig snap. Whipping around, I draw my gun and take aim, expecting to find an animal. Instead, on the other side of the fence, I see a gray-haired man. And he's smiling at me.

CHAPTER 16

BEFORE I CAN say a word, the man throws a small bag over the fence and disappears into the brush. I stare at the bag, trying to decide if this is another test. Do I look in the bag and risk something exploding or leave it and walk away?

The sack is small and made of a coarse brown material. Not anything like the fabrics used to make our Commonwealth Testing bags or any of the bags I saw in the Testing supply room. I think about the man who threw it. His clothes were faded but in good repair. His skin was sunbaked and weathered, but his muscles looked strong from hard use. More like my father. Less like the Testing officials I've come in contact with.

So who is the man? One of the rebels Michal mentioned in Magistrate Owens's house? History tells us there were differing opinions about how to revitalize the country after the Seventh Stage of War ended. Those who survived struggled with how best to proceed: to band all the survivors together under another centralized government or to allow each group of survivors the freedom to choose their own way forward. Those who disagreed with the choice of the majority struck out on their own. Could the man I saw be one of the survivors who live outside the United Commonwealth authority? If so, why is he throwing a bag over the fence marked as United Commonwealth territory for me?

After several minutes, curiosity wins out. I pick up the bag, hoping to find some clue to the man's identity inside. Instead, there is a loaf of bread, a small hunk of white cheese, a bag of raisins, and a bottle of water. I open the cap to the water and sniff it. The scent is clean and pure. A few drops of my chemicals confirm it.

I contemplate the items in my hands. The almost magical appearance of water when we are running so low is a blessing. So are the other supplies. But there is no way I can share them with my companions. Not without provoking questions about where the food and water came from. If it was just Tomas, I could have him remove his identification bracelet. Will doesn't know about the listening devices implanted in the bracelets, and we haven't known each other long enough for me to guess how he will react when he finds out about them. He might tip off the listeners and give away the only advantage we have—not to mention letting the Testers know we have received help from outside the fence. I can't help but wonder what the penalty for that kind of assistance might be and if other Testing candidates will be subjected to that punishment if they, too, run into the gray-haired man.

Not sure what else to do, I pour some of the fresh, clean water into the canteen. Then I store the bottle and the sack of food in my bag until I can best work out how to share them with my friends. Back at our camp, I stoke the fire and skin the rabbit while thinking about the gray-haired man and the sack of food he gave to me. Who is he? From my fellow candidates I've learned that Five Lakes Colony is far better stocked with provisions than many other colonies. So why is the gray-haired man sharing his food and water with an unknown girl? Does he know why I am on this side of the fence? Does he know there are others out here on the corrupted plains? Does he understand this is a test that some of us will not survive? By the time I get the rabbit roasting and wake my companions, I still have no answers.

Will is giddy at the sight of the cooking meat, dancing back and forth on the balls of his feet. He reminds me of my brother Hamin on Christmas Day. It makes me wonder if it is that similarity that causes me to trust him.

No one questions the amount of water in the canteen as we eat breakfast, pack up, and walk back to the road. With everyone's stomach full, I feel less guilty about the food hidden deep in my Testing bag. But I find myself walking behind them, watching the fence line for signs of the man who gave me the food.

After ten miles, we have yet to spot water although we do find a tree bearing small, hard apples. We fill our bags with the apples and some wild carrots I find growing nearby, and then we set off again. After another five miles I begin to suspect that any nearby water sources will not be close enough to the road for us to spot. The Testers aren't making it that easy.

The ground around the road is packed flat, which makes me say, "I think one of us should take a bicycle and scout for water off the road. Whoever goes can cover more territory and get back before it's time to camp for the night."

"I'll go," Will volunteers.

Tomas immediately rejects the offer. "No offense, Will, but once you have one of the bicycles, who's to say you won't ditch us and speed your way to the finish line."

"You're right. I could do that." Will smiles. His tone is affable, but I can see in his eyes something flat, dark, and angry. "I wouldn't, but I can understand how you might not trust my word given the circumstances. Even if your girlfriend here does. I'm also guessing you won't trust me to stay with her while you go scouting."

"You guessed right." Tomas's mouth curls into an answering smile. I can't help but notice the way his hands are clenching at his sides. "There's no way I'm leaving Cia alone with anyone. Not even you."

Will stops in his tracks. His eyes are cold. His hands ball into fists. "So, where does that leave us, Tomas?"

Before Tomas can respond, I say, "It leaves the two of you idiots here sweating out our last drops of water while I go in search of more." If the words come out harsher than I intended, I'm not sorry. Will and Tomas look ready to fight, and while I'm grateful that Tomas wants to keep me safe, this whole macho thing is out of place considering our circumstances. Even with the hidden bottle of water, our chances of survival decrease every mile that we don't find another water source.

Taking out the near-empty canteen, I throw it at Tomas and say, "I'm going to bike about ten miles ahead, set a couple of snares, and then go off the road to look for water. I'll leave a marker by the side of the road near the snares in case you get there first. Try to act like the adults you're supposed to be while I'm busy keeping us all alive. If you can't handle that, you both deserve to fail this test and we all know what punishment that brings."

I throw my leg over the bicycle and start pedaling. Tomas shouts for me to wait, but I don't turn back. The two of them will have to work out their differences on their own. The fact that they both have weapons concerns me for a brief moment, but I shove the worry aside and keep pedaling. My anger fades as my wheels propel me farther from my friends. This test is designed to help us learn about the land we need to restore to health, but it also gives us and the Testing officials a strong look into our character. Yes, the boys were out of line, but I overreacted. While I'm not proud of it, I have just learned not only that I have a temper, but that I would happily run headfirst into whatever danger I might find alone just to prove a point. Perhaps I have a bit of growing up to do, too.

When the Transit Communicator says I've traveled ten miles, I tie a piece of sheet to a bush near the side of the road, walk fifty feet beyond it, and set several snares. With that task done, I start pedaling over dirt, grass, and rocks to the northwest in search of water.

The sun is hot as I canvass the landscape. The air is thick with moisture. If we're lucky, it will rain. I'm grateful for the secret bottle of water as I zigzag across the cracked earth, and I'm still annoyed enough with both boys that I eat the hunk of cheese and part of the bread for lunch without any guilt.

I get off the bicycle and walk while studying the ground for signs of animal tracks. While my fellow Testing candidates and

I are only passing through, the animals live year-round in this barren stretch of land. They must have a source of water in order to survive. I find what looks like raccoon tracks and follow them west. After about three miles I am ready to give up when I see a small dip in the terrain nearly two hundred yards to the north. The grass around the dip looks marginally healthier than the brown, crackly stuff I've been traveling over, making my hopes rise as I ride to check it out. And I'm glad I did. The dip I saw is the bank of a shallow stream. A couple of tests, the additions of the right chemicals, and I'm able to fill my water containers. I'm tired but triumphant as I return to my bicycle, consult my compass, and begin the trek back to the road.

I am so pleased with my efforts that I don't register the sound of something moving behind me. When I do, I barely have time to pull my gun free of my bag's side pocket before my bicycle is hit from the side, sending me careening to the ground.

Scrambling out from under the bicycle, I see an animal leap and I roll to the right. Whatever the thing is, it hits the ground with a snarl. Before I can blink, it is up and launching another attack. This time I don't move fast enough. I scream as the creature's claws slash deep into my left arm. Whatever this thing is, I know I cannot outrun it. Even if I could get back on my bicycle, it's doubtful I'd be able to outdistance something with such speed. The animal snarls as I roll out of its grasp, push to my feet, and race to put distance between us. I turn and extend the gun in front of me as it barrels toward me. As I aim, I finally get a look at it. Long legs matted in a tangle of brownish hair. Long arms that are extended toward me with three-inch claws

I already know are razor sharp. A hunched back. Curled lips revealing blackish teeth. More brownish hair on the torso and back. And the eyes . . .

My finger pulls hard on the trigger, and I barely keep my footing as the gun jolts. The eyes of my attacker go wide. There is anger and fear as the wound in its chest blossoms with bright red blood. My enemy sinks to the ground and with its last breath lets out a cry that sounds like a call for help. Which it might be. Because now that I have looked into the dark blue eyes of my attacker I know this isn't an animal. The eyes are too intelligent. Too much like the ones I see looking back at me in a reflector. The body was twisted and deformed, but there is no doubt. I just killed a human being.

There is no time to deal with the swell of emotions I feel as an answering call sounds from somewhere to my right. Near the water I collected. Which only makes sense. If I had to pick a spot to make my home in this wasteland, that would be a logical place. My arm is on fire. Blood streams down it, but I don't have time to tend to the injury. Not with the guttural sounds of other mutated humans coming closer.

Racing to where my bicycle fell, I yank it upright and straddle the seat as three more clawed humans appear over the rise. My feet push hard to gain momentum, and I can tell the minute the one I killed is spotted. There is a cry so filled with pain and loss that it makes me blink back tears. Then the cry is replaced by a snarl, and I know they see me and have begun their chase.

They are much faster than I am. Whatever chemical reaction warped their bodies and twisted their fingers into claws has also given them incredible speed. They run with their bodies bent at the waist. Their arms hang low to the ground. Their all too intelligent eyes are fixated on me. The sight of my three attackers closing the space between us is terrifying. Sweat pours down my body, stinging the wound on my arm, as I force my legs to pump up the incline. Years of playing games with my older and faster brothers has taught me that the top of the hill will give me the best vantage point from which to defend myself.

The closer they come, the louder their snarls. And something else. Something more human—words. None that I understand, but the sounds are too clear and purposeful for them to be anything else. The three are communicating with language and using it to plot their attack even as I am plotting mine.

The heat, the loss of blood, the exertion to make it up the steep hill all make me dizzy. The world swims in and out of focus as my heart pounds loud and hard in my chest. I know that if I slow up for even a moment I will die. That alone keeps me pushing the pedals around and around. I rise up off the seat for the last stretch of hill, using my whole body to propel the bicycle up, up, up. The minute I hit the top, I jump off, let the bicycle clatter to the ground, and spin to take aim.

For a moment my finger stills over the trigger as I watch the three travel up the hill toward me. My throat tightens as I hear them shout guttural words back and forth. I straighten my shoulders and set my aim on the one on the left. The trio is getting closer. Only twenty yards away. But still I don't shoot. I don't want to kill them. They are human. Maybe not the same version of human that I am, but we come from the same ancestry. Everything I've been taught makes me want to find a way to communicate with them. To help them.

Instead, I pull the trigger.

The one on the left clutches its leg and hits the ground with a yelp. The middle one turns back to look at its fallen comrade, and I fire again. This time I hit the torso and the second attacker goes down in a heap. The last lets out an anguished cry and lunges up the hill with its teeth bared. I spot the wetness of tears streaming down its face as my bullet enters its skull.

The last is dead. The other two have been injured enough to keep them on the ground, but for how long I do not know. Part of me wants to bury the dead one, like I did the Testing candidate we found, but there isn't time for that. I need to get away before the other two rise or more take their place. Stumbling, I remount the bicycle and pedal away, barely noticing the tears that threaten to blind me.

Traveling downhill is easier, but I am aware of the blood streaming from my wound. I do not look at it, for fear of what I will see. I just keep pedaling and coasting until I spot the road. When I reach it, I can barely stand, let alone pedal. Sitting on the hard, hot surface, I finally fish out the medical kit and strip off my top to assess the damage. The five parallel cuts on my upper arm are jagged but shallow and at least seven inches long. It's bad, but not as bad as I feared. While the injury hurts, I can still move my arm. None of the muscles or tendons has been cut, and my stomach churns with relief.

Some animal scratches can fester if not treated properly. While my attacker was human, I'm careful to clean every inch of the wound and apply lots of anti-infection ointment. The ointment hitting the wound sends blazing pain up and down my arm. My eyes water. My nose runs. I can't wipe either because my one good hand is working at securing a clean bandage around the injury. Once that is done, I struggle into my other shirt. The fabric catches on my identification bracelet and I vaguely wonder if the people listening were excited to hear the gunshots. Do they think I killed another candidate? Does that raise their opinion of me as a leader? Do they understand that I am injured? Do they even care?

My entire body wants nothing more than to stay seated, but I slowly rise to my feet, store my Testing bag on the bicycle, and check my Transit Communicator. I've traveled more than forty-five miles today. Will and Tomas are somewhere on the road to the east. And they need the water I've found. Knowing their survival depends on me makes me move the pedals round and round. And if I am totally honest with myself, my reasons for backtracking are much less noble. I'm scared to be alone. Scared to face the things that might come in the dark. Scared to face my own conscience after taking human life.

But I might not have a choice. My legs are sluggish as the sunlight fades. I eat the rest of the bread and some of the raisins, sip water, and check the Transit Communicator again, trying to decide how long it will take to reach Will and Tomas. If they stopped to search for water or food, they might be miles away. Too far for me to reach before the sky turns black.

My muscles are heavy as I scan the sides of the road, looking for a place to camp. Something that is defensible, but still has a good view of the road just in case Tomas and Will keep walking after dark. After another two miles I see a clump of trees, oak or maybe elm, near the fence line about seventy yards off the road. I tie a piece of the white sheet from the cot to a branch and stick it into the ground as a marker. If Tomas and Will see it, they will know I am nearby.

The leaves on the trees are a yellowish brown, but the trunks and branches look sound. While I might sleep more comfortably on the ground, I decide to climb the sturdiest-looking of the trees and hope to find a place to camp in the branches. Of course, much depends on whether my left arm is strong enough. I stash my bicycle in some tall brown grass and decide to try. As I jump to catch a low-hanging limb, my left arm sings with pain. I bite my lip to keep from crying out, but I don't let go. Instead, I grit my teeth, pull myself up, and climb the way my brothers taught me.

The tree I've chosen is thick with heavy branches. I find a spot where several limbs are close together and perch with my back up against the trunk. Not the most comfortable bed I've ever had, but one I'm fairly certain I won't fall out of if I manage to sleep tonight. The moon comes out. I yearn for my mother's hands stroking my hair through the night the way she did whenever I was sick. Thinking of home, I keep my eyes fastened to the road in case Tomas and Will are still traveling, but somewhere during the course of my watch I fall fast asleep.

Hands reach for me. Slash my arm. Instead of screaming unintelligible words, the person I shoot calls me by name. Tears stream from its intelligent eyes as it begs me to take pity. But I don't. I shoot and kill again and again.

I jolt awake, my face wet with tears. My heart slows as I realize I am not on the hill. There are no eyes filled with pain accusing me with their dying stares. I am alone.

The moon is still shining, but I can tell by the haze of gray in the sky that daylight will not be far behind. Squinting toward the road, I see my makeshift flag still standing on the sidelines. Tomas and Will are nowhere in sight.

My injured arm protests as I shift around on my branch, preparing to descend. It screams the minute my boots make contact with the ground. I swallow several more pills before once more cleaning the cuts. The wounds don't look any worse than yesterday, which makes me feel a bit better as I apply more ointment and struggle to rewrap the bandage. A thud on the ground behind me makes my heart stop, and I leap to my feet with my gun held firm in my hand. I turn my head back and forth, looking for the source of the noise, and find it. On the ground near the fence is another coarse brown bag identical to the one given to me yesterday. This time I don't hesitate before opening it. Water. Two apples. Another loaf of bread and cheese. And what looks like a piece of roasted chicken. No note. No sign of my benefactor. Just the food and the water and the hope they provide.

Breakfast consists of chicken and an apple. I feel better after the meal, and after shoving the rest into the bottom of my bag, I break camp. The pain pills take the edge off the agony of the wound. My arm is still sore, but the pain is manageable. Pulling my marker from the side of the road, I climb onto my bicycle and set off to the east in search of my friends.

I find them two miles down the road looking tired, but alive. I can tell the minute Tomas spots me. Even at this distance I see his face light up. My heart swells with love as I race down the road, dismount my bicycle, and throw myself into his waiting arms. His mouth finds mine, and for a minute I forget that

Will is standing next to us. I abandon myself to feeling alive and in love. When I do remember, I walk over to Will, give him a kiss on the cheek, and hand him a canteen filled with water.

"See, Tomas. I told you that she was fine and that she'd find water." He takes several swallows from the canteen and flashes a smile. "Your snares also worked like a charm. Two squirrels and some kind of mutated fox. Too bad your snares couldn't land me some wheels, but those are the breaks, right?"

"I've been thinking about that," I say as Tomas notices the bandage peeping out from under my shirt.

"What happened?" Gently he takes my arm and pulls the shirtsleeve up to reveal the entire length of bandage. "Are you okay?"

"I'm fine," I say. "Turns out I wasn't the only one who was interested in using the water source I found." Without going into a lot of detail, I give them a rundown on my injury and escape from the stream. Tomas asks a couple of questions, which I answer as briefly as I can. At no time do I mention the attack was perpetrated by another kind of human. And I completely eliminate the trio of humans who lay chase after I killed their friend. To do so would open myself up to questions I don't want to answer, especially not with Testing officials listening in.

Once I'm done, I ask them about their travel. From the look Tomas and Will exchange, it is clear something went wrong. "What? Did you run into trouble, too? I was worried you wouldn't have enough water to get you through the day."

Tomas looks away as Will says, "The two of us shouted a lot after you left. We might have even thrown a punch or two.

Then we decided to put aside our differences and get moving. About lunchtime we ran out of water. We also ran into another Testing candidate."

"Who?" I ask, looking down the road. My heart quickens. "Anyone we know?"

Will shakes his head. "A guy from Colorado Springs Colony. He wasn't exactly thrilled to see us, but he wasn't all bad—right, Tomas? He did share his water."

Tomas just shrugs.

"Where did he go?" I'm not surprised that Tomas wasn't willing to let another Testing candidate travel with them, but now there is someone trailing behind us who knows we are here. Not having met the person or sized up his intentions, I can't help my anxiety.

Will takes another slug of water and frowns. "I tried to get Tomas here to agree to let the kid join us, but he wasn't inclined to trust anyone else. We left him about fifteen miles back. He was looking pretty tired. I think he planned on resting for a while. I don't think he'll catch up to us anytime soon."

The strain in Will's smile. The way Tomas won't meet my eyes. Both speak to what my gut has already told me. Something is very wrong. My next questions are met with short, vague answers and I am left wondering what secrets Tomas's and Will's silences are hiding.

I hand a water bottle to Tomas and store the empty canteen Will gives me in my bag. Then we set off down the road. Will tells us he'll understand if we want to ride, but I suggest we stick together for a while longer. After my run-in with the local inhabitants yesterday, I'm glad for the protection both Tomas and Will provide. Late in the afternoon we spot a cluster of buildings in the distance to our right. Possibly what is left of a small town.

"Well, that's my cue," Will says with a quick grin. "If I can find something with wheels, I'll catch up to you guys by tomorrow night. If not—well, I'll see you at the finish line. Okay?"

Tomas tells Will to be careful and mounts his bicycle. His smile gives no doubt as to his feelings. Tomas is happy to see Will go. Will hands me half of the roasted meat from last night and then gives me a hug goodbye. While his arms are wrapped tight around me, he whispers, "Watch your back, Cia. Your boyfriend isn't the nice guy he's pretending to be. I'll try to join you soon. Until then be very careful."

I want to ask what he means. What he saw. What he and Tomas did that has put shadows in both their eyes. But I can't because Will is loping away from the road toward the buildings far in the distance. Whatever secrets are being kept I'll have to figure out for myself.

Tomas isn't in the mood to talk as we glide to the southwest. The fast pace he sets tells me he is attempting to put as much distance between us and Will as he can. Or maybe he is trying to put distance between himself and whatever happened when the two were alone. I have to work hard to keep up with Tomas and often lag behind. My arm is throbbing and my entire body cries out for rest, but I don't stop until the sky turns from bright blue to gray.

As I unpack the roasted meat, Tomas says, "The moon's been brighter the last couple of nights. We probably can ride a little farther if you're up to it."

"Why? I mean, I want to get to the end of this test as fast as we can, but you're acting like something is chasing us." A flash of twisted claws enters my mind. I shake it free and ask, "What happened while I was gone?"

"Nothing." Tomas shrugs. "Look, we lost a lot of time in that city maze, and who knows what other things the Testers have arranged to slow us down. I figure we should travel fast while we can."

The point is valid, but his light tone is contradicted by the tightness of his jaw and the hands clenching and unclenching at his side. And that's when I see it. A smear of brown on the hilt of his knife.

Dried blood.

My insides churn as I think about the Testing candidate they ran into. The questions Tomas won't answer. Will's warning about Tomas not being exactly what he seems. I shake loose the rising fear, telling myself I've known Tomas for years. He's kind and caring. The blood is probably from cleaning the snared animals. And even if it isn't, there are other justifiable reasons for the stain. I should know after what I have done. I should just ask Tomas and set the worry aside.

But I don't. I eat my meat and clover, drink some water, and remount my bicycle so we can pedal another five miles before we rest.

When we do make camp, Tomas insists on one of us keeping watch. After what I have seen roaming the plain, I don't object. He takes first watch and stands next to a tree. In the moonlight, I can see him brushing aside tears. While my first instinct is to go to him, I know he thinks that I'm asleep — that his grief is his own. My heart aches that he won't share his pain and the source of it with me. Although, how can I object? I have secrets too. Secrets that make me fight sleep. And when sleep pulls me under, those secrets chase me in my dreams.

Tomas shakes me awake from a dream filled with gunshots and bloody knives. He gives me a kiss and asks if I'm okay. I'm not, but I smile and tell him my dream was no big deal. More secrets. Since I'm awake, I tell him to get some rest while I keep watch. I sit next to the same tree he chose, but instead of watching the road, I set my eyes firmly on the fence line as I wait to see if anyone appears. No one does. The day dawns. We mount our bicycles and begin to pedal.

Despite Tomas getting several hours of sleep, his eyes look red and tired. He brushes my attempts at conversation aside, and when he does speak it is only to worry about our lack of food and water. I do my best to stay optimistic as a bridge comes into sight. Beyond the high-arching road lies another city. My mouth goes dry with fear. Another test?

The bridge climbs over land for several miles before stretching over a wide river. From far above the water looks cleaner than any we have seen in the Testing area. This river must have been purified by a colony north of here. Unfortunately, the bridge we take to cross the river keeps the water tantalizingly out of reach. The only way to reach the water safely is to travel back several miles to where the bridge began. Perhaps that is part of this test. To see if we will recognize that getting the water takes more effort than finding another source. Then again, a desperate candidate might not care. I'm thankful we are not that desperate.

We are rewarded at the end of the bridge with a less than sparkling but, according to my tests, drinkable pond. In the distance, perhaps two or three miles, looms the city. After the last trek through city streets, we are acutely aware of our diminished supplies. Even with my secret stash of food, we could not survive for more than a few days.

As much as Tomas wants to race away from whatever he left behind, he says, "Why don't we camp here for the night? We can wash and maybe catch some game before we start into the city."

I am quick to agree. Leaving Tomas to fill and treat the water bottles, I head off to the southwest to set snares and look for other fresh foods. There is a small wooded spot several hundred yards away where I set my snares and begin my search for roots and greens. I am digging up some wild carrots when I spot movement in the wooded area beyond the Testing fence. The man with gray hair appears from behind a tall bush. He approaches the fence and beckons me. Without a second thought, I dump my bag on a tree stump and remove my identification bracelet. I place it on top of the bag, and then walk the fifty yards to the fence to meet whatever fate has in store.

CHAPTER 17

I DON'T BOTHER to take my weapon. If this person wanted me dead, he could have killed me days ago. The man's gray hair gives the appearance of age, but his eyes and the lack of lines on his face tell me he is years younger than I first guessed. He's wearing a gray sleeveless shirt, which shows off strong arms, and brown loose-fitting pants. In his hand is a bag much like the ones that he has tossed over the fence to me.

Pushing my hair out of my face, I say, "Thanks for the food."

The man smiles. "You're more than welcome." I wait for him to continue, but the silence stretches between us.

Jamming my hands in my pockets, I ask, "Who are you?"

"I'm a friend who wants to see you survive this journey. My name isn't all that important."

Maybe not to him. His unwillingness to share it with me sets me on edge. "Well, thanks again for the food."

I turn on my heel to leave and hear, "If you wait, I'll explain why I can't tell you my name and why I want to help you."

My feet stand still. I look at him and wait.

"My name will mean nothing to you, but it might mean something to those who evaluate your performance when this test is complete. And while I trust you would not willingly share my name with the Testing officials, you might not have a choice."

"Why?"

"They told you about the interview after the fourth test?" He waits for me to nod. "Before the interview begins, they will give you a drug to encourage you to answer the questions honestly, without holding back anything you wish to keep secret."

While there are things I've done during this test I would rather not talk about, nothing I've experienced thus far would cause me difficulty if I'm forced to speak. My ability to remove the bracelets might cause the Testers concern, but wouldn't they see that as a sign of my resourcefulness? Even this strange man and his gifts of food are not dangerous to me. Dr. Barnes stated we could not leave the testing grounds. Nowhere in the rules did he mention not accepting food thrown over the fence.

Straightening my shoulders, I say, "I have nothing to hide."

"Are you sure of that, Cia?"

The sound of my name on this unknown man's lips makes my heart clench. I had assumed my encounters with this man were random. The fact that he knows who I am suggests something entirely different. "How do you know who I am? Are you a Testing official?"

He laughs. "Far from it. I'm someone who believes the Testing process is wrong and wants to help you survive—not just to the end of this test, but through the challenges the University will bring."

Up until now my goal has been to survive the Testing in order to make it to the safety of the University. The idea that the University might be filled with more tests sends a chill straight to my heart. But while questions about the potential dangers of the University spring to my lips, I know this isn't the time to ask them. I will worry about that if and when the time comes.

Instead, I ask something equally if not more important. "If you are against The Testing, why are you throwing us food and water? Why not help us escape?"

"As I believe the esteemed Dr. Barnes explained, Testing candidates cannot leave the Testing ground. The fences are harmless enough until a Testing candidate goes over them." The man reaches into his pants pocket and pulls a silver identification bracelet from his pocket. The symbol is a triangle with what looks like a drawing of a human eye at the center. A memory nags at me from after the third test. Tomas pointing out the students in his group. A boy with a shock of untamed brown hair and a sweet smile. "The boy scaled the fence about a hundred miles back. He was dead by the time he hit the ground. The only thing we could do was bury him the way you and your friend buried the girl candidate you found."

My muscles go still. "Only a Testing official could know Tomas and I did that."

"Not all Testing officials agree with the current procedures. One even disabled several skimmers in an effort to keep officials from arriving at their designated colonies in time to pick up candidates for The Testing. Unfortunately, the part we had him disable was not as difficult to repair as intelligence led us to believe. Otherwise you would still be in Five Lakes Colony and I would be having this discussion with a different candidate."

Was he talking about Michal? Is he the one who told this gray-haired man about me? Something tells me asking will not get me the answer. This man is here for a purpose. I have already been away from the Testing officials' listening device for too long. Too much longer and they might question my stillness. It is time to learn what this man's purpose is.

"Why are we having this discussion?"

For the first time he smiles. "Because, Cia, we know your family has secrets you don't want the Commonwealth to know." The bag he has been holding comes sailing over the fence. "Inside that bag is a small vial. It contains a liquid that we believe will counteract the interview drug. Take it the morning of the interview if you want to keep you and your family safe."

The tacit threat to my family scares me to the core. But fear won't help me. I tamp it down. I look at the bag in my hand and then back at him. "How do I know this isn't another test?" If it is, the liquid in the vial will probably kill me. Punishment for a wrong answer.

"You don't." There's sadness in his voice. "You have only my word that I am not part of the United Commonwealth." He takes a step back from the fence. "Hide the vial in your spare clothing before you cross the finish line. One of my friends will make sure it isn't discovered by the Testing officials and is safely hidden in your possessions again before the interview begins. Good luck, Malencia. I hope we meet again."

Without another word, he turns and walks away. I watch until he disappears into the tall grass before retrieving my identification bracelet and my Testing bag. The sun is starting to set. I need to get back to Tomas, but I take a moment to think over everything I heard as I empty the brown bag. Yes, there is a small, unmarked vial corked with a black stopper. Carefully, I unwork the stopper and take a sniff. It smells faintly of roses.

I shove the vial deep into my pants pocket and look at the other items. More water. Instead of bread and cheese, I find a small container of raspberries, a heaping bundle of wild carrots, and several small yellowish fruits that I think are pears. The wild carrots and raspberries are plants I might find here in this area. I wonder if the pears are as well. I move away from the fence, and after a fifteen-minute search, I find not only a pear tree but also a thick bush ripe with raspberries along with several spots where an abundance of wild carrots grow. The bag isn't food just for me. It's food to be shared. The man beyond the fence must also know I never told Tomas about the bread and cheese. The man knows a great deal.

He implied he also knows my family's secrets. Was he talking about my father's nightmares? Or that Zeen is smarter than all of us and that knowledge was hidden from Dr. Barnes and his Testing officials? That leaders of Five Lakes conspired to keep their graduating students safe? Knowing there is a chance I might be asked about those things in my interview makes me break out in a cold sweat. Or maybe this is all just another test. Maybe the man is trying to scare me into drinking the liquid in the vial and failing.

This is a problem I will have to address at some point. But not now.

Arms filled with supplies, I trek back to camp and wait for Tomas's reaction to the bounty. I'm not disappointed as he helps me put the food on the ground and then picks me up and swings me around. The shadows of the past two days disappear, and it feels like we are back home in Five Lakes—safe and happy and whole.

We eat the last of the roasted meat and fill our stomachs with juicy raspberries and pears. We plan to collect more tomorrow before heading into the city. I check Tomas's backside, which seems much improved, and my own arm, which doesn't look so good and hurts like hell. I wash the wound clean in the pond, swallow a couple of pain pills to ward off the worst of the sting, and slather on more ointment knowing deep down that it will not do much good. But I have to try. Right? Tomas helps me rewrap my bandage, teases me about the berry stains on my mouth, and kisses them away. He is so like his old self that I find myself yearning to tell him my secrets. But I can't. Not yet. First I need to know. "What happened with you and Will after I left?"

"Will told you what happened."

"A lot more happened than either of you mentioned."

I feel Tomas stiffen. "Are you calling me a liar?"

"No," I assure him. "But I know you and Will weren't exactly getting along when I rode off." Tomas moves his arm from around my shoulders, gets to his feet, and stares into the distance, doing his best to shut me out. Which hurts. I scramble to my feet and touch his shoulder. "Look, I know it's hard to trust someone under these circumstances, but I trust Will."

"You shouldn't." Tomas's eyes meet mine with blazing passion. "Didn't your father warn you not to trust anyone?"

Tomas's words stop my heart. He knows that someone is listening and that if by luck they hadn't been paying attention to our conversation before we reached Tosu City, then not taking care with his words now might put my father—my whole family—in jeopardy.

Swallowing hard, I say, "I trust you. And my father warned me that competition might blind some people, but that doesn't mean Will is one of them."

"How can you be so sure? Because he makes jokes and was upset when his brother didn't make it through the first round? So what? You don't know what he's capable of. When we found your snares, he unpacked his bag to look for his knife. In the bag he also had a purification kit, a medical bag, a pair of binoculars, and a map book like mine."

"And?"

"The numbers don't add up. We were allowed to choose *three* items. Three that we could add to two personal items. The knife. The gun. Add them to the others."

I do the math. "Maybe he found the knife or binoculars along the way."

"They both have Testing logos etched into them. Just like your gun. My knife. Which means he ran into at least one Testing candidate."

The girl we buried flashes in front of me. I shake the image away. "Maybe a candidate lost their bag or he saw one asleep and decided to take their things." Not exactly an admirable choice, but one I can almost live with. "Look, people do strange things under pressure. Just because he had a few extra possessions doesn't mean he hurt whoever he came across. The two of you met a candidate while I was gone and nothing happened to him, right?"

"Yeah." Tomas drops his gaze and says, "Right."

With all my heart I want to believe him. But I'm not sure I do. Tomas, who from my earliest memories has always been calm and collected, is filled with tension and anger and despair.

Trying to sound upbeat, I add, "I know you don't trust Will, but I want you to consider that there might be another explanation. The United Commonwealth is looking for a new generation of leaders. Even leaders have to trust sometime." My tone, if not my words, seems to calm Tomas, and we settle back onto the ground to prepare for sleep—Tomas's arm wrapped around me, my head resting against his chest. But there is one question I have to ask before closing my eyes. One test I need Tomas to pass. "What was the other candidate's name?"

I feel Tomas's heart quicken under my cheek. His muscles tense. After a few moments, he whispers, "I don't think he said. If he did, I don't remember."

He is lying. He would have asked for a name. He would have given his own in return. Habit. Common decency. The Five Lakes way. My stomach clenches with disappointment, and I fight the urge to retreat from his arms.

It is not surprising that both of us only pretend to sleep.

The snares are successful. Two rabbits and an opossum. While Tomas cleans and sets the game over a fire to roast, I gather more fruit and greens for our journey into the city. There are no morning kisses or gentle looks. Tomas is withdrawn as we pack up camp and begin to ride, which gives me lots of time to think.

The sky is overcast. My eyes drift more than once to the fence line as I look for signs of my mysterious benefactor. I'm not surprised when I don't see him. But I do believe he or someone he knows is watching. Rebels? He spoke of not being a member of the United Commonwealth. Of not agreeing with its methods of Testing. And yet he chose only to offer food and a vial of an unknown drug. Other than the friend who will keep the drug hidden, there is no offer of further assistance. No offer of escape. If he and the people like him could sabotage United Commonwealth skimmers, surely they could find a way to circumvent the penalty for escaping the test. Of course, according to the man my presence here is proof of their inability to beat the Testing officials. Still, even knowing the odds were against success, I believe there are candidates who are sufficiently scared, hungry, or ill and would leap at the chance to flee.

Or would they? We all left families back home. Families bound by the laws of the United Commonwealth. The government compensates our families when we leave for The Testing. I wonder if the law states what would happen to a family whose Testing candidate chose to escape.

A large metal arch towers over us as we follow the main road that travels around the outer rim of the city. The buildings stand taller than those in the city we passed through days ago, but these look to be in far worse shape. The scorched nature of some of the wreckage tells the story. This city was bombed.

According to Tomas's map book, the name of the city was St. Louis. Neither of us remembers if our history books say what kind of bomb was used here. Some bombs destroyed what was in their path. Others laid waste to water and soil. The worst contained poisons with potencies that, unless physically counteracted, do not fade over time. It is the last option that keeps our bicycles pointed to the west and our eyes fastened on the road that veers around the city. With a sufficient amount of water and food, we do not need to risk whatever tests this city contains.

The next few days we settle into a pattern of foraging for food, traveling, and camping. We find several small streams that help us wash away the stains of travel, and while we do not go hungry, our clothes begin to hang from our bodies. I wrap a long piece of cot sheet around the top of my pants to keep them from slipping onto my hips. Tomas is forced to do the same. We talk of only the most superficial things. Every once in a while I catch Tomas staring at me as though longing to say something. But he doesn't. And neither do I.

I jump at every sound even though there are no more animal attacks or strange humans—although twice we spot what look like other Testing candidates on the northern horizon. We pedal faster to avoid confrontation. The man from the other side of the fence does not appear again. Just day after day of travel. The shadows beneath Tomas's eyes get heavier. While he laughs and smiles, I can see the strain under everything.

My nightmares get worse. Friends, family, and foes find me in my dreams, but I am learning to bite back the screams that come with waking. I find myself touching the vial of liquid in my pocket to calm myself. More disturbing are the cuts on my arm. For the first few days I tell myself I am imagining the difference, but after a week passes, no amount of wishful thinking can change what is undeniable. The cuts have gotten worse. The scabs growing over them turn green and ooze a yellowish liquid. Whatever chemicals twisted the humans in this area have now infected me. I take more pain pills, drink more water, and hope I can make it to the end of this test without the infection doing permanent damage.

After more than a week of riding, we spot another large collection of buildings on the horizon. Here both the northern and southern fence lines are visible. The Testers are limiting the amount of space during these last two hundred miles. If there are other Testing candidates nearby, we are almost certain to come in contact with them.

Footprints and what look like tire tracks on the side of the road tell us at least two, maybe three, candidates have passed through this area. While we have moved fast, they have been faster. Now they could be lurking somewhere in this city's streets.

We wait until dawn before following their lead through the first streets. The city looks decayed, but the buildings are in moderately good repair. Until we turn a corner and the buildings come to an end. In their place is a deep crater that stretches as far as we can see. Ringing the edge of the crater are buildings like the ones we just passed through. Several streets deep. All that is left of a place where people once lived and worked and thrived.

We stare into the emptiness with our fingers clutching our handlebars. Miles and miles of scorched emptiness. While the land behind us is corrupted, there are still plants that have adapted. Things live. In front of me there is not a speck of plant life. Nothing lives here. I try to imagine what once stood in this space. How any leader could order a bombing that results in this—the kind of destruction that cannot be fixed with the right chemistry equation or a new breed of plant. The earth is resilient, but it's hard to imagine a time when this place will be anything but a terrible reminder of what we as a people can do.

With the crater stretching for miles, we have no choice but to take one of the roads that travel around it. This means going through the maze of streets filled with buildings. For no real reason, we choose to go to the right, walking our bicycles instead of riding. I am glad for the decision to walk. My arm is aching more. So is the rest of my body. The pain pills push back the chill for hours at a time, but it always returns. Maybe walking will help my body rest enough to fight the infection inside me.

After we zigzag through several blocks, I ask, "Do you think the people who bombed this city really understood the damage they were causing? Do you think they realized winning might mean killing everyone and everything—even themselves?"

Tomas shrugs. "Does the answer really matter?"

"Maybe," I say. During the past week, I've thought a lot about that question. Perhaps because the closer we come to the end of the test, the closer we are to becoming the next leaders of our generation. Many of my fellow candidates had demonstrated their belief that the end justifies the means. I have a hard time understanding that, but one thing is certain. The past cannot be changed. My nightly dreams are a testament to that. And sometime during the wakeful nights, I have realized that the length of this test is not arbitrary. The third test helped them learn what they needed to know about our ability to trust, strategize, and cooperate with others. From our behavior during that exam, I have no doubt the Testing officials could predict which candidates would use the provided weapons for survival and which would turn them on their fellow man during this test. While the fourth test measures many of the same areas as its predecessor, it's also designed to gauge not only the choices we make, but also how we live with those choices once we've made them. Do we learn from our mistakes and use that information to carry us successfully to the end of this exam, or will they swallow us under? From the shadows under his eyes and the slump of his shoulders, I know Tomas is being swallowed whole.

The image of Ryme's lifeless body flashes in front of me and I feel a stab of fear. Ryme was swallowed by whatever doubts plagued her. While I am not sure what memory is haunting Tomas, I am certain by the despair in his eyes that it has the power. I don't know what he has done, but whatever it is, he does not deserve to end up a victim of The Testing.

Taking a deep breath, I explain, "The whole point of this test was for us to see what terrible things were done and for us to learn from those mistakes. Right?" Tomas cocks his head to the side, and I forge ahead. "The best leaders make mistakes and then learn from them. The best leaders never make the same mistakes again. The only way you can learn is if you understand the mistakes that were made."

Tomas looks down a street that ends at the crater and considers my words for a long while. When he looks back at me, I see some of the tension is gone. "I think the leaders knew they'd destroy the buildings and kill the people. The rest . . ." He sighs. "I can't believe they intended to completely destroy a world they wanted to live in. They had to realize they were making a mistake. They just didn't know how to stop."

I look around at the buildings and nod. "Maybe that's the mark of a real leader. Admitting a mistake has been made and finding a way to stop it at all costs."

We've traveled over halfway around our side of the circle

when a shiver travels up my spine. I reach for the fever pills in my medical kit and shiver again. This isn't the fever. This is something very different. When I was little, my brothers made a game of talking me into doing things our mother wouldn't approve of—like sneaking bread from the pantry or taking her best sheet and turning it into a pirate's costume. I could always tell when Mom caught me by the tiny shiver I felt as her eyes settled on my back. The same shiver I feel now. Someone is watching.

Gaping windows, open doorways, cracks in the walls surround us. I see nothing in the ones we pass, but I slide my gun out of my bag anyway. The wind picks up. The sky turns gray. A storm is coming. Perhaps that is what is making the hair on my neck stand on end.

The wind whips a strand of hair free from the knot I've been wearing it in. I push the hair off my face, and that's when I see it. A face framed by a doorway. Large, intelligent eyes sunk in a wrinkled, sunbaked face. Tufts of dark brown hair on the head, the neck, the arm I see. My blood churns as I see the familiar razor-sharp claws at the end of the hand. Several inches long. Sharp. Poisonous.

The wind howls. No. Not just the wind. The wind has merely masked what I refused to hear as we walked. The low murmur of voices. Guttural sounds carried on the wind that tell me there is more than just this one. Slowly, I turn and study the shadows, counting the faces I see. Five. Ten. Two more in a second-story window. Too many for us to survive if they attack. But they haven't yet. They are waiting for something.

Tomas has yet to notice the faces. His eyes are fixed on the road, looking for danger ahead of us—not in the windows three stories up. I hold my breath as a light rain begins to fall. Tomas swears and suggests we climb on our bicycles so we can move faster. But I don't dare. Thus far the occupants of the buildings have done nothing more than watch. Perhaps walking seems unthreatening. But riding? I was riding when one attacked. If riding triggers their aggression, I will not repeat the offense.

"Cia, did you hear me? I think we should ride."

I give a small shake of my head, put my hand on his arm, and whisper, "Look in the windows." He stops walking. The quick intake of breath tells me he has spotted someone. Leaning closer, I say, "There are dozens of them."

"They look almost human." Tomas's hand fingers the hilt of his knife, and I see the watcher in the window shift.

"They are human."

"How can you be sure?"

The rain falls harder, plastering the clothes to our bodies, making it more difficult to see the eyes following our every move. A watcher steps away from his spot in a doorway. His movements are fast and smooth. Tomas reaches again for his knife, but I put a hand on his arm and shake my head as the watcher comes to a stop ten feet behind us. His eyes are unblinking as he waits for our next move. My chest tightens and it's impossible to catch my breath as step by agonizingly slow step we begin to walk again. Thunder rumbles. The cuts on my arm burn. Two more watchers join the first in the street. They slowly follow behind us.

The rain falls harder still. Lightning streaks across the sky and reflects in the watchers' wide, never-blinking eyes. Another falls in behind us. Then another. Soon there are more than a dozen. Never moving faster than us. Walking with their strange hunched but fluid gait. They keep their distance, at least ten yards behind, but are ever present with their claws and their overwhelming numbers.

It is Tomas who first notices the distance between the watchers and us is growing wider. They do not leave the street, but their gait slows until it comes to a stop. Dozens of them stand in the street as we pick up our pace. Perhaps this too was a test. Maybe the Testers were curious to see whether we would attack these people without provocation—out of fear of the unknown instead of a real threat.

I see one more watcher in the doorway of a building twenty feet in front of us. Thunder rattles the windows as the watcher stares at us with unblinking eyes. I barely register the rattle of gunfire until the person's face is torn to shreds.

CHAPTER 18

Strong arms pull me to the ground. Tomas drapes himself over me, acting as a human shield, as the sound of gunfire continues. From the asphalt, I see the watcher's sightless, bloody body hit the ground. Then I hear the cries behind us. I do not know the words. But I understand. Outrage. Anger. The need for vengeance. The group is no longer dozens of yards behind us. They are moving forward. Fast.

Tomas scrambles to his feet first and holds out his hand. I take it as another rattle of bullets sparks the pavement and sends wounded watchers to their knees. The bullets chew apart limbs, torsos, heads—creating a gore unlike any I have ever imagined. The mutated humans shriek as bullets cut their comrades off at the knees. I catch a glimpse of blond hair, a tall, muscular build, and the dark metal machine gun atop a three-story building as Tomas pushes my bicycle toward me and yells to ride.

But I can't. I know the boy wielding the gun. It's Brick.

"Stop shooting," I scream, waving my arms to get his attention.

Cries of anguish come from windows and doors that line the streets and mix with my screams as more watchers arrive. Dozens and dozens of them. And while I should be scared of their vengeance, all I can do is scream for Brick to stop firing and stare at the horror he has wrought. It is impossible to tell that the tissue and flesh on the ground were just moments before standing in front of us. The smell of blood makes my stomach rebel. From the retching I hear next to me, I can tell Tomas is not in much better condition. Doubled over, I see the rainwater streaming down the road toward us swirling with red blood. Red. The same as ours. Human. All human. All dead.

Amid the thunder and the guttural cries, it takes me a minute to realize Brick is shouting down at us. "I have you covered, Cia. Run! Hurry. Get out of here before they attack you. Go!"

"Stop," I scream. Tears clog my throat. Revulsion threatens to choke me. All these people dead. Killed by a boy I helped to survive. "You're killing people. They weren't hurting us. They're just people."

But Brick isn't listening. He has opened fire again, farther down the street, at people who despite this horrific provocation are not attacking. All the living want to do is care for the dead. And now they, too, are among the fallen.

Tomas grabs my arm. I lose my grip on my bicycle, and it clatters to the ground.

"Pick it up. We can't help them, Cia. We have to go."

I barely keep my balance as I cast looks behind me, willing Brick to stop. But he doesn't. Rattles of gunfire echo through the air. How many more dead? Because of me. Because I saved Brick's life and he in turn believes he is saving mine.

More than once I stop pedaling as the enormity of the massacre I witnessed overwhelms me. Tomas's patient voice is the only thing that keeps me moving forward. All I want to do is curl into a ball and weep.

And I do. On the outskirts of the city, Tomas spots a small building that looks sound and insists we stay there for the night. The downpour has ended, but our clothing, hair, and shoes are soaked through. He finds enough wood to build a fire on the stone floor near a window and encourages me to change out of my wet clothes. I follow his request even though my other shirt is stained from my first encounter with those people—when I too killed.

My body isn't up for food, so I pull my legs tight against my chest and stare at the fire, trying to imagine my family safe and warm in front of theirs. Tomas insists on treating my arm. He digs out some pain pills and makes me take them. Maybe the pills will stop my body from shaking. Thunder still echoes in the city streets as Tomas tells me how much he loves me and holds me as I cry myself to sleep.

My dreams are filled with gunfire and rivers of blood. When I wake, I remember the dreams were real and nausea rolls through me. I know I need to eat, but my stomach curdles at the thought of meat. I force myself to eat a pear and drink some water. Our boots are still damp, but we put them on, store the rest of our belongings, and step outside. The sky is a brilliant shade of blue. The wind is cool and refreshing. There are even a few flowers blooming under the brilliant sun. A perfect day that mocks the horror of the night before.

Out of habit we consult the map, wheel our bicycles to the road, and begin to pedal. According to the Transit Communicator, we have just under two hundred miles before reaching the end of the test. We pedal hard, as much to reach the end as to get away from the death behind us. As we ride up hills, we can see the fence line to the north moving closer. Perhaps as little as a mile separates the two boundaries. Yes. Our Testers want us to face each other. I wonder whether the Testers will have to make a choice when this is over. With what I have seen, it will be a miracle if twenty of us cross the finish line alive.

We travel throughout the day with only minimal stops. My arm is worse. I am sweating more as we ride, and my fingers on my left hand grip the handlebars with less assurance. But I force my legs to move around and around. I will our wheels to go faster and faster to the end. We meet no other candidates during the day, and there are 150 miles left to travel when we stop. Tomas holds me close again at night, kisses me gently, and whispers that if we keep up this pace we can make it to the end in three days. Just three days. I tell myself I can make it and hope I am right.

The sky is gray when we once again set out. My legs feel weaker, my arm more inflamed. I take more pain pills. Use more ointment. Know that both are useless against the poison festering inside me. Will they know how to treat the wounds when I get to Tosu City? Tomas says they will, but he will say almost anything to keep me from giving up. Funny, but giving up is the last thing I will do. Not after everything we have witnessed and the things we have been forced to do. Giving up would be like admitting none of it mattered. And it needs to matter. It needs to be remembered. But, now that we are so close to the end, I worry about the memory wipe my father said is coming. As we ride, I recall everything I've learned about the workings of the brain from our teachers and from Dr. Flint and when we break for lunch, I tell Tomas I'm tired and need a nap. Instead of lying down, I take off my bracelet and walk fifty yards away. After a few minutes, Tomas does the same.

"What's up? Is your arm worse? We can slow our pace a little if you need a break."

I ignore the pain that has moved from my arm to my shoulder and down my torso and say, "We're almost to the end."

His face breaks out into a wide smile. That familiar single dimple makes me want to cry. "I know. Another day. Maybe two and we should be there." He feels my forehead and frowns, which only tells me what I already know. I'm burning up. "They'll fix up your arm as soon as we get there, Cia. You'll be good as new in no time."

I might be. But I can't worry about that now. "According to Dad, they're also going to fix our memories so we don't remember any of this."

"Maybe taking away these memories isn't as insidious as we first thought. Maybe they're trying to help us survive. Do you really want to live remembering Malachi die or watching Brick with the machine gun?"

"No," I say honestly. A lifetime of nightmares isn't my idea of a good time. But neither is being reprogrammed to forget what I lived through. What Malachi died for . . . What Brick did for me . . . "But I need to remember. Forgetting that it happened doesn't change anything. Nothing can change the past. My father's nightmares prove the memory wipe isn't complete.

Now instead of being haunted by what he did and didn't see and do, he can only guess and wonder. Isn't that worse?"

Tomas kicks at the ground in front of him. I can see him struggling with my words and I can understand why. The idea of forgetting is seductive.

Looking up, he says, "Your father's and Dr. Flint's nightmares make me think the memory wipe isn't being done with surgery."

I tend to agree. Dr. Flint says that the long-term and short-term memory centers of the brain are easy to find, but that every brain is slightly different. Trying to alter a specific path in the brain that only affects three or four weeks of memory would be tricky on one patient, let alone the hundreds who have graduated from the University.

"Drugs? An audio pulse? Hypnosis?" Counteracting all the options seems impossible, especially out here.

"My bet is drugs."

So is mine, especially after talking to the man on the other side of the fence. I consider telling Tomas about the man, the vial he gave me and the truth serum the Testers will dispense to us. Withholding the information feels like a betrayal. Only, I don't know how to explain why I have not shared this information with Tomas up until now. I had good reasons, but Tomas might not understand. The last thing we need right now is hurt feelings or recriminations. I will have to find another time to tell him.

Instead of sharing my secrets, I ask, "How can we fight a drug we don't know or understand?"

"I don't know if we can. I guess once we get back to the Testing Center we'll have to figure out how they plan on administering it. Maybe one of the staff will tell us if we ask in the right way. If they put the drug in water or something, we'll have to act like we drank it. Then pretend we don't remember anything from before our arrival at The Testing." He takes a step toward me and runs a hand over my cheek. "I've done and seen things out here I don't want to relive the rest of my life, but I can't imagine not remembering the first time I kissed you."

His lips find mine with a passion that takes my breath away. Maybe it's the fever that causes me to shiver as he kisses my cheek, my neck, my lips. But I don't think so. I wrap my arms tight around his neck and return his kisses with my own—hot, urgent, needy. A deep yearning fills me as I struggle to get closer, although we are wrapped together so tight, I doubt air could pass between us. But it doesn't feel like enough. And when Tomas steps away, we are both left panting and wanting more.

But more will have to wait. We've been away from our microphones for long enough. Any longer and the Testing officials will wonder about our silence. Tomas places one last, incredibly sweet kiss on my lips, takes my hand, and walks me back to our camp.

When we arrive, I pretend to wake up, ask questions about what happened while I was asleep, and listen with a smile as Tomas weaves a tale about a squirrel he tried to capture. I don't know if those listening are amused, but I am.

We eat lunch and mount our bicycles, hoping to travel another thirty miles before dark. Only, I'm not sure I'm going to make it that far. The pills are no longer controlling the sizzling pain in my arm. Or if they are having an impact, my arm is worse than I imagined. Ten miles along, I find my body slowing down. Tomas encourages me to keep pedaling, and I do try. But my pace doesn't pick up. It is all I can do just to stay balanced and moving forward.

Another ten miles along the road, it is Tomas who stops and points out a shape running along the northern fence line. I squint into the sunshine, trying to make out the details of who it might be. Certainly another Testing candidate. By the gait I believe the candidate is male. Tomas then points behind us. Far in the distance is another figure stumbling along the road. Friend or foe? We keep moving forward, hoping to avoid answering the question.

Two more miles and I can no longer pedal. My head is spinning. My throat is dry. The wounds on my arm scream so loud it is hard to focus on anything else. I tell Tomas I have to stop.

Unwrapping the bandage, I prepare for the worst and find it. The wounds are swollen and hot to the touch. When I was a kid, I fell and opened a large gash on my leg. Dr. Flint was away from the colony, so Mom patched up the wound and made me stay in bed. Several days later, my leg looked a lot like my arm currently does. Luckily, Dr. Flint had returned and knew what to do. He gave me a small dose of something for the pain, broke open the scab, and squeezed yellow and white pus out of the wound along with a small piece of metal. The contaminated metal was the source of the problem.

I'm certain the scabs on my arm now trap whatever poison is infecting me. And there is no Dr. Flint. Only Tomas, me, and my need to survive.

Tomas starts a fire. He boils water and pieces of the towel I took from the Testing Center to use for bandages since I have used all the ones in the medical kit. Meanwhile, I sit down, take several more pain pills, and ask Tomas for the scabbard to his knife. He gives me a strange look, but slides the knife out, unstraps the case, and hands it over. Before I can question what I'm about to do, I bite down on the thick leather, grab the top of my left arm, and squeeze.

Had I not been seated, the pain would have brought me to my knees. As it is, my stomach heaves, my eyes tear, and my lungs gasp for air as my fingers dig into my flesh. Bit by bit the scabs break free of the skin and pus—yellow and green and swirling with milky-looking blood—streams out. I gag at the stench of meat left too long in the sun. I realize the meat smell is coming from my arm and begin to cry. But I don't stop squeezing. Pus runs down my arm. Tomas takes the bandage I removed earlier, dips it in water, and begins to dab away the infection as it oozes out. But no matter how quickly he works, there is more to take its place.

The world swims in and out of focus. I double over from the pain. And still I squeeze. My fingers move alongside the middle of the wounds and squeeze again. Then lower still.

Tomas talks to me, but his voice sounds miles away. I can't make out his words. Time loses meaning as I force the infection from my body drop by putrid yellow drop. I only stop when the wounds stream blood red. No yellow. No green or white. No infection—for now.

I free my fingers from their viselike grip and let Tomas clean the stinging open cuts with hot water. He uses the last of the ointment and wraps my arm in sterile wet cloths. He rocks me back and forth and whispers that everything will be okay. That I should sleep. He'll make sure I stay safe.

My dreams are filled with equal combinations of horror and happiness. Ryme and Malachi help me bury the girl without eyes. Zeen forgives me for stealing from him and reminds me to call home with the Transit Communicator when I get the chance. Roman grins as he walks through a door and abandons me to a group of watchers who scratch me over and over with their claws and then explode before my eyes. My father's arms rock me for hours the way he did when I was little. The rocking stops. He cocks his head to the side and tells me I have to get up. Someone is here.

My eyes snap open.

I can feel Tomas breathing in the dark beside me—slow, steady breaths that speak of a deep, restoring sleep. Taking care with my arm, I push my body to a seated position. I flex my fingers on my injured hand. They move easier than yesterday. The rest of the arm and shoulder doesn't feel as swollen, and either the medication has finally kicked in or the worst of the pain is gone. I blink back tears of relief, and out of the corner of my eye see something shift in the shadows. Holding my breath, I wait for it to move again. I catch a glimpse of its size in the fading moonlight. Big. Human. One of the mutated inhabitants of this area or a fellow Testing candidate? From the way the shadow moves, I think it's a candidate.

Our fire has burned out and we are camped in a ditch behind a set of bushes, which probably makes it hard to spot us. But daylight isn't far away, and the candidate doesn't look like he's in a hurry. He's slowly picking his way across the ground about fifty yards away and is coming in our direction.

Slowly, I reach out my arm, trying to find my Testing bag. I am panicked when I realize it's not nearby. Tomas must have moved it after I'd fallen asleep. And with it, my gun.

I squint into the darkness, trying to locate the bag, but its dark color camouflages it from sight. Without knowing our new neighbor's intentions, I don't dare move around. Lying back on the ground, I nudge Tomas and whisper in his ear, "Another candidate is out there." His eyes spring open, alert and fearful. Then he nods to let me know he understands. Together we hold our breath and wait.

The snap of twigs and the rustle of leaves tell us our fellow candidate is closer. The first gray rays of dawn chase the darkness as I peer under the bushes. No one is there.

Tomas raises an eyebrow and shakes his head. He doesn't see him either. The other candidate must have already passed us by and is traveling toward Tosu City.

"I think we're safe," Tomas whispers. A branch snaps under him as he sits up.

I hear the whistling of the knife flying through the air a moment before I see it in the pale light. That extra second saves my life as I dive to the side and watch the blade sail into the bushes behind me. Our attacker gives an angry shout as I scramble to my feet and look around for my Testing bag. Tomas draws his knife and races forward as I spot the bag sitting on the ground next to my bicycle over fifteen feet away. The sound of metal on metal tells me our attacker has another weapon and Tomas and he are now engaged in battle.

Tomas cries out as the attacker's long, wide knife bites into his side. And that's when I get a look at the other candidate. His face is thinner and his cheeks hollow, but I would recognize that sneer anywhere. Roman. And now he is pulling his knife back and preparing to strike Tomas again.

My fingers fumble with the fastenings of my bag as blade sings against blade. I frantically dig through my belongings and hear another shout. This time Roman is the one bleeding, but he doesn't grip his wounded arm or flee. Letting out an angry growl, Roman lowers his head, charges, and tackles Tomas to the ground. A scream rips from my throat as a knife barely misses Tomas's neck. For a moment I am paralyzed, watching the two wrestle in an effort to gain the upper hand. And Roman does. He pins Tomas to the ground and raises his knife just as I pull my gun from my bag and take aim.

A shot rings out. Blood blooms on the right temple of Roman's forehead. The sneer is gone, replaced by surprise and then emptiness as the knife drops from his hand and he pitches forward — dead.

Holding his side, Tomas crawls out from under the dead boy and lets out a sigh of relief at being safe. But we aren't safe. Tomas doesn't know what I know. I didn't take aim in time. I was not the one who fired the gun.

CHAPTER 19

"GET DOWN," I yell as I look from side to side, my entire body humming with tension and fear. "I didn't fire. There's someone else out there with a gun."

"That would be me."

Spinning, I aim and tighten my finger on the trigger before the familiarity of the voice hits me square in the chest. The cocky tone that could only belong to one person out here.

Will.

I lower my weapon and see him strutting toward us, twirling a pistol around his finger. And while I know Tomas doesn't want me to like or trust Will, I can't help wrapping my arms around him. "You have no idea how glad I am to see you," I say. "I'm not sure I would have been able to save Tomas. Thank you."

Although I'm not sure whether I'm thanking him for saving Tomas or for sparing me the need to take someone's life. Probably both.

Will steps back and slides the gun into his pocket. "I'm sure you would have managed without me. In a strange way, it's a good thing this idiot was stupid enough to attack you guys. I would never have found you without all the noise. I've been looking for days and figured the two of you had already gotten to the end of the test."

"No such luck," Tomas says, holding his side.

"Yeah." Will gives Tomas a nasty smile. "I know you hoped you'd seen the last of me. Guess I just proved you can trust me after all."

For a minute, Will and Tomas look at each other. Tomas is the first to look away as he says, "I guess so."

"Good." Will laughs. "Then why don't we let Cia here take a look at that cut before you bleed to death. If you die, I won't be able to lord my heroics over you. What fun would that be?"

At the mention of Tomas's injury, I rush to examine it, doing my best to ignore Roman's lifeless body crumpled on the ground. Tomas's cut is long but shallow and won't need stitches. Which is good, because after the past couple days I don't know if my fingers would be steady enough to perform the job. Will offers me the use of his medical kit, and I quickly clean, medicate, and bandage the wound.

Once I'm done, I hand the supplies back to Will and say, "You caught up to us. That must mean you found wheels. Right?"

"No wheels." Will gives me a big smile. "I found something even better. Want to take a look?"

Not too far from the road sits a small, single-passenger open-cabin skimmer. Kind of like a hovering version of a scooter. My father has three of them at his lab for light field use. They are good over short distances, but long distances make them overheat and they can't hold much more than 160 pounds, which limits their usefulness. My father and two of my four brothers are too heavy. They can't even get off the ground. But Will and his lanky frame are perfect for the design.

"Where did you find it?"

I hear the suspicion in Tomas's voice, but Will doesn't seem to notice as he explains, "Two days after I left you guys, I ran across a big stone building with a huge metal door. It took me a while to get the door open, but it was worth it. There were four of these babies inside. None of them were in working order, but I was able to use parts from the other three to fix this one. Looks like the Commonwealth stashed a lot of vehicles and other things in the second half of this test. I've seen a couple Testing candidates riding these, and one of the guys I ran into found a bunch of automatic weapons in a cabin just before the last city. I guess the first part of the test was about survival. The second is testing how fast we get to the end and how many competitors we'll take out along the way."

"How many candidates do you plan on taking out before the end, Will?" Tomas asks the question so quietly, I almost miss it.

But Will doesn't. With a serious expression, he answers, "The only competitors I plan on eliminating are ones who pose direct threats. Kind of like our friend over there." He hooks his thumb toward the body on the ground. "Or do you think he deserved to live?"

Will gives Tomas a smug, almost challenging smile. So much for hoping Will's heroics would put the two on the same side. I step in between the two and say, "Look, according to the Transit Communicator we have about eighty-eight miles left to go. Instead of sniping at each other, our time would be better spent eating breakfast, packing up, and getting the hell out of here."

"Fair point, Cia." Will flashes an easy smile. "I'm willing to put our differences behind us if Tomas is."

Silently, Tomas nods, and I let out a sigh of relief. I'm not naïve enough to think the two won't find opportunities to fight along the way, but I'm hoping they'll keep it to a minimum.

While I set out breakfast, Will rummages through Roman's Testing bag and finds clothes, two bottles of water, a compass, a fishing kit, several tools, and a bow with a quiver of arrows. All marked as Testing candidate supplies. Evidence the boy attacked and at least wounded one other candidate. We dine on pears and rabbit and divide the new supplies among our own bags. I keep the knife and bow and arrows if for no other reason than I don't want my two adversarial companions to have additional weapons to use if their sniping gets out of control. Then, while Tomas and Will aren't looking, I remove Roman's identification bracelet and slip it into my bag alongside the one that belonged to the girl Tomas and I buried. Roman was untrustworthy. He came into The Testing intent on winning at any cost. And while I hate what he did to reach his goal, I realize I hate the Testing officials more. Roman didn't deserve to be a future leader, but death seems an extreme penalty to pay. For good or ill, his life should be remembered.

Tomas and I put our bags on our bicycle racks, Will heads for his skimmer, and the three of us meet up on the road. There are two shadows on the horizon behind us. Other Testing candidates? If Will is right, they could have vehicles that will overtake us soon. We have to get moving.

Will's solar-powered skimmer is faster than our bicycles, but he keeps pace as we pedal. I can't help but wonder why. Knowing how fast my father's open-cabin skimmers travel, I'm pretty sure Will could be at the finish line in a matter of hours. While he might feel some kind of responsibility to me for my part in keeping him in The Testing, saving Tomas this morning has more than paid the debt. Although maybe Will doesn't see it that way since, technically, he didn't save my life. I don't know. Whatever his reasoning, I'm grateful to have another pair of eyes watching the horizon for signs of danger. And it's good he's watching because Will is the first to spot a glint on the road ahead. A tripwire that our wheels would have triggered.

We get off our bicycles and wheel them off the road, around the trap, and then back onto the smooth surface. Will's skimmer hovers over the trap, and we continue along. We pedal a bit slower as we watch for signs of other dangers. Tomas hates the delay. So do I, but adding a few hours to our journey is nothing compared to the alternative.

The plants and leaves become greener, the trees less twisted, the grass and water more plentiful as we get closer to our destination. Markers of revitalization. My arm aches, but the signs of our goal being so near help me ignore the pain and fatigue.

An explosion from somewhere far behind us shakes the trees. Gunfire and shouts echo across the landscape from the northwest. Reminders that we are not alone in our quest and the danger is not yet past. We keep watch during the night and rise early, hoping today will be the day we finish this exam. I check the Transit Communicator frequently to mark our progress.

Forty-five miles left.

Thirty-five.

Twenty-five. We drink water as we ride, ignoring our hunger. We can get food after we have passed this test.

Fifteen miles remain, and the sun starts its decent. The sky is streaked with purple and pink. We keep going, squinting into the setting sun, on the lookout for anything that poses a threat.

Ten miles.

It is only by chance that I see the flash of metal next to the wide trunk of an oak tree. I scream to Tomas and Will as cracks of gunfire split the air. Sparks fly on the road in front of us, and I pull my handlebars to the right to avoid running into their path. The quick change in direction is too much for my repaired bicycle. The front wheel wobbles and cracks. I land flat on my back and gasp for air as the wind is knocked from my lungs. My left arm screams from the impact. Tomas shouts my name as gunfire begins again. Louder. Closer. More terrifying than before because I can barely breathe, let alone move.

But I do move because I don't want to die. Tomas and Will shout from somewhere nearby, but I don't look for them. I can't. I roll onto my injured arm, ignoring the wave of dizziness and pain as I reach for my Testing bag. My fingers find the gun. I come up to my knees and look for the shooter on the other side of the road.

There. The barrel of the gun peaks out from behind the tree as the shooter prepares to fire again. I aim at the arm holding the gun and pull the trigger. A female cry of pain tells me my aim is true. I can't help the surge of triumph that streaks through me as the gun and the girl's arm disappear behind the tree. I keep my arm extended and my finger ready to pull the trigger as I watch the tree, waiting for signs of our attacker.

"She's making a run for it," Will yells.

I blink—then understand. While I have been waiting for more gunfire, the candidate has faded into the trees and mounted a skimmer similar to the one Will is driving. She must have stashed it there before taking her spot behind the tree. I pull the trigger and fire shot after shot as the skimmer fades into the setting sun. The candidate and her skimmer are gone. Unless another candidate eliminates her in the next couple miles, she will finish the test and pass on to the next one. This girl who stopped and hid here, specifically for a chance to kill her competition, might become a University candidate—a future leader of the United Commonwealth. I fight back a scream and realize the only way to keep her from being a University student is for more than twenty of us to pass this test. Then I can only hope the Testing committee will choose those who have not resorted to deadly tactics. For us to be included in that number, we have to get to the end. Which means we'd better get moving.

I climb to my feet before remembering the wreckage of my bicycle. A quick glance makes my heart sink. The fading light cannot hide the damage. The entire front wheel assembly has broken free. There is no fixing it. "I guess I'll be walking the rest of the way," I say, trying not to sound as discouraged as I feel. According to the Transit Communicator, there are only eight and a half miles left to travel. The distance is minor compared to the miles I have already crossed.

"Don't worry, Cia." Tomas appears next to me and takes my hand. "You won't be alone. I'll walk with you."

"You don't have to," I say, but I am glad he volunteered. The idea of walking by myself in the darkness, not knowing what lurks in the shadows, is terrifying.

He gives me a light kiss and says, "Yes. I do." Then he turns to Will. "I guess this is where we part company again. Cia and I wouldn't want to hold you back."

Will smiles. "Funny, but I was just going to say the same thing."

It's the smile that alerts me to the danger. Cold. Calculating. So unlike anything I've seen from him before. I shove Tomas to the side just as Will raises his gun and fires. But I'm not fast enough. I feel Tomas flinch as the bullet enters his abdomen. His eyes are wide with surprise and pain as he doubles over and sinks down to his knees.

My gun is up and targeted as Will shifts his attention to me. "What the hell are you doing, Will?"

He smiles behind his gun. "Isn't it obvious? I'm getting rid of my competition. I didn't lose my brother and come all this way just to be told I'm not good enough to make it into the University. I made that choice early on. Only you wouldn't die. Thankfully, a couple of the others were easier to kill before I ran out of quarrels. Both Gill and I are championship crossbow marksmen. He always takes first, but I give him a run for his money."

Chicago. The crossbow shooter. The wound in Will's shoulder. A gunshot where I hit him. The pieces fall together with terrible clarity.

"And you think I'm just going to let you shoot me now?"

My voice is remarkably steady considering the rage churning in my veins. I finger the trigger of my gun, trying to channel that anger into killing a boy I thought was my friend. "I've already proven I won't go down without a fight."

Will's smile widens. His white teeth gleam in the growing darkness. "You're smart, Cia, but you don't have the killer instinct. I could walk away right now and you wouldn't fire at me."

"You wanna bet?" I yell. "Go ahead and try me." The trembling of my hand belies my bravado. And for a moment, I'm certain Will is right. I cannot kill him. I am going to die out here on the Testing grounds.

"Cia."

It's the whisper of my name by the boy I love that stops the trembling. Tomas is still alive.

Will straightens his shoulders and takes aim. My finger tightens. The gun in my hand kicks a second before Will fires. My bullet punches into his right side, sending him staggering backwards as his shot whizzes by my ear into the darkness. Will screams and starts running toward his skimmer as I fire again. His stagger tells me I've once again connected with my target, and I hear his gun clatter as it hits the ground. I shoot again and again as the skimmer lifts off the ground and zips forward. Two more shots and he is out of range, streaking toward the finish line.

The last of the gray light is fading as I kneel next to Tomas. The adrenaline coursing through my body fades, leaving me weak and tired and scared.

"Is he gone?" he asks.

Feigning more confidence than I feel, I say, "With any luck

he'll black out from blood loss and crash his skimmer before he gets to the end. Where did he shoot you?" A pointless question since I can see where Tomas's red-streaked hands clutch his right side. I roll him over and find a bloody wound on his back. The bullet passed right through. One less thing to worry about, I tell myself as I pull the rest of the towel I took from the Testing Center out of my bag, rip it into pieces, and hold one against the wound. With the flow of blood stanched, I rack my brain for everything I learned from Dr. Flint about human anatomy. An ear pressed to Tomas's chest tells me his heartbeat is quick but steady. His breathing sounds strained but there are no gurgling noises to indicate his lungs are filling with blood. Both are good signs. But neither will matter if I can't get him back to Tosu City.

There are other Testing candidates traveling this way. With the fence lines so close together, there are few if any places we can hide that will ensure our safety. The only answer is to get him across the finish line as soon as possible.

Folding several strips of fabric, I create pads to absorb the blood and press them to Tomas's wounds. While he helps hold the pads in place, I dig out his other shirt, wrap it around his torso, and tie it tight. Handing him a bottle of water to sip, I say, "We have to get you to Tosu City. Can you walk?"

"I can try."

But it's clear after a few stumbling steps that walking is not an option.

Tomas sinks back to the ground and shakes his head. "It's no use. I'm not going to make it."

"You just need time to rest," I say, but I know that isn't true. Time is our enemy. Every second that ticks away means more blood loss. More chance of infection. Fellow Testing candidates approaching with weapons in hand. A greater chance of dying.

He takes my hand and pulls me closer. "I know you don't want to hear this, but you're going to have to leave me here. Once I get some rest, I might be able to walk the rest of the way—"

"I'm not leaving you." I try to pull back my hand, but Tomas isn't letting go.

"Yes, you are. You're going to finish this test for both of us. I want you to go. Please. Before another Testing candidate comes along."

Tears bubble close to the surface, but I choke them back because I won't give in. "I can't. This is my fault. I told you to trust Will. I have to make this right." I kiss him firmly on the lips to quiet whatever argument he wants to make and give him the last three pain pills so he can rest easier while I think. He closes his eyes, and I start to pace.

Tomas can't walk.

If he doesn't get to the end of this test soon, he won't make it at all.

Even though one bicycle is broken, the wheels still function. There has to be a way to use them. Tomas can't operate a bicycle. Not in his condition. But maybe, if I work it right, he can sit behind me while my feet do the work.

With the possibility of other Testing candidates nearby, I hate the idea of lighting a fire, but the night is cold. Tomas needs the warmth, and if I'm going to turn our bicycles into something that can transport him, I need the light. Tomas is asleep on the ground as I dig through his bag for matches. I find the matchbox at the bottom of the bag along with something metallic. From the feel of it I'm guessing it's a Testing identification bracelet. Briefly, I wonder if Tomas took the bracelet off the bag of the girl we buried. Perhaps, like me, he wanted something tangible to remember her. To keep the bracelet from getting lost, I shove it deep into my pocket. Then I turn my attention to the fire. My brothers showed me how to bank a fire to minimize the amount of light it produces. I try my best to replicate the process, but I'm not sure how effective it will be. Keeping my gun within reach, I drag the two bicycles close to the light and get to work.

I jump at each snap of a stick. Every howl of the wind sends me reaching for the gun. But no one disturbs us as I assess my supplies and decide on a solution. A cart for Tomas to sit in would be ideal, but the metal and tools I have at my disposal make it hard to create one, especially if I want to do it fast. The most likely option would be to modify the one working bicycle into something that the two of us can ride. And I have an idea.

My eyes are grainy and my hands caked with grease when I finish. The moon has shifted, telling me dawn is near. The bicycle seat has been wrapped with Tomas's extra pants to give him a slightly wider and more comfortable perch to ride on behind me. To accommodate the extra weight on the back of the bicycle, I have salvaged the two back wheels from my broken bicycle and screwed their assembly slightly behind and to either side of the back wheel. The training wheels I used as a kid inspired the plan, but it took hours and a lot of wire, screws, and bolts and six test rides to get it to work. Of course, the real test will be the ride to the finish line. I only hope my handiwork will help us get there.

Tomas's forehead is feverish, but not scarily so as I rouse him from his sleep. I cut up some pears and leftover meat and make him eat as I explain what I've been working on. "All you have to do is put your arms around my waist and hang on. I'm going to do the rest."

I don't give him a chance to protest as I empty out all but the essential items from our bags. When I'm done, there is a pile that includes a pot, a pan, the bow and arrows, several empty water bottles, the book of maps, the gray-haired man's burlap sacks, and the now empty medical kit. I wince as I put Tomas's tool kit in the pile, but I have my pocketknife if I need basic tools and, really, if the bicycle breaks down, I'm not certain any tool would help fix it. At this point, I just have to hope for the best. Putting my hand in my pocket, I remember one final chore and shove the vial with its unknown drug into my spare pair of socks. I don't know what will await us at the end of this road. Whatever it might be, I know it is best to be prepared.

With everything ready, I help Tomas to the bicycle. I don't bother to douse the fire. If someone finds our camp and the supplies there, so be it. The two new wheels help keep the bicycle upright as I maneuver Tomas onto the seat. I get on in front of him and have him wrap his arms around my waist. As an extra precaution, I've cut my other shirt into strips and braided them into a rope, which I now loop around the two of us. If we go down, we'll go down together.

The gears groan as I push my feet forward. The extra weight makes it hard to gain momentum. Tomas leans his head against my back as I shove my right foot forward. Then my left. Inch by inch we move. I am not discouraged. Moving at all is a victory. Right foot. Left foot. I push with all my might, and we begin to teeter forward. After several more pushes, we start to coast. The road slants downward, and we gain momentum. Not as fast as we traveled before, but faster than I dared hope as I worked through the night.

Zeen's Transit Communicator is strapped with wire to the handlebars.

Seven miles left.

Six.

Five.

The sun is high in the sky. Sweat drips off my forehead as I push forward. Tomas's grip around my waist slips, and I stop the bicycle to check on him. He's shivering, and hot to the touch. I make him drink half of our last bottle of water before starting back up. Somewhere behind us there are gunshots. I use the fear they bring to keep my feet moving.

Four miles left.

The fence lines have narrowed so that there is only about ten yards of space on either side of the road between them. There is no sign of Will or his skimmer. I know I injured him, but it must not have been enough to stop him. Unless . . . Could he be well enough to lurk near the completion mark, waiting to finish what he started?

Three miles.

I ask Tomas if he can balance on the bicycle without hanging on to my waist. When he agrees to try, I unfasten the rope and stand to apply more force with each push.

Two miles.

Tomas starts to lose his balance, and I sit back down. I reattach the rope and keep pedaling.

One mile.

I see purple and red in the distance. Testing officials are waiting for us. The end. They have to be standing at the end. Behind the people the buildings of Tosu City sparkle and shimmer as they climb into the sky. Tomas's head slumps against my back. I feel his weight pull against the rope, but I can't stop. If I do, I might never get him back onto the bicycle. I doubt he could survive me dragging him to the end.

With one hand, I balance Tomas's unconscious body as I use my other to steer. My arm, my muscles, every part of me is on fire. But I won't give in to the pain or the fatigue. My feet keep moving. The people in the distance come into focus. I see smiles. A few concerned expressions. They all stand behind a white line. The finish line.

I ignore the people and focus on the line. I will it to come closer as I push my feet over and over again. We are so close when I feel Tomas slide to the left. My injured arm doesn't have the strength to catch him and pull him upright. Because we are strapped together, his momentum pulls me off the seat and we crash together to the ground. I hear gasps. A few cries of worry. I see Dr. Barnes standing at the front of the group, wearing an expression of mild interest. Not one person comes to our aid. The white line is less than fifty feet away, and from their place behind it the Testing officials stand and watch.

I know I am tired and scared and in pain, but at this moment all I can feel is rage. It is white and hot and powerful. I look at each face and vow to make them pay for Ryme and Malachi and all the others. For the girl whose name I don't know but whose body I buried. For the watchers who were gunned down without provocation. And for Tomas and these fifty lousy feet that are so damn important to the Testing officials that they would watch him die after all he has survived.

I untie the rope and push myself off the ground. Carefully, I unstrap the bags from the rack, sling them both over my shoulder, and on shaking legs walk over to Tomas. I refuse to look at our audience as I roll him onto his back. He moans as I slide my hands under him. The sound tells me he is alive. I plan to keep him that way as I grab his arms and pull. I lean backwards to use my weight as leverage. Inch by impossibly slow inch I slide him, my eyes fixed on the hard black pavement. Twice I have to put him down to catch my breath. When I look up, I see another Testing candidate appear on the distant horizon. The sight urges me on.

And then I see it. A solid snow-white line slashing across the black of the asphalt. The finish line. One last pull. I watch Tomas's feet cross the threshold and sink to the ground next to him as Dr. Barnes's smooth voice says, "Congratulations, Malencia Vale. You and Tomas Endress have passed the fourth test."

CHAPTER 20

One hundred and eight candidates entered the Testing Center in hopes of attending the University. Today twenty-nine of us sit in the dining room, although the whispers we hear in the halls tell us there is still a chance more will arrive.

Testing officials tell me it has been nine days since I crossed the white line and passed the fourth test. I've been unconscious for most of those days. Turns out, the poison in my arm put me in far more danger than I realized. Had I not squeezed most of the toxin out of the wound, I would be dead now. As it was, it took the doctors several hours to determine whether the medications they pumped into me would clear the remaining poison from my system. An accelerated healing tool helped close the wound, but the damage the contamination caused to the tissue prevented the tool from also removing the scars. I will be forever marked by The Testing, as if that was ever in doubt.

Tomas fared better with his wounds. Whatever medical advancements they used left him free from scars. Although, from the way he and Will look at each other, I wonder if more scars aren't inevitable. I'm thankful Testing protocol dictates that all weapons be removed from the candidates' possession immediately after the completion of the fourth test. This rule is the only reason I can close my eyes at night.

I see Will's eyes following me from across the room. When he notices me watching him, he gives me a smile and winks. He's seated with a group of candidates, most of whom I've never spoken to. One is Brick. He has yet to speak to me and I am glad because I am not sure I could speak without seeing the massacre he wrought in my name. I wonder if he understands that the lives he took were human and if their bloody faces haunt his dreams the way they do mine.

On the other side of the room is Stacia. Her face is just as unreadable as it was during the test. She doesn't sit with her travel companion, Vic, but instead is seated alone. Redheaded Vic is seated far across the room. Tracelyn, the girl who missed her boyfriend and so badly wanted to be a teacher, is nowhere to be found. I can only guess that whatever happened to her is the reason for the haunted look in Vic's eyes and the knowing smile on Stacia's lips.

Tomas and I do not talk to the others as we wait for the fourth test to end and the final interviews to begin. We spend mealtimes together and, when allowed, walk the grounds outside. In between talk of home, Tomas whispers in my ear that he might have found a way to retain our memories. While he was in the hospital, he overheard his doctors talking to a Testing official about the medication he and some of the other wounded candidates were taking. The Testing official was concerned because the medication had been known to interfere with the upcoming Testing procedures. He insisted Tomas and the others be strictly monitored so their systems will be clear of the drugs by the time the final University selections are made.

"They thought I was sleeping. The next time the nurses brought my medication, I pretended to take it. I managed to save one of my pills. I'm going to try to get a few more during the next couple medical checks. Some of the nurses are more easily distracted than others. It'll depend on which ones I get."

I'm not surprised that Tomas's dimpled smile and clear gray eyes could distract the nurses from their duties. His kisses are certainly a distraction to me. Over the next two days, Tomas adds one more pill to his stash and five more candidates cross the white finish line. Each time one walks in, I feel my heart lift—hoping the last of the Five Lakes candidates has made it back. But it is never Zandri's face in the doorway. And when an announcement comes during dinner, telling us interviews will begin tomorrow, I know she won't be returning.

That night Zandri joins the cast of my nightmares. Her blond hair is spread out on the cracked brown earth. Her mouth open with surprise as birds peck away pieces of her eyes.

My eyes snap open as I bite back a scream. It takes me several minutes to realize I'm in the Testing Center. No longer on the plains. No longer in danger. Then I remember.

The interviews are today. The danger is far from over.

I stare at the ceiling, holding my Testing bag until dawn breaks. Without a roommate, I don't need to sleep with the bag, but old habits die hard. When light streams through the window, I slide my legs over the edge of the bed and head to the bathroom. I take a shower and then dig through the pocket of the pants I wore yesterday. My fingers close over the vial containing the liquid I was instructed to drink before my interview. As promised, it was among my possessions when I was released from the medical facility.

Sitting on the floor, I roll the vial between my fingers and think back to the gray-haired man's words.

Before the interview begins, they will give you a drug to encourage you to answer the questions honestly, without holding back anything you wish to keep secret.

I said then that I had nothing to hide, but I was wrong. While I personally might not be in danger from my answers, others could be. If Testing officials ask about my father, Zeen, or our former teacher there is a chance my answers could betray or condemn. If this vial offers a chance at keeping them safe, I have to take it. Unless, of course, I believe Dr. Barnes and his Testing officials planted this drug in my hands as one more test? Will consuming it be punishable by illness or death? I wouldn't put it past them. I have a choice to make. Do I drink the liquid or leave it untouched?

By the time the loudspeaker announces breakfast, I have yet to make a decision. But one will be required of me and fast. Soon they will wonder why I haven't left my room and ask questions I can ill afford to answer. I have to decide what I believe.

I unstop the vial, then drink the contents. My family's safety comes first. If this is the wrong answer, I will know soon enough. Grabbing my bag, I climb to my feet and head toward whatever the day will bring. For good or for ill, The Testing will end today.

Breakfast is a rowdy affair. Most candidates sit together in the middle of the dining hall as though proving they have nothing to fear from the evaluations. Will is in the center of the group, cracking jokes. He stops to watch as I walk by, take a table in the back, and wait for Tomas.

Nibbling on a piece of bread, I wait to feel the effects of the drug. I don't notice Will until I hear a chair scraping the floor across from me and see him drop into it.

He takes a bite of an apple and considers me across the table. "I thought you'd like to know I almost died. The last shot you fired burst my appendix. Good thing I don't really need it to live. Otherwise, I wouldn't be here." When I don't respond, his smile disappears. "Okay, I know this probably sounds stupid, but I'm glad I didn't end up killing you like I planned."

"You're right. It does sound stupid." And because I can't help myself, I say, "I trusted you."

"Yeah. That's your Achilles' heel. Leaders are supposed to inspire trust. They're not supposed to actually believe in it."

"You trusted Gill."

Pain flashes deep in his eyes. Then it is gone, replaced by a nasty grin. "My Achilles' heel. After he left, I couldn't focus on the second round of tests. They'll call me out on that in my interview, but I think I demonstrated in the third and fourth rounds that I have an ability to focus on the goal."

"Zandri didn't mention you doing anything in the third round."

Will laughed. "That's because she went first. It wasn't until you came out and mentioned Roman's trick with your group that she started to put the pieces together. When the third test ended and none of the other members of our group returned, Zandri realized what I'd done."

I stare at Will as his confession sinks in. Will made the same choice Roman did—to betray his teammates and eliminate the competition. I should have realized this, but I had been so distracted waiting for Brick to return that I hadn't paid enough attention to my friends. If I had, Tomas would never have been shot. Then again, without Will, Tomas and I might never have survived our encounter with Roman.

"I thought you were a nice guy, Will."

"I am a nice guy." He laughs.

"Nice guys don't kill."

"Killing was the easy part. Kind of like killing a wolf back home. You just aim and fire and your problem is solved."

"You think it's that easy?" Bile rises fast and hot in my throat. "The blond girl you killed with your crossbow wasn't an animal. She had a family. Friends. People who loved her. She was trying to survive the test as best she could. Just like you."

I wait for him to defend his actions. Tell me how it was all necessary. His choice to get a spot at the University.

Instead, Will lowers his voice and says, "Her name was Nina. She was from Pierre Colony. One of the girls who made it to the end went to school with her."

"Nina." I think about her bracelet in my bag and am happy to have this piece of information. Knowing her name doesn't make her any less dead, but it matters to me.

Will nods. "And no. You're right. It's not that easy. The act of killing is simple. Living with it . . ." He looks off beyond me and sighs. "Well, maybe that's what the whole test is really about. Leaders are forced to kill all the time. Then they have to learn to live with the decisions they make. Just like I'm going to learn to live with mine."

"You really think that was the point of the fourth test? To learn if you could kill and live with it?"

He shrugs. "I guess we're going to find out. Right?"

I think about Stacia's words that so closely echoed Will's and then of Dr. Barnes, who watched Ryme's body being cut down while believing it was for the best that she died. And I'm scared Will's right. That killing and learning to live with it was the point. Since I, too, have killed I do not have to worry about meeting the criteria. But I am no longer certain I want to be a leader. Not if my country values murder above compassion.

I see movement near the dining hall entrance, glance up, and, for the first time today, smile. Tomas. His jaw clenches as he spots Will, but he doesn't come right over. Instead, he grabs a plate and fills it. If Will is smart, he'll get lost before Tomas arrives.

Will follows my glance and groans. "I should have known you'd find a way to save him like you saved me. For the record, I'm not so happy to see him alive. No offense." He leans forward and adds, "I hate to say it, but he still doesn't deserve your trust, Cia. Or your love. Hell . . ." He looks around the room before his eyes settle back on me. "None of us does."

Before Tomas can reach the table, Will gets up, gives me another one of his winks, and heads off to rejoin the group.

Tomas sets his plate next to mine, but his eyes are focused on Will. "What did he want?"

Good question. One I'm not sure I can answer. But I try.

"To tell me he's glad I'm alive. He's not so happy to see you, though."

A smile crosses Tomas's lips. "Well, isn't that too bad? Because I plan on staying here for a really long time."

"I for one am happy to hear that."

"I kind of hoped you would be." He looks around the room at the kids laughing and asks, "Are you ready for the interview?"

I hear Will's laughter ring through the hall and wonder if he was right about what the Testers are looking for. Shaking off the worry, I say, "It's just answering a few questions. After everything else, how hard can that be?"

"Good morning." Dr. Barnes smiles at us from the lecture hall stage. "Congratulations on passing all four tests. I cannot tell you how impressed we are by your intelligence, your resourcefulness, and your dedication. During the fourth exam you had a chance to see beyond the borders of your revitalized colonies and witness firsthand the challenges our leaders face. The tests we put before you were challenging and the consequences for failure high, but the challenges and consequences that our leaders face are higher still. We know what we have asked of you, and we are delighted so many more of you than expected have made it this far."

I think of how small a group we are compared to when we started. It makes me wonder how few must have survived in years past for Dr. Barnes to expect less.

"Of course, you are all wondering about today's interview. I'm happy to tell you that the interviews will be short and relatively simple. Thus far you have demonstrated your intellect and your ability to strategize. You've shown us your ability to survive under strenuous conditions and problem-solve when things have gone awry. We know you are smart. Now we would like to know more about you the person. We are going to ask questions about you, your family, and your colony as well as the decisions you've made during your time here at The Testing. Please be honest and open. In essence, we are asking you to just be yourself. Nothing you say will be wrong, unless, of course, it is a lie. As members of the United Commonwealth, we ask that our leaders be honest and forthright. Today, we ask the same courtesy of you."

I can't help but wonder how they will enforce this rule and what punishment will occur if we are not completely honest.

Dr. Barnes, however, has moved from that point on to the rest of the instructions. "Each of you will be interviewed by a panel of five Testing officials. Each evaluation can last as long as forty-five minutes. Please do not read anything into the time we take to question you. When your evaluation is over, you will be escorted back to your designated sleeping quarters to wait for the results. I warn you—our decision making might take a great deal of time. We ask that you be patient as we work to select those we feel are the very best candidates for the University. Some of us are known to be stubborn."

He gives us one last warm smile. "The best of luck to each one of you. I look forward to working with many of you when you attend the University next year. I know we are going to do great things together."

Dr. Barnes exits the hall and a gray-haired woman in a blood-red jumpsuit takes the stage. "When your name is called, please stand and exit into the hallway. From there, a Testing official will escort you to your evaluation room."

"Victor Josslim."

Red-haired Vic climbs to his feet. He keeps his head down as he walks out. I can't help but notice how thin and pale he looks compared to the boy I met a week into the fourth test. He's changed. We all have. And as more names are called, I hold tight to Tomas's hand and wonder if that isn't why the Testers remove our memories. To turn back the clock. To turn us back into the kids who optimistically came here believing they could change the world.

I feel Tomas stiffen as his name is spoken. My lips brush his cheek for luck and then he is gone and I am left to wait for my name to be called. And that's when I remember. Tomas has the pills. Both of them. Our one chance at keeping our memories of The Testing alive if we make it through the interview. I can only hope the Testing officials will allow us to see each other again before our memories are altered. If not, I hope Tomas will take them and remember for both of us.

One by one the room empties. I try to sit still, but I can't help fidgeting as I think about the questions the Testers will ask and wonder what kinds of answers they're looking for. Dr. Barnes said no answer we give will be wrong, but I know that isn't true. Fourteen more candidates will be eliminated during this phase. The Testing committee has to be looking for something specific. I just wish I knew what it is.

"Malencia Vale."

My legs are uncertain as I stand and walk to the hallway. My heart thunders in my chest. I repeat Dr. Barnes's words "just be yourself" in my head as I follow a Testing official to a doorway at the end of the hallway. He asks me to wait for a moment and slips through the door. Inside is the murmur of voices. I bite the edge of my thumbnail and stifle the urge to pace off the nervous energy building inside me.

After several minutes, the door swings open and a voice says, “Please come in.”

Just be yourself, I think as I take a step across the threshold. But instead of calming me, the words make my heart pound harder. Because I’m not sure I know how to do that. I’m no longer the girl who left Five Lakes Colony, who believed that Graduation Day actually made a child into an adult. I certainly wasn’t an adult then, and now . . .

After everything I have seen and done, I’m forced to admit I don’t know exactly who I am. But I know I need to find out fast because this final interview requires that I show them. And that test has just begun.

CHAPTER 21

The room is small and white. White walls. White floors. No windows. A long black table sits along one side of the room with five Testing officials seated behind it. Two in red. Two in purple. And Dr. Barnes beckoning me farther inside.

"Please, come on in, Cia. Take a seat."

In the middle of the room is a single black chair that faces the Testing officials. Next to it is a small black table and a glass of clear liquid.

"Please have a drink."

All eyes follow me as I cross the room and take my seat. Dr. Barnes nods as I pick up the glass, making it clear the polite request is an order. There is no choice but to drink whatever the glass contains.

Water. Perhaps something else. There is a metallic aftertaste along with something slightly bitter. Almost immediately I notice the tension leaching out of my muscles. After being on my guard for so long, the relaxation in my limbs feels wonderful. I find myself smiling and decide there is more than just a muscle relaxant in the mix. Whatever else they gave me must cause euphoria and an overwhelming sense of well-being.

"Truth serum." The words are out of my mouth the moment I think them.

Dr. Barnes nods. "So far today, you're the first candidate to pick up on that without my telling them."

"Or maybe they were too scared to mention they noticed." Again, the words are gone before I think to control them.

Dr. Barnes laughs. "That is certainly a possibility. That's why we give you the drug. It is designed to help your mind and your body relax. We know how stressful this process is. We don't want the tension to interfere in our getting to know the real you."

The haze of euphoria clears, and this time I think before admitting, "I'm not sure I know who the real me is."

"That's what we are here to find out. Tell us about your family, Cia."

My family. I take a deep breath and carefully consider my answer. That I can stop and think before speaking makes me believe the liquid in the vial has counteracted the worst of the truth serum. Now I need to give them the answer they're looking for. They must already know about my parents and my brothers. So what do they want to hear?

I decide to keep it simple. I list my family members. The other Testing officials ask a couple of questions about Five Lakes Colony, and I answer them as best I can. Their questions focus mostly around my father—what he taught me, what he told me about his Testing experience. I admit that he told me he remembered very little. "But he did warn me some of the other candidates would be very competitive."

They ask follow-up questions, and though my muscles are loosened, my mind stays alert enough for me to avoid answers that could put my family in jeopardy. When Dr. Barnes mentions he has heard that my oldest brother has spearheaded several projects for my father and asks me whether I think he should have been tested for the University, I do not hesitate. I lie.

"My father tries to give all of his workers credit for projects they work on whether they deserve it or not. I love Zeen a lot, but his work is sloppy and doesn't merit the credit it receives."

I am relieved to navigate this pitfall when the next opens up in front of me. This time they ask about my father. Did he want his children to follow in his footsteps? Was he excited I was chosen? I keep my answers simple and upbeat. No mention of my father's dreams or his unhappiness at my candidacy. Nothing to cause Tosu officials to think twice about my father's memories of his time in The Testing.

The questions shift to The Testing itself.

Why did I alert Brick to what I believed was Roman's deception?

To do less would make me a poor teammate.

What was my reasoning behind burying the unknown testing candidate?

My parents taught me to treat life with respect.

Did I come in contact with people from outside the Testing barriers?

No.

How do I feel about my decision to trust Will?

Trusting Will was a poor choice. I will choose more wisely in the future.

As I answer, I am constantly aware of Dr. Barnes's eyes studying me, weighing every word.

When he finally speaks again he asks, "Tell us about your relationship with Tomas Endress."

The question surprises me. Carefully, I answer, "The two of us are close friends. He says he loves me, but I think that's because I remind him of home."

"Surely you feel more than friendship for Mr. Endress. Why else would you have risked your life by taking the time to save his?"

I bite my lip and try to decide what Dr. Barnes wants to hear. Finally, I say, "My family taught me to help others at all costs. It's the Five Lakes Colony way."

Dr. Barnes leans forward. "Do you think taking time to rework your bicycle in order to save his life was a smart decision?"

"It worked," I answer. "We're both alive."

"Yes. You are." He smiles. "But I'm concerned you might be too emotionally attached to candidate Endress."

The benign tone cannot mask the menace behind the words. Even the Testing officials flanking Dr. Barnes shift uncomfortably in their seats. The silence stretches between us, making it hard to breathe. It must be my turn to say something, but no question has been asked—and without knowing what he is asking, I cannot hope to answer correctly. And something tells me this answer is the most important of them all.

Finally, when the silence becomes unbearable, I admit, "I don't understand."

"Emotional entanglements can be challenging in these kinds of situations. For instance, what will happen if you are accepted to the University and he is not?"

My heart thunders. "I will be pleased for myself and disappointed the Testing committee didn't recognize Tomas's potential. He's smart and resourceful. The United Commonwealth would benefit from having him attend the University."

"Should we be concerned that your disappointment could impact your performance at the University?"

How to answer the question? My mind races. Whatever I say will not only impact my life, but affect Tomas, too. To say I am going to be indifferent will be a lie they can easily identify. After all, as Dr. Barnes pointed out, I did save Tomas's life at the risk of my own. The truth serum they gave me is supposed to render lies impossible. If I answer with an obvious lie now they will know something has gone amiss and wonder why. I resist the urge to wipe my sweaty palms on my pants and force my mind to focus.

There is only one answer I can come up with. "All leaders have to live with disappointment at some point or another. If I have to learn that lesson early, I won't enjoy it, but I will do my best not to let you down."

The other Testing officials look at one another as I wait for whatever else Dr. Barnes has in store. He rolls a pencil back and forth on the table in front of him as he studies me. I remain still and meet his stare with one of my own. Someone in the room coughs. Another clears her throat. Those are the only sounds as the minutes tick away.

Finally, Dr. Barnes says, "I think we've gotten all the information we need. Unless any of my colleagues have something to ask?"

Every head behind the table shakes from side to side, flooding me with confusion. Dr. Barnes told us the evaluations could take forty-five minutes. I doubt twenty minutes have passed since I walked into this room. They never asked about my performance in the first two tests and only asked a handful of questions about test number four. Does their disinterest mean I've failed? It must, because they are pushing back their chairs. I want to ask them to wait. To explain that people who elicit trust only to betray should not be leaders. To tell them that while I am no longer the same girl who dreamed of coming to Tosu City, I am someone who should be selected for the University. Not because I want to be a part of this system. I don't think I do. Not anymore. But because I want the chance to live.

Before I can speak, Dr. Barnes says, "Before you go, I should ask if you have any questions for us."

This is my chance to impress them. This is the time to ask something that will show the depth of my observational skills or demonstrate my ability to think on my feet. But while I know that this is my chance to shine, the temptation to fill one important blank is too great. Maybe it was talking about Five Lakes Colony and our tight-knit community or maybe it was learning Will took the time to discover the name of the girl he killed. While the chances are slim, someday I might go home. If the pills Tomas has sneaked from the hospital help me retain my memory, I will be able to tell Malachi's family about his time at The Testing. I will be able to tell them how he died. Zandri deserves no less.

So instead of discussing the fields of study or questioning what my life will be like while attending the University, I ask, "What happened to Zandri Hicks during the last test? How did she die?"

A ghost of a smile plays on Dr. Barnes's lips, and he lets out a small laugh. "And here I thought you had that figured out. Perhaps the answer will come to you after this interview is over. After all, you do have her identification bracelet in your bag." He checks his watch and sighs. "And with that, this interview is at an end. Congratulations on making it this far in the process, Cia. It has been a pleasure to watch you perform."

I'm escorted out of the room before I can ask what he means about Zandri and her bracelet. My legs threaten to buckle as the official leads me down the hall. This must be a typical response either to the drug or the stress, because the Testing official puts an arm around my waist as he leads me back to my designated sleeping quarters. And then he is gone, leaving me alone with my worry of failure and Dr. Barnes's parting words to keep me company.

Zandri.

Dr. Barnes thought I already knew what happened to her. How could I? I never once saw her on the Testing plains. There is no way I could have ended up with her identification bracelet.

Upending my bag on the bed, I search for clues to what I'm supposed to have learned already. There are my clothes, the Transit Communicator, my pocketknife. There is a fragment of white sheet lodged in the corner of my bag. But all other evidence that the fourth test ever took place is gone. Except for three small identification bracelets that rest in the side pocket.

My fingers outline the design on the first. The triangle with an eight-spoked wheel I took from the girl we buried. The girl Will killed with his crossbow. The girl I now have a name for—Nina. A girl from Pierre Colony who came here to take a test and was murdered by the United Commonwealth. Will might have pulled the trigger, but the Testing officials allowed it to happen. Over the years, how many other candidates have murdered to keep themselves alive? And how many more have died to help the Testers pass judgment on the merits of the candidates?

The thought makes me angry. So much so that it takes me a while to remember the two other bracelets in my bag. One of which Dr. Barnes claims is the answer to my question. I put Nina's bracelet to the side and study the other two. The first displays Roman's symbol—an X surrounded by a circle. On the other, smaller bracelet is a triangle with a stylized flower. I think back to our ride to Tosu City. Zandri was flirting with Tomas while her fingers toyed with her bracelet. A bracelet with this design. A bracelet I don't remember picking up. Where did it come from?

I think through the events of the fourth test day by day. The run through the wreckage that was once Chicago. The beautiful, booby-trapped oasis. Nina's sightless corpse. The hulking, wolflike animals giving chase. Meeting Stacia, Vic, and Tracelyn. The city with its domed building and mazelike streets. The stream where I was forced to kill. Will. Brick's bullets tearing the mutated humans to shreds. Roman's attack. The girl firing at us so near the end. Will shooting Tomas. My desperate attempt to alter the bicycle to get him back to Tosu City. The ride.

Wait. My fingers worry away at the sides of Zandri's bracelet as a memory hits. A memory so unimportant next to Will's betrayal or Tomas's wound emptying his blood onto the soil. I needed matches, so I searched Tomas's bag in the dark and found a metal object. An object I believed to be Nina's other bracelet that Tomas must have taken as a remembrance just as I had done.

Only, I was wrong. The bracelet belonged to Zandri.

How did it end up in Tomas's bag?

Of the three and a half weeks it took to complete the fourth test, Tomas and I were together for all but a day and a half. Could he have picked up the bracelet while wandering the streets of Chicago? If so, why didn't he tell me? Did he not want me to know that Zandri had failed the test so soon after it began? Did he fear that I would believe failure was inevitable?

Maybe. Tomas would have worried for me. He would have wanted to keep me focused and safe. But I am not sure this is the answer. There was one other time Tomas and I were separated. And I know.

The bracelet.

The dried blood on Tomas's knife.

The haunted look in his eyes.

Will's words that Tomas is not who I think he is.

The candidate that Will and Tomas met while I was gone. Not some unnamed male from Colorado Springs Colony.

Zandri.

The pieces click together with a force that knocks the air

from my lungs. I can't move. I can't breathe. I can only clutch the bracelet that belonged to the beautiful girl whose talent everyone from Five Lakes Colony admired. The girl who flirted with Tomas. The girl he must have killed.

No. My heart doesn't want to believe it. Tomas wouldn't kill anyone. Not unless he didn't have a choice. I left Will and Tomas together. Isn't it more likely that Will, a proven killer, was the one to murder Zandri? Maybe there was some kind of altercation. Maybe . . .

The possibilities jumble. The combination of drugs in my system is making it hard for me to think clearly. I get up and walk the length of the room, staring at the bracelet in my hand, trying to uncover the truth behind it. As much as my heart wants to think Tomas had nothing to do with Zandri's murder, his unwillingness to share what happened on that day makes it hard to believe otherwise.

Betrayal and fear, anger and heartbreak. The emotions hit hard and fast, buckling my knees, sending me to the floor. But I refuse to cry. The camera is still in the ceiling, and I will not give Dr. Barnes and the officials behind the screen the satisfaction of seeing me break. And, really, aren't they the ones to blame for Zandri's death? They put us in their game and asked us to survive. Whatever Tomas did, I am certain he didn't do it to win a place on the University roster. He must have thought his life was in jeopardy.

I jump at a knock on the door. When I open it, I am handed a large tray of food and told the committee is still deliberating. The Testing official leaves, and I hear the sound of the lock sliding into place. And I wait.

The meal is extravagant. A large steak charred on the outside but pink and oozing with juices in the middle. There are slices of potato—the version Zeen created—with the skin still on, fried to a golden brown. Cold shrimp is served with tiny slices of lime and a small dish of melted butter. A salad of fresh vegetables and walnuts is tossed with something tangy and sweet. A frosty glass is filled with something clear and bubbly. There is also a clear bottle of water and a piece of cake.

This is a meal meant to celebrate making it this far in The Testing. Never have I felt less like celebrating.

The camera above makes me cut the steak. I'm certain it is delicious, but it is all I can do to chew and swallow without gagging. I take a drink of the bubbly liquid and immediately put the glass down. Alcohol. The same drink Zeen brought to cheer me on graduation night. Then the drink tasted bitter with disappointment. Today it tastes of home.

I drink the water and take tiny sips of the alcohol to keep Zeen close. I eat bits of the salad, but ignore the cake. The idea of celebrating while Zandri's identification bracelet sits in my hand is enough to make me ill. The passage of time is marked by the setting of the sun. I watch as the last rays disappear and wonder if the decision will be made before tomorrow's sunset.

An official collects the dinner tray. Once again I hear the loud turn of the lock. With nothing but the moon to keep me company, the minutes drag by. I think about Zandri and Malachi. I analyze every moment of my interview, turning each word over for some clue as to whether I have passed or failed. I fall asleep curled around my Testing bag.

The dawn brings a new tray. No decision has been made. The Testing official tells me to be patient before leaving me alone to pace the floor.

Trays come. Trays are taken away. No news.

I relive my days in The Testing, looking for clues as to what could have propelled Tomas to take Zandri's life, and find nothing. While Zandri was brash and headstrong, I can't imagine her attacking Will or Tomas. She was friends with Tomas. She might have even loved him a little. And now she's dead. Tortured by my waking thoughts, I try to lose myself in sleep, but find Dr. Barnes and the Testing officials waiting for me there, too. One by one they evaluate the performance of the dead candidates.

Ryme. Nina. Malachi. Boyd. Gill. Annalise. Nicolette. Roman. Zandri.

A pile of bodies lies in the corner when the evaluators turn to me. Dr. Barnes shakes his head. He tells me I showed great promise. It's too bad I trusted the wrong people. Leaders cannot afford that mistake. He tells me I failed as another Testing official pulls out a crossbow, takes aim, and fires. The quarrel punches through my stomach, and I scream myself awake before I hit the floor.

Locked in a room with no human contact other than the official who brings my meals, I feel the tension gnawing at me. I pace for hours and then sit for hours more and stare at the walls, willing a decision to be made. But no decision is forthcoming, and a small part of me wonders if this waiting is also a test. Are Dr. Barnes and his friends sitting behind their screens, watching to see how we handle it? Do other candidates pace as I do? Are my nightmares a strike against me or does uninterrupted sleep show an undesirable streak of indifference?

I stare at the camera above, not caring if the officials see that I know it is there. Or maybe I want them to know. To see

I am smart enough to figure out that they are watching. As sleep eludes me, I think about the candidates who have died, and the memory wipe that is coming if we cannot outsmart it, and wonder for the first time if the candidates who failed the first two rounds of Testing were eliminated or if the Commonwealth simply erased any memory of this experience. Over the past one hundred years, the United Commonwealth population has grown, but has it grown enough to eliminate dozens of its most promising citizens every year? And if those candidates aren't eliminated, where do they go?

After the morning tray has come and gone, I tire of the eyes that follow me and the ears listening to my awakening screams. Giving my audience behind the camera a small smile, I probe my bracelet, find the clasp and watch it fall from my wrist onto the bed alongside those that belonged to Zandri and Nina. I remove the second bracelet from my bag, place it with the others, then I take my bag and lock myself in the bathroom.

The feeling of being alone—really alone—eases some of the tension from my shoulders. I take a shower. I curl up on the floor and nap. With nothing else to do, I go through the items in my Testing bag. These are things I brought from home. Things my mother sewed. My father touched. My brothers worked with. Things that helped define who I used to be. No longer afraid of being judged by the cameras, I allow my tears to fall as I touch each one and hold it to my cheek, trying to recapture the person who first packed this bag. I miss the hope she felt. The optimism. The brightness of the future in front of her. If Tomas's pills don't work, will taking away the memories of The Testing bring her back? Can losing my memories truly wipe the shadow from my heart?

Maybe, and for a moment I allow myself to yearn for that blissful ignorance. Dreams filled with peace. A future free of too much knowledge.

I jump at the sound of a male voice and turn to see where it is coming from. It takes me a minute to realize the voice is speaking from the device clutched tight in my hands.

"The soil in sector four is showing signs of sustaining life, and the radiation levels are almost nonexistent. The new formula appears to be working."

Zeen. His voice is strong and healthy and so wonderfully familiar. I ache, hearing the sound of it. I must have hit a button that started a playback of Zeen's voice. The Transit Communicator is also a recorder.

"Tell Dad there are sick animals in sector seven. Might be from the new berries we cultivated there. We should run tests."

I remember hearing about that problem over dinner—a week or maybe two before my graduation. They argued, laughed, and debated the problem long into the night, even allowing me to add a few thoughts of my own. I felt so grown-up to be included. So ready to take on the world. How silly that seems now.

For a while I am content to listen to Zeen's voice as he records his thoughts on the sections outside of Five Lakes that my father and his team are working to revitalize. A disgruntled word makes me laugh. Mentions of Dad or my other brothers cause tears. And I wonder—how does the recorder work? I know the device can communicate with the one Dad has in his office, but I've never heard Dad mention that it doubles as a recorder.

It takes me a while to find the button. A small area in the

back that looks to be a part of the casing but has been turned into something more. Something not originally designed to be a part of the device. Something created by Zeen.

The screwdriver on my pocketknife helps me reveal the rest of his handiwork. I can't help smiling as I admire my brother's ingenuity. A tiny black box has been nestled among the other wires and chips. By the way he spliced and connected the wires, I can see how he rigged the communication microphone to record voices and the earpiece to act as the playback speaker. All of it is done with seamless precision. Had I not squeezed so hard and mistakenly triggered the playback button on the back, I would never have recognized the recording device was there.

A knock startles me. Carefully, I slide the items into my Testing bag, go into the darkened bedroom, and open the door. The woman on the other side is holding a tray and wears a concerned expression. "Is everything okay in here?" she asks.

I guess my disappearance into the bathroom has not gone unnoticed.

"I'm fine," I assure her, but from the commotion coming from down the hall, I fear someone else is not. Has one of the candidates ended the tension like Ryme did? Though I should no longer care, I worry for Tomas. I can't help it. No matter how The Testing has changed him, he will always be the boy from home who was kind to everyone. I want him to live.

The Testing official hands me the lunch tray, tells me no decision has been made, and locks the door. For the first time, I don't mind the solitude. I eat the chicken swimming in a delicate tomato sauce and the fresh vegetables before once again closing myself off in the bathroom.

For a while I take comfort in my brother's voice as he lists the day-to-day tasks that need addressing. But the reality that another candidate may have died soon has me pacing the floor. Perhaps I should see it as one less candidate standing in my way to the ultimate goal. But I can't. To me it is one more promising mind whose fate will soon be forgotten. Like the others who will be forgotten. Unless someone remembers. If the United Commonwealth and the Testing officials have their way, no one will. At least no one who cares.

I look at the device in my hands and have an idea. It takes me a few minutes to figure out which series of buttons starts the recording device. Once I do, I begin to talk. In a quiet and often unsteady voice I remember Malachi. His smile. His shy demeanor. His sweet singing voice and his death. Ryme. Her corncakes. Her cocky attitude. Finding her hanging from the ceiling in our room. The first of the Testing murders. I tell of waking up in the box. Walking out onto the broken streets of Chicago. The crossbow quarrel aimed at me. My terror. How the gun kicked in my hand.

I find the recording device can only record so much. I have to pick and choose what I tell. I agonize over which memories to preserve. It breaks my heart when I have to rewind and erase a story to preserve a different one. They all deserve to be remembered, but only a few can. More than once my tears force me to stop the recording. My heart stings. My lungs burn and my throat is raw when the recorder is full. But the memories are there. As much as the machine will hold. For someone to learn and remember.

Will they send the device back to my parents if my candidacy is unsuccessful? I doubt it. But maybe I can ask Michal to get it to them if I'm gone.

With my pocketknife, I etch a small design in the back of the device before shoving it in my bag. I then pile my clothes and other belongings on top and wash the evidence of my efforts from my face. When the Testing official brings dinner, she again asks after my welfare. I assure her I am fine and take the tray. Before she closes the door she says, "A decision has been made. The next class of University students will be announced after breakfast."

Pass or fail, this will all end tomorrow.

CHAPTER 22

For the first time in weeks, there are no nightmares. Just dreams of home and a sense of peace and relief that this all will end soon. The knock at the door wakes me. A new tray with a request that I be dressed and packed in an hour. Someone will come for me.

I pick at the meal. Fresh strawberries. A thick, hot grain sweetened with raisins and walnuts. Tangy orange juice. Rolls thick with cinnamon icing. I try to enjoy it all, but a nervous tension begins to push aside my newfound well-being and I can eat only a few bites.

I fasten the clasp of my identification bracelet around my wrist. The second bracelet I place back on the strap of my bag. I think of my father and how he must have felt while preparing for his verdict. And I wait wondering if I will see Tomas before the officials remove our memories. Will he be able to pass me one of the pills? Will he see my newfound suspicions in my eyes?

When the knock comes, I am ready. Bag over my shoulder, I follow the dark-haired woman down the hallway. The small meal I consumed rolls in my stomach as we enter the elevator and ride in silence to the second floor. My escort's expression stays neutral. No smile. No look of warning. Nothing to give away the fate that has been determined for me.

The door at the end of the brightly lit hallway is open and my Testing official tells me to go inside. They are waiting.

I shove my hands in my pockets to keep them from trembling and walk inside the large room with my escort trailing behind me. There are at least a dozen Testing officials seated behind a large table. Dr. Barnes sits at the center. A small white envelope is on the table in front of him. His expression is unreadable as I walk to a solitary chair placed in front of the table.

As I sit, Dr. Barnes gives me a warm smile. "I'm sorry you had to wait so long for us to make a decision, but we wanted to get it right." Slowly, he takes the envelope, walks around the table, and comes to a stop in front of me. My heart thunders as he says, "I'm sure you're anxious to receive the results of your Testing, so I won't delay any further."

He lifts the envelope flap and pulls out a white sheet of paper. He stares at it for a moment as though weighing the judgment before handing it to me. My fingers fumble with the paper. It takes me several tries before I can read the single word printed in bold black print in the center.

Pass

I did it.

A smile crosses my face, and my heart skips. I hear murmurs of congratulations from the officials in the room. Dr. Barnes tells me how proud he is and shakes my hand. Then something pinches my neck and the world goes black.

I failed.

My fingers trace the five lines etched in my left arm as I study them in the reflector of my University student quarters. Three rooms—bedroom, living space, and bathroom—that have been assigned to me for the first phase of my studies. Signs that I passed my Testing. The most important achievement of my life. And yet, I remember none of it.

I must have tried to avoid the memory loss. And still I failed. All I remember is the trip to Tosu City in the black skimmer. A scruffy, mean-eyed boy tripping Malachi. My roommate and her corncakes. And then nothing until the moment when I find myself in a room sitting among what I can only assume are other Testing candidates. My eyes fly around the room, looking for familiar faces, as a gray-haired, bearded man in a purple jumpsuit climbs onto a lit stage. He gives us all a warm, delighted smile and says, "Congratulations. I am happy to say you are the twenty candidates who have been chosen to attend the University next year."

Surprise. Delight. Confusion. And then understanding. The Testing is over. I passed. Dr. Barnes tells us we will be moved from the Testing Center into our new living quarters as soon as the meeting is over. There will be a celebration afterward so we can get to know one another. But I already know one of the candidates. My heart leaps with joy as a pair of gray eyes meets mine. And when he holds out his arms, I fly into them—happy that a familiar face is here. I will not embark on this adventure alone. Tomas is with me.

That was almost three weeks ago. Tomas and I have spent part of every day together, exploring the city and learning about each other. Just thinking about seeing him again today makes my insides flutter.

A knock on my door makes me jump. I roll down my sleeve, hiding the five jagged scars, and answer the door.

"Hey, you're not ready." Stacia's dark eyes narrow as she takes in my white tunic and brown pants. "You can't go to the party looking like that. What will everyone think?"

"The party isn't for another hour." I laugh. "Don't worry. I'll be appropriately dressed."

"You'd better be." She frowns before stalking off, but I see the smile lurking under the serious demeanor. Stacia's frown has kept most of the other candidates, including Tomas, at bay. But for some reason, I decided to talk to her and we seem to get along. I can't help thinking that we must have met during the six-week Testing period. Maybe our friendship began then and we are just continuing it now.

Closing the door, I decide Stacia's right. I should probably get ready for the party. After all, it is for me.

Between meeting University instructors, taking tours of the facilities, and moving into our apartments, none of us has had time to shop for new clothing. We've been given a few spare items from other University students, and Dr. Barnes has said we will be able to purchase new garments during the next few weeks. So I dress as usual in pants, but change into a borrowed blue shirt that covers my scars. I leave my hair down because Tomas mentioned that he likes it loose. As the only two Five Lakes Colony students who passed, we're naturally drawn to each other. But there is something more than just the talk of home. Something warmer and richer and more exciting than friendship. Perhaps it's silly for me to think our feelings might be love. But they might be. And now that The Testing is over, there's nothing to prevent me and Tomas from finding out.

The next time Stacia knocks, I have clasped the silver identification bracelet etched with a single star, the symbol of a first-year University student, onto my wrist and am ready to go. The chatter of voices greets us as we step outside, and when we turn the corner I can't help grinning. I see a banner wishing me *Happy Birthday*, a large cake filled with candles, and people smiling. Tomas. Dr. Barnes. Our entire University class and a number of the Testing officials are here to celebrate my birthday.

Someone spots us. Everyone turns, and together they begin to sing. I don't know if all colonies sing this song to mark the occasion of one's birth or if Tomas has taught it to them, but the song evokes memories of home. I can't help but cry.

When the song is over, a gentle finger wipes the tear that falls down my cheek. "Hey, this is supposed to be a happy occasion. Maybe the song wasn't such a good idea after all."

"No." I smile up at Tomas. "It was perfect. Honest."

"Really?"

He brushes his lips against mine, and I smile. "Really."

"Hey," a teasing voice calls. "Other guys want to give the birthday girl a kiss too."

Tomas frowns as Will walks up, plants a kiss on my cheek, and swings his arm around my shoulders. Will's long hair is pulled back at his nape and his eyes flash with humor, which is good to see. As soon as Dr. Barnes finished congratulating us on our acceptance, Will raised his hand and asked about his brother, Gill, who came to The Testing with him. When Dr. Barnes explained that only Will had been accepted and, like all unsuccessful candidates, his brother had been assigned to a new colony, Will went nuts. It took four Testing officials to remove him from the lecture hall and several days before they considered him calm enough to move into his University quarters. Some of the students whispered that the officials were planning on calling back one of the unsuccessful candidates to replace him. But Will returned, and I'm glad he did.

Will gives me a second kiss on the cheek, and when Tomas protests he laughs. "Your boyfriend here is just jealous that the two of us are paired together for city orientation. Personally, I think you're too good for any of us, Cia. But what do I know?"

Will's words feel familiar. I find myself, not for the first time, cocking my head to the side, trying to recall something that hovers just out of reach.

Tomas tells Will he has no need to be jealous. Other candidates join us. A large, quiet boy named Brick hands me flowers. Then the conversation switches to our upcoming orientation. Before classes begin, all students spend four weeks meeting with Tosu City officials and representatives from every colony. We will also travel the city, learning about the place we are to call home for the next several years. The students are paired up for their assigned meetings and tours. That Will is my partner doesn't sit well with Tomas. Not because he thinks there is anything romantic between us. Tomas gets along with most of the other students in our class, but Will seems to rub him the wrong way. I hope the two of them will work out their differences over the next weeks and months ahead.

Someone pulls out a solar radio, and the dancing starts.

Even Dr. Barnes gets into the swing of things and twists and twirls with another Testing official who before they leave is introduced as his wife.

By the time the sun threatens to set, my feet are sore from dancing and I've eaten far too much birthday cake. I'm thinking about going back to my rooms when I see a familiar face lounging against a tree. I tell Tomas I'll be back in a few minutes and walk across the courtyard to where Tosu City official Michal Gallen is standing.

"Happy birthday."

"Have you been here all along?" I ask.

He shakes his head. "I figured it would be best if I waited until some of the guests had gone home. Otherwise, you wouldn't have time to talk. Congratulations on passing The Testing. Not that I'm surprised. You're smart. You're strong. I knew you could make it."

The sense of déjà vu hits me again. But as I try to grab on to the memories, they scatter like the wind.

"What's wrong?"

I shake my head. "Nothing. Just, I could swear I've heard you say those words before. Funny, right?"

He smiles, but doesn't deny it. Instead, he says, "I brought you something." He pulls a package from behind his back and hands it to me. When I start to unwrap it, he shakes his head. "Why don't you wait until you're alone or we'll both end up in trouble. University policy states students will have minimal contact with their families, but I couldn't see the harm in bringing you this."

My family. I turn the present over in my hands with wonder. "How? Did my family contact you?"

"There was something I had to take care of in Madison Colony last week. I heard your father was going to be meeting with some people there, too, and decided to give him a call. He asked me to bring your family's gift to you."

The words are benign. A nice guy doing a nice thing for a girl far from home. But just a few minutes ago he didn't deny that there are things he's said to me that I no longer remember. I feel the gift in my hands and know there is more being said here than what it seems.

For a moment our eyes lock. I search his face for answers as someone shouts my name. I turn to see Tomas and some of the others waving their desire for me to return. "I'll be there in a minute," I yell. But when I turn back, Michal is gone.

A few of the other students tease me about a Tosu official bringing me a gift. I explain that he was our escort to The Testing, but that just makes the girls giggle harder. Even Tomas raises an eyebrow, but I give him a look that says I'll explain everything later and keep the origin of the gift to myself. Michal has broken the rules to get this gift to me. I don't want him to get in trouble for his efforts.

The sky darkens, and the party breaks up. Tomas walks me to my door, gives me a tender kiss, and then gives me something even better—his love. When I tell him I think I might love him back, time feels like it stands still as Tomas stares deep into my eyes as if searching to see if I am telling the truth. After one last kiss and a promise to see me in the morning, Tomas leaves. And, finally, I am alone with my gift. A gift from home. While I have forgotten the passing of the days that led to my birthday, my family did not. I open the box and find two cards and a bouquet of dried roses in a small cast-iron pot. Flowers my father and brothers created in the pot that my mother says was handed down from her mother. I couldn't ask for a better gift.

Setting the flowers on the table next to my bed, I read the cards. One from Daileen telling me how much she misses me but promising to see me here next year. Then one from my family. Three of my brothers have scribbled a line telling me they miss me or wishing me a happy day. Zeen's inscription says he's proud of my achievements and sorry for his behavior on the night I left. He also wants his Transit Communicator back.

Laughing, I grab the device out of my Testing candidate bag and turn it over in my hand. No doubt Dad has already gotten a new device for Zeen. But sure, I'll send it back. Just not before teasing Zeen a bit first. After all, what are younger sisters for?

I dump the device back into my bag and shove it under my bed. As I head to the closet to grab my nightclothes, I hear a clicking sound.

Drat. I must have turned the Transit Communicator on when I pushed the bag.

Sure enough, I managed to switch on the two-way radio feature that is too far out of range to communicate with the one my father has in his office. I know because I tried. Who knows, maybe after a year or two at the University, I'll figure out a way to boost the signal so I can talk to my family whenever I want.

I'm about to put the device away again when something catches my eye. A scratch on the back of the device. Something I don't remember seeing there when I took it from home. The scratch is only a centimeter long, but its jagged shape reminds me of something. The lightning bolt on my candidate identification bracelet. As my finger runs over the scratch, I feel a slight give in the metal. A button? Sure enough. It's disguised well, but there is definitely a button hidden on the back of the device. No wonder Zeen wants this one back, I think. Because he turned it into something else. I must have figured that out during The Testing and left a mark as a reminder.

Grinning, I plop down on the bed, push the button, and wait for something unbelievable to happen. Because with Zeen, it's always something unbelievable.

And it is unbelievable.

I blink as the small room fills with a voice that sounds like my own and listen as the voice speaks words I don't want to believe.

THE TESTING GUIDE

A PREQUEL TO
THE TESTING

BY JOELLE CHARBONNEAU

Today is the day.

I lean against the trunk of a thin, healthy tree and watch the sun crest over the horizon. Thirty feet from where I sit, I can see where green grass meets cracked earth. Brown, scraggly plants. The twisted branches of trees that fight for life in the corrupted soil. An area where my father and his team have yet to ply their revitalization efforts. But they will. My father is hoping I'll be here to help. I have different plans. Today will determine whether all of the studying, pushing myself to learn more, will pay off. It has to.

The wind catches the edges of the papers in my hand and pulls my focus back to where it belongs—studying. If I am selected for The Testing today, I need to be prepared. Being ranked first in my colony's graduating class and being chosen to go to Tosu City will mean nothing if I am not prepared enough to pass The Testing and continue on to the University.

I touch the words on the cover of the booklet in my hands:

THE TESTING PREPARATION GUIDE. A knot of guilt forms in my gut as I think about the head teacher of Five Lakes Colony, Mrs. Bryskim. Just yesterday she was saying how proud she was of me for graduating first. How proud my father must be to have his oldest take after him. I wonder if she'd express that same pride if she knew I stole this booklet out of her desk drawer?

Not that I wanted to. Stealing is not the Five Lakes way. But what choice did I have after Mrs. Bryskim refused to let me borrow it? I thought she understood how much I need to be chosen. To succeed. That I have to get out of Five Lakes colony and make my mark on the world. I don't want to work for my father for the rest of my life. I need the chance to make my own mark on revitalizing our damaged world. To do that, I have to be selected for and pass The Testing. This booklet will help me grab hold of the future that is waiting for me.

I flip to the opening page and read the first question: *Describe each of the Seven Stages of War.*

Easy.

In my head I list the stages—the first four stages of man-made warfare that started on the other side of the globe and tore apart civilization as people knew it. Then the next three stages, when the earth, corrupted by radiation and biologically engineered weaponry, fought back. Windstorms. Tornadoes. Earthquakes. Hurricanes. Until finally the earth quieted and the rebuilding process could begin.

I smile as I consider how far we've come in more than a hundred years. Then I move on to the next question. *Explain kinetic theory and write the formula that best explains how to determine the temperature of a gas.* It isn't a difficult question, but not as easy as the first. Pulling a piece of chalk and a black slate from my bag, I get to work. Though I would prefer to write on paper, I can't. Not for this kind of practice. Paper is precious. In school, paper is used only for the most important tests. Once the test scores are determined, the paper is immediately sent off to Ames Colony for recycling. Trees are too precious to waste on frivolous things.

"Zeen."

My head snaps up at the sound of my name coming from our dwelling's kitchen window. "I'm out here, Mom," I yell back, and go back to reading the next question.

"You'd better be in here in the next five minutes or you'll be late for graduation."

I start to yell that I have plenty of time, but then I notice the position of the sun in the sky. Damn. I shove my chalk, slate, and the booklet into my bag, sling it over my shoulder, and head for the house. I will have to study later. Mom is right. Graduation is important. I don't want to be late.

My mother fusses over every detail. I let her even though the way she frets and fiddles makes me want to scream. No matter how I brush my hair, it's not right. Finally, Mom takes over, which makes my brother Hamin snort with laughter. We'll see how funny he finds it in two years when Mom does the same to him.

Finally, after more than an hour of buffing dirt and grime only my mother can see from my boots, and a lot of jokes from my twin brothers, Win and Hart, Mom declares me presentable. A glance in the reflector tells me she's right. My blond hair is neatly swept back behind my ears. My chin is whisker-free.

As I straighten the deep purple sleeve of my tunic, I smile. Purple. The ceremonial color of adulthood. I am a man.

As the rest of the family hurries to get ready, I pull the booklet from my bag and take a seat at the scarred oak kitchen table, hoping there is time for just one more question.

"Are you nervous?" asks my favorite voice in the world.

Without regret, I push the booklet aside and smile into my little sister Cia's deep brown eyes. "Not a bit. All I have to do is stand on stage and listen to a bunch of speeches. That's nothing to be nervous about."

"Then why have you been getting up so early and studying like your life depends on it?"

I laugh. Although her tiny stature and dark curls make my sister look younger than her ten years, she is smarter than almost anyone in Five Lakes. Except for our father, the magistrate, Dr. Flint, and me. It doesn't come as a surprise that she has noticed my Testing preparations while others have not.

"I'm just making sure I'm ready in case I get chosen for The Testing, kiddo."

Cia's teasing smile fades. "You're going to get chosen. Everyone says you're the smartest student to graduate from Five Lakes in the last ten years. I overheard Mom talking to Dad about it this morning. She's sure you're going to be chosen and you'll go away forever."

The tears lurking in my sister's voice have me pulling her up onto my lap the way I did when she was a toddler. "What did Dad say?"

"He told Mom that she should be more concerned with what's going to happen if you don't get chosen. He doesn't think you'll be happy living in Five Lakes with us. That's not true, is it?"

I do the only thing I can. I lie. "I'll be happy no matter what. I promise."

"Good." Cia wraps her arms around my neck and hugs me tight. Which I'm glad for, because it means she can't see the anger that must show on my face. Our father went to the University. He should be pleased that I have worked hard to be chosen in order to follow in his footsteps. But instead of being proud and hoping for my success, my father is planning for how he will placate me when I fail.

I have worked too hard. There is no one who has worked harder. I can't fail.

But I do.

I stand on the stage so proud. So confident. I look out at the gathering of our entire colony—just over a thousand people strong—and smile. I don't care how long the presentation is or how many announcements the magistrate and other leaders need to make. This is the only yearly opportunity to address the entire colony. Why should I begrudge them their announcements about building a barn or constructing a new fountain in the square in honor of the man who helped purify our water? While my fellow graduates fidget, anxious for the event to be over, I stand with my hands clasped behind my back. Patient. Because the prize I've waited so long for is coming.

Only it never arrives. No Tosu Official takes the stage. No announcement about Testing candidates selected. Nothing but the stab of defeat followed by bone-chilling shame.

The minute the sky turns dark, I slip away from the graduation celebration. No more smiling to hide the bitterness of disappointment. No more pretending to be excited to start work with my father.

For the first time, I am grateful for the isolated location of my family's dwelling. Normally, I get irritated being so far from friends. Today, the long walk by hazy moonlight gives me time to think. My father offered me a job working with him. Everyone expects me to take it. It's only natural. I want to be part of the country's revitalization. My father is doing important work.

And yet, I don't want to stay in Five Lakes, where I know every face and everyone knows mine. I could apply to Tosu City and hope they find a job for me in another colony, but the chances of that happening are rare. If I want to see more of the world than Five Lakes, I have to do it on my own.

When I reach our home, I am glad to know no one will disturb me as decide what choices I still have left for my future. I pass through the living room into the bedroom I share with my brothers and sister and flip on the light Cia built out of spare wire and solar panels. As I cross the threshold, the purple tunic I'd been so pleased to wear hits the floor. I give it a kick under the bottom bunk of my bed and try to decide what to do next.

I should get ready for sleep, but instead I find myself pulling on my work clothes and my most comfortable boots. I take several more shirts out of the wooden trunk at the foot of my bed. Three pairs of socks. Two pairs of pants. I grab my bag, pull the practice test out, and throw it on the floor. Funny how just hours ago those pages seemed so important. Now they are nothing compared to the need to pack. To leave Five Lakes Colony behind me. To run far and fast from my failure. To do it now.

"I had a feeling I'd find you here."

The sound of my father's voice makes my heart stop. I'd been so focused on gathering my things, I never heard him come in. Taking a deep breath, I turn and face the man I've always been told I look like. The man I've always wanted to make proud. "I thought you'd still be at the party."

"Did you intend to leave without saying goodbye?"

The bag in my hand feels impossibly heavy. "I don't know." The truth of the words makes the shame inside me grow.

My father nods. "I know you wanted to be selected for The Testing, but I'm relieved you weren't. Especially after seeing you now." He points to my packed bag. "Your passion is one of your greatest assets even as it is your biggest flaw. You always lead with emotion and think through the consequences later. It's the reason you'd never have survived The Testing."

Anger flares hot and deep in my stomach. "I know how to take a test. I would have passed."

"The Testing is about more than the right answers. A great deal more."

"How would I know what The Testing is about?" I throw the bag to the floor. "You never talk about it. It might have helped me get selected if you had, but never once did you tell me what The Testing was like."

"That's because I can't." My father runs a hand through his hair. The hurt in his eyes drains away, leaving sadness and something more haunting behind. "The United Commonwealth has procedures in place to ensure that successful candidates can never reveal their Testing experience. But I can tell you this—the Testing doesn't always reward the smartest or the fastest to finish the test. Unlike you, I was not at the top of my colony's class. There were candidates smarter than me who walked through The Testing Center's doors. Whatever happened inside was too much for them. They never walked out."

My father's admission that he wasn't the smartest of his class surprises me. I always assumed he was. Now I am forced to wonder what else about my life is not as it seems.

"Look," my father continues. "I understand you're disappointed, but leaving Five Lakes isn't the answer. At least not today."

I cock my head to the side. "What's that supposed to mean?"

Dad's eyes meet mine. "There are things outside the safety of Five Lakes Colony that you don't understand. That you aren't prepared to deal with. You've only seen glimpses of the damaged world that exists out there."

"Whose fault is that?" Frustration storms through me and punches through my words.

"Mine." My father shouts back. "I take responsibility for keeping you sheltered, and I will not apologize for making choices that have kept my children safe. There is more than poisoned water, rabid animals, and a lack of food waiting outside Five Lakes."

"Like what?"

"Promise you won't run off in anger. That you'll stay in Five Lakes and let me help prepare you for what exists beyond our colony's borders. If in a couple years you still want to leave, I swear I won't stand in your way." Before I can answer, he adds, "Don't give me your answer now. Sleep on it. The world will still be waiting tomorrow."

With that he's gone, taking my anger with him. All that remains in its place is the weary ache of misery.

Stay home and hope to find answers?

Leave on my own and discover the secrets my father hints at?

Fatigue jumbles my thoughts together. My head pounds. Bitterness churns my stomach as I try to focus. When I can't, I am forced to admit Dad is right. I cannot make the decision now. Tomorrow. Tomorrow I'll be rested. If I choose to, tomorrow is soon enough to leave.

My brothers are still sleeping when I wake and carefully slide out of bed. Cia's bed is empty. Not a surprise, since Win is snoring. Carefully, I slip out of the room and smile as I spot the tiny body curled up in front of the fireplace. In that moment, my choice to leave or stay is made. While I love my parents and brothers, Cia is special. I'm the one she comes to when she's worried or confused. She's the one person I know needs me. So for now, I will stay and learn what Dad has to teach. Once Cia is older and Dad has shared what secrets he knows . . .

Who knows.

I'm so focused on my own problems that I barely notice the booklet clutched in Cia's hand. The same booklet I studied yesterday morning. Cia must have found it on the floor in our bedroom.

Careful to step around the floorboards that squeak, I cross to where Cia is sleeping. When I reach to take the booklet from her hands I notice how tightly she holds it. As if it is as important to her as it was to me.

So, instead of retrieving it, I go in search of my father to tell him that I will stay, and leave the study guide clutched tight in my sister's hands. After all, what harm could encouraging her dreams do?

Malencia Vale

TEST 1 - HISTORY
Authorized by THE TESTING
for
The United Commonwealth

Q: Explain the First Stage of the War of the Nations.
A: The assassination of Prime Minister Chae fractured the Asian Alliance and sparked a power struggle among the other nations and a civil war. During the civil war, bombs were dropped on the Korean States, destroying most of the population and causing the meltdown of two nuclear reactors.

Q: What were the first two genetically altered crops to be cultivated successfully in the fields outside Tosu City?
A: Wheat and corn.

Q: Explain the cause of the Fifth, Sixth, and Seventh Stages of War and their impact on North America.
A: Use of nuclear and biological weapons increased the pressure near fault lines. This sudden rise of pressure caused earthquake swarms and aftershocks that began in what was once the state of California and traveled across the continent. Earthquakes also disrupted the ocean floors, triggering the first of the floods that signaled the start of the Sixth Stage and submerged what remained of the coastal states, destroying most of the population. The Seventh Stage was marked by a shift in the weather patterns. Tornadoes, radioactive windstorms, and droughts caused the population to decrease even further and tainted all but the hardiest of plants, animals, and food sources. When

the weather calmed, those who survived could finally begin to rebuild.

Q: Why was Tosu City chosen as the site for the United Commonwealth capital?

A: Because of the non-strategic nature of the state of Kansas, the city of Wichita was not targeted during the first four stages of war. While earthquakes and tornadoes ripped apart the north side of the city, the majority of the city was untouched, making it the ideal site to start the rebuilding process. The city name was changed from Wichita to Tosu to symbolize the hope of a people set on rebuilding what was lost.

Do you think you have what it takes to pass
THE TESTING?